P9-DVO-677

DWYNWEN'S FEAST

Also by I. H. Smythe:

Stories for Animals
Poetry for Animals

I.H. SMYTHE

DWYNWEN'S FEAST

iUniverse, Inc.
Bloomington

Dwynwen's Feast

Copyright © 2010 by I. H. Smythe

All rights reserved. No part of this book may be used or reproduced by any means, graphic, electronic, or mechanical, including photocopying, recording, taping or by any information storage retrieval system without the written permission of the publisher except in the case of brief quotations embodied in critical articles and reviews.

This is a work of fiction. All of the characters, names, incidents, organizations, and dialogue in this novel are either the products of the author's imagination or are used fictitiously.

iUniverse books may be ordered through booksellers or by contacting:

iUniverse
1663 Liberty Drive
Bloomington, IN 47403
www.iuniverse.com
1-800-Authors (1-800-288-4677)

Because of the dynamic nature of the Internet, any Web addresses or links contained in this book may have changed since publication and may no longer be valid. The views expressed in this work are solely those of the author and do not necessarily reflect the views of the publisher, and the publisher hereby disclaims any responsibility for them.

Any people depicted in stock imagery provided by Thinkstock are models, and such images are being used for illustrative purposes only.

Certain stock imagery © Thinkstock.

ISBN: 978-1-4502-7694-8 (sc)
ISBN: 978-1-4502-7697-9 (dj)
ISBN: 978-1-4502-7695-5 (ebook)

Printed in the United States of America

iUniverse rev. date: 12/03/2010

To the Big Guy Upstairs –
my husband, Steve.

He's big, he's upstairs.

Saint Dwynwen (died AD 460)

One of twenty-four daughters of the Welsh King Brychan Brycheiniog of Brechon, the virgin Dwynwen, perhaps inspired by her mother's fecundity, decided to become a nun. Thereafter she became the patron saint of two separate groups, and only two: lovers – and sick animals.

"If music be the food of love, play on."

—Shakespeare

Preface

Faithful Reader:

Aren't you sweet! Oh how gratifying it is to know that you've not lost interest in your beloved Oliver after all, and that the postbag continues to be stuffed with letters begging me to clarify, once and for all, the reason *why* I refused to accept the prestigious International Restaurant Critic of the Year Award. Apparently my copious op-ed pieces and letters to the editor have not been sufficient; like an enticing array of hors d'oeuvres and canapés, they have served only to whet the appetite but not to satisfy it. Fair enough. It is for you, then, that I have assembled the following pages, though interestingly the project was initially suggested to me by my children – three boys and a girl known privately to me and my wife as LTC 1, 2, 3, and 4 (LTC being an abbreviation for "long-term consequence"). I expect their motives are less noble than yours, however, and that far from desiring greater understanding of the situation, they think a literary project might simply deflect my attention away from them (I have, on occasion, been accused of tyranny); and so I am indulging them – and you, Faithful Reader.

This book is a mystery, both in the general sense that all books are mysterious – the visible (brain) made invisible (thought) and then visible once again (book) – and in the specific sense that there is a mystery (indeed, more than one) embedded in the pages of this tome. Though I ought immediately to add that by "mystery" I do not mean a body in the trunk of a Renault, or Colonel Mustard holding a revolver in the conservatory, or ectoplasm on the carpet (and, with four children, who would believe the old ectoplasm ruse anyway), or something impossibly grandiose as sometimes happens in novels, such as the revelation that I am, let's say, a direct descendant of Jesus Christ himself. I probably *am* a descendant, mind you, as are most of us after two thousand years of interbreeding, but that is *not* our focus here. By "mystery" I mean to suggest concealed motives, suspenseful situations, and terrible secrets, all of which I have chosen to reveal through the selective use of primary sources: unedited music and restaurant reviews, letters, e-mails, and even the transcripts of actual dreams. I have faithfully reproduced my own and also those of Mr. Rafe Wilde, the other protagonist in the unfolding drama. Lucky for us, Mr. Wilde doesn't read books and assumes that nobody else does either, which is surely the only reason he has allowed me to reprint his letters, e-mails, and that one ultra-embarrassing music review. Or was it because he was utterly blitzed (how well I know his weakness for ouzo) that he let me download everything from his laptop and use it for my own literary purposes? Hmm. Come to think of it, I'm not sure now that it didn't just slip my mind to mention this little project to him – but no matter. Let's keep it between ourselves, Trusted Reader, and Mr. Wilde and his lawyers need be of no concern to us.

You ought also to know that there are clues to said mysteries scattered liberally throughout this book, though understand that by "clue" I do *not* mean hints delivered in code or cipher. Please do not feed my every sentence into an anagram generator; or hold each page over a candle to reveal the secret message scrawled in lemon juice; or imagine that when I say, as I do, "The bean salad was ravishing!" that by "bean salad" I actually mean, say, "mistress." Do not read the text reflected in a mirror in order to determine if the butler did it (did what? I've already told you not to look for a body in the Renault, besides which I've sold it now – the Renault, not the body). By "clue" I mean a subtle suggestion that leads to greater understanding, that's all – and ultimately what you must understand is this: that not even a restaurant critic can have his cake and eat it too.

Ah, I see the lunchtime crowd is arriving even as I write this (my very own BLT sandwiches – Beauty, Liberty, Truth – are on the menu today), and thus I take my leave. (It still feels strange to be writing in this kitchen, mind you, especially with Mr. Wilde's face painted all over the walls, although the opportunity to give him a ketchup mustache whenever the spirit moves more than makes up for the imposition.)

Sincerely yours,

Oliver Black

Writing from the kitchen
of the erstwhile Beds Beds Beds Factory Warehouse

Chapter One

La Jonquille Comes Up Roses
By Oliver Black

Picture the following: It is precisely 7:30 PM on a Saturday evening, and I, in my finely aged and inconspicuous Renault, pull up to the curb in front of the most aggressively baroque of buildings; one has the impression of nothing but columns and fountains, carvings and statuary. A young valet dressed in red-striped black trousers and a pill-box hat politely offers to escort my vehicle to greener pastures while I attend to the business within. Note that I am impeccably dressed in a black tuxedo with satin lapels, an immaculate white shirt, a black bow-tie and a top hat. I am sporting a monocle and a cane. There is a carnation in my lapel. The moon is full, the planets aligned; Jupiter is in the seventh house.

I push open the heavy oak doors and enter the establishment. My senses are immediately stirred by the delicate fragrance (daffodils?) and by the dainty strains of the clavichord (Couperin?). I am promptly greeted by a charming hostess teetering on three-inch heels and wearing a little black dress and pearls – a tiny woman whose grasp of English is fleeting but who understands perfectly the language of hospitality. She takes my arm and steers me adroitly past a veritable museum of Watteau and Fragonard prints in absurdly ornate gold frames, past an imposing marble statue of Louis XIV, the Sun King himself (poised Christlike, with arms raised, as if pronouncing a benediction over some bacchanal proceeding) and through the imposing, leaded-glass French doors through which I hope to find digestive redemption.

The doors open onto a thrilling sight – high ceilings, gilt mouldings, marble fireplace, brocade chairs, original art in gold frames. Upon the round, heavy-legged tables are generously starched, creamy-white damask tablecloths, crisp napkins arising from replicas of Baccarat crystal goblets, and an impressive array of gleaming silver utensils. I note six knives, six forks, and seven spoons in graduated sizes and in strict parallel at each table setting. The gilded plates are, naturally, in the style of Louis XV. On each table there are sprays of baby's-breath surrounding long-stemmed, fragrant daffodils shooting out of masterfully executed imitations of elaborately decorated Sevres vases.

Though it may not be so for the average diner, I was reminded of home.

But this is not, in actual fact, home; it is the renowned eating establishment La Jonquille and it is the chef-d'oeuvre of the incomparable French chef, Octavio Babineau. Chef Octavio has devised a *prix fixe menu* – meaning, Savage Reader, that there are preselected dishes presented as a multicourse meal at a single set price. There are a total of five courses, and diners may choose between two items per course (at least one vegetarian, one not). Incredibly, the updating of *le menu* is a quotidian affair, so that each evening the offering is entirely different from the evening previous. There is also an encyclopaedic, seventy page wine list with beverages priced from $26 to an astonishing $11,000 per bottle. Like the thrill of ingesting the potentially deadly blowfish, the danger of accidentally ordering the wrong bottle of wine (Pop! "That will be ten thousand dollars, please . . ."), a simple error that could put one in hock for years to come, if not cause catastrophic financial ruin, adds a certain intoxicating thrill to the dining experience. Imagine the possible downward spiral, from the pop of the cork, to the burly liquidators coming to remove one's furnishings, to the hostile divorce and estrangement from one's children, to the shopping cart full of bottles and garbage, to the filthy sleeping bag in a cardboard box under a bridge. All this because of a bottle of wine. Alas! Dining well does not come without risk.

The maître d' (towering, regal bearing, waxed moustache) presents me and my fellow diners with the menu (embossed, gold-trimmed) for the evening, the bare text of which I shall reprint here with the gracious permission of Chef Octavio.

Ode to a Grecian Salade
Asparagus Soup infused with lemon essence and topped with
chive foam

Pasta Poème with Heirloom Tomatoes, Winter Beans, and Ripe
Cheeses
Trout on the Hook with Foraged Truffles and Sebastian Road
Blackberries

New Mexican Antelope diced with South American Cantaloupe
Manicotti gorged with blossoms and greens

Recalling a Glimpse of Picasso on the Pont Neuf
Daffodil Duck Breast with Genevieve's Apple-Stuffed Calf on
Sauce Rouge

Crème Josephine
Traditional Napoleon Biscuits

Are you beginning to comprehend the scope of Chef Octavio's peculiar genius, Dear Reader? Don't be an ass – of course you're not. You cannot possibly even dimly understand this man's rare gift until you have partaken of his diverse creations. Any committed sensualist knows that mere words are incapable of conveying the experience of the body (see Wittgenstein's *Tractatus* for details).

Thus, I began with the soup, a marvellously fragrant dish that made my mouth water, that made my lips quiver, that made my whole being rise up and shout the eternal *yes* to asparagus! (Curiously, it also made my urine smell funny for about twenty-four hours. This may be an indelicate topic; nevertheless, about 40 percent of any given population is affected by asparagus in this manner, and one ought to be aware of it lest one think oneself dying of some unique and malodorous urinary tract malfunction.) I then proceeded to the Pasta

Poème – a cleverly presented dish in iambic pentameter that ended with a heartbreaking couplet. (I jest, but the description of this particular dish as a thing of great lyric beauty is not hyperbolic.)

How could I resist the manicotti, force-fed flowers like some unfortunate paté goose? When my plate was delivered, I did not at first recognize it as my meal; I thought that the floral centrepiece had been delivered to the wrong location at the table. *Incroyable!* It was like eating a bouquet of flowers, but flowers partially melted, buttered, and delicately seasoned. It was a revelation, like discovering that sunsets and rainbows are not primarily a feast for the eyes but rather a feast for the belly. Imagine stumbling upon the fact that clouds make an exquisite dessert, that stars taste particularly good sprinkled on cereal, that the best way to begin one's day is with lava on toast! When one eats Chef Octavio's manicotti gorged with blossoms and greens, one feels that the whole point of the existence of the flower has gone completely unnoticed. Let flowers henceforth be eaten!

Naturally it was impossible to resist the charm of a dish entitled "Recalling a Glimpse of Picasso on the Pont Neuf." Of what ingredients might such a dish consist? Apparently, Monsieur Picasso was particularly fond of Sole à la Meunière, and indeed this is exactly what the ever astute Chef Octavio served. You ought to be aware, Dear Reader, that on one occasion after Picasso had finished his fish in butter sauce, he was overcome with the urge to create; he obtained some clay (and let this be a lesson to all aspiring artists: one should never step out the door without clay, paints, brushes, 8x10' canvas, naked model, smock and beret – one never knows when inspiration might strike), and he pressed the fish skeleton into it, making fossil-like imprints, which eventually became part of a highly attractive platter, now worth more than the average Reader's entire, lifetime-accumulated income.

I am saddened to report that at this point in the meal, I briefly quarrelled with the maître d', arguing that vegetarians do not eat anything that at one time had a) a mother and b) a face, and that obviously fish are not exempt from this consideration. (You remember that there is always to be at least one herbivorous and one omnivorous selection per course.) Chef Octavio must have overheard our vociferous exchange because he flapped out of the kitchen specifically to lower his bushy eyebrows and flare his bull-like nostrils directly at the maître d' in a way that skillfully summed up the-customer-is-always-right philosophy without so much as a word being uttered. Octavio apologized profusely for this oversight, and I assured him that the gaffe was a purely technical one and quite irrelevant to me as a diner. The now hostile maître d', however, had removed my plate in a fit of pique, and therefore – alas – we shall never know just how ingenious the sculpture I might have created from the bones would have been.

No matter, Grieving Reader. For just when it seemed that no other gustatory pleasure was really and truly possible, incredibly something that can only be described as a cookie was presented – but, Dear God, what a cookie! Could there be a greater shock than to discover that the humble cookie could be the climax, the denouement, the raison d'être of this masterfully orchestrated succession of flavours? No, there could not. I should be no more surprised to discover that the consumption of this cookie was the climactic moment of my entire existence; it was, I insist, *that good*. Thus I will end with the customary verse, this time in praise of The Cookie and its divine completion through destruction – a moment of consummation, of consecration – a moment which shall be forever housed in its own holy shrine.

O Cookie! My Cookie!

O Cookie! My Cookie! Round like the moon,
I ruminate on thee, my words untaught.

O exquisite biscuit! Moist, soft, and sweet,
Like the moon thou art full, yet I am not.

Oh how I long to see thee waning gibbous!
Thus shall I ravish thee with teeth and lips.
In Elysian fields of chips and dough,
Thou shalt be a satellite 'round waist and hips.

As proof of a Designer most divine,
Thou art evidence, sweet, and calorescent.
Eyeballs, giraffe's necks, watches can't convince,
Thus I reduce thee to a waning crescent.

Sweet mastication! Leaving crumbs so few,
I devour thee, my love, and make thee new.

Before departing (and, as always), I take a card from its gold case and deftly place it under my plate for the maître d' to discover. Only then does the unsuspecting staff realize that the keen eye of Oliver Black has been upon them. There is no escaping the inevitable; there will, most assuredly, be a review. But fear not; the indomitable Chef Octavio Babineau need not tremble in dread before his most insightful and influential diner. Beauty, Liberty, and Truth! There exist only these three commandments, Scrupulous Reader, and though ever simmering and sautéing within the natural limits of human awareness, La Jonquille heroically strives to be a living embodiment of all three. With its wine list, its herbivorous menu, and its beautiful Cookie, it points us in the general direction of perfection, and it is for this reason that I give both restaurant and chef abundant praise.

La Jonquille is located at 1100 Paradise Drive in the northwest quadrant of the city. There is only one seating per night, and the cost per person is a mere $150. Dress is formal; wear your bow tie and tux, your *sequined gown and satin gloves. Children are welcome as long as they can be trusted to be as still as marble statues and as silent as the grave for at least three hours. Do not annoy the maître d'. Are reservations necessary? Let's just say that to show up without a reservation is to de-* *clare oneself a country bumpkin of the highest order. Like Socrates, I should not prefer exile but insist upon death rather than suffer the humiliation of arriving without a reservation, and so should you, Dear Reader.*

From: rafe.wilde@thedawnpost.com
To: angel.day@agape.org
Subject: Bibbidy Bobbidy Bed

Hey There, Angel Baby:

Well praise Jiminy! After a period of time that has limped forward with all the speed of a geriatric snail – a snail on ice, wearing skates, at his first skating lesson, *and* he forgot his little chair – anyway, after what's seemed like an eternity, I've finally attained the unattainable, mounted the insurmountable, perved the impervious! After twelve interminable weeks of frenzied seduction – of whining and dining, of urging and splurging, of campaigning, entertaining, abstaining – I finally managed to convince you (extended drum roll please) to get into my bed! *And with me in it, no less!* Oh, my Angel! That glorious moment when you finally agreed to climb on board ranks right up there with the top ten greatest moments of my life. (I've bumped off #7 – first test drive in my 1974 red Ford Torino – in order to make room just for you.) You don't know how many times I've imagined us horizontal, how many times I've imagined your perfectly proportioned and cosmetically unaltered body prostrate next to mine! (On average, probably about every seventeen seconds, actually – unless your mom's around, of course, and then I'm too busy bobbing and weaving and, frankly, admiring her footwork.) Oh, my nubile beauty! I've been poring over my mental come-on compendium and obsessing about all the deliciously filthy things I want to do to you between the sheets for what seems like an entire lifetime now – and I don't mean a human lifetime, here – I'm talking geologic time, Baby, the lifetime of a planet, of a star, of an entire universe of planets and stars!

And, as you well know, Angel, *I'm still just obsessing.* Don't get me wrong – that I finally, technically, got you into my bed has left me engorged with gratitude. And I think the fact that, strictly speaking, we didn't do anything even remotely sexual isn't your fault; I blame that psychotic bed, which I'll definitely be exchanging today for something more reliable and less technologically advanced. A heated bed is a dumb idea, anyway. An overheated, defective bed is especially torturous (was it really 125 degrees under the covers?), although I can imagine a faulty model like this is currently all the rage in hell, which is, coincidentally, precisely where this bed is going. What was I thinking when I bought this asinine contraption, anyway? The whole idea of two beds in one is misguided to begin with, what with your side going up, and my side going down, your feet going up, my feet going down, your head up, my head down. *You* weren't doing that, were you? No, of course not – it couldn't have been you. It was the bed going batshit, and that's why I'll be contacting Satan and his minions immediately and demanding that he cart this thing back to the store where I bought it – a place called Beds Beds Beds, whose head office is located in an industrial park somewhere in the underworld. I guess I should have suspected something was up when I noticed all the staff members had little horns poking out of their heads and were wearing red tights. (Kidding, kidding. Their tights were black. Oh, and sorry, Babe. I just remembered you don't like it when I joke about Satan, and evil, and sin, and all that other cool, fashionable, incredibly marketable stuff that gets a big two-thumbs-down at that nutty evangelical church of yours.)

Anyway, just a couple of things: Do you think you could get

that hideous, Bible-thumping bog woman who calls herself your mom to eliminate your sundown curfew, especially given that the sun sets at about 5:30 these days? Also, it was really fun helping you with your homework (hey, I love science as much as the next guy – especially anatomy, if you get my drift – hubba-hubba) but do you think next time you could leave the textbooks at home? Nobody ever uses anything they learned at school anyway (I'm living proof), and you said you just want to get on with your modelling career full time – so next time we're together, why don't you practice gliding sylphlike down the catwalk and into the waiting arms of your oversexed tom?

Meow!

And also – yes, the rumours you heard are true. I'm leaving *The Herald* – *of my own free will* – and I'll be writing popular music reviews for *The Dawn Post* instead. It's no big deal; I just need a little more money, what with the cost of beds these days (cha-ching!), but I vow to continue my devotion to a lifestyle of sex, drugs, and rock and roll – without the drugs, of course (allergies). And without the sex either, apparently.

Love ya, Pussy Cat,

Rafe

From: rafe.wilde@thedawnpost.com
To: sales@bedsbedsbeds.cybersleep.net
Subject: I Like It Out of My Sight

To Whom It May Concern at Beds Beds Beds:

Right. This latest contraption you've sent me (model 2B, the "As You Like It" adjustable bed) is just not working out. First of all it overheated and wouldn't shut off, causing my girlfriend and me to roast like two sex-crazed sausages. Then each side of the bed had a spaz attack – at one point I found myself folded in half against my will, with my head touching my toes (and although I am famous for my physical prowess in bed, this does not normally include rubber-band-like flexibility) – at another point I was, again involuntarily, bent over backward in an arch, a posture of which any yogic grandmaster would be proud. Neither of these positions are ideal postures for lovemaking, by the way, given that they render one helplessly immobile. (Note to self: this could be a good thing . . .) Basically, my girlfriend and I wasted our whole lovemaking session in utterly incompatible positions at a variety of misaligned heights and angles. And it was the *bed's* fault – my girlfriend was *not* playing with the controls. She wouldn't do that – she's too totally hot for me, which is not surprising given that any woman is on the verge of spontaneous combustion when she's with The Great Rafe.

My point is simply that I'd like less of the up and down and more of the in and out, if you get my drift.

I am ordering bed number 69C out of your online catalogue (the "Sircle of Sleep" round bed), and I expect it to be delivered before beddy-bye time tonight. I also expect this other piece of mechanical doo-doo to be carted away and ritually sacrificed, in an elaborate ceremony involving volcanoes and virgins, to the twin gods of Lower Back Pain and Thwarted Sexual Encounters. It's the least you can do, given that you actually owe me (morally and probably also legally – I'll be contacting my lawyer about this) at least one free appointment with a top-notch chiropractor and at the very least two mind-blowingly explosive orgasms (although, realistically, given my supernormal sexual capacity, more like half a dozen). My lawyer and I will be discussing means of payment.

Flaming hell. Just get 69C here, all right?

Rafe Wilde

From: rafe.wilde@thedawnpost.com
To: conrad.norton@herald.net
Subject: The Safe Return of Blankie

To My *Former* Employer:

Well, well. Your vindictive, retributive little scheme didn't work; given that I'll still be doing exactly the same job and yet getting a substantially heftier pay cheque, I'd have to conclude that in throwing me overboard, you actually did me a big favour, you malicious son of a bitch. I don't actually care what paper I work for, you colossal dork, as long as I get paid. So many thanks for inadvertently providing fresh pastures and for substantially improving my standard of living, you titanic piece of dung.

However, I understand that you've cleared out my office and have callously chucked my double divan, you spiteful bastard, as well as my overstuffed cushions, my Indian throw, my comforter, and my hot water bottle in the shape of Elvis. I require the safe return of all of these items immediately, you execrable jackass. Most importantly, *I demand the return of Blankie.* That you could toss an artefact from the 1960s just goes to show what sort of a heartless scumbag you really are.

Failure to return these items will result in legal action, you vapid, flaccid, malevolent prick.

Sincerely,

Rafe Wilde

The Topsy Turtle
3773 Oak Street

Feast of Bertrand Russell

Dear Mr. Wilde:

I have recently been informed that you have been convinced, by fair means or foul, to abandon your position at The Paper Whose Name Shall Never Be Mentioned, and to join the ever jolly staff of critics here at *The Dawn Post*. This is excellent news indeed! I have read *Rafe Reviews,* your ever insightful critiques of the popular music scene, with interest for many years now, and I am pleased as punch (recipe available upon request) to welcome you aboard.

In case you've never heard of me, and I don't mean to be smug when I say that this is hugely unlikely, my name is Oliver Black, and I have been the food critic here at our illustrious rag for almost twenty years. I understand that we have at least a couple of things in common: firstly, that we immigrated as small fry to the Americas from across the pond; and secondly, that your triumphant career spans precisely the same period of time as my own, but that there is a gap of eighteen years between us (I am now fifty-six – you, therefore, are thirty-eight). What a precocious youngster you must have been! And what an old codger I have apparently become! The only similarity in our ages is that the digits of each, taken separately, add up to eleven – a banal truth that I shall be careful never to mention again, lest I bore you into unconsciousness and you suffer a concussion as your head crashes to your desk.

(Are you aware that it is possible to bore people actually to death? This is just a friendly warning: at all costs avoid our junior editor, the indefatigable Mr. Nathaniel Midge, whom everyone calls Nat – the silent *g* is implied. His co-workers are known to carry nooses in their handbags just in case they have to euthanise themselves rather than endure yet another of his infamous monologues, the topic of which is inevitably his fascination with the minutiae of everyday life. Should lunch be served at 12:00 or 12:15? Should the lamp be turned off with the switch on the cord, the one on the wall, or the lamp itself? Should buttonholes properly be vertical or horizontal? Dear God, help us all! How many times have my colleagues had to cut me down from the light fixture just as I was about to kick away the chair? The mere mention of his name causes most of his associates to slip into a coma; even his initials are a hazard, and his colleagues avoid thinking of the letters N. M. while driving.)

But I digress. Mere age, of course, matters not a jot to the discerning reviewer. Genius is not restricted to those between twenty and forty, he said, somewhat defensively. And I dare say that you and I, Mr. Wilde, are kindred spirits. We are, as they say, on the same page, and that page is number 137 in the book *Sustenance* by Monsieur Renée Depardieu, a tome which has been my New Testament lo these many years. Monsieur Depardieu writes (and here I am quoting by heart):

I do not intend hyperbole when I say that the position of Restaurant Critic is one which is comparable in importance to that of the greatest and most influential of political or religious leaders. The Restaurant Critic is, in sooth, a guru to whom people turn when they need the most basic and yet the most essential information possible. Where shall I take my body? What shall I put in it when I get there? In essence, How shall I live?

Judging by the quality of your reviews I can only assume that this is precisely how you feel about the role of the popular music critic, in spite of the fact that our approach to our work is remarkably different – I work undercover so as not to influence the subjects under my laserlike focus; you parade about in flamboyant attire and stretch limousines with wildly cheering, semiclad young women and TV cameras in tow, and are more immediately recognizable than most of the musicians about whom you write. And yet I feel that the restaurant, and therefore the food critic, is in a uniquely powerful position, given that the peak experiences of an individual's life so often occur there. Proposals, receptions, wakes, divorces, mergers, shakedowns, fatal chokings – even accidental births as happened when my youngest son suddenly slid out of my wife in between the departure of the chilled cucumber soup and the arrival of the fruit kebabs (regrettably abandoned). It is for this reason that I write my reviews with the passion and dedication of an apostle writing scripture (even numbering the sentences, just in case), and after all these years of devotion to the craft, I find that even my dreams are plagued by newspaper columns that stand in loose relation to my everyday life – strange and heavily ironical, but evidence nonetheless of my enduring zeal.

Tell me if you would, my young chap: What, exactly, is your philosophy of criticism? What do you perceive your mission to be? To the untrained tongue my task appears to be embarrassingly straightforward, but in reality it is a hotpot of complexities. The gastronomical universe is vast; every year in our fine city, an unbelievable two hundred new restaurants open, which makes a grand total of 730 restaurants about which the gastronomically educated public demands information. Conveniently, this works out to two restaurants per day, every day, each year (a somewhat less convenient 1.995 per day during leap years). The numbers alone are staggering and can only lead to deep bewilderment and even estrangement from the restaurant scene. My job is to be a one-man reconnaissance party, to foray ahead and gently root out the enemies of good taste and thence to shepherd the flock to sweet and succulent pastures where they might graze contentedly upon the finest cuisine this city has to offer.

By the way, we already have a common acquaintance – a Ms. Savage, who has the good fortune of being my daughter's piano teacher. I understand that she was also once your piano teacher but that, at age twelve, you opted to end your "mutual torture" as Ms. Savage put it, and to pursue other avenues of expression. Ms. Savage has some fascinating memories of Little You, all of which tumbled out unbidden upon mention of your name and, hopefully, most of which you have sensibly deleted from your own memory banks. (I say that no child, no matter how many superficial facts point to his essential and inescapable culpability, should be held ultimately responsible for the complete mental collapse of an adult.) Still, a decidedly lacklustre beginning in music in no way impeded your future progress, and you are by far the most celebrated popular music critic working the live scene today.

I shall raise a glass (of Chateau Black '87) in celebration of your appointment.

With admiration,

Oliver Black

The Dream Post
Study Reveals That 95 Percent of All Suicide Bombings Are Preceded by Extremely Boring Conversations

Washington, D.C. – A recent top-secret government study reveals that the vast majority of suicide bombers blow themselves to smithereens for entirely nonpolitical reasons.

Polls show that suicide bombers who have accidentally survived their own attacks are usually motivated by the intense boredom brought on by the incessant chatter of strangers in such places as bank line-ups, bus stops, and discos. In an interview with career suicide bomber Ahmed "Lucky Bastard" Husayn, who is now a torso living in New Jersey, researchers discovered that most bombers don't wait for special occasions but, rather, wear their explosives at all times in case of an ugly event, such as accidentally sitting beside an old lady on a crowded bus who won't stop offering you the other half of her banana. In light of these findings, officials are warning the public to be wary of boring others to death and to take seriously such comments as, "If you offer me that banana one more time I'm gonna go ballistic." Other reasons given by bombers for blowing themselves up include gum disease, computer problems, piano lessons, and general dyspepsia.

From: rafe.wilde@thedawnpost.com
To: suzanne@heartmail.com
Subject: Otiose Sesquipedalian Verbosity

Hey There, Suzanne Baby:

You won't believe the letter I just got from this Oliver Black character – you know, that hoary old restaurant reviewer for *The Dawn Post* who's written about nothing but food since the moment just after the Big Bang, when spices were spontaneously created (just in time for Campbell's Primordial Noodle Soup). I've never even met Mr. Beauty, Liberty, and Truth, but he writes me this jumbo-size, suspiciously chummy letter, which I did *not* receive by e-mail but, unbelievably, *by post* (*Hello, Mr. Black! Welcome to the late quaternary*), asking me asinine questions like "What exactly, Young Chappie, is your philosophy of criticism?" Hell's bells, Suzanne – how should I know? I might be forced to make something up to impress him. "What is my philosophy of criticism? My Dear Mr. Blackie Chappie: come into my atelier and allow me to explain that a nugatory and inchoate précis is inevitable when speaking of my cherished métier. The critic qua critic, as opposed to the critic qua chimpanzee, must never admit obfuscatory, pusillanimous animadversion. Likewise postmodern otioseness and recondite cupidity. *Mais non?* Only by grasping the gestalt – that is, the propinquity between criticism and its anti-pode – can one begin to understand the critic in all his sesquipe-dalian verbosity." Whoa! That's damned convincing, isn't it? If I'd known that channelling Oliver Black was that easy, I could have bumped him off years ago and taken over his cushy job with its cushy salary. Or I could at least have broken into his office and left an incriminating message on his answering machine, just for fun: "Hello, this is Oliver Black – I'm in *medias res* with my ecdysiast at the moment – please leave a fustian communiqué at the What Ho . . ."

Alternatively, I could just tell him the simple truth – the truth being, essentially, that I know what I like and I like what I know. (Isn't that the root philosophy of every critic?) Hey, but get this – do you remember that I told you I've been dreaming in the form of newspaper articles for years? It turns out I'm not the only one – Oliver Black says he dreams in columns too. It must be a profes-sional hazard, like musicians who develop tinnitus and can never again shut off the ghetto blaster. It's unnerving to know that I have *anything* in common with a guy who writes like he does in those antiquated reviews of his – that is, like some sort of nine-teenth century, Old World crackpot. What a pompous ass! Still, I have to be careful to appease him at all costs because he wields a hell of a lot of clout at the paper. And, as you know, Suzanne, I desperately need this job.

Listen. Nobody else has to know why I "chose" to leave *The Herald*, but I want you to know and to believe me when I tell you that *I did not technically sleep with the publisher's wife.* This is the honest-to-god truth, Suzanne. Can I help it if the woman accosts me in her own home and practically drags me upstairs to her enormous and unbelievably comfortable bed (remind me to get one of those feather tic thingies) and then attempts to rip the clothes right off my body? Can I help it that my form-fitting, black leather pants just happen to have a Velcro fly? That her hubby and my former employer (Conrad Norton, that is) just happened to walk in at the very moment she pulled me helplessly on top of her naked body was a stroke of unbelievably bad luck. I'm just glad we could strike a deal: Mr. Norton keeps this nasty little episode private, and I don't say a word about the various illegal substances I found stashed in his pillowcase.

Anyway, Suzanne, I know it's been years now since we've been together (since you dumped me, that is), but you're still my best friend, and I really need your emotional support – and your body if at all possible. (Hey, there's no harm in trying.) Are you still going out with that stuffy, wet-blanket of a heart surgeon? The freak who uses "Hey, Baby, what's your blood-type?" as his pick-up line? The freak who takes you to the blood donor clinic for cookies and juice on a date and who scrubs before dinner? The freak who can sew better than you can? As for me, I'm seeing the girl who's on the cover of *Teen Fare* this month, a stunningly hot babe named Angel. I know what you're going to say (what you always say, every time): "She's too young for you!" Yeah, yeah, talk to the hand, Baby. It doesn't matter anyway since she's vowed to save herself for Mr. Right – and even though I've offered to change my last name, she hasn't budged.

Anyway – she may be a goddess, Suzanne, but she's not you. Hardly anybody is.

With those great big sad sighing sounds I always make in the face of rejection,

Rafe

PS: Oh yeah. That Black guy even mentioned my old piano teacher, Ms. Savage. It's weird because I thought she was dead – not that she died after I finished piano; I mean I thought she was dead while I was actually taking lessons from her. Ha! Anyway, wish me luck – I'm going to fire off a deeply respectful *letter by post* (fucking hell, where do you buy those stamp thingies anyway?) to our Victorian English gentleman right now – and let us pray, sister Suzanne, that I stay on his good side.

PPS: I've got a really important question I want to ask you, but I'll save it for my next e-mail. No time now since I just remembered I owe my mom an e-mail too, and you know her: if I don't write every few days, she assumes the worst – not that I'm dead, but that I don't love her anymore.

PPPS: We've got to straighten out Petey's custody papers, once and for all. That damned bird's driving me crazy.

---

617 Firebird Suites
Poplar Lane

Hey There, Mr. Black:

Well, well! Odds bodkins and what ho! I was seriously blown away by your letter, Old Chap! I mean, it's no big surprise that I've been a huge fan of yours for years, but I had no idea that someone like you would even be remotely interested in the kind of stuff I write about. I hadn't imagined you as a great lover of the pop music scene; from the way you write, I figured you would have been a classical music fiend – strictly an eighteenth and nineteenth century sort of a guy. But wait a second, something just twigged – are you are in some way related to the members of that new neo (new-neo?) gothic band in the city called Black Chalice, who all have the last name of Black? Probably not, it's a common enough name, but it might explain why you read my reviews. So maybe your interest in popular music is a sort of second-hand thing. Or can it be that you actually have no interest in music whatsoever, and it's just my fabulous writing you can't resist – and, of course, my ability to grasp the gestalt – that is, the propinquity between criticism and its antipode – while never admitting obfuscatory, pusillanimous animadversion. Likewise postmodern otioseness and recondite cupidity.

I've got to tell you that the bit of your letter that really sent shockwaves through my body was the mention of Ms. Savage, that lunatic-asylum-escapee who was chiefly responsible for my weekly crucifixion. I thought I'd managed to eradicate that cloven-hoofed, forked-tongued, horned beast from my consciousness forever, and I can't say I'm terribly pleased that she's managed to escape from the private hell to which I condemned her. Hey, does she still breathe fire? Is she still invisible in mirrors? Does her gaze still turn students to pillars of salt? Take my advice and get your daughter out of there before she starts howling at the moon, or developing a taste for fresh kill, or something worse.

Sorry I don't have time at the moment to answer your specific questions, but I've got a contract to sign (and, yes, my coming to *The Dawn Post* was an issue of money, and I'm going to be making truckloads of it), a concert to get to, a review to write, and a girlfriend to satisfy (ho ho). My first *Rafe Reviews* column should be in tomorrow's paper, and though one review can be merely a nugatory and inchoate précis, I hope you like it.

Toodle pip!

Rafe Wilde

PS: Given that it's the twenty-first century, I was just wondering – have you ever heard of e-mail? If so, you can get in touch with me at rafe.wilde@thedawnpost.com

PPS: Who the hell is Bertrand Russell, and why are you going to eat him?

From: rafe.wilde@thedawnpost.com
To: alma.wilde@command.net
Subject: Rubber Sheets

Hey, Mom:

Thanks for your latest e-mail and sorry it's taken me a few days to get back to you. So, are you *serious*? Whoa. I think it's freaky that you're finally clearing out my bedroom, the Holy Shrine to Little Rafe, which you haven't laid a finger on for the last twenty years. Spooky! Why are you doing it now, anyway? Are you finally calling my bluff and renting it out like you always threatened to do if I didn't do my piano practice, or if I left my Star Trek action figures in the tub, or if I didn't keep my hair cut above my ears (and then, when you lost that battle, my shoulders, and then my shoulder blades, and then my waist, and then my butt)?

I have to tell you that I feel more than just a little nervous about it – I don't remember what the hell is in there except for every glass in the house (unwashed), a thousand pizza boxes, ten thousand banana peels, dried vomit, porn, drugs, rock 'n' roll – just the usual stuff you'd find in the bedroom of any perfectly normal and psychologically healthy teenage boy. Why don't I just send you the money, and you can hire a team of competent explosive experts to blow it up – you know, those guys who can implode skyscrapers so efficiently that slightly deaf pedestrians strolling by don't even notice that a fifty-storey building has just dissolved. A suicide bomber would have the same effect (note to self: commence Operation Petey). How about termites? Actually, after twenty years, everything has probably just fermented, decomposed, and liquefied – why don't you just drill a hole in the floor and drain the damn thing? Trust me, ten minutes in that room would be toxic, twenty minutes would be deadly, and that's just because of the bad feng shui. Plus, after twenty years of contact with Deep Purple albums and sweaty gym shoes, the dust mites will have mutated into some tentacled, stalk-eyed, mom-sucking life form. Forget your sponge and feather duster – what you need is a spray bottle of sulphuric acid, an oxygen rebreather, one of those bulky white protective suits worn by government agents investigating areas of possible alien invasion, and a wrecking ball.

That being said, thanks for sending me a box of my old stuff. I fell to my knees and kissed my old Black Sabbath eight-tracks and my Heineken Beer T-shirt from the seventies. You at least know the value of these irreplaceable artefacts, as opposed to my asinine former employer, who heartlessly tossed Blankie in a dumpster outside the office. Miraculously, your valiant son was able to retrieve it, using only his gargantuan brain and a 2×3 greenish piece of paper, in a display of superherolike genius (I paid some little kid to crawl in there and get it). And getting some of my baby stuff was pretty cute, although I don't really need my old rubber sheets, in light of the fact that I gave up bed wetting about thirty-five years ago. But thanks anyway!

I apologize for not telling you about my change of employment, but I decided to make the move in a bit of a rush, and I haven't even signed a formal contract yet – I was going to wait to tell you the news when everything was all settled. Essentially I'm doing exactly the same job for a different paper but for even more money. And, no, so far my persistence is not enough to woo back Suzanne, so in the meantime I'm still seeing a supermodel named Angel. You'd like her – she has the two things you value most: lofty moral values and a deep understanding of the importance of personal hygiene. She's also, incidentally, a total knockout (and, let's face it – that's what *I* like best!)

Hope you're well and trouncing those geriatric tarts at bridge.

Blankie sends his love.

Your son,

Rafe

From: oliver.black@thedawnpost.com
To: rafe.wilde@thedawnpost.com
Subject: Cats, Pop, and the Saints Go Marching Out

Dear Mr. Wilde:

Many thanks for your delightful (if occasionally inchoate and obfuscatory) reply. Indeed, Sir, I am well acquainted with electronic mail and use it daily to contact persons on the other side – of the earth, that is, not those who are on the other side of the grave (or have I just invented the original idea of software that claims to contact the dead?) – as well as to contact those persons who are merely on the other side of the house. Admittedly, I distrust computer memory so completely (it requiring far too much faith in things unseen) that I insist upon a hard copy of everything of possible lasting significance. My e-mail thus becomes almost indistinguishable from ordinary post, especially because it is impossible to put a sheet of paper down in this house without it ending up covered with cats, literally and pictorially. We have a superabundance of cats in this household, and they inevitably sit on every idle page, each cat giving its own personal stamp of approval – but more importantly, there is no force on earth powerful enough to prevent my daughter, Olivia, from drawing cats on every sheet of paper placed upon any flat surface. Personal letters, bank statements, legal documents, investitures – they speak to Olivia as she walks by, demanding cats and more cats, and she can do nothing but submit to the power of blank space. (In the margins there is opportunity – a lesson from a child that might legitimately be an entire philosophy of life.) She Who Draws Cats has all the aesthetic sensibilities of a mediaeval scribe – no text must be left unadorned – and even her numbers and letters inevitably end up with ears, a tail, and whiskers. The psychological usefulness of this custom cannot be overstated, and how often my fury has been quelled when, let's say, upon rereading my electricity bill and coming to the outrageous total at the end, I have discovered a fat and roguish cat, customized to harmonize with the subject, and a speech bubble apologizing for robbing me blind. Fury turned furry. Olivia's cats seem to make everything right, which is a good thing, as they are ubiquitous.

Now, concerning your letter – I couldn't help but notice that the paragraph you wrote about your former piano teacher was particularly inspired. I too have fond memories of my old piano teacher, the decrepit and perpetually scowling Mrs. Kowalski. Just the mention of her name never fails to bring back the delightful sensation of my knuckles being rapped with a pencil. It's no surprise that someone who enjoys torturing small children should become a teacher of piano, of course, but I can't say that I've noticed this tendency toward sadism in the lovely Ms. Savage. Are we really talking about the same sensitive, charming, witty, long-legged, slim-waisted, blonde bombshell of a woman who is my dear little Olivia's piano teacher? I can understand her description of *you* as "her worst nightmare" (you pride yourself in being something of a hell-raiser) and "the ultimate penance" (she claims that in six years you never practised once – true?), but Ms. Savage can hardly be construed as the sort of Medusalike creature you claim her to be.

It was particularly astute of you to notice that my surname corresponds to those of the members of the band Black Chalice; yes, all three are the fruit of my enterprising loins. Selwyn is nineteen, Merlin is eighteen, and Damien is sixteen, and although I am responsible for their ages, it will come as no great surprise that I am in no way responsible for their names. These are of their own invention and are suitable, they tell me, for a band in which all the members clothe their bodies strictly in black, hang inverted crucifixes about their necks, and have artificially lengthened canines (the dental bill was astronomical). You were incorrect to assume, however, that my interest in popular music (specifically rock and roll) is merely the outcome of my relationship with my sons – a "sort of second-hand thing" as you put it. People are often surprised to learn of my devotion to the best of popular music; I am not the type, I am told. Apparently I ought to be wearing polyester pants, sipping conservative amounts of sherry, and listening to Mozart string quartets with my incontinent geriatric friends. (I confess only to a passion for sherry and polyester.) But why? I am a child of the 1950s; I was alive when rock and roll was invented, when the likes of Chuck Berry and Little Richard set music free and Elvis did the same with the hips of a nation: I was in the trenches when the British invaded, and I saw the Beatles live when you were probably still in nappies; it is I, not you, who is a contemporary of The Stones, The Who, The Police, and it is I who grooved equally to the beat of each. (And, if that wasn't enough, there was Mrs. Kowalski, who served as a weekly advertisement for the benefits of avoiding classical music at all costs. Just a few measures of the *Minuet in G* still conjure up an entirely explicable visceral dread: Tuesday evenings – piano night – still cause nausea and profuse sweating.) It is surely *my* genuine fascination for the best of the popular music genre that at least partially explains my *sons'* ambitions, and that also explains why I have read *Rafe Reviews* with consuming interest all these many years. Classical music? I have only come to recognize it for what it is – that is, the Gateway to the Sublime – after ridding myself of the spectre of Mrs. Kowalski, whose arsenal of teaching methods (boredom and disapproval chiefly among them) were calculated to annihilate every shred of affection for the genre. But Oliver Black cannot be estranged from that which is true and beautiful forever; a reunion with the classics was inevitable, and no mere teacher of piano could prevent it. And besides, a knowledge of *all* music – like my knowledge of astrology (which, being a skeptic, I abhor), of religion (ditto), of weather, of neuroscience, of interior decorating – is essential for me to do my job. The world is my bailiwick, Mr. Wilde, and I must be expert in, essentially, *everything,* especially as it pertains to the complex task of ambience-setting in my restaurant reviews.

Now, Mr. Wilde, do tell me – are you pulling my leg? You honestly don't know who Bertrand Russell is? My dear boy, where have you been? What have you been doing with your time? Bertrand Russell is one of the greatest critical thinkers ever to have walked the earth, and possibly the tastiest, though I have no interest in eating him, especially since he's been dead for ages and would undoubtedly have gone off by now. The date of my letter to you just happens to be his Feast Day – that is, the day I celebrate his life and work – according to the calendar of saints that ever sits on the desk before me. You see, it was my conviction that celebrating the lives of worthy individuals was a capital idea but, sadly, I found the traditional Catholic saints to be a rather shabby bunch indeed, composed as it is of anorexics (the true enemy of the food critic), bulimics, masochists, Christians, neurotics, and psychotics of various hues, and traditional martyrdom inspiring not courage or fortitude but, usually, queasiness (there being far too much emphasis on the consumption of excrement and vomit, on disembowelling and dismembering – that sort of thing).

Therefore, I cleverly devised my very own calendar (à la Comte) with my very own saints, one which is based not upon outdated virtues, such as smiling and commenting vigorously on the endless compassion of the Almighty even whilst being eaten by lions or thrown into the fiery furnace (admittedly a vital skill for the early Christian – and certainly there is a lesson here for all those in the service industry), but based rather upon achievement, intelligence, and good works. For example, I made Bertrand Russell the patron saint of skeptics and mathematicians. Frederick Nietzsche, whose name I hope you know – and if you don't then I'm afraid you'd better reenroll yourself at Sunnyvale Elementary immediately, and this time pay attention for God's sake – is the patron saint of atheists and bachelors. Tomorrow is the Feast of Jane Goodall – the patron saint of chimpanzees. J. S. Bach, Helen Keller, Mary Wollstonecraft, Abraham Lincoln, Leonardo da Vinci, Rachel Carson, Albert Schweitzer, Dewey Decimal – they're all here. Note that I don't believe in death as a prerequisite for sainthood – the old thinking was that in death one can no longer embarrass or discredit oneself, but surely there are always others eager to embarrass or discredit one posthumously. Also note that I have not excluded those worthy traditional saints – I have my own reasons for holding Saint Dwynwen fast to my bosom, I revere Saint Nicholas of Tolentino, and I celebrate the great feast day of Saint Lawrence with an excess of effervescent glee. (Some mischievous wag, with a very black sense of humour indeed, decided that the unfortunate Lawrence ought to be the patron saint of cooks and chefs, due to the fact that he himself was barbequed in his robes like a potato in its jacket. "Eww!" you might comment, to which I would reply that we ought not to be in the least surprised. Prudence, mercy, justice, fortitude, temperance – the Almighty recommended many popular virtues in His book on the subject, but for some reason [impishness, whimsy, misanthropy, senility – and Alzheimer's in the omnipotent is never a pretty thing] it somehow slipped His mind to mention one of the mightiest virtues of all – that is, *tact*.) Yes, my saints are an inspiration and example to me, and I have always put their names atop my correspondence as a form of subtle public service announcement; however, of late I find myself spending bloody great wodges of time explaining who my saints are and justifying my choices to my pugnacious colleagues – henceforth, I intend to advertise the feast days of my saints only when the spirit moves, and not as a rule.

On a more mundane note, I expect that you have already signed your contract with Our Most Esteemed Publisher, but in case you haven't, a word of advice: read it with excessive care. Many of my comrades have been too trusting of our cunning publisher, have foolishly ignored the fine print, and have paid dearly for it.

My compliments in advance on your latest review; it will undoubtedly be the glorious highlight of the morning's entertainment section.

With all best wishes,

Oliver Black

The Dream Post
Piano Teacher Cleared of Assault Charges

Topeka, Kansas – Sixty-three-year-old piano instructor Mrs. Enid Kowalski was exonerated of any wrongdoing in court yesterday after being accused of aggravated assault against her former piano student, eight-year-old Jimmy Johnson.

The gripping thirty-day trial ended after the presiding judge heard convincing testimony from famed musicologist Dr. Ludwig Schlüssel. "The *Minuet in G* has three beats to the bar," Dr. Schlüssel explained, "and after ten months of hearing it with four beats to the bar, Mrs. Kowalski just snapped, understandably. Frankly, I'm surprised it didn't happen sooner."

"A teacher can only take so much," agreed Judge Davey Crotchet. "Mrs. Kowalski is a fine instructor with an impeccable reputation, and it is only to be expected that the normally mild-mannered teacher would take definitive action after witnessing the repeated desecration of such a fine piece of music. Anyone in her position would feel justified in taking a child's head, placing it inside the piano, and then slamming the lid down over and over while screaming, 'You'll burn in hell!' as Mrs. Kowalski did. I exonerate her now and would do so again and again in future."

After hearing the verdict, Mrs. Kowalski dropped her countersuit against Jimmy Johnson, in which she claimed he was attempting to drive her

to an early grave with his
insistence on playing B naturals
in the key of F major.

Little Jimmy will be resuming his lessons with Mrs.
Kowalski on Monday.

From: oliver.black@thedawnpost.com
To: selwyn.black@freenet.org
merlin.black@freenet.org
damien.black@freenet.org
Subject: Bread: I Earn It, You Eat It.

Feast of Karen Carpenter

Hello, Boys:

Here is an amusing riddle for you to solve. How is a teenage boy like the common American house sparrow? Answer: It eats twice its own weight in food every day. There are two vital differences, however, the first being that the father sparrow doesn't have to pay for the groceries, and the second being that the juvenile sparrows have not invited bloated hordes of strapping teenage boys around, all of whom are expecting to have nosh shoved down their throats like so many adolescent cuckoos. Good God, Boys! Must you and your companions – boys with appetites like famished caterpillars, like black bears after a protracted winter's sleep, like particularly peckish blue whales – must you swarm into the kitchen like a plague of locusts and leave nothing in your wake but a cloud of dust and a morsel of food that would not even satisfy a Who's mouse? Must you cluster in the kitchen like the unfortunate homeless with their tin cups, warming themselves around a fiery barrel on a cold winter's evening, guzzling hefty containers of milk, of juice, of soda, of salad dressing – of anything potable you can possibly root out of the fridge? (Except, of course, water, which you avoid as if it were, say, antifreeze.) Do you realize that I have not personally eaten a banana out of our fruit bowl for the last decade? This is because, between the three of you, we go through an average of nine bananas every day, sometimes even a spectacular twelve or an incomprehensible fifteen! And this is just bananas! Containers of cookies have been dispatched before your mother has a chance to take them out of the grocery bag. Pretzels have been set upon before she even has a chance to take the grocery bags out of the trunk of the car. Bags of potato chips have been clawed open and devoured even before the bag has made it from grocery cart to trunk! You hover around people with bags of food like vultures circling a carcass. And yet, even though you eat enough to feed an extended Biafran family – not to mention their goat, their chicken, and Frenchie, their poodle – you remain as scrawny as captives surviving exclusively on one potato a month in a particularly brutal POW camp.

In addition to the installation of troughs and strategically placed salt licks, be warned that I intend to supply nosebags in which the daily feed is placed in order to better regulate your daily rations. In the meantime, is it too much to ask that you actually chew your food before swallowing instead of just sucking it up like so many silent vacuum cleaners? Perhaps it is too much to ask, in which case why don't I just install three conveyer belts in the kitchen to deliver an endless stream of sandwiches and cupcakes into your permanently gaping maws? There would be no need to restrict ourselves to dainties of course; we could include food the size of watermelons and pumpkins, given that I'm quite sure I've actually seen the three of you, when you are especially determined to stuff something immense into your faces, unhinge your jaws like pythons and swallow it whole.

Perhaps you might at the very least even the score a bit and scarf down the occasional feast at the home of one of your friends – all of whom, it seems to me, are curiously reminiscent of grouper fish. Have you noticed this? Probably not. Alternatively, you should be aware that shamans sometimes go without food for three or four days in order to produce visions and various trippy hallucinations. Why not give it a try? Or how about a good old-fashioned hunger strike on behalf of something you really believe in – say, the right of women to go topless in public? I realize that for you the experience of hunger is as terrifying as having a leg amputated without anaesthetic, that you three fear hunger in the same way that a hippopotomonstrosesquipedaliaphobic fears long words (a cruel but amusing condition given that the name of the affliction is itself the cause of the symptoms, as if just saying the word "vertigo" caused dizziness). I understand that, for you, the rumblings in your stomach that occur between meals are as compelling as the rumblings of Vesuvius itself and are accompanied by the same imperative to halt them at all costs (in this case, by stuffing the mouth of the volcano with various comestibles – not to be confused with combustibles) before thousands die in the ensuing tragedy.

I sympathize, Boys, given that I, too, was once an insatiable youth; I, however, contented myself with what was provided at mealtimes and, like Dickens' Pip, was only once tempted to steal something out of the pantry and was subsequently tormented by the same guilty conscience. Would I have to do time for a stolen bun? My own crime was especially heinous given that my parents could barely afford anything as luxurious as an actual bun; believe me when I tell you that, rather than habitually eating bakery buns, I usually had to make do with wax reproductions.

In summary: what I want to say is that food doesn't just grow on trees. I cannot, since it does; nevertheless, I think you take my meaning.

Thank you so much.

Scroogishly,

Dad

PS: Will the three of you be attending Mousetrap's concert this evening? If so, let me know what your impressions are so that I may compare your thoughts with those of Mr. Rafe Wilde, who, by the way, has been seduced away from the Evil Empire and is now writing his reviews for *The Dawn Post*. Another victory for Beauty, Liberty, and Truth.

From: oliver.black@thedawnpost.com
To: lucy.black@artnet.org
Subject: Kudos and Kiddos

Good Morning, My Love:

When I awoke this morning, you were already hard at work in your studio (no doubt painting something woefully unsuitable for inclusion among the masterpieces at the Louvre, because its unprecedented quality and vision would make even the greatest da Vinci look shabby and amateurish), and I didn't want to disturb the genius at her easel. Did you read the review of your exhibition in the paper this morning? I noted with genuine glee the presence of the words "sensational," "clever," and "profound" used in a (futile) attempt at description and summation. Brava, my darling. In celebration, I intend to prepare an elaborate meal, the like of which has not been seen since mythological times when the gods of Olympus would gather in the great hall at the palace of Jupiter and feast upon the finest domestically grown and pesticide-free nectar and ambrosia. Perhaps we might even shoo our sons away for the evening, given that I find the miniature barbells thrust into the tongue and lower lip of our eldest enormously unappetizing – not to mention the bizarre clothing choices of our youngest (is it my imagination, or has he worn the same, unlaundered T-shirt since he was a newborn?) and our supposedly overlooked middle child who, being the middle child, is apparently following the tradition of the Middle Ages and bathing only on feast days and holidays. I am strongly reminded of Saint Agnes, who went to her grave at the age of thirteen having never washed. But perhaps Saint Jerome was indeed correct, and the cleanliness of the body implies the uncleanliness of the soul, in which case our Merlin is second only to God Almighty Himself in the purity department (aisle four, next to the antibacterial hand soap). And what do you think of the dreadlocks he is attempting to cultivate, apparently through the judicious use of dust and spit? He is neither black nor Rastafarian – would you care to break the news to him, or shall I? Ah well, no matter. As bewildered and impotent parents have done since time immemorial, we can always cultivate a world-weary demeanour and utter in an omniscient tone the expedient expression, "It's just a phase." This will cause us to appear calm and in control of the situation, as if just such a phase had been planned all along. Dreadlocks? Ha! It's just a phase. Full-body tattoos? Bestiality? Homicide? Piano teaching? A phase, a phase! I note that it is the very same expression my own mother used when she would catch me after dinner, holed up in my attic room, furiously scribbling reviews of the meals she prepared (Macaroni casserole bland and unadventurous – beans jejune – *what was that meat?*) and which she would subsequently tear to shreds and scatter to the four winds, after taking me over her knee of course. Mother was never wrong; that my food critic phase has lasted fifty years only makes her even more right than if it had petered out early and is a sound testimony to her razor-sharp insight.

So, my love, about dinner – shall we dine in our own great hall tomorrow evening, by candlelight and Chopin, at sevenish? Our dear, unspoiled Olivia may be present, naturally, and if you would like our three sons to attend, I will not object; I will merely prepare ten times the reasonable quantity of food, so that when they begin hoovering everything in sight, there will still be some left for the rest of us. (Note to self: investigate Heimlich manoeuvre, re: ingesting plates and cutlery.)

Your loving husband,

Oliver

From: oliver.black@thedawnpost.com
To: damien.black@freenet.org
Subject: Getting Shirty

Hello, Damien:

I was just composing an e-mail to your mother when, out of
the blue and for no reason that could possibly pertain to you
directly, the words of an old song by Harry Wincott just popped
into my head unbidden. Somehow I thought that you might
appreciate them.

The Little Shirt My Mother Made for Me

I shan't forget the day that I was born,
'Twas on a cold and frosty winter's morn,
The doctor said I was a chubby chap,
And when the nursey put me on her lap,
Oh, she washed me all over I remember,
And powdered me all over carefully,
Then she put me in my cradle by the fireside,
In the little shirt my mother made for me.

Last summer I went on my holidays,
Upon the briny ocean I did gaze,
The sea it looked so nice I thought I'd go,
And have a dip but in a minute . . . Oh!
All the girls on the beach at me were staring,
And some were taking snapshots I could see,
It was a good job for me that I was wearing,
The little shirt my mother made for me.

Have a nice day.

Dad

From: oliver.black@thedawnpost.com
To: wendell.mullet@agricorps.org
Subject: Black Mail

Find deposited into your account the *usual* monthly sum and not a penny more, you ruthless swine. (No compliment intended.)

From: rafe.wilde@thedawnpost.com
To: suzanne@heartmail.com
Subject: Unrequited Love

Hi Suzanne:

I got another letter, by e-mail this time, from that screwball Oliver Black. He's a bit of a wanker, but surprisingly, he's pretty interesting (although I wish he wouldn't keep bringing up that poisonous, fang-toothed, scaley, oversized reptile, Ms. Savage). Hey, did you know that Oliver Black is the father of the three guys who make up the band Black Chalice? Weird! It's like finding out that an entire eardrum-splitting heavy metal rock band was fathered by Charles Dickens.

So, remember that question I mentioned in the post-postscript of my last e-mail? Okay, so, here it is. What I really want to know, Suzanne, because not knowing is making me just the teensiest little bit dangerously psychotic, is: Why don't you want to go out with me anymore? No, seriously, why? I need a straight answer, once and for all. I've been going over and over the possible reasons in my head ad nauseam for the last five years, and I just can't figure out why you don't want to be with a sexy, pseudo rock star like me, particularly given my stellar credentials. I mean, honestly, look at me! I'm like some sort of animate reproduction of a Greek statue in tight leather pants, what with my chiselled features, my fabulous shoulder-length mane of wild black hair, my piercing blue eyes, my adorable dimples, and my dazzling smile – all *your* words, by the way, from an e-mail you sent to me when we were first going out and which is now framed in gold above the mirror in my bathroom. I treat it like a legal document, as a binding and enforceable body of evidence that I am a total babe magnet, in the unlikely event that anyone has any doubts. Actually, it reads more like a victim impact statement – "My life has never been the same since . . . You've affected me in ways you could never . . . When you did It I couldn't stop screaming [for more] . . . et cetera." I think everyone should have a reference letter like this – a sort of official endorsement, a professional certificate of ability – hanging on the wall with lots of extra copies to hand out at parties, leadership conventions, church picnics, whatever.

But back to my original question – so why do you want to be "just friends" as you once put it, a phrase that conjures up all the excitement of an afternoon tea party with Blankie and Petey? (Oh, and speaking of Petey, that one sentence you taught him to say is really getting on my nerves. He's *your* parrot, remember? So why, after five years, is he still eating *my* crackers and jingling *my* jingle bell?) Anyway, you once referred to my "weird little quirks," presumably all of the sexy, cool ways that make me way more interesting than most people. Okay, so maybe there was something that happened between us that put you off, though I can't for the life of me think what it might have been. I thought everything was going so great for us, except for a couple of weird things – like the occasional tension over the housework issue, my attachment to Blankie, and your jealousy over Juan, the foster child in Guatemala my mom gave me for my birthday. (Get your own goddamn foster child.) Other than that I really can't imagine why you wouldn't want to be with me, Suzanne. I mean, wasn't it you who said I look exactly like Keanu Reeves? Or was that me? Whatever.

Anyway, my point can best be summed up in that hot new Black Chalice tune, *Just in Case*, which is "a nod in the direction of Pascal's Wager," whatever that means. (How much do you want to bet that Daddy Black wrote the liner notes?) I love the bit after the "Just in case I've got the hottest buns" refrain, with those wild chords and that pounding drum beat and Selwyn Black screaming:

> *I might just be the best thing*
> *That's ever happened to you,*
> *Baby, you can't know for sure.*
> *A game is being played, and heads or tails is gonna come up.*
> *Whatcha gonna pick, Baby, whatcha gonna pick?*
> *By reason you can't wager on either;*
> *By reason you can't stop either from winning.*
> *You gotta wager, Baby, a choice has gotta be made.*
> *If you gain, you gain all;*
> *If you lose, you lose nothing.*
> *Try then to convince yourself,*
> *Oh Baby, try to convince yourself.*
> *I'm the best or I am not*
> *I am hot or hot I'm not.*

Genius.

Anyway, look for my first review tomorrow morning in *The Dawn Post*. And while you're at it, dump Doctor Thrombosis and come back to me.

Love,

Rafe

PS: No, really, Suzanne – dump him. If you do I'll take you to

La Jonquille, that snooty French restaurant, where we'll order a burger and fries just for fun, and then we'll celebrate our love in my new round bed (which I keep falling out of – thank God it's not an upper bunk) with the slippery red satin sheets and fluffy pink duvet, and afterward we'll dump an entire bottle of bubble bath in the Jacuzzi and eat chocolates that are the exact colour of your hair and your eyes. Please?

I love you.

Mousetrap Snares
Good Review
By Rafe Wilde

Faithful shock-rock pilgrims from around the globe tramped by the thousands into The Dome yesterday evening for the express purpose of having their eardrums battered into submission by this nation's premier metal band – and nobody left the building that night without getting what they came for, i.e., irreversible hearing loss. Yes, rock music's most destructive band, the legendary Mousetrap, staged a truly memorable concert (for those of us not taking date-rape drugs, that is) with plenty of electrifying thrills for all their loyal fans. These devotees found what they were seeking: fast and nasty thrash metal that brings you to your knees and makes you beg for mercy before it grabs you by the nuts and pushes in your eyeballs with its thumbs.

For twenty-five years now, this black sheep band has been performing nerve-shattering, extreme machine versions of light pop classics originally made famous by the likes of The Carpenters, Air Supply, The Captain and Tenille, John Denver, Anne Murray, and Celine Dion. Some of their best-known hits include "The Wind Beneath My Wings," "You Light Up My Life," "Feelings," "To Sir with Love," "Annie's Song," and a medley of favourites made popular by Helen Reddy, including "I Am Woman" (interestingly, there are no female band members). Waves of nostalgia broke over the crowd as the band sang all of these speed metal smash hits, but they also added an impressive amount of new material, including a section devoted strictly to musicals ("Send in the Clowns," "Memories") and TV themes ("Gilligan's Island," "The Simpsons"). It was a riotous musical onslaught, a sonic cyclone, that included thundering, fuzzed-out guitar riffs, primal-screech vocals, WWF-style keyboard playing, and pulverizing, testosterone-driven drum solos.

It was painfully good.

When Mousetrap arrived on stage in their muscle shirts and jeans so tight that rumour has it none of them have any feeling left in their lower limbs (though they are eager to let the public know that their genitals are still fully functional), they launched immediately into the song that has become their anthem, "Having My Baby." Band member Randy Sexlightning's frantic and amazingly agile tenor solos were in constant dialogue with the whine of the electric guitar, played expertly by Mousetrap's mysterious, androgynous, anonymous, albino guitarist. Drummer John Thomas used every part of his body to produce sounds, using his head to whack the cymbal, his ass to whump the bass drum, even licking the snare drum with his impressive tongue. Dick Thundersex played the keyboards with his boots and then, at the end of the piece, kicked them all to smithereens in the tradition of so many fine keyboard players before him. In fact, all of the instruments (or, at least, clever facsimiles) were frenetically smashed to pieces at the end of every set. The stage itself was designed like a giant mousetrap or, rather, like the popular game of the same name, and at the very end of the show Mr. Sexlightning turned a crank, thereby setting in motion a series of horrifically destructive events that appeared to blow up each of the band members in turn. It was pure magic.

After the show I had the privilege of interviewing two of the members of the band (a third member was comatose, and a fourth is apparently so deaf that interviews are now impossible without the tedious exchange of a notebook).

"We're decomposers, really," admits lead singer Randy Sexlightning in a stereotypical Cockney accent, though the band originally hails from Saskatoon. "We deconstruct popular tunes by guys like Barry Manilow or Neil Sedaka, and then we smash up the stage and all the instruments to sort of symbolize what we're doing with the music. It's really beautiful."

R.W. "And what do you say to those captious critics of your music who claim that you have nothing original to say, that all this has been done before and you're living in and off the past, that you're a parody of a parody, and that you're essentially nothing, really, but a colossal joke?"

R.S. "To any critic who said that, mate, I'd have to say f--- off. And as further proof of my argument, I'd point out that I have enough money to buy everything he'll ever own about a thousand times over. Plus I've slept with his wife. Case closed."

When asked about some of their stage antics, like stomping on stuffed animals with football cleats, keyboardist Dick Thundersex said, "Oh yeah, well, we were going to use real animals but then we all became Jains and they believe we were all little bunnies and chickies in past lives, and how would you like to be stomped on? So then we couldn't use animals, really, because it would wreck our karma. You know, it's sort of like – kill a chicken, get killed by a chicken."

R.W. "You're *Jains*?"

D.T. "Yeah, absolutely, one hundred and ten percent."

R.W. "Wow. But my sources tell me that Jainism is the most ascetic, self-denying religion around. How can you be Jains? You use drugs and alcohol, you eat meat, you engage in wild orgies . . ."

D.T. "Yeah, that's right. But, I mean, when I said we were Jains I didn't say we were *good* Jains. Nobody's perfect, mate, and saffron's not my colour, really. But I do have my little broom and my little wooden bowl, and I did shave my head."

R.W. "Your hair is down to

your waist."

D.T. "Oh yeah, right, I didn't shave it. I thought about it but then I didn't actually do it, did I? Yeah, that's right."

R.W. "So how did you actually become a Jain?"

D.T. "Well, it was down to my girlfriend here, really. She thought moksha sounded fun and everyone at the temple was so nice, really, and so she became what they call a Digambara."

R.W. "And what does that mean?"

D.T. "It means buck-naked. She took a vow of nudity, mate, and I'm all for that."

R.W. Pause. Examine girlfriend. "She's completely naked . . ."

D.T. "Absolutely."

R.W. ". . . under the fur coat . . ."

D.T. "Yeah, that's right."

R.W. "I see." Pause again. "So you sweep the stage free of any insects before the show?"

D.T. "Oh, yeah, absolutely. You see all the guys in the band up there with our little brooms, sweeping and chanting. I couldn't live with meself if I stepped on a little ant."

R.W. "You ate a steak for lunch."

D.T. "Is that what that was? See, sometimes good manners gets in the way of my religion. I eat what I'm given, me."

R.W. "And does your religion have any impact on your music?"

D.T. "Oh yeah, absolutely. We'd never sing anything by Meatloaf, for example."

R.W. "Okay, just one last question. Is what you're doing meant to be taken seriously, or is it just satire?"

D.T. "Our music's just what you think it is, mate."

After the concert, I spoke with several fans who had been hurling their bodies off the stage and surfing recklessly into the mosh pit below. "It's the only way to fully experience Mousetrap," one ecstasy-riddled fan claimed. "Music demands response, man. The body's gotta move, otherwise you miss the point."

"I loved it when, like, he drilled through the grand piano with a jack hammer and then smashed it to pieces with a pick-axe," another fan said.

"Look, I got a black note!"

Mousetrap's new album is entitled *Cheesed Off* and will be released in stores sometime next month.

I'm giving this concert a 6 out of 7.

The Dream Post
McNoddle's Retrenching
After Attempt to Open New Restaurant

Apple Valley, New Jersey – In a daring new move calculated to show how McNoddle's is living up to its "Have It Their Way" slogan, the worldwide franchise attempted to open up a new restaurant yesterday that was to cater exclusively to the Jain community and operate on strict Jain principles. "The monks and nuns from the local temple are just super people," said McNoddle's spokesman, Tex Heiferman, yesterday, just prior to the opening of the new McJain's, "and we at McNoddle's want to prove that there is no culture or religion in the world that can't be assimilated into our fast-paced McEthic of immediate gratification." The sexy new spiritual look was enhanced by the teenaged staff members, all of whom were required to dress like one of the twenty-four Tirthankaras and to follow at least three of the five vows (their choice) of nonviolence, truthfulness, nonstealing, chastity, and nonpossession while behind the counter. The Happy Feast was to be replaced by The Compassion Feast, which consisted of one leaf of iceberg lettuce, specially handpicked to avoid damage to the mother plant. "Given that starving yourself to death is a virtue in Jainism, we keep the portions nice and small. Really, it's a win-win situation for everyone – ancient Indian food at modern American prices." Increasing the profit margin even further was the fact that Jain patrons bring their own little bowls wherever they go. "We don't even have to supply the dishes!" exclaimed Mr.

Heiferman, rubbing his hands together in the universally understood expression of excessive greed.

The mood was one of jubilation yesterday as bald and barefoot Jain monks queued around the block, eager to get a taste of this newfangled McKarma. All was well until several Jain monks actually lined up at the counter and ordered their food. Only then was it discovered that the monks are not allowed to carry any money whatsoever and are only allowed to beg. "This is America, people," Mr. Heiferman said as he swept the bewildered little men out the door, locking it behind them. "In America we don't call people like you ascetics – we call people like you bums. Go on! Get outta here!" Mr. Heiferman was later heard muttering, "Those people in marketing have a lot to answer for."

After this disappointing experience, and with the knowledge that the McNoddle's demographic department is apparently not doing any field work whatsoever but is simply using information it finds on the Web, McNoddle's is rethinking its decision to open a restaurant that was to cater specifically to the Klingon Empire. (Later, Mr. Heiferman admitted that the problem is not so much the possible fictitious nature of the empire, but the fact that "the Klingon's main delicacy is Gagh, a dish composed of raw, live worms – worms that just keep wriggling out of the bun, dammit." McNoddle's, whose new competitor, Ferengi's, is eating up the market, also has doubts that the tenets of Klingon philosophy, especially the outrageous ideal of "Success with Honour," can be assimilated into the McNoddle's Ethic.)

From: rafe.wilde@thedawnpost.com
To: angel.day@agape.org
Subject: Mum about Mum? Uh, Uh.

Hey There, Angel Baby:

I just wanted to tell you how much I loved our date last night. You are so flipping gorgeous, your perfect body drives me insane with desire, and I totally love the way your lipstick, your barrettes, those little pink shoes, and your fingernails are *all exactly* the same colour. Wow! How do you do that? When did you have time to go to Crayola University and get a PhD in colouring? Anyway, only one teensy little thing would have made our date better for your Rafey Wafey. Can you guess what that is? No, it's not that I minded you painting your toenails during the Mousetrap concert – I found that incredibly cute/sexy. No, it's this: Would it be okay if your mom didn't come with us next time? I mean, your mom's a total riot, and I love her over-the-top, frumpy-homeless-person look, but I find her conversation to be more than just a little bit creepy, you know? The way she just gives me this sort of deadpan stare and says stuff like, "What concord hath Christ with Belial?" and I don't know what the hell she's talking about, so naturally I try to make a little joke – "Christ hath no Concorde; only a Boeing 747," at which point she hisses *"What will ye? Shall I come unto you with a rod?"* which might have been amusing if she hadn't actually been holding one. (No, I told you, it was *not* just a body-of-Christ baguette, okay?) Or how about when we were waiting for the concert to begin, and she was glaring at me with those pale, watery eyes and then said something like, "Doth not even nature itself teach you that if a man have long hair, it is a shame unto him?" And then when you said, "Do ye look on things after the outward appearance?" and your mom said, "The wise man's eyes are in his head," well, then I was just completely freaked out. It's totally spooky when you two do that Bible-speak thing, you know. It makes me feel like I'm trapped in a scene from *Carrie*, especially when she starts spouting off about blood and spitting out menacing Bible verses like, "Without the shedding of blood, there is no remission of sins" (nice rule, by the way – what sadist made up that one?), and then I notice she's holding a crucifix with a Jesus whose head's sharpened to a deadly point. Very maternal. Your mom's a panic, really, and I love having her around all the fucking time, but maybe next time we go on a date, she could have a quiet night sitting at home (is that a real pew in your living room?), reading the scriptures and singing the hymns and slaughtering goats or whatever she does to get off on a salvation kick. Come on, Angel. Just tell her your soul is totally safe with The Great Rafe, and as for your body, I vow to personally inspect every single inch of it at the end of every date to make sure not even a single hair on your head, or on any other part of your body, has been damaged in any way. Internal exams are also free of charge. You won't find a better deal than that.

Love ya – mean it,

Rafe

From: rafe.wilde@thedawnpost.com
To: suzanne@heartmail.com
Subject: Inside Out and Upside Down

Suzanne:

Hey, I didn't see you at the Mousetrap concert last night – did you go, or is it not quite the kind of music that appeals to that colossally pretentious cardioboob boyfriend of yours? I know his type well, Suzanne, the type that won't even consider going to a concert if he finds out any of the instruments require electricity, or there's no conductor, or it's not in Italian. I'm right, aren't I? If there aren't at least fifty people onstage doing things to catgut and blowing into various kinds of tubing, he's just not interested. And there's nothing he likes better than listening to those tone poems by depressed Norwegians, unless it's spending his Saturday afternoons listening to the opera on public radio and weeping. We both know it's true. Still, you should have been there, Suzanne – both to hear the music (which was ear-drum-splittingly great, by the way – my head's still happily buzzing like a hornet's nest) and to lay your eyes on my current one true love, Angel – and, even more interesting, on her maniacal mother, who insisted on coming with us to the concert. Actually, she comes almost everywhere with us – movies, restaurants, prayer meetings – I've only had Angel alone once, and then, of course, my bed malfunctioned, meaning that I got screwed, but not in the way I had intended.

Speaking of malfunctioning beds brings me to the point of this e-mail, which is the ever-burning question of why you don't want to date me anymore. You refuse to tell me what the problem is ("*You* figure it out" being your standard and hugely helpful reply), but I think I've got it anyway. It was the incident with that ancient, demented wall-bed, wasn't it? Oh yeah, that's it. I couldn't believe it when it snapped up right in the middle of the greatest fuck ever (talk about coitus interruptus – they should advertise the bloody things as an extreme form of birth control) although I think the fact that *I did manage to complete the act while suspended upside down* is a testimony to my stupendous manhood. I admit it was a bit embarrassing when emergency rescue services had to become involved, and I was as steamed as you were when I saw us on the six o'clock news (did you see my hair? Bloody hell!) but, hey, it was free publicity, and in my job I take it where I find it.

Anyway, Suzanne, you know you'll always be the only one for me, in any orientation.

I still love you.

Rafe

PS: I still hate Petey.

From: oliver.black@thedawnpost.com
To: damien.black@freenet.org
Subject: The Milk of Human Crossness

Good Morning, Damien:

You are exactly 6175 days old today (plus three hours and thirty-seven minutes as of the time of this e-mail). Congratulations! You have set a new world's record! For at least 6175 days, you have failed every single day to perform the ridiculously elementary function of putting the milk back in the refrigerator! Well done, my lad! It is this sort of obstinate perseverance that will ensure your future success in whatever endeavours you undertake.

Expect your allowance under your door at 0800 hours tomorrow morning. Expect the usual amount, minus the cost of seven cartons of spoiled two percent.

You owe me four dollars.

Sincerely,

Dad

PS: Did you read Rafe Wilde's review of the Mousetrap concert? I found the interview particularly droll. But tell me this, Damien: which member of the band do you suppose is deaf as a post? In other words, what do drummer John Thomas and composer Ludwig van Beethoven have in common? Besides a love of rhythm and raging syphilis, that is? Yes, that's right – after the bitter loss of their hearing, exchanges could only occur via pen and notebook, so let this be a caution to you, my boy. I suggest that, whenever you play the drums, you first protect your *own* drums by clapping over your ears those attractive airport-maintenance-worker earmuffs that are (or, at least, ought to be) so in vogue. You've seen me wearing such earmuffs at my desk often enough, so I know from experience that it's almost impossible to hear *anything* unpleasant when one's ears are sandwiched between them. What a godsend is silence! And how handy they are when you boys come into my office and make unwelcome requests for more money or later curfews. (What? What? What? What? *What?*) So, do feel free to grab a pair from the box I keep beside my desk, and next time you get the urge to beat upon the old animal skins, remember John Thomas's flaccid apparatus and protect your own throbbing membranes.

From: oliver.black@thedawnpost.com
To: lucy.black@artnet.org
Subject: Missing My Missis

Hello My Darling:

Upon waking this morning and seeing my tuxedo still draped over the chair in our bedroom, I decided that I would put it on and pretend to be our butler, Dogbane – you know, the imaginary fellow we made up in the first years of our marriage and who exasperates us so when he doesn't answer the doorbell or bring us breakfast in bed. (You always liked to point out that you get what you pay for, and we pay him nothing – but how can we provide recompense if he is never here? It's a problem of logic, my dear, and his existence in the realm of myth alone thickens the soup considerably, creating, one might say, a viscous circle.) So just imagine your ridiculous Oliver, dressed to the nines at 7:00 AM, silver tray of biscotti and coffee balanced professionally in one hand, knocking at your studio door with the other, and then discovering, alas, that there is no one within – indeed, discovering that you are not in the house or on the grounds at all. This was a shock, and then a humiliation when one of our dishevelled sons emerged from his bedroom at the exact moment I was passing, exclaimed, "Yeah, this is more like it, Old Man," relieved me of my tray, and slunk back into his room.

Dearest Lucy. You have been so withdrawn of late, and it is not my intention to pester you with endless questions concerning your whereabouts. Do forgive me if I sound like Apollo chasing after his beloved Daphne and, upon reaching her, finding only a tree, or in this case, something derived *from* a tree – that is, a piece of paper upon which you had written the note that I found on the dining room table this morning. In it, and for reasons you do not care to disclose, you tell me that we cannot have our celebratory meal this evening. All right, then, how does Sunday suit you, say at about seven? We could dine sans sons as I had previously suggested (and with or without your mother, naturally, but you know she's always welcome), or if you like, we could create more of a party atmosphere. Not only could all of our offspring join us, and your mother, but we could also invite Mr. Rafe Wilde and Consort to share in the festivities. I know the boys would be pleased with the idea of meeting a celebrity in the music biz, particularly one who will undoubtedly have such influence over their musical careers. Please let me know if you have any objections, my sweet.

By the way, I believe I forgot to mention that the forever roaming Branksome telephoned yesterday from a small volcanic island surrounded by a coral reef and a crystal sea of blue-green liquid glass located somewhere in the South Pacific. According to Branksome it is one of the clammiest places in the universe, second only to Venus. In order to demonstrate this concept, he suggests that we fill up a bathtub with warm water, borrow some snorkelling equipment, submerge, and then whilst still underwater, attempt to towel off. Tricky, isn't it? Branksome says that should we ever visit this part of the world, we ought to take our snorkelling equipment and be prepared to wear it *at all times*. That's how humid it is. Anyway, he is apparently thawing out after his adventures in the Antarctic, where for six long months working in conditions that would give even the hardiest of Kurds pause, he was involved in the tagging of every single penguin in a colony of about two hundred thousand. That he should find such an activity in the least bit enjoyable is a testament to the fact (and this is underappreciated by geneticists) that two children born of exactly the same parents can often belong to two entirely different species. How else can one explain Branksome, the restless and wanderlusting bachelor (and so shall he ever be), and me, the contented and firmly rooted family man, dedicated to hearth and home? Or look at the difference between our Olivia and any one of her brothers – she so sweet and adorable, the very embodiment of young Venus herself, and they so Pan-like, especially in odour. How is it, by the way, that they are so popular with their peers? There is one answer only and it is this: music is power. Put an electric guitar into the hands of a young man, put that young man on stage, and instantly he is transformed into a godlike being with powers of sexual attraction rivalled only by Zeus himself. If only I had understood this in my youth, I myself might have become a rock and roll musician rather than a humble food critic. (I suppose there is still time; at the very least I could encourage the boys to set some of my culinary poetry to music. Imagine "O Cookie, My Cookie!" as a classic rock anthem.) Happily, you fell in love with me regardless, even though my hands held not a guitar and a pick, but a menu and a pen.

My dearest duck: You always said that art was a religion to you; it would therefore be wrong of me to keep The High Priestess from her labours any longer. You were never one to rest on your laurels, but given that your latest success is still so fresh, I wonder what it is that you could possibly be working on so steadfastly? (The upcoming exhibit in Vienna, the tenured professorship, perhaps grocery shopping for three boys who eat like Calydonian boars . . .) Anyway, my peach, I eagerly await news of your latest creations.

Your loving husband,

Oliver

From: oliver.black@thedawnpost.com
To: rafe.wilde@thedawnpost.com
Subject: Phoney Baloney

Dear Mr. Wilde:

My answering machine is not precisely like a similar model that was on display at the booth beside Alexander Graham Bell at the Centennial Exhibition of 1876, but it is something like that. That I have not yet purchased a new one is inexplicable, even to me, but I believe it might have something to do with the fact that I enjoy annoying my sons. They can almost never tell exactly which young lady has called them, and this has resulted in many hilarious episodes worthy of inclusion in any American situation comedy.

This evening I received a garbled message on the answering machine, and I imagined, incredibly, that the voice on the other end identified itself as none other than Rafe Wilde. I thought this must be impossible, or at least unlikely, given that you have never contacted me by telephone in the past. There could be no reason for you to call, surely, unless you possess the power of second sight and had decided to reply to my dinner invitation before I had even issued it.

Please confirm whether or not it was indeed your good self on the other end of the telephone. Why don't you do this by e-mail, in order to avoid another fruitless interaction with my antique answering machine, and the even greater risk of one of my sons answering the phone and pretending to listen attentively whilst claiming to be taking a message. (Nota bene: If a young man discovers that a telephone call does not relate in some way to his burgeoning sex life, he is given to paroxysms of indifference, and any communication conveyed via his insouciant hand is only slightly more likely to get to me than putting a note in a bottle and throwing it into the Bering Sea.)

Cheers,

Oliver Black

From: rafe.wilde@thedawnpost.com
To: angel.day@agape.org
Subject: Breaking a Date

Angel:

I called earlier but you weren't home – instead I got your mother on the phone who practically deafened me by screaming, *"And I find more bitter than death the woman, whose heart is snares and nets, and her hands as bands, and the sinner shall be taken by her,"* but she hung up on me when I told her I was hoping to be taken by the woman, and the sooner the better. So, here's the deal: I have to break our date tonight, which I was really looking forward to, especially because I bought a whole case of Grenadine just so I could ply you with an endless supply of Shirley Temples. Something pretty nasty has happened at *The Dawn Post*, but it's a grownup problem and nothing to worry your pretty little head about (for God's sake, don't frown – I couldn't stand a crease in *your* forehead on *my* conscience).

Love ya,

Your Rafey

From: rafe.wilde@thedawnpost.com
To: suzanne@heartmail.com
Subject: Making a Date

Suzanne:

Where the hell are you?! I've e-mailed, I've phoned, and dammit I hate that stinking answering machine message of yours. (It's so old I hear Petey in the background, screeching that one goddamned sentence – which isn't funny anymore, Suzanne, and never was, except at first, when I thought you were joking.) Anyway, this is not a test of my emergency broadcast equipment, all right? This is a heavy-duty, industrial-strength, weapons-grade fuckup, and I need to talk to you *now*. *Please,* Suzanne. Just meet me tonight at The Nut and Squirrel, around 9:00, okay? This time the sky has *really* fallen.

Rafe

Chapter Two

From: oliver.black@thedawnpost.com
To: selwyn.black@freenet.org
Subject: Mutilation as Recreation

Feast of Saint Sebastian

Hello Selwyn:

Dear God, not *another* piercing. Your mother tells me that you now have holes in *seven* parts of your body (which bit has been mutilated this time, I dare not speculate) and that you have elaborate plans for another five. I shan't be surprised if next time we meet I see you sporting a hugely attractive bone through your nose or large iron rods through your kneecaps. Are the bumps under your turtleneck actually bolts in your neck? Is the arrow through your head pretend or genuine? But perhaps I ought not to give you any ideas.

You should know that when you were born, I vowed that there should never be such a thing as a generation gap between us, as there was between me and my progenitors. However, I find that with the recent fascination for piercing everything that it is possible to pierce, not to mention the plethora of unsubtle tattoos spread over the formerly unspoiled flesh of the young (a practice I find particularly disturbing in young ladies), a gap, nay, an abyss between us is inevitable. I choose not to poke holes in any part of my anatomy, having discovered quite enough natural orifices to suffice; you like nothing better, it seems, than to intentionally puncture your flesh in order to create permanent wounds in which to insert various artefacts. If you were the only young person engaged in this bizarre ritualistic behaviour, I would certainly wonder where your mother and I had gone wrong when you were still a boy; perhaps we overlooked a morbid fascination for splinters and paper cuts. However, given that such behaviour is widespread among your peers, I can only conclude one of two things: either I just don't understand it (doubtful), or your generation has been infected with an alarmingly virulent meme, which for some reason causes you and your contemporaries to believe that mutilating yourselves is a jolly good idea. Such mutilation quite possibly has an evolutionary advantage; perhaps it is a signal to others that you *are* young (you will not currently find many grandmothers with a pierced tongue), and that you are therefore a desirable reproductive partner. Or like reckless driving and excessive alcohol consumption, abundant piercings may well serve as a sexual signal to others of your generation in a different way; that you can put yourselves in so much danger and handicap yourselves so severely with, for example, pierced tongues and genitals, and yet *still* function (almost) normally, means that you must be a young, strong, and (otherwise) healthy individual – a superior genetic choice. Of course, the explanation may be simpler: it may be that all of you have far too much time on your hands and need to direct your attention outward, rather than gazing at the hoop in your navel.

Couldn't you do something less permanent? Temporary measures would have the added advantage of endless variety. May I suggest jewellery? Hair ornaments? Mehndi? Or, if these simple measures are not to your taste, what about a radical change of clothing? Perhaps you could design and wear one of those flamboyant phallocarps worn by the men of the Ketengban tribe of New Guinea. How marvellous you would look with your penis sheathed in bright reds and yellows and embellished at the end with leaves and Fun Fur or some other decorative ornament. Like the Ketengbans, you could have a different one for each day of the week, or go one step further, creating even larger, more festive varieties for the holiday season. (A mini Christmas wreath is obvious, but why not consider tinsel, bells, and even little speakers that play the "Boar's Head Carol" or "The Friendly Beast?")

Do think about your options. Meanwhile you should know that your mother has hidden her pincushion, and I have put the staple gun out of reach.

Sagely,

Dad

From:　　oliver.black@thedawnpost.com
To:　　　hyacinth.butterworth-scone@thefaultline.org
Subject:　Adulation

Dear Madam:

I received your kind letter in the post today and wanted to reply immediately to the question you posed. Not surprisingly, the answer is an unwavering and unequivocal yes. *Yes,* I would be profoundly honoured to receive the Restaurant Critic of the Year award from the International Restaurant Critics' Association.

It is gratifying to know that you recognize, Madam, that life is no picnic for the restaurant critic. It is not all pudding and cream puffs, a fact that is recognized by other critics but is largely unappreciated by the ill-informed public. I find that it is not so much like being a common journalist as it is like being a foreign correspondent, don't you agree? In truth, we risk life and limb daily, wading through rivers of rich white sauces, trudging over vast deserts of pancakes and breads, sinking into the quicksands of custards, marching through minefields of pastries and pies, and stuffing ourselves with God only knows what as our bloodstreams thicken, our arteries clog, and our bowels howl in protest. And living in the heart of cattle country as we do, with the mania for bovine flesh rampant as it is, the unfortunate food critic, who is not a dietician after all, is expected to consume one poor beast after another after another (though as you know I have *always* squeamishly drawn the line at veal, since the prospect of eating a motherless infant sentenced to life in a wooden crate does not inspire salivation, but rather sorrow). What a toll the daily consumption of what I fondly refer to as the Triple Bypass Special must take on the body over the course of a lifetime! The saturated fats, the excess protein, the various hormones and antibiotics and herbicides and pesticides! The dragon of diabetes is only one of our many enemies; other food-related illnesses lurk just inside the next restaurant. Dear God! I dare not think of all the ghastly things I have ingested for the sake of my fellow human! I feel like a canary in a coal mine, in between the moments of culinary splendour, that is (and I readily admit that it is these that make the job worth the risk).

So, Dear Lady, I thank you for recognizing my contribution to the literature (as well as my lion-hearted valour, given that I have had job-related food poisoning requiring hospitalization at least five times during the course of my career). I look forward to receiving this tremendous honour from your hands in only a few weeks' time.

Sincerely,

Mr. Oliver Black

From: oliver.black@thedawnpost.com
To: branksome.black@rebel.net
Subject: Troubles at The Topsy Turtle

Dearest Branksome:

It was excellent of you to call the other day; how remarkable that one can now contact the civilized world from the nether regions of the universe by merely pushing a few buttons. Science brought us the microwave oven, the ceramic flat-top stove, and now this. I say hurrah for technology.

I am relieved to know that you are as warm and cozy as a Hottentot on toast in your temporary south sea refuge. You most certainly deserve a rest from your heroic avian labour, and not only this, but also the other business (of which I will not speak here, except to say a well-deserved "Bravo, Old Chap"). As I mentioned in our telephone conversation, the universe appears to be unfolding as it should here in the Black household. My extraordinary wife is still seeking that full-time professorship and producing paintings worthy of the Uffizi; my daughter is steadily evolving into the next Glenn Gould (who himself might have appreciated the nonlegato effect produced by the three or four cats inevitably napping on the strings inside the piano); my sons, though riddled with puncture wounds, are rising as one up the pop charts; and due to my scintillating and provocative restaurant reviews, I have been named Restaurant Critic of the Year. There is no hint that anything here is other than in the pink – at least, so it would appear to the external observer. But alas, Branksome, as you well know, appearances can be deceiving. (I use you as corroborative evidence of this fact – who would think, upon looking at you, that you are actually a relatively decent chap?) Upon hearing your voice after these many weeks, I was reminded that it was always you, my dearest brother, to whom I could turn with the simple problems of my childhood – that is, when you were not too preoccupied with plans for my impending torture. Dear Boy, how you loved your rubber darts and bullwhip! Relations between siblings are notoriously complicated, are they not? Never mind. The point is, Branksome, that there exists a philosophical matter, which is not, however, merely theoretical and above practical import, about which I would greatly value your opinion. You have always given me jolly good advice, both legal and personal (urging me to marry Lucy, for instance, being a conveniently combined example of both) and lately I find that I am once again in need of your counsel.

The problem is, I regret to say, my Weltanschauung. "Check the fuel-pump," you will wryly reply (how well I know you after fifty-odd years!). But, in all seriousness, Branksome, my Weltanschauung is not at all well; it is confounded, incongruous, befuddled. I find I no longer act idealistically, but expediently. I know

what you will say. You will quote that notoriously overused passage of Whitman's: "Do I contradict myself? Very well then I
contradict myself. I am large, I contain multitudes." You always
did love to quote the great poets, like a guilty priest madly quoting Scripture, but we both know that you always choose this particular passage when you want to justify questionable behaviour.
You are forced to claim bankruptcy, to deny paternity, to abandon the wreckage, and instead of boasting like you normally do
about your Aristotelian-like flawless rationality, you furiously spit
out Whitman until you find yourself stuffed like some hapless
Thanksgiving turkey, full of contradictions so violently opposed
to one another that it's amazing you don't simply blow up. Instead of quoting the poets and philosophers known for champion-
ing reason over passion, we get the mystic Pascal and the heart
that has its reasons that reason knows nothing of. And how often
this progresses to defensiveness and self-pity – even as children
you pitied yourself for being born on a Wednesday (and therefore
being full of woe) and envied my birth on a Sunday (giving me the
advantage of being loving and wise and good and gay), and therefore you made me your personal slave in order to redress the
imbalance.

But I digress. How often our conversations proceed thus! I
blame an overabundance of brotherly love, besides which it is
only natural for the elder brother (by a full fifteen months) and
the wiser brother (me again, by epochs) to want to sculpt the
fragile character of the younger and more reckless. Has it not
always been my responsibility to keep you in check and to remind
you to include human beings, other than yourself, within your
circle of moral concern? Indeed, it has. Yet the situation is rife
with ambiguity; perhaps I really ought to be *encouraging* your
natural instincts since, in truth, it is your greatest weakness (i.e.,
flippant indifference toward your fellow human beings) that is
your greatest strength!

Still, Dear Branky, for once I mean to speak of myself, not of
you. So by way of explanation of my situation, I am including a

copy of the text of a letter received by me only a few days ago. It reads as follows:

Mr. Black:

Is it possible that you did not fully comprehend the content of the letter I sent to you on the fifteenth of this month? Perhaps your brain has finally given in to the inevitable mental stupor to which all of your kind eventually submit. Still, can anyone, even a freak like you, be that obtuse? Did I not make it clear that ignoring my demands will result in the immediate public revelation of The Information that will further result in a catastrophic professional explosion? To wit, you will be out of a job, unable to secure another, and despised by all. I would not be at all surprised if your family also abandoned you; frankly, I don't know many women who would relish being married to an imposter such as yourself.

Your last review was a betrayal of mammoth proportions. The word "sabotage" cannot be construed as an overstatement. However, I'm willing to overlook this latest disappointment in return for triple the usual payment.

Don't forget which side your bread is buttered upon, Mr. Black.

Rather frightening, isn't it? I shan't write more about my predicament at present (*Muri oculos habent*), but I trust I make the situation plain enough to you, who know me so well. (If not, at least I know you love a good puzzle – or is that me?) In so doing I find that, just like the time you attempted to fasten me to a corkboard by throwing darts at the perimeters of my clothing, I am once again at your mercy. Still, I remain convinced that with your meritorious credentials, you are by far the best person to provide advice. You have climbed mountains, conquered oceans, loved women, tagged penguins. You are a man of the world, Branksome, and the man for the job.

Respond immediately. Do not bother with either Pascal or Whitman.

Your devoted sibling (with the scars to prove it),

Oliver

PS: I did something entirely out of character the other day – but no. Not here, not now – not you.

PPS: I also need to confer with you about Lucille, but I'll save that particular business for another letter; just now I have another note to write that is far more exciting than any note I ever write to you, Dear Brother.

My Only True Love,

One hand upon your breast, the other upon your thigh and inching ever closer to heaven. Have mercy. Twenty-five years is surely long enough to wait for consummation.

Forever,

Oliver

From: rafe.wilde@thedawnpost.com
To: oliver.black@thedawnpost.com
Subject: Cue Career Death Knell

Hey Mr. Black:

Flaming fucking hell! How could you do this to me, you rancid, fetid, nauseating abscess – you oozing pus factory – you chunk of sickly sewage, clot of diseased offal, lump of mouldering mucus. *I hate you, I hate you, I HATE you*, you . . . – yeah, well, you get the idea. Just imagine at least twenty-five more insults combining the themes of stench, stupidity, and embarrassing body parts and their excretions. And then you'll know what I said to "Our Most Esteemed Publisher" when I stormed into his office this morning, contract in hand, demanding to know what the fuck is meant by the very last footnote – at the very bottom, on the back of the very last page, in the indecipherably minuscule print. Shit! Why didn't I pay attention to the part of your e-mail that urged me to be careful when it comes to signing contracts? And, apparently, I can't do a thing about it, unless I try to sue the paper, which my lawyer says I should definitely do if I enjoy the sight of my own entrails.

Listen: When I agreed to write *Rafe Reviews* for *The Dawn Post*, I understood that I'd be doing *exactly* the same job that I've always done – you know, writing music reviews about the whole popular music scene. Rock, reggae, hip-hop, soul, metal, gothic, indie, funk, industrial, psychedelic, progressive, punk, hardcore, rap, grunge, glam – that's what I cover, right? I mean, why else would anyone hire me? Apparently, however, *I* misunderstood the terms of the contract, a document that apparently states, in print that requires an electron microscope to read, that I am now *the* live contemporary music critic for *The Dawn Post*! Do you under-stand what I'm saying here, Mr. Black? *Rafe Wilde is no longer a critic of the popular music scene.* Oh no. Now Rafe Wilde is the critic of the *entire* live contemporary music scene, the whole god-damn thing – which means that if a piece of music was composed in the last hundred years, and somebody plays it in a live concert, I cover it! I'm supposed to write reviews about *every genre of music* that gets a live performance. *Every genre*, Mr. Black. Get it? Just in case the fatal implications have eluded you, allow me to spell out what this means for what *was* a glorious career.

Right. My entire professional life has been spent hanging out at the funky jazz clubs and blues bars and stadium style rock con-certs that are my second home, and I've naturally become known to my fans as the quintessential cool critic. *You* know this – hell, *everybody* knows this. Rafe Wilde *is* the King of Cool, the Sultan of Swank, the Don of Funk, to list only a few of my many monikers. Sure, I occasionally stray from hip pop venues without undue harm to my reputation; for example, the occasional country and western review doesn't damage my image, given that there is nothing sexier than Rafe Wilde wearing cowboy boots, bootleg jeans, and a black Stetson – but *not* chaps, spurs, string tie, and cap gun – and here you see that the line between cool and uncool is razor sharp and wafer thin. I've *never* crossed that line, Mr. Black, or allowed myself to be pushed over it for that matter. (Anyone at a country and western event who tries to make me *square* dance, for example, will quickly find his head on a *circular* satin pillow, lying in a *rectangular* box.) Let's not kid ourselves – we all know it's all about *image*. It's not about how you look in the mirror, but how you look in the public eye that matters. It's all about reputation, and at the moment *my* reputation as the Titan of Trendy is being held by the testicles and dangled out the window by the fucking lunatic-publisher of *The Dawn Post*.

Case in point: my very first assignment is to make my way out to the suburbs of East Bumblefuck and to locate, in among all the identical vinyl-sided garages attached to identical vinyl-sided houses, the Happy Valley Community Hall (a *community hall – in the suburbs* – you following me?) and then to write a review of – get this – the Buffalo Jump Barbershop Quartet. *Barbershop*, Mr. Black! *Bar-ber-shop*! The guys with little bow ties and little striped vests and pencil thin moustaches – and always a little guy who sings like a girl, a fat guy who sings like a foghorn, and two guys in between who sing about shoo fly pie and apple pan dowdy in every fucking song. So where does *this* register on the cool-o-meter? Right! *It doesn't register at all*. And what's worse, the very next day I have to review the music of an extremely uncool ethnic festival, and it's one of those ethnic countries with incredibly embarrassing national dress and customs – *and I have to pretend that it's not slowly killing me to be there*, even though their ridiculous little hats and hosen are a veritable *Kryptonite* for the kool.

But I can take all of that – yeah, sure I can. I say bring on the folk and world-beat, the Celtic and bluegrass, the gospel and the ambient, the illbient and the trance. Bring it on and watch Rafe Wilde the alchemist transform gold into platinum. But there are limits, Mr. Black – and I reach *my* limit at my third assignment, which is destined to ruin my reputation as the King of Cool faster than a porkpie hat and a buck-and-wing dance. My third task is to write a review of a concert of the most hopeless sort of music of all, though here I'm using the word "music" lightly and with every grain of salt in the shaker. I'm talking about modern art music – you know, new music, experimental music, avant-garde music, serious contemporary classical music – it has many names but new music by any other name would still smell as – well, let's just say it would still smell. I'm talking about that plinkety-plonkety, binkety-bonkety, contemporary donkey music – music without an actual melody, without an actual beat, *without any-thing that identifies it as actual music.* Don't pretend you don't know what I'm talking about – you know what I mean about this so-called music, expressly composed for the pompous, the sui-cidal, the psychotic, the elderly – *the deaf!* I'm talking about those List E pieces from our old piano days, my friend – that nonsensi-cal noise, full of meaningless clatter and empty gestures, randomly flicked onto the page by a conspiracy of deranged, sadistic white guys who hated music so much that they tried to destroy it by rid-ding it of everything that makes it into music in the first place – but then, in a clever move calculated to confuse the issue, they still called it "music." I guess we should be thankful they didn't infiltrate other professions, otherwise we'd all be driving cars without wheels, flying in planes without wings, reading books without words, eating food without taste.

I explained all of this to (well, yelled all of this at) "Our Most Esteemed Publisher," and all he did was attempt a benign smile (a smirk, really) as he handed me a stack of back issues of *The Peri-odical of Modern Music.* Christ! Have you ever seen this magazine? I doubt it because due to public interest there's only one copy per issue, but let me tell you it's exactly like reading a "Save the Panda" edition of the World Wildlife Fund magazine. "Inside this issue: the decline of the Modern Composer – read about his fight for survival in a hostile world, where he is outcompeted by every other musical species!" These new music composers are like animals at the edge of the gene pool, hoping for the birth of a supercomposer who will save their kind from extinction. It might happen to one of them, but meanwhile they write these articles about new music venues that read exactly like articles on panda habitat reforestation, complete with photos of doomed composers, each one like the photo of some pathetic endangered beast.

Anyway, the point is this: Is there anything less hip, anything more pretentious, *anything that will end my career as the King of Cool faster*, than being seen at some miserable little concert of contemporary "classical" music? Rafe Wilde, no longer cool but looking dapper, natty, spruce, in his bow tie and cummerbund, getting claustrophobia in some pokey little community hall and listening to music so sterile you could convert it to pill-form and use it as birth control. Isn't it obvious that if music *sounds* like shit, it *is* shit? And what am I going to say about that godforsaken avant-garde noise anyway? Jesus H. Christ. It's no surprise that they're paying me a small fortune, but no amount of money would be enough to cover this gig.

I need my girlfriend right fucking *now*.

Rafe

PS: Actually, the point is – can you help?

The Dream Post
Danger of Hiring Unqualified Employees
Brought to Light

St John's, Newfoundland – An official government study released yesterday (chiefly researched by Miss Sweet's precocious grade five class at Newfoundling Elementary) demonstrates how shoddy hiring practices in modern mega-institutions (newspapers, hospitals, governments) have led to the employment of totally unsuitable and underqualified persons. "We see it all the time at the university," explained the dean of the philosophy department, Dr. I. B. Fuddle. "The recent cutbacks have meant having to combine previously separate positions in the department, and so, as an example, I recently hired Mrs. Myrna Hoople, the large-bottomed, beehived, sensibly shoed social sciences cleaning lady, to teach our courses in Advanced Logic and History of Thought from Plato to the Present. I was looking forward to Mrs. Hoople making a 'clean sweep' of the department, teaching Logic and various graduate courses while taking over dusting and vacuuming duties from Professor Macintosh, chores which he has performed tirelessly since the cutbacks of '92."

Sadly, however, Dr. Fuddle's reasoning in this matter was unsound, and now nothing strikes terror into the hearts of the department members like the rattling approach of Mrs. Hoople's trolley of cleaning supplies and philosophical abstracts. The amiable professors, who used to be found ambling about the philosophy department in their pipe ash–stained cardigans, are now usually found squatting on their desks like skittish animals of prey as Mrs. Hoople hoovers vigorously around them, ranting and raving as is her custom. "Haven't you read Kant?" she often scolds her colleagues. "'Act only according to a maxim by which you can at the same time *will* that it shall become a general law!' Hello? What do you have to say to that, Mr. Bigshot Professor? I say, what if everybody's office was a pigsty? Well? Were you born in Plato's cave? Are you one of Rousseau's savages? Some sort of Nietzschean superman who doesn't have to empty the wastepaper basket?" The professors are continually horrified at Professor Hoople's pseudophilosophical mish-mash and have tried to counter – at first by reasoned argument, and later by hurling copies of *Attacking Faulty Reasoning* directly at her bun – but Professor Hoople is a spry sixty and can dodge flying books and logical postulates with equal alacrity.

The situation has worsened since Professor Hoople is herself now on various hiring committees and is making sure that all her friends get top positions in the department. "Just yesterday the philosophy department hired Ping Pong, a former short-order cook from Hong Kong," explains Dr. Fuddle, "a fellow who speaks no English whatsoever but whom we understand is devoted to short-order logic, which is the summing up of each philosopher's entire body of philosophical thought in a single Chinese character."

Not only are universities affected, but so are other mammoth modern institutions, such as banks (not wanting to be accused of discriminatory hiring practices on the basis of dress and name, one bank recently regretted its decision to hire an individual in striped pajamas named Sticky Fingers Louie) and, as previously mentioned, newspapers, which have been known to hire underqualified critics and reporters who seriously skew public opinion by – among other practices – taking seriously the findings of children.

From: rafe.wilde@thedawnpost.com
To: sales@bedsbedsbeds.cybersleep.net
Subject: No Circumsomnambulating around the Issue

You Bumbling Cretins at Beds Beds Beds:

Good morning, Putrescent Balls of Vomit. Did you sleep well?
I sincerely hope so, because *I* sure as hell didn't, and you're going
to need every advantage a good night's sleep affords in order to
deal with the wrath of Rafe Wildebeest. *Fucking hell.* Don't you
think I have enough problems in my life without having to worry
about getting a decent night's sleep? It was a joke, wasn't it, selling me this farcical excuse for a bed. "Let's make a laughingstock
of the music critic," you thought, "and sell him a *round* bed, a
piece of furniture that was designed exclusively for the comfort of
the spherical. And when he tires of *that* gimmick, we'll sell him
our triangular number, The Isosceles Solution, or maybe The
Pentagonal Principle, or how about The Sleep Star Seven? And
when he doesn't fit into any of *those* beds, we'll offer him our
special Personalized Adjustment Service, where we come out to
your home, carefully measure both you and your bed, and then
lop off any extra bits of you that are hanging over the edges."
Need I point out that most human beings are not octagonal, not
pyramidal, not rhomboidal, but roughly rectangular in shape?
Given this unavoidable reality, is it not obvious that we require
roughly rectangular shaped beds? Maybe this elementary notion
has eluded you since you undoubtedly sleep on the beds you sell
and are therefore dealing with the mentally debilitating effects of
chronic sleep deprivation.

Do you know how unbelievably disorienting it is to sleep in a
round bed, a bed with no up or down, no left or right, no top or
bottom? How can you make sense of your exact location in a bed
when the only thing that still applies is gravity? Some part of my
body is forever dangling off the edge, usually a couple of limbs
and also my head, which often lolls dangerously over the side,
leaving me to choke on my own vomit. And I'm constantly hitting
my head on the night table – thank god it's inflatable or I'd have
to wear a football helmet and mouth-guard to bed every night.
The only way to stop myself from falling out of bed is to sleep
exactly in the middle, but why in the name of the Sandman should
I need a ruler, a compass, and a GPS (Girl Positioning System) just

to get comfy?

And besides all of that, I discovered that normal bedding doesn't fit, which you might have mentioned at the time of purchase. So I had to drive all over town looking for round sheets, a round comforter, round pillows, round mints for the round pillows, round everything – which I couldn't find, and so I had to beg the invisible mending lady across the hall to make them for me – and then I was plagued with nightmares that not only would I not be able to orient myself in my bed, I wouldn't be able to see the fucking thing either. And all this for an astronomical price, I might add.

So I've taken it upon myself to roll this circular bed from hell into a large puddle just outside my back door where you'll find it when you deliver model 79a (the vibrating bed called Helga's Hands). Who knows what I'll sleep on in the meantime.

Irked again,

Rafe Wilde

___

From: rafe.wilde@thedawnpost.com
To: suzanne@heartmail.com
Subject: Here Comes the Shun

Hey Suzanne:

Okay, so where are you anyway? And why won't you answer a simple question? I've left about seventy-five messages on your answering machine this morning alone. You're probably at your heart surgeon boyfriend's mansion getting a free physical exam in his bedroom on his hugely comfortable king-size gurney. And I can't talk to Angel about it because she's on an afterschool photo shoot, besides which in order to fully convey the legal subtleties of my situation, I'd have to use words with more than three syllables in them. Anyway, I really need to talk to you about my new job, which is not at all the job I thought it was going to be. I feel like an oil rig worker who's been told that, from now on, he's going to be drilling teeth. Or maybe a heart surgeon who's been told he's going to be working for Hallmark making valentines. (You like that one, don't you?) The point is I've been betrayed, Suzanne, and it's a betrayal of colossal proportions. Now I know exactly how Jesus Christ felt just after he ate the last supper aboard the Titanic.

I've got another problem, too, which is that I've gotten rid of my bed – you know, the round one, which I'm beginning to think was a replica of The Wheel that the Beds Beds Beds people copied from some torture museum. "Buy now and receive a cats' paw, thumbscrews, and punishing boots – at no extra charge!" Actually, it's a good thing you didn't sleep over when I had it, or we probably would've knocked ourselves out as our heads crashed together in a moment of debauchery and disorientation. My new bed won't arrive for a couple of days, so meanwhile I'm forced to sleep on my old futon, which has become so compacted over the years that now it's exactly like sleeping on a slab of granite, only much less comfortable. Please, Suzanne. I ask you, as my best friend – can I sleep over at your house? You have that fantastic wooden sleigh bed that always made me feel as if it was snowing outside but we were cozy and warm and racing along over the Russian steppes together. (Look, a reindeer! A communist! Tsar Nicholas II!) We wouldn't have to have sex or anything, honestly. I would leave that decision up to you, although realistically, one look at my firm, naked, gyrating form next to you will render you helpless with desire. (Not my fault.)

So, *please*, call me as soon as possible. That heart surgeon boyfriend of yours doesn't need you; he's got all his nurses and surgical tools and internal organs to keep him company. But *I* need you. I need your support, your pity, your bed. Come on, Suzanne. Have a heart (a phrase that has a whole different meaning coming from your boyfriend, especially if he says it while reaching into his pocket, at which point I'd make a run for it).

Luv,

Rafe

From: oliver.black@thedawnpost.com
To: rafe.wilde@thedawnpost.com
Subject: "Of all the horrid, hideous notes of woe, Sadder than
              owl-songs or the midnight blast, Is that portentous
              phrase 'I told you so.'" —Lord Byron

Dear Mr. Wilde:

Now, now. Language, language. Temper, temper. Firstly, let me just say that I did warn you about our wily publisher, didn't I, and perhaps from now on you will take the word of Oliver Black with the seriousness it deserves. Secondly, just because the New Music Society is playing, in only three weeks, a tribute concert to the music of Mr. John Cage, a man who is one of the most famous composers of the twentieth century and about whom you know (I'm guessing here) absolutely nothing whatsoever, this is no reason for you to panic and lose whatever cool you claim to possess. Your position is far from hopeless, and I believe you have at least three options open to you. If *The Dawn Post* is paying you such an extraordinary amount of money, why not hire somebody else to go in your stead? Or if this strategy is unsatisfactory or, indeed, illegal, why not consider working as I do and attend these disreputable concerts in disguise? It is truly astonishing what deception can be accomplished with a fake nose, a false moustache, and wax lips.

Of course, you could attempt to attend any unseemly concerts as Rafe Wilde himself and write your reviews as you always have – with precision, wit, and insight. How can you do this, you wonder, when you know so very little about the music you are attempting to review? Elementary, my dear Wilde. You get yourself an education – take a course, read a book, secure a private instructor of music history. (I have in my possession the name of a particularly fine teacher of precisely the sort of which you are in need; shall I pass it on to you?) The point is that you are a resourceful and intelligent chap. You don't need any help from me. And besides, it may very well be that the mighty hordes of cheering admirers will accept this new facet of the maturing critic and will read your reviews with enthusiasm, if only for the literary content. What is true for me is also true for you: indifference to my reviews is restricted to the tongueless, or to those whose palates have been mysteriously erased by sinister unknown means. Only the deaf will find your reviews of exiguous interest.

I do believe, my dear Rafe, that you may be overreacting somewhat to your new position of contemporary live music critic. Forgive me for saying it, but you sound rather like a petulant child who is insisting on his hotdog and chips just as he is about to be escorted into a three-star restaurant for his first authentic dining experience. What I mean, Rafe, is that one must be careful not to tar every note of modern art music with the same brush, mustn't one? I readily admit that the worst of contemporary music is ghastly, and those composers responsible (mostly academics composing for other academics), along with their counterparts in the visual arts and architecture, should be force-fed a diet of their own creations until they finally crack and admit the truth – i.e., that they got carried away with a hilarious practical joke that became increasingly misanthropic the longer they realized that people were actually too stupid to catch on. It is true that, on the one hand, the worst of such music is so stupefyingly irritating, one can easily imagine it used as a device equal in destructive capability to any chemical or biological weapon. Perhaps in future we shall have musical warfare where each side will blast the other with increasingly bad music until the worst piece of the century is played, thus securing victory. Imagine soldiers frantically trying to cover their ears as they fall senseless to the ground screaming, "No! Not that! Anything but –" (Ooh – I dare not speak its name. It's fine and dandy to provoke feelings of terminal dread, but one mustn't overdo it.) On the other hand, such music can be so stupendously dull that one wants to ask if it was really written by composers intending it to be taken seriously as art, or was it, rather, concocted by fiendishly clever scientists in their sleep labs, searching for a fool-proof cure for consciousness? But as I say, my young chappie, one must not assume that all music written in the last hundred-odd years falls into either of these categories. There are challenges unique to the avant-garde, but so often one's investment in overcoming these challenges is repaid a hundredfold. Do not resist the unknown, Mr. Wilde, and do not make the mistake of mocking that about which one knows very little. After all, music is music, is it not? And never forget Theodore Sturgeon's observation, which subsequently became immortalized as Sturgeon's Law, when some know-nothing accused the genre of science fiction of being "ninety percent crap": "Ninety percent of everything is crap," he wisely remarked, and certainly this is no less true of modern music. But the other ten percent, Rafe! One can feel only pity for those who wander through life imagining that the peak of musical achievement happened with, let's say, "Puberty Love" by The Osmiroids, only to die without hearing a note of what the very best contemporary composers have to offer.

Now, Mr. Wilde, thus far in our correspondence you have successfully evaded every question I have asked of you. However, I feel I simply must know the specifics of the evil that the beastly Ms. Savage inflicted upon poor little you. Two of my three sons studied piano with her, you know, and both of them begged to quit, and were given permission so to do, at about the same age as you were when you were released from your alleged torment. (My third and youngest son, now known as Damien, never studied the piano; even in utero he enjoyed flailing away, and my wife prophesied that he might someday become a boxer or some other kind of person whose calling in life is to beat the tar out of peo-

ple. Predictably, he went on to become a whacking enthusiast –
rhythmic, uproarious, *loud* – and it is no surprise that it is he who
is the drummer in the band.) Now my dear little Olivia, at the
delicate age of eight, is at the mercy of the apparently psychotic
Ms. Savage for a full half an hour a week. Am I paying for the
gradual erosion of her self-esteem and her musical sensibilities? It
seems impossible for me to believe; Ms. Savage always seems so
eager, so congenial, so passionately nice. Is there some sort of
hideous Jekyll and Hyde transformation occurring in my absence
of which I ought to be made aware?

I have three further questions to which I hope you will respond in your next missive. Firstly, would you like a cat? I find in
times of affliction, nothing restores one's peace of mind faster
than the rumbling waves of contentment that emanate from a cat
within purring distance. Cats are like stress balls: you pick one up,
give it a squeeze, and everything's right with the world once
again.

Secondly, who is this extraordinary girlfriend of yours who is
capable of taming the Wilde beast? And, thirdly, would you and
said girlfriend care to dine *chez nous* next Sunday evening, say
about sevenish? I would welcome the opportunity to meet you in
the flesh, and you, I dare say, would welcome a meal prepared by
the experienced hand of Mr. Oliver Black himself. Some restaurant critics fall into the profession in their university days, as they
cannot cook for themselves and are forced to dine out; I, however, began my career in the kitchen and was preparing exotic
dishes when I was no more than a slip of a busboy. Come on
Sunday, and I shall reveal to you the mystery of the quince.

Expectantly,

Oliver Black

From: oliver.black@thedawnpost.com
To: lucy.black@artnet.org
Subject: Gruntled Reminiscing

Dearest Lucy:

Once again I expected to find you in your studio, my petal, and once again my hopes have been dashed. Never mind. I merely wanted to make you aware that I have invited Mr. Rafe Wilde and companion to dine with us this coming Sunday evening at seven, and I issue this e-mail as a formal notice – please, Darling, join us for a dinner in your honour. I promise you shall not be disappointed with the evening's fare; I am making your favourite: vine leaves stuffed with rice, pine nuts, veggies, and my inscrutable special sauce, which I always prepare in pitch-blackness in the dead of night, like some kind of deranged food scientist. Of course I shall prepare vast quantities of the boys' favourite dish – Tomato Woodchuck – so that there will be some proper food left for the rest of us. By the way, I am beginning to suspect that their huge appetites are due to the fact that not only are they boys, and teenage boys to boot (Freudian slip), but also musicians. Have you ever examined a group of musicians after a gig, Lucy? It's shameful. No matter how heavily laden at the beginning, by the end of the evening the table is always so disgracefully devoid of food that one could swear the band (or the orchestra – they're the absolute worst) had actually gotten to their knees and licked the serving plates clean with their tongues. No insect ever bothers with a post-concert wine and cheese twice, and even the tiniest microorganism knows he's going to leave woefully empty-handed. Anyway, my treasure, that's neither here nor there. The point is that all the family is welcome, and as a special treat, I shall even hose the boys down in the back garden before the meal. It will be an occasion to remember, I assure you.

Speaking of occasions to remember, my own, I was reminiscing earlier today about that fabulous fortnight we spent in

Mexico, *nine* years ago now, the first (and only) trip we have ever
taken away from our copious offspring. Perhaps Branksome's
travels have put me in mind of it, but by gosh, Lucy, we had a
marvellous time! Remember? The fine bleached sand, the gentle
turquoise surf, the thatched-roof beachfront cabana – it was
another world! Do you recall the day that we went wandering
along the streets of that lazy little town beside our resort, past the
shops with their colourful scarves and trinkets, the hole-in-the-
wall restaurants with their quesadillas and corn tortillas, and then
past some sort of religious retreat centre where a single row of
people were sitting in the lotus position on little mats and just
staring straight ahead at the wall? Do you remember it, Love? We
instinctively bowed our heads, tiptoed reverently past, and then
pranced to the beach where we found the perfect palm tree under
which to park ourselves for a morning of swimming and sunbathing. We also found a largish sort of salt marsh connected to the
ocean by a small trickle of a stream. While you bathed your
bikini-clad body in the sunshine, I decided in a fit of boyish
enthusiasm to widen the rivulet a little in order to allow better
drainage from stagnant pond to roaring ocean. I worked away for
a quarter of an hour or so, stealing glances every so often at you,
my wifely wahine (never has the Nobel prize for fashion been so
deserved as by the inventor of the string bikini), and then we
decided to meander along the beach in order to find the ultimate
picnic spot. We walked for an hour – found it – paddled, lunched,
lounged – and then walked back along the water's edge, hand-in-
hand, the surf lapping at our feet. How astonished we were when
we came back to where we had begun and found that my little
three-inch-deep, ten-foot-long trench was now a gigantic chasm,
still ten feet long but now at least six feet deep and six feet wide!
Big enough for children to be playing in it, for teenagers to be
carving graffiti all over it, for the authorities to be puzzled by it!
Had I, a casual tourist, unwittingly altered the Mexican landscape
forever? It was an intoxicating though somewhat worrying
thought.

We were quite heady with the thrill of it as we sauntered back into town and once more passed the religious retreat where the same group of people had apparently not moved a muscle for the last five hours, and had continued to sit as still as tombstones, staring at the wall. What were they doing? Were they praying? And if so, what was the hold-up? Perhaps they had connected to the Almighty only to hear, "Please hold the line – your prayers are important to us and will be answered in the order in which they were received." Do you remember what happened next, Darling? I couldn't resist. I had to know what these people were up to, and so I gingerly opened the glass door, stuck my head in, and whispered, "Excuse me, but what are you people doing?" No one seemed to hear me except for the young fellow nearest the door, who, without moving his body an inch, merely turned his head slowly toward me and announced, simply, "We're sitting."

"They're sitting," I whispered to you as I closed the door, and we were barely a respectable distance away from the building before we broke down into great heaving sobs of laughter. Tears came to our eyes as we contemplated the answer. They were sitting! Of course! Why had we not seen it ourselves?

I remember that we had difficulty recovering our composure after this little episode; we remained quite giddy, and everything seemed hilarious to us as if we had imbibed too much red wine, which we then proceeded to do. After a fine bottle and an excellent meal, we slept off our stratospheric spirits back at our cabana and, when we awakened, decided to take a little vespers constitutional along the beach. We walked back to the very spot where you had sunbathed and I had accidentally engineered that colossal and spectacular drainage system to find – nothing! Not a trace of it! The ocean had erased all evidence of my canal! It was a sobering moment for us, a moment of perspective, of focus, but also, I think, of relief. How small we are! How ephemeral our petty achievements! We walked back to our cabana, bathed in perspective, and conceived Olivia. It just seemed like the thing to do, did it not?

Oh, my dearest love. How I would love to be back in that little thatched-roof cabana of ours, on that cozy double bed, with flower petals beneath us and the mosquito net drawn around us. Now, I don't mean to be too forward, and I'm reluctant to ask it, but shall we rendezvous after I return home from an evening of exquisite dining and supping? (Ah, how I love my work.) I miss you for all sorts of reasons, of course, but it has been such a long time since we have been properly together as husband and wife, and it would be marvellous to be physically proximate. I hope you will not be too fast asleep when I come home this evening, darling Lucy.

Your ardent husband,

Oliver

PS: Say, do you remember the poem we composed on the beach the next day while sunbathing together – that crazy little bit of verse inspired by our sitters? I well recall what fine sport we made, puzzling over the question of religion in general and various religious practices in particular. (Good Lord – do you suppose, Lucy, that our sitters are still there? One can imagine the very same people, now bearded and grey, moss growing on their north sides – do you think they've progressed through the novitiate stage and on to the higher disciplines, perhaps squatting or the more complicated and demanding activity of standing up?) I recall that we wondered as astonished observers, and we gave our little bit of comic verse a little twist at the end in order to prove our essential goodwill to all. I reprint it here in hopes that it brings back the memory of that happy time.

The Religious Are So Amusing!

The Religious are so amusing! with their funny little ways,
Their alms, their psalms, their jihads, and their witchipoo

flambées!
Their brooms, their bowls, their bells, their books devoted to
the dickens,
Their passion plays, their judgment days, their sacrificial
chickens!

The Religious are so amusing! with their supernatural notions,
Their inquisitions, superstitions, martyrish devotions.
How I like their long, stern faces! "Don't do this" and "Don't
do that,"
And I like the funny man who wears the funny pointy hat.

The Religious are so amusing! Look! They've books without
errata!
They've incantations, flagellations, they've even got stigmata!
They're very big on virgins – the priest, the monk, the nun,
And other sorts of masochists who don't much like much fun.

The Religious are so amusing! and I think it's simply swell
That they'd rather go to church on Sunday morn than go to
hell.
They like to make a racket, then pray quietly in their pew,
But they hate it when you sneak right up behind them and yell
"Boo!"

The Religious are so amusing! at all naughtiness they scoff,
And if you have a foreskin, then they'll prob'ly whack it off.
They look so smugly sad at the misled, the damned, the liar,
For all but them are doomed to boil in Satan's deep fat fryer.

The Religious are so amusing! with their celestial bosses,
They like grape juice, unleavened bread, and people up on
crosses.
Sometimes they ring my doorbell, then beneath my bed I
hustle,

And stroke my little Darwin fish and pray to Bertrand Russell.

The Religious are so amusing! they love things pecuniary,
From art to coffers full of gold to tacos shaped like Mary.
Bedfellows, ne'er! With unbelief and skeptical codswallop,
Trustworthy faith is proof and sluttish reason is a trollop.

The Religious are so amusing! I just think they're simply
    super,
And in no way do I mean to be a celestial party pooper.
It's the *skeptic* who'll be stunned to find religion's not a fraud!
And shocked this doggerel's holy writ penned by Almighty
    God.

                                        Almighty God

    PPS: I am reminded of Wilde's remark (no not *Rafe* Wilde –
the other one): "Rhyme . . . can turn man's utterance to the
speech of gods." Well, there you have it. Proof in the very signature.

From: rafe.wilde@thedawnpost.com
To: alma.wilde@command.net
Subject: Doom and Broom

    Hi Mom:

    I dropped Blankie on the floor today, and he landed in a
frown shape – and that's when I knew it was going to be a dismal,
depressing, melancholy crap day. (Sometimes the fact that I can
read Blankie like a psychic reads tea leaves almost feels like a
curse, you know?) Anyway, do you remember when I was taking
piano lessons with that spawn of Satan, Ms. Savage, and one of
the requirements was studying modern music history? Remember

how I got the lowest mark ever recorded by the Conservatory of Music on that test (an impressive minus 96 percent because they subtracted a mark for every wrong answer, and although some generous examiner gave me points for spelling my first name right, I've always kicked myself for forgetting the "e" in Wilde)? Well, I wish I'd paid more attention now because *The Dawn Post* is, *against my will*, making me the all-inclusive critic of the contemporary music scene. It ain't just rock 'n' roll anymore, Mom. It's everything from the last hundred years that I'm supposed to be some kind of expert in, including all of that avant-garde crapola – the stuff that sounds exactly the same whether or not you play it backward or forward, you know what I mean? The kind of music that you don't have to like, you just have to "understand." The kind of music whose one and only criterion is that it sounds like a really bad smell. You know, artsy fartsy, heavy on the fartsy. Bloody hell, why don't they just make me a rat exterminator while they're at it? Or the head of a math department? Or some other execrable job that doesn't interest me in the least, that I'm not qualified to do, and that I actively despise? Christ! It's like I've been drafted, and whether I like it or not, I'm about to be choppered into Iraq.

So it's a damn good thing you included my old piano books in the latest box of stuff you sent; finally, they may actually be of use as something other than kindling. Speaking of which, thanks for sending another box of stuff from the Holy Shrine of Little Rafe, which if I lose my job, I can always post on eBay and make a killing. I am deeply humbled to be in possession once again of my pet rock, my *Charlie's Angels* poster, and my purple snakeskin platform boots. I'm finding my old matching *Starsky and Hutch* mugs to be a bit of a downer though, although I'm not sure why. A pair of totally nongay swinging bachelor buddy/cops spending their days gleefully squealing around corners in a 1974 red Ford Torino on the streets of Bay City is a *good* thing. My therapist would probably ask if I was reminded of some long-forgotten childhood dream. He'd want to know if it was because I got the red Torino – natch – but I never found a Hutch for my Starsky. Hey, I think I've just saved myself $350 – cha-ching!

Gratitude aside, Mom, I still don't think you should be risking your life in that stinking cesspool I used to call my bedroom. I worry that like some unsuspecting diver in a lake full of underwater weeds, you'll become hopelessly entangled in my green shag rug and only be discovered weeks later by the Mod Squad, clutching a Pink Floyd cassette in one hand and a lava lamp in the other. Plus I worry that you might discover something truly embarrassing and/or disgusting (in fact, I'd say that's a given); on the upside, you might actually turn up that $3,000 worth of illicit drugs I stashed somewhere in my room when I was fourteen. For a friend.

God, I can't believe I was ever such a slob! Did I tell you that Rosita, my maid, still comes over once a week even though all we do is sit in my sparkling kitchen and drink tea and talk for three hours? She's a sort of cover for the fact that I do my own housework – who needs to know that it's actually me who keeps my pad as pristine as an operating theatre? I think it used to bug Suzanne a bit, but honestly, women can be such pigs! How many times did I find the spoons in the fork section of the cutlery drawer and fruit in the vegetable crisper? And the way she used to iron my towels drove me crazy! You're supposed to iron the creases *out*, not *in*, I'd tell her. Still, I made it clear that I really didn't mind undoing her little homemaking mistakes given that doing housework is just so totally orgasmic. Some people think housework isn't manly – what's not manly about *that*? What's not manly about a washing machine with a 1,000-RPM spin cycle? A dryer with a jet engine from a 747? A dishwasher that could double as a hydroelectric dam? What's not manly about polishing furniture – all that stroking and rubbing – and that lemon fresh scent! Sometimes I'll knock over a potted plant on purpose just so I have an excuse to use that souped-up vacuum cleaner of mine, the monster truck model with the V6 engine I had installed that can suck up a dust bunny at a hundred yards. I have to be careful not to suck up my furniture. How many cats have I lost to this thing? I could suck up a black hole if I wanted to – actually, I think this thing *is* a black hole, the kind that's so loud you have to wear construction-worker ear protection or risk instantaneous deafness. What I really love is wearing my big hiking boots and my deer stalker when I vacuum. "I'll get you, you dusty little bastards!" I yell as I shove my nozzle under the couch and annihilate entire civilizations of unwelcome microbes. Really, doing housework is like playing God, isn't it? Now I know why women spend so much time at it; it's sexy (especially in a French maid outfit), it's fun, and when you're doing it you feel like you rule the universe.

But no time for housework now. I better shoot off an e-mail to Oliver Black (you know, the restaurant critic for *The Dawn Post*), who actually warned me about our unscrupulous publisher – and is now being incredibly smug about it – and who has suggested that I take some modern music history lessons from some kind of expert. And he's invited me to dinner, which will be a good opportunity to show off Angel, as long as she doesn't insist on saying grace, that is, because by the time she's finished our food will have petrified – or worse yet, ask *me* to say grace like she once did when I was at her house for supper. Do you think I could remember the one prayer you taught me? You know, "God is great, God is good, let us thank him for our food." Not a chance, so I said the only other verse involving food that came to mind. "Dear Heavenly Father: Trick or treat, smell my feet, give me something good to eat/If you don't, I don't care, I'll pull down your underwear. Amen." It went over well with Angel's army of brothers and sisters, but praying in public is not an experience I care to repeat – unless it leads to smelling Angel's feet and pulling down her underwear, of course, in which case you can make me a lay preacher and call me Sexton Wilde, if you get my drift.

With love from your boy,

Rafe

From: rafe.wilde@thedawnpost.com
To: oliver.black@thedawnpost.com
Subject: RSVPing

Dear Mr. Black:

Thanks a lot for your calm, well-reasoned response to my admittedly hysterical diatribe, and I'm really sorry I yelled at you. (!!!) You're absolutely right, my contract is not a death sentence, but that being said, I still think I have every right to be seriously pissed off. I don't know exactly what I'm going to do yet, but yeah, sure, give me the name of this teacher of art music history; maybe he can explain exactly how these new music people get around the city's noise pollution by-law.

I'll definitely be there at seven (what the hell is a quince anyway?), and of course I'll bring my girlfriend, Angel. Just wait until you see this little hottie, old man; your eyes will pop out of your head and dangle there on springs, guaranteed. Will the boys in the band be joining us? Tell them they can look, but they can't touch my Angel, or I'll have to hack them to death with a chainsaw. (Just kidding. I don't have a chainsaw, only a handsaw, and this makes the job much more tedious.)

I admit that I've been avoiding the topic of Ms. Savage, mostly because I find it so gut-wrenching to think about, so thank *you* very much for continuing to hound me about it. I admit, reluctantly, that she didn't actually wear a necklace made of the severed heads of her students – I told my mom that once, but I made it up. Did she really threaten to make me wear a dunce cap and then make me beg for the Crown of Thorns model rather than – *the other*? Did the piano bench really have a pedagogically approved ejection seat that would catapult me out the front door if I hadn't done my theory homework? And if she knew I hadn't done my theory homework, would Ms. Savage leave the front door closed on purpose? (Smack!) No. Ms. Savage never hit, never yelled, never even delivered the expected lecture about how I never did enough practice (this was true, of course; I tried very hard never to do any). The torture was purely psychological, as my analyst will happily tell you (if you have a spare hour and $350), but I'd really rather not go into it just now, thank you. If your kid was my kid, unless she had done something truly evil, like devouring the raw afterbirth of an unclean spirit, I'd never punish her by subjecting her to the total and unremitting insanity of a woman who's been forced for twenty years to listen to music being butchered for countless half-hours every week. What must that do to a person? It's like guys who work in slaughterhouses; can we really trust *them* not to kill *us*?

See you Sunday.

Rafe Wilde

PS: No, I don't want a cat. I find their fur clogs up the vacuum cleaner, especially when it's still attached. Plus a cat might eat my foster parrot. (On second thought . . .)

From: oliver.black@thedawnpost.com
To: rafe.wilde@thedawnpost.com
Subject: The Importance of a Good Barber

Dear Mr. Wilde:

Aha! Although your comments were concise (and your slaughterhouse comment particularly astute), they were revealing nonetheless, and I think I just may understand your aversion to Ms.

Savage. You see, it has long been my conviction that musicians in general, and piano teachers in particular, are of two sorts: either sadists or masochists. I had the great misfortune of having a sadist. You, I now believe, had the far less pitiable misfortune of having a masochist. Perhaps someday you will share your nightmare with me in full. However, I do believe that my little Olivia will not suffer unduly under the tutelage of Ms. Savage; it is Ms. Savage who will do the suffering, but it is for taking the musical sins of the world upon herself that I pay her. Every wrong note is another jewel in her crown.

I understand completely, by the way, about cat hair clogging up the works, and I admit that, in my enthusiasm, I oversimplified the assertion that cats relieve stress. They can also induce it, especially when they learn to fly, like our little Amelia Earhart. Using any high point as a perch, she launches herself onto passers-by and crashes into them, as into a coral atoll. She then attempts to ride about on the shoulders but generally slides off down the back, leaving one feeling as if one has been lashed, not by a cat with one tail, but a cat-o'-nine. This hurts like billy-ho, of course, but one forgives the insult immediately as our Queen of the Air is a great beauty – an odd-eyed white with one amber eye and one sky blue. I'd never give Amelia away, of course (I love too much!), but if you change your mind, you're welcome to a different cat – perhaps Christopher Hitchens, who acquired his name after he ate a Bible and threw up all over the Persian carpet.

I am delighted to read that you no longer view your contract to cover modern music as a death sentence, though your initial reaction was entirely understandable. It doesn't matter if one is being ambushed by flying cats or new ideas – or both – one naturally feels alarmed, fearing the worst from the various points descending rapidly from on high. I wonder, though, if this new music won't be a great boon, Mr. Wilde, and lead you on a path toward greater engagement with the arts and away from mere idle diversion. After all, it was modern music that lead *me* to engagement – literally – ever since Samuel Barber introduced me to the extraordinary woman who became my darling wife, Lucille.

May I? You see, it was a gorgeous day at the height of summer, and I was driving about in a red convertible, borrowed from my brother Branksome. I was caught in a traffic jam and, glancing casually in my rear-view mirror, I saw for the first time my enchanting Lucille – a petite blonde beauty, but a beauty deeply troubled, biting her trembling lower lip, her oversized sunglasses unable to hide the dampness on her cheeks. The most deeply melancholic music began to waft in on the air, and I realized that she was blaring not the oh-so-predictable rock ballad or heavy metal monstrosity but, rather, Barber's elegiac *Adagio for Strings*. Do you know it? If you do, you might find it odd that such a gloomy rain cloud of a piece should draw two lovers together. True, it isn't exactly music to trip through a copse by; it's more like music to trip over a corpse by, but it has the most gripping effect, Rafe, and if it doesn't make you weep with raw emotion, then you might as well get yourself a toe tag right now and check yourself into the metal drawer that awaits you at your local morgue.

Anyway, you can well imagine how the traffic started to move, faster and faster, how the emotion continued to build, how the peak was reached, and suddenly how I did it – how I slammed my foot on the brake so hard that there wasn't a moment for Lucille to react, and she went crashing into the back end of Branksome's convertible (whoops) more or less totalling both cars in the process. Obligingly, the orchestra kept playing and neither of us moved – eyes locked in my rear-view mirror, we both knew that we had to reach the end of the piece, that to stop now would be a kind of sacrilege. And what did our vehicles matter now? Obviously they were smashed beyond repair – "scuttled for love," as I explained to Branksome later, just before he punched me in the face. Finally the *Adagio* sighed one last time, we wiped away our tears, and we emerged from our demolished automobiles in order to get on with the dreary business of apologizing, assessing damage, exchanging insurance policy numbers, and attempting to justify the accident to the police ("Surely, officer, you understand I just had to meet her . . ."). Bracing myself for the onslaught of righteous fury to be unleashed in my direction, I approached this woman with caution – but before I had the chance to express any (false) regret or to ask if she had been hurt, my future wife looked me straight in the eye and said – and I quote: "I always said it was a smashing piece." Well – that was it. It was all over for me. Getting into the police car, I remember my first question was "Do you perform weddings?" Thanks to Samuel Barber, Lucille and I were married exactly one year to the day later – naturally Branksome was the best man and, incidentally, the chauffeur.

Thus ends the personal anecdote – I return now to the business of your first critique. I believe that you need considerably more data (one datum would be a start) before you begin writing reviews that will be immortalized on the pages of *The Dawn Post*. To this end, I should be happy to honour your request and give you the name of the finest modern music teacher within a thousand miles. Her name, happily, is Ms. Gabriella Savage.

Sincerely,

Oliver Black

PS: So glad that you and your Angel will be able to join us for dinner on Sunday. I feel these first meetings go so much more smoothly if there's a formal topic presented for discussion, don't you? I would therefore like to propose the following quote by the immortal Frank Zappa, in which he proposes a definition of rock and roll journalism: "People who can't write, doing interviews with people who can't think, in order to prepare articles for people who can't read." What say you?

From: oliver.black@thedawnpost.com
To: lucy.black@artnet.org
Subject: The Kettle Black

Dearest Lucy:

I apologize for the tone of this missive, which may, I fear, be interpreted as one of tiresome nagging. Nevertheless, since we so seldom find ourselves in each other's company lately, I thought I should remind you that Rafe Wilde is coming to dine with his current companion, an entity of apparently mythic beauty named Angel, and it would add so much to the evening if you could be there, given that this is meant to be a dinner in your honour. I hope you don't find my gushing pride intolerable, my darling, but I can't help it. Not everyone can brag about having his own private Artist in Residence, you know. And you have become such a successful artist, and have always been so captivatingly beautiful, so stylish, so gracious and intelligent, that I can't help but want to show you off just a little bit. Perhaps Wilde was right (no, not *that* Wilde – the other one) when he claimed that it is only through art that we can realize our true perfection. No wonder you are so utterly perfect! "Look," I want to say to the world. "This creature of such staggering talent, virtue, and intelligence is *my wife*! She has borne *my* children, all four of them! *She loves me!* Ha! Top *that* if you will." And, of course, no one can possibly top it because no one else is married to you. (As far as I know – I suppose you *might* have a harem of Charles Atlas lookalike lovers kicking sand in each other's faces, tucked away in the attic, but I'd find this hugely surprising given both your aforementioned virtue, and the fact that the attic is three feet high at its tallest point. Perhaps these loft lechers of yours are like Charles Atlas in every way possible, except that they're all hunchback homunculi. *Omnia fieri possunt.*)

My dear, my dear. When I was first courting you, it was Branksome who noted that I went to mush whenever you were around, that I got all soft and dewy-eyed in your presence and lost my characteristic edge almost entirely. So shall it ever be, it seems. I still swoon at the sight of you, especially when I catch a

glimpse of you engaged at your easel, your catlike blue eyes narrowed in a look of complete concentration, your sleek strawberry
blond hair tied carelessly back with a ribbon, and you dressed all
in black except for those elaborately beaded slippers that you
found in some practically microscopic shop on our Mexican
holiday, and which you always wear to pad around your studio.
Ah! Just the thought of you like this makes me want to appear at
your studio door cradling a meadow of flowers, a baguette, a
bottle of wine, and a tasteful volume of Victorian love poetry!
How I want to skip gaily about and toss my hat spiritedly into the
air! Dear God, I need a copse to trip through right this second!

Which brings me, once again, to the fact that every evening I
come home from my duties (often quite late, I admit), and every
evening I find either that your indispensable mother is holding the
fort, or that you are already draped o'er the arms of Morpheus
and dead to the world – or, at least, to me. I had almost begun to
imagine that you were avoiding me, but surely this can't be the
case. You have never been busier – this is a fact and, I believe, the
reason for your frequent absence. Now, I know that you are
weary of my asking it, but are you absolutely sure you're all right?
I can't help but think that there is some mundane physical reason
for your change of behaviour lately. I don't mean to imply that
you don't look as fresh and as beautiful as ever – actually you
look even lovelier of late, if that's possible – but your entire spirit
seems to be so curiously altered. I wish you would confide in me,
my love. Must we keep secrets now, after twenty-five years together?

Oh dash it all! If ever there was an instance of the pot calling
the kettle black, this is it, I'm ashamed to say. Here *I* am urging
you to confess, when it is *me* who has the terrible secret! Well,
not so terrible, perhaps, but I'm afraid it will give you quite a
shock given that it's so utterly out of character. I almost confessed
to Branksome in an e-mail the other day, but I realized in the nick
of time that confiding something like *this* to someone like *him* is
like confessing to a monkey that you've tasted a banana. So?

Anyway, I don't know what came over me, and I only hope you can find it in your heart to forgive a passing sin. I don't have the time, or the heart, to write about it here – it's too dreadful – I'd rather just prostrate myself at your feet this evening, after I return home from dining at The Mad Cow (of all horrors), with tongue in spasm and review screeching hot from the pits of hell.

Guiltily,

Oliver

From: rafe.wilde@thedawnpost.com
To: suzanne@heartmail.com
Subject: Navel Gazing

Suzanne:

I can't believe how mean you are, not letting me sleep over for just a few nights at your place. I suppose that big fat show-off boyfriend of yours, Dr. A. Orta, is sleeping over instead. Fine. Just don't let him anaesthetize you while you're sleeping and re-move your vital organs and sell them for a fortune on the black market, okay? Some guys do that, you know. And don't worry about me. My old futon didn't work out, and the bathtub didn't either (though at least I discovered, when I woke up soaked in the middle of the night, that either the faucet has a slow leak or I really do need those rubber sheets my Mom sent me), but at least my new bed should finally be arriving tomorrow (not that you care).

Even though you won't let me sleep over, I still owe you big time for coming out with me the other night and talking me through this asinine contract business. The whole thing's still a mess, but thanks anyway for donating your shoulder to cry on for a bit, a gesture of sympathy which had the added advantage of me being able to look down your shirt. Hey, when did you get your bellybutton pierced? Anyway, there's something about that nutcase Oliver Black that's starting to make my head throb and my eyelid twitch. The guy is a windbag of gale-force proportions as it happens, and he keeps hounding me about my old piano teacher, actually recommending that I should take lessons from her again. Yeah, right. I can't see myself voluntarily placing my body on the piano bench and offering myself up as a human sacrifice to that diabolical banshee any time soon. But what positive action I *am* going to take – besides getting shitfaced, of course – remains a mystery.

I guess I'd better send a reply to Mr. Black right now – and even though he's seriously beginning to twist my knickers, I better hope I don't offend the old blowhard. I'm also hoping, of course, that today will be the glorious day you break up with that wanker boyfriend of yours. He may be a doctor, Suzanne, but when it comes to a prescription for good lovin', Rafe Wilde is just what the doctor ordered.

XOX,

Rafe

PS: Petey doesn't say hi. He says what he always says, and I'm *this* close to getting a bag of Shake and Bake and firing up the crock pot. By the way, is it red or white wine that goes with parrot?

From: rafe.wilde@thedawnpost.com
To: oliver.black@thedawnpost.com
Subject: Savage Idea

Dear Mr. Black:

With all due respect, Sir, did you actually read my last e-mail? If so, did I not convey clearly enough just how much I loathe the beastly Ms. Savage? You don't seriously expect me to resume my student-teacher relationship with that ancient hag (what is she now – 106?) from hell, do you? Surely you jest, Pops. Some of the most humiliating moments of my life took place in front of that cow. (Maybe they'd take *her* at the slaughterhouse.) Take lessons from her again? Repeat some of the ugliest moments of my life? No, I don't think so.

And, as for that Zappa quote, sure I'll take it on and give you one to wrestle with in turn. Definition of pompous anachronisms: "Individuals who don't listen, bothering other people who are too polite to say anything, in order to irritate those people with their outdated notions." Damn! I wish I could remember who said that.

Rafe Wilde

From: oliver.black@thedawnpost.com
To: rafe.wilde@thedawnpost.com
Subject: Re: Savage Idea

Dear Mr. Wilde:

No, I do in no way jest. I am very much in earnest. Don't you see? This is your shot at redemption. This is your chance not, perhaps, to erase your past, but to place it within the broader context of sin and forgiveness. There exists on this planet a person who believes that Rafe Wilde was placed on this earth for the express purpose of providing unwelcome opportunities for acute mental suffering. What must the knowledge that such a person exists do to your sense of self? How can you even live knowing that there is someone in this world who thinks of Rafe Wilde as some stupidly recalcitrant musical ignoramus?

And what, pray tell, do you mean by "ancient hag?" Ms.

Savage is the same age as my wife, a mere forty-eight, and is at her intellectual, physical, and dare I say sexual peak (my wife, that is; I cannot speak for Ms. Savage, but she certainly appears to possess all the attributes of aesthetic goodness.) Ms. Savage is an attractive, accomplished, altogether wonderful woman; the only fly in the ointment is a man, constantly buzzing around the kitchen and all over the food until you just want to smack him. The poor woman is unsuitably partnered to an individual who is a genius in the realm of haute cuisine, but edacious to a degree that even the Ravenous Bugblatter Beast of Traal would find excessive. It's a bad match, given that she's the sort for whom food is not important – a bizarre notion for those of us for whom food defines our life experiences (for example, as much as I love my wife, I remember almost nothing about our wedding day – except that the bean salad was ravishing!). All this information about Ms. Savage's private life is neither here nor there, of course; the point is that your outdated views on the subject of your former piano teacher are in dire need of updating and revising. You are like a computer with a faulty automatic update function – after all these years, you are still running version 1.0. Your brain is buggy, Rafe, and I say it's best to do something about it before it gets maggoty as well.

And as for your quote: Naturally I recognized it immediately (though admittedly you paraphrased rather wildly.) It was spoken by Franklin Delano Roosevelt to his wife upon deciding to run for the presidency against that pompous anachronism Herbert Hoover. Naturally I will address the implications of what was said – i.e., the defeat of Hoover and the instigation of the New Deal. You might want to bring a notebook and pen, but please note that I have forbidden recording devices since the time I discovered Merlin's trick of hiding headphones underneath the masses of his dreaded locks.

Earnestly,

Oliver Black

From: oliver.black@thedawnpost.com
To: lucy.black@artnet.org
Subject: Smut

Dearest Lucy:

Well. That was quick, wasn't it? Apparently, if I want to get a response from you badly enough, all I need do is commit a secret offence and then offer to 'fess up. Oh the power of the withheld confession! If ever I should seek a job in politics, Lucy, I will be sure to run on a platform of wild debauchery, and agree to confess every sordid detail if, and *only* if, I am elected. My victory would be assured, for what chance would a politician stand who says to the people, "I have so much to offer you" (yawn, we've heard it before, thank you) against a politician who says, "I have so much *to confess* to you?" And just watch the atmosphere change in any room, but especially in the bedroom, if one utters these words. Hmm, I wonder. Perhaps I shouldn't give it away so easily – after all, criminals and talk show participants are often paid hundreds of thousands of dollars for their confessions. Why should I not be paid for mine? The confession is a sort of modern-day currency, really (though the Catholic Church has been on the confessional gravy train for years), and only the fact that we share the same bank account puts the boot to the idea of you paying me for mine. Ah well. I'm just rambling on in order to delay the inevitable, obviously. I wish we could put my depravity off until this evening, but since you tell me you can't possibly wait, I shall come clean forthwith, though I hope I can still count on your vote in the next election. Ah, my love! If only putting you out of your misery didn't mean putting me in the thick of mine.

Here it is, then – a confession as repellent as any stoat on toast. I, Oliver Black, of 3773 Oak Street, attempted to rent an exceptionally naughty video of the sort that is sold at those shops that cater to adults only, and which I have always avoided as if they themselves were covered in highly contagious open sores. Disgusting, I know, but hear me out! You see, I became haunted by the idea that, when it comes to romance, you had come to find me boring and predictable, and in a moment of desperation I imagined that a little jolt of sexual electricity might be enough to re-awaken your ardour. It was simply a misguided effort to spice things up and to catch your attention (before I knew that merely putting the word "confession" in the subject line of an e-mail would do it).

Allow me to explain in full. One evening, after the family was tucked up in their beds, I donned one of my many disguises and slipped out of the house, navigating my way by a circuitous route to the closest den of iniquity, an establishment called, simply, Zippers. I entered with trepidation, scanned the racks with indecent haste (the only kind possible in such a place), and with possibly comic speed picked out a title with a picture on the cover of some very pleasant looking lesbians who seemed to be enjoying each other's company immensely. My heart was not set on lesbians, you understand, but so many of the other covers featured women in frankly ridiculous poses, looking pouty and unhappy, possibly because their breasts had been inflated like balloons and they were finding anchoring and navigating well nigh impossible. In addition to problems related to manoeuvring large objects through space, they also had to deal with restrictive clothing (six-inch heels, tightly laced bodices, steamy black leather under studio lights) and were also undoubtedly discomfited to find themselves wearing studded dog collars, which would seem to imply that they themselves were dogs, which I should think would be an enormous insult. Whatever the reason for their universal petulance (which was, perhaps, just simple concern that the spikes on their collars might pop their bosoms) I rejected them outright, grabbed the lesbians, and went to the counter to pay for them.

"Name," demanded the spotty youth behind the counter.

I was startled at having to identify myself, assuming that I could make such a transaction with cosy anonymity. "Mr. Black," I replied, nervously.

"B-l-a-c-k," confirmed our young chap, whom I noted was wearing a trainee badge and who proceeded to type my name with excruciating slowness – with one index finger – into his computer. "Okay, right. Mr. Black. That's you, right?"

"Right."

"On Oak Street, right?"

"Yes, that's correct," I replied, disconcerted.

The plodding adolescent poked at a few more buttons. "And will you be putting this on your Red Light Account this evening?"

I immediately broke into a sweat. *"Red Light Account?"* I asked, outraged.

"Yes, for our . . . valued repeat customers," he explained, pausing to consult a list of appropriate phrases.

"I don't know what you're talking about!" I protested, at which point he aimed the computer monitor in my direction and I saw that indeed I, Mr. Black, living on Oak Street, had rented about two hundred titles in the last six months, all of them, interestingly, containing the word "lesbian."

"You *are* Mr. Black from Oak Street, aren't you?" the hateful youth asked.

"Of course I am!"

"Mr. Selwyn Black?"

Ah. Mr. Selwyn Black. At this point in the proceedings there was a *lunga pausa*, an Italian phrase taught to me by Mrs. Kowalski and which has always sounded to me like a lunging pause, the kind of pause that leaps up and grabs you by the throat. We were both silent, eyes locked. Eventually I nodded my head slowly and replied, "Yes, that's right. I am indeed Selwyn Black."

The boy turned back to the computer screen. "You've rented

this one four times, you know."

"Have I?"

"Yeah. And remember it doesn't actually have any lesbians in it."

"No matter," I assured him. "Just put it on my account."

The transaction proceeded at a glacial pace. Indeed, the real world seemed to dissolve and, for what might have been two minutes or what might have been two decades, I saw before me a parade of disgusted and scandalized faces: yours (of course), my grade one teacher, my own long dead mother, Jesus Christ, P. C. Growler, Mrs. Kowalski. My brain dredged up, in succession, every person I have ever known or imagined – living, dead, historically controversial, entirely mythological – whom I would be horrified to see walk through those Zippered doors. Mercifully, after what felt like an eternity of psychological lambasting, the simple procedure of renting a pornographic video eventually came to an end. As I walked away from the counter, the dim-witted adolescent called out, "Hey, man, I love your music!" I cringed, exited, and slid the video into the return slot on the way out.

My dearest love. In a moment of madness I attempted to bring into our sacred love-relationship something that depicts women as nothing more than dehumanized sexual objects dominated by well-endowed males who care about nothing except their own pleasure. Do you suppose that you will ever be able to forgive me?

Yours forever (which, by the way, is the length of time I will be grounding Selwyn),

Oliver

The Dream Post
Traditional Way of Life Under Threat

Gomorrah, California – A special government report released yesterday reveals that many people who earn their livelihood by traditional means are finding their way of life endangered by various modern pressures.

"First it's the trappers' way of life that's jeopardized, then the farmers, then the cod fishermen, and now us. There are people out there who are a menace to our livelihood, and it's time someone spoke up about it," says Max Dingle, founder and owner of Zippers Pleasure Emporium franchise.

"Classy, nonsluttish people with good taste and imagination, who go in for real sexual experiences rather than cheap commercial imitations, are the enemies of our time-honoured industry," says Mr. Dingle. "I mean, our business relies on keeping things dumbed down and on helping men in particular to spiral ever further into the bottomless pit that is human sexuality. Those social freaks who are immune to the hype –

and who have never even been to a pleasure centre because they find our products alternately revolting, silly, or just plain funny – are a millstone, let me tell you."

The real problems for the porn outlet began when the business next door moved out and another one took its place. "Everything was A-okay when the Doggy Style Pet Grooming Centre was our next-door neighbour," explains Mr. Dingle, "but when the Friends of Kali Feminist Bookshop moved in, all hell – or its Hindu equivalent – broke loose."

When asked if women concerned with issues of exploitation and objectification began to picket the premises, Mr. Dingle waved his arms and shook his head. "No, no, nothing like that. I mean, they're women, right? Their tactics are much more covert and underhanded. You see, we have posters in our windows of big busty babes with these 'Come and get me for seven days at only $4.99' expressions on their faces, right? So these feminists put a poster in their window with no pictures or nothing, just a big sign that says 'Find Real Women Here!' Real women! Well, I ask you, how are we supposed to compete with that?"

Mr. Dingle rolled his eyes with disdain when confronted with the idea that, surely, real women and fantasy women appeal to two separate kinds of customers. "No, you don't understand. See, because of that godforsaken place, my customers are disappearing – literally! I mean, curious men go into the bookshop – *but they never come out again*!" Extrapolating on this extraordinary claim, Mr. Dingle offered this theory: "I don't have exact numbers, but it seems to me that twice as many women are coming out of that damned bookshop as went in, and I think the only explanation is sex reassignment surgery. It may sound farfetched, but the chance to have breasts is pretty irresistible, isn't it, and once you're an enlightened woman concerned with the well-being of her sisters, you tend to avoid porn stores like mine, don't you?"

When asked about his plans for the future, Mr. Dingle sighed and said, "Unfortunately, I'll probably be closing down, both because of that stupid bookshop, and also because of the grief I'm getting over the whole porn thing from the new lady in my life – a gal with sensational breasts, by the way – my wife, Leroy."

From: rafe.wilde@thedawnpost.com
To: angel.day@agape.org
Subject: Dinner at Oliver's

Hey There, Angel Baby:

Wow. Is your mom clairvoyant or something? Does she have the third eye? I just got a freaky phone call from her a few minutes ago, a call that leads me to suspect that she has supernatural psychic powers. I sort of lost her after her opening diatribe – *"What? Know ye not that he which is joined to an harlot is one body?"* – but the gist of it is that she seems to know, by some mysterious means, that I want our date tonight to end with me ripping off your clothes and pummelling you into my mattress. Amazing! She also tried to talk me out of asking you to dinner altogether (*"And if any man hunger, let him eat at home!"*), and when you see her later, you can tell her that the answer is still no – *no,* she cannot come for dinner with *us* at Oliver Black's house. And yes, all right, I will have you home by 10:00 PM, following the specific route from Mr. Black's house to yours as laid out by your mother, thus ensuring that any postprandial coitus is rendered impossible, or at least uncomfortable. Oh well. As I assured your mother, there will be other nights. Ha! As for this one, I can't wait to show you off, especially to Oliver's boys – the three of them are going to wish they'd never been born when they understand the life of misery and disappointment they will forever lead knowing that none of them will ever possess the girl with the face that can launch a thousand rocket ships.

So, just a quick briefing before dinner tomorrow evening. Please don't talk about you-know-what (your nutty beliefs) and you-know-who (the son of God). Also, remember how I told you to turn the numbers of your age upside down? I didn't mean for you to tell everyone that you're 61; that would be reversing the numbers, wouldn't it Angel Sweet? I meant for you to turn that tiny little 6 into a great big 9, but keep the 1 in front of it, okay? That's 19, get it? Good girl.

Love you, Babe.

Rafe

From: oliver.black@thedawnpost.com
To: selwyn.black@freenet.org
                merlin.black@freenet.org
                damien.black@freenet.org
Subject: Fodder Knows Best

Hello Selwyn, Merlin, and Damien:

I hereby request your presence en masse at a dinner in honour
of your mother this Sunday evening at exactly seven o'clock. I am
inviting Mr. Rafe Wilde and companion to dine with us. Please
wash up for the occasion (you will find "soap" in the "shower")
and spiff yourselves up a bit (I freely throw open my closet doors
to you for this event; within you will find dress shirts, suits, and
various accessories including an impressive quantity and variety of
neckties; I tried it once and found that, when laid end to end,
they reach all the way to seventeenth century France.)

Please note that tardiness will incur a severe penalty, such as
public flogging. The same fate awaits those who use their utensils
in the incorrect order. Any young man found blowing his nose at
the table shall be put in the stocks forthwith, or suffer some other
equally severe humiliation at an undisclosed later date. Failure to
wear matching socks will result in immediate disinheritance.

Isn't this fun? I can't imagine how fathers and sons used to
communicate before the advent of electronic mail.

Infallibly yours,

Dad

Chapter Three

From:　oliver.black@thedawnpost.com
To:　　damien.black@freenet.org
Subject: *No*! And Again I Say *No*!

Feast of Saint Hilary of Poitiers
(the patron saint of backward children, if you must know)

Good Morning, Damien:

You will undoubtedly argue that there is no question on the table at present that demands a response from the Head of the Household; nevertheless, the answer from me is still a hydrogen-bomb, asteroid-impact, supernovalike, universe-shaking no. *No*, you may not have the image of a naked woman tattooed between your shoulder blades and down the length of your back. The whole idea is preposterous. Unless you have your eyes surgically transferred to the back of your head (and I wouldn't be surprised to learn that you've already given this procedure your serious consideration), you won't even be able to see it. Is this some sort of display behaviour for the benefit of other males, perhaps to make up for other perceived physical deficiencies? Is the purpose of such a mutilation to noisily proclaim your heterosexuality? You needn't. That you begin slavering like a mad dog in the presence of any attractive female is advertisement enough. (The stack of pornographic magazines in the box marked "Private – Do Not Open" in your closet also serves as further proof of your sexual preference.) Is the point of such a tattoo to attract members of the opposite sex? I wonder who it is you hope to attract. Rhodes Scholars? Vassar graduates? Nobel nominees?

Let me put it to you another way: how would you feel if you were attempting to seduce a young lady who had an image of the perfect male tattooed on her torso? Tanned, muscular, superhumanly endowed, et cetera. (I needn't remind you of the unkind nickname given to you by your own brothers, need I, Stringbean.) Would the presence of her fantasy boyfriend inspire optimum

confidence? Would it not serve to deflate both your confidence
and another, even more significant participant? Would it not, on
some deeper level, make a mockery of your union?

Repeat after me: I will not tattoo a naked woman on my back.
I will not tattoo a naked woman on my back. I will not tattoo a
naked woman on my back. Recite it like a mantra. Write it in all
the colours of the rainbow on an enormous chalkboard five million times. Dangle it from each earlobe and bind it around each
knee. Engrave it on your headboard, burn it into your brainstem.
Under no circumstances have it tattooed on your back.

Sternly,

Dad

PS: If you absolutely insist on getting some sort of permanent
doodle or scrawl, why not get something unique and practical in a
spot where it will be of some utility? For example, you could be
the first in your class to have permanent crib sheets available for
every exam; why not have a periodic table of the elements, a list
of capital cities, the Hillis Plot, a table of weights and measures,
logarithms, multiplication, sines, cosines, and tangents engraved
on your inner forearm? How about the precepts of Einstein's
theory of general relativity carved into your palm, like commandments on a stone tablet? Planck's Constant? Buys-Ballot's Law?
Finagle's Factor? Or here's an idea: why not have the location of
your internal organs mapped on your torso for ease during surgery? Or what about etching into your flesh a sort of survival kit
in case you get lost in the wilderness – a recipe for dandelion
soup, perhaps, or illustrations of poisonous fungi. How to catch
and milk a mountain goat. When to perform an emergency ap-
pendectomy. How to appease a cannibal. Or perhaps you might
consider some slightly more esoteric knowledge – the exact proportions of the perfect martini, for example, or how to take the
temperature of a cat. Or why not carve into your skin something

of even greater daily urgency, such as – oh, I don't know – maybe
a permanent reminder *to put the milk back in the fridge?* Ah ha!
Now there's a tattoo-worthy sentiment if ever there was one.
You'll recoup the cost of the tattoo itself in only a few weeks and
be forever left with a sound bit of advice that will be of far greater
benefit than any anatomically exaggerated female forever riding
piggyback.

From: oliver.black@thedawnpost.com
To: rafe.wilde@thedawnpost.com
Subject: Alimentary, My Dear Wilde

Dear Comrade in Criticism:

I was so glad that you could come for dinner with the stunning
Angel, and my only regret is that my lovely wife could not be
present in order to partake of our simple but sumptuous (if I do
say so myself) repast. You seem better educated than most of my
colleagues about food (the quince notwithstanding), and you
certainly seem to be well-acquainted with an impressive range of
Chardonnays. You, in turn, were pleasantly surprised by my extensive knowledge of all things musical, were you not? I hope I
managed to convince you that a lack of appreciation of modern
(or even what is now called postmodern) "classical" music is often
due to an ignorance of the theoretical underpinnings; those who
whine and complain that they shouldn't have to "understand"
music, but merely enjoy it, are like children with as yet uneducated palates. My little Olivia, for example, is still devoted to
macaroni and cheese-substitute, and if it is not served with every
meal, she's apt to wind up in a catatonic state. Under my tutelage
she will overcome this youthful simplicity, as did my sons (note
how they tucked into their dolmades with all the ferocity of
piranhas at a submerged cow). If only the unfortunate Beethoven
had had someone like me, or even actual me, as a mentor; appar-

ently macaroni and cheese remained his favourite dish even unto death. This is not so surprising as the greatest musicians, and especially their teachers, are so often found to be the greatest savages; we need look no further than Mrs. Kowalski for confirmation of this fact.

You noted the absence of animal flesh at table, with the exception of the extraordinary number of cats weaving themselves like champion square dancers around the table legs and those of the diners. The vegan nature of the meal was strictly to accommodate my idealist daughter who, at the mentally uncluttered age of five and in a burst of sophisticated philosophical insight, declared that because she loved all animals, she thus thought it wicked to also murder them (*her* words) and thence to disguise them as food and to eat them. Almost overnight she became a vegan warrior princess, campaigning ferociously and relentlessly for the absence of animal food in the house, and eventually the entire family had to abandon flesh entirely or risk having her pass out at the beginning of every meal. Stamping her little feet to get our attention, she would announce, "I'm holding my breath until you stop eating that *awful*" (she meant offal, of course, but the manner in which she spat it out suggested both words and their respective meanings), and within seconds she would begin to turn azure blue, her tongue lolling out of her mouth and her eyes rolling up in their sockets for effect. Well, what could we do? Two other things happened at about the same time: 1) she began an animal rescue service, which explains both the copious number of cats in the house as well as the fact that there is rarely anyplace to sit around here anymore; and 2) she began to study my calendar of saints and to name her strays after them. You already know about Amelia Earhart and Christopher Hitchens, but that's just the beginning. Not only will you find at least one cat curled up on every chair, but open the cupboard under the sink, and who do you find? John Stuart Mill. Open the sock drawer – Dian Fossey. Pull back the shower curtain – Stephen Fry. There must be at least a dozen of them now; who could imagine so many feral felines in the few streets between our house and her primary school? Oh, and just in case you were wondering, the cats are vegan without exception, and I challenge you to find a healthier bunch of reformed carnivores with brighter eyes and more lustrous coats anywhere in the civilized world. In fact, the dolmades and the cats were stuffed with almost identical ingredients; the exception is the essential protein taurine, synthesized in the lab and added as a supplement, just as it is in commercial cat food, by the way, since taurine is destroyed during the rendering process. Is this too much information for you? Forgive me; not everyone can keep up with the lightning-fast intellectual and compassionate genius of a five-year-old.

I do hope you enjoyed our vegan fare. I felt that not only the meal but also the conversation was exceptional; my deepest thanks for sharing in depth your philosophy of criticism (which can be reduced to one word – honesty – can it not?), your insights into the world of the rock and roll musician (how many times a night? Surely not), and also for the enlightening tour of the landmarks of your body. I hope you didn't think I was being rude when I abruptly ended the tour just after you lifted your shirt and displayed the humanoid female tattooed between your shoulder blades, but one has to think of the little ones (and here I refer to my sons, who are as suggestible as participants at a tawdry hypnosis stage show, which would have been obvious had your tattoo contained instructions to, let's say, act like a chicken.) Many thanks also for the astonishing hostess gift that you thoughtfully brought for my dear wife. Most dinner guests bring the obvious bottle of wine, box of chocolates, or potted plant; how much more imaginative to bring a cherished set of vintage coffee mugs, wittily wrapped in a copy of today's paper, featuring the actual mugs of that legendary American crime fighting duo, Starsky and Hutch. You are far too generous, my good man; surely you cannot possibly bear to part with a matched set which, in only a few years time, is guaranteed to drive any expert on the *Antiques Road Show* into a frenzy of professional bliss comparable only to finding a Ming vase in a Shaker desk. No, Dear Rafe – *je refuse absolument!* I insist that you return them to your china cabinet and ensconce them in their rightful place, in between your over-sized Cannon soup tureen and your *Dukes of Hazzard* salt and pepper shakers (and note the correct spelling and pronunciation – not Hazard but Hazzard – implying that the emphasis should be on the second syllable. Dukes of Haz*zard*. Ah, much better.) You will currently find your mugs carefully bundled and secured in the trunk of your car, with our deepest thanks and with infinite appreciation for restoring them to their true home.

And finally, my humblest thanks for providing the experience of proximity to that goddess of youth and beauty, the positively mesmerizing Angel. You were right, my boy, she is a young lady of almost impossible pulchritude; never in all my life have I beheld such an air-brushed beauty as she, a resplendent Venus without pores, without imperfections, even without veins it seems (how amazing that there is no external evidence that she even possesses a circulatory system). How wondrous are the cascading chestnut locks, the emerald green eyes that appear to emit light rather than to reflect it, the row of pearls that are her perfect teeth. That my three boys were transfixed by her dazzling charms was obvious; in the presence of such elemental beauty, they became as primitive man, unable to do anything at all but grunt and poke at the earth with a stick.

In conclusion, Dear Friend: Many thanks for a most excellent evening.

Vale, mi amice,

Oliver

PS: But do tell me if you would, Mr. Wilde, do you find the incessant hair flicking, nail filing, earring fiddling and lipstick refreshing just the teensiest bit distracting? And what about the age of your enchanting mistress? Are you at all worried that Child

Protection Services might oppose her (presumably attempted) seduction on the grounds that she still sucks her thumb and believes in the Easter Bunny? And does the fact that she has the Holy Bible tattooed just above her left breast (clearly visible through that aggressively captivating and hair-raisingly translucent chiffon blouse) have any implications for your relationship? Just wondering.

The Dream Post
Anthropologists Make Startling Discovery

Bethlehem, Israel – Two thousand years after three wise men followed a star from the east bringing gifts to the lowly stable where the saviour of the world was born, anthropologists have discovered three unopened containers of gold, frankincense, and myrrh shoved behind a bottle of shaving lotion and several pill jars of expired medication at the back of what is quite clearly an ancient bathroom cabinet.

"Hello!" exclaimed professional Jewish mother Mosette Mumonides when she heard of the unearthing. "Are we dealing here with three wise men? Or three wise guys? Let me guess – their wives didn't help them pick the gifts. Am I right? Am I right?"

"The need to choose appropriate gifts was as important two thousand years ago as it is today," remarked mild-mannered anthropological etiquette guru Bubbles Soupspoon, "and one suspects that The Magi made the common faux pas of neglecting to consult the authorized gift registry."

Ms. Soupspoon bases this assumption on the fact that frankincense and myrrh are nothing more than glorified tree resins and that gold, a highly prized and precious element, would have been an insanely dangerous commodity to give to a young couple living in a stable in the days before the invention of the safety deposit box.

"Oh, thanks very much for

the lovely *tree sap*!" an irate Mosette Mumonides exclaimed in sarcastic imitation of the Virgin Mary. "Did you buy it at the mall? Or did you root around for it in a tree stump on the way here?"

"Even the Virgin Mary, with all her supernatural connections, had absolutely no idea what to do with frankincense and myrrh," said Ms. Soupspoon condemningly.

"And as for gold," added Mrs. Mumonides, "what good is gold to a woman, a virgin no less, who's just given birth? Aye aye aye! She doesn't need gold! What she needs is an ice pack!"

The discovery also reinforces the importance of occasionally cleaning out household cupboards and proves that it is theoretically possible for that jar of Cheez Whiz, for example, to remain at the back of the fridge for all of eternity.

From: oliver.black@thedawnpost.com
To: lucy.black@artnet.org
Subject: A Report from the Front Line
              and a Request from the Rear

Dearest Lucy:

I am attempting *not* to feel like Captain Bligh after his first officer mutinied and left him surrounded only by savages at dinnertime, but I confess to finding such a mental exercise daunting in the extreme. Forgive my snivelling, Dearest Love, but I felt your absence at table yesterday evening rather keenly, I'm afraid. I know you were not avoiding me due to the ignoble Zippers incident – that I completely miscalculated your reaction, and that upon reading my confession, instead of gnashing your teeth whilst gouging my eyes out of the family photo, you apparently doubled up and wept with laughter still causes my face to burn just a little bit. All right, perhaps my attempt to rent a pornographic video wasn't the diabolical offence I had imagined it to be. So why, then, were you not at dinner? You tell me that you were called away at the last moment to an important meeting that you were loath to miss. And what meeting would this be, Darling? I was not aware that you belonged to any group of which meetings are a regular feature, particularly emergency meetings on Sunday evenings that last till well after midnight.

But never mind. This is the modern world after all, not ancient Greece where the newly married bride was delivered by chariot to the household of her husband, at which point the axles of her chariot were symbolically broken. Your axles are still fully intact, and I pride myself in never having stood in the way of your pursuit of interesting life experiences, as long as such experiences do not include other men, bizarre religious practices, or excessive saturated fats. ("Well, where's the fun in that then?" you might well remark.) I shall tell you in detail about last evening's dinner with Mr. Wilde when next we are together – suffice it to say, he lived up to the reputation that his last name would suggest, except for his strange habit of absentmindedly polishing the silverware, his postprandial dish stacking, and his predeparture picture straightening. And I don't mean to make too much of it, but I also had the impression that Mr. Wilde was not being his authentic self – that he was wearing the mask, so to speak, and behaving like a stock character in a movie featuring the stereotypical rock critic. One regularly meets people who act as if they have hidden depths when they actually have none at all; Rafe Wilde strikes me as the sort of person who acts shallow, but who isn't. He appears to be trapped within the confines of popular culture and is so busy trying to be cool that he has forgotten how just to be himself. His personality seems to have been eclipsed (one hopes temporarily) by various popular obsessions, human sexuality being chief among them. The boys lapped it up of course, but poor Olivia spent most of the time with my hands clapped over her delicate little ears. (I eventually sent her away from the table with Rafe's girlfriend Angel, and they amused themselves for the rest of the evening playing veterinarian – there wasn't a cat left in the house who didn't have all four legs in splints and a patch over one eye.)

Now, my dearest love, do you suppose that we might make plans to compensate for this lost occasion sometime in the very near future? I realize that you have a number of upcoming speaking engagements, in which you will undoubtedly clarify and correct what centuries of other great thinkers have got horribly wrong (and how I would love to hear your address entitled "Why Art Should Be a Religion, But Isn't – Yet"); however, I wonder if you might be able to set aside just a few quality moments for your fawning husband.

Darling: recall those idyllic years when we were first married, before the babies came and each precious life, each blessing from above, exploded into our lives like some kind of hideous, noisome volcano. (Lord above! Do you remember that I had some woman embroider "Temporarily out of order – sorry for the inconvenience" onto each diaper?) Recall those beautiful precolic years before the invasion of our four angels from heaven with their mountains of plastic toys, stuffies, picture books, and endless objects that squeak loudly in the dead of night when they are trodden upon whilst tiptoeing to the loo? The time before we could recite the entire oeuvre of the immortal, and deeply insane, Dr. Seuss by heart. The time before the rivers of breast milk and other bodily fluids began to flow like the Amazon. Recall those few short years, Lucille, when we felt exclusively like lovers rather than merely as partners in a corporation, when we used to spend practically every waking moment in each other's presence. Do you remember? We were rarely separated longer than it took one of us to brush his or her teeth. Oh my sweet love! What a rare and beautiful thing it is when two people can spend so many years together and avoid pissing each other off, even a little bit!

My point is, Darling, that I do hope to recapture the magic of our early years together when we used to dine and write and paint together and (dare I say something that is obviously such a perversion, even in an oversexed newlywed couple) while away the late night and early morning hours – in our bed, under the covers, breathing heavily – playing Scrabble. Good heavens, we were obsessed! It got to the point where we could only speak in unusual words of seven letters or fewer, and every sentence was followed by a lightning-fast calculation. "Dipso, Darling," you might say, "there's some calx on my quipu. Five hundred and forty-seven on a triple word score. Ha!" How well I remember raising the stakes by increasing the value of each letter, and I expect that we became the first Scrabble players in the history of the game to break one million. And do you remember when we decided to spice things up by adding a rule that stated that the loser of the game had to become the obedient servant of the winner – but that we had to change the rule because I kept eagerly forfeiting the game? Ah, my love! Being in your radiant presence is such a joy; perhaps I can be forgiven for my obsession in light of the fact that you are irresistible, and this is in no way my fault.

Why doesn't your mother look after Olivia tomorrow evening – or we could give her the evening off (because she's been looking after Olivia a lot lately, have you noticed?) and hire a sitter instead. Not one of the boys, of course – I don't want to come home only to find our little angel's musical sensibilities forever corrupted, in a rock band and playing the tambourine à la Tracy Partridge. (Why don't I call our junior editor, Mr. Midge – sleep is anathema to Olivia, but Nat Midge can be relied upon to bore anyone into insensibility within thirty thousand words or three minutes.) And then you and I could attend a concert together since, among other classics, the orchestra is playing Barber's *Adagio* – the very piece that brought us together in the first place, you recall. And then, after a fine meal, we could stroll along the river, arm in arm, and dream of what the future might hold for the two of us and for our unfashionably large brood. I just want to be proximate, Lucille, to hold your hand, to kiss your cheek, and to know that you still have even just a sliver of interest in me, and that I haven't become to you as a puddle of warm Limburger cheese, aged and goatish.

All of my love,

Oliver

From: oliver.black@thedawnpost.com
To: lucy.black@artnet.org
Subject: . . . And Another Thing

Dearest Lucy:

There is one other item I need to address, an item that I could
not include in the above missive as it would have spoiled the
whole tone but would therefore have served as an excellent example of precisely what I was getting at – that is, the ability of
children to ruin everything, just when it's at its most perfect.
(Dearest love: only you would understand that I am exaggerating
wildly. Obviously I am devoted to our children and firmly believe
that they are stellar examples of the species, though what species
that is, exactly, I have never been sure.)

Now, just in case you haven't heard, I think I ought to warn
you that Damien has a stupefyingly harebrained scheme that involves a picture of a naked woman, his lily white flesh, and a tattoo parlour. But never fear, my treasure! I have already shot off
an e-mail forbidding the very thought of such an outrageous and
misguided act. Heaven help us! Why is it that young people want
to turn themselves into living sandwich boards with all manner of
illustrations, symbols, slogans, mottos, and maxims plastered all
over their bodies, and all in that particularly ugly shade of
garbage-bag green? Do they not have enough wall space? Have
they not heard of campaign buttons? Badges? Bumper stickers?
Novelty T-shirts? "We want to express our uniqueness," says
Damien. (Note the plural.) Rubbish, I say! These young people
flock by the hundreds of millions to be branded; there isn't a
human being under the age of twenty-five left in the entire west-

ern world who is devoid of these marks of nonconformity. How I want to prove them all wrong! How I want to have my eyelids pierced and an aubergine tattooed on my posterior! Just imagine the effect this would have, Darling. The multiple infections leading eventually to the removal of the eyeballs! The gradual sagging and withering! What was once an aubergine deteriorating into nothing more than a splotch, a stain! Would this not put our sons off the idea for the rest of their lives? Would they not rebel against the whole ghastly trend? Indeed, they would. Sadly, however, although I strive to be an exemplary father, I find I must stop short of self-mutilation. (A mother can never say this, of course, given that childbirth is inherently mutilating. By the way, have I told you recently how grateful I am that you descended into hell four times in order to retrieve each of our children? I've not forgotten my debt to you, my courageous love, and every day I bash my head savagely against a brick wall in order to experience a mere fraction of your agony. Dear Brave Girl! Any deity, be it good or evil, who wanted to campaign on a platform of eliminating the pain of parturition would be more than welcome to put a sign on my lawn, by God.)

Sincerely,

Your partner in the corporation

My Only True Love,

I've not yet had the pleasure of a reply from you so, in the event my note went astray, here it is again: One hand upon your breast, the other upon your thigh and inching ever closer to heaven. Have mercy. Twenty-five years is surely long enough to wait for consummation.

Forever,

Oliver

From: rafe.wilde@thedawnpost.com
To: suzanne@heartmail.com
Subject: Don't Make Me Beg (Please? *Please?*)

Hey There, Suzanne:

Have you ever been at a party and some guy you thought was essentially harmless offers you a cupcake, and you take it and bite into it and only then discover that it's actually a ball of fibreglass insulation with concrete icing and a crushed glass topping? "I hate it when that happens," you're probably saying. Well I hate it too, which is why that gasbag Oliver Black is really starting to piss me off. You would not believe the e-mail I just got from him! It was his way of "thanking" me for coming to his house for dinner, a dinner to which I would have invited you (if you'd bother to answer your phone once in a while, and return voice messages, and text messages, and e-mails, and rocks chucked through your bedroom window). Firstly, he just can't shut up about music, a subject about which he obviously knows *nothing*, because anyone who says, "Rock and roll isn't so much about music as it is about posturing," is an idiot and a wanker. Secondly, he admits to having stuffed the dolmades with cat food (*haaackkk* – that's the sound of me coughing up a fur ball). And thirdly, he dares to question my relationship with Angel, as if it's any of his goddamn business. Because I'm my mother's son (i.e., well-mannered and thoughtful to a fault, if you don't count trashing the occasional hotel room, which I don't), I was actually going to write him a gracious thank-you note, you know, a sort of "Thanks for the lovely meal, you must give me the name of your china pattern, my turn next" – that sort of thing. Maybe I *will* write him a note, but it'll begin something like this: "Dear Nosey Bastard: That's funny – I don't remember electing you Minister of Personal Affairs for the entire planet. And don't you worry about that Bible on Angel's breast, you freaking lecherous old pervert; it means nothing. She's got the New Testament on her thigh and the Old Testament on her ass; it's just her thing, okay? She's a hot-blooded woman who takes her modesty off with her thong under-wear, and there's nothing she likes better than me nailing her to the bed with my substantial nail, all right? And she's not too young either. She's old enough to drive – to drive me crazy with lust, that is! Maybe somebody's jealous because his own wife evi-dently thinks so little of him that *she couldn't even be bothered to show up for dinner.*"

You know, Suzanne, *you* could have spared me all this if *you* had come for dinner with me instead of Angel, but oh no, you had to go on a date with – oh who was it now? Happy? Sneezy? Dopey? No, no – *Doc.* That's it. On the other hand, taking Angel did add some entertainment value to the evening. All three mem-bers of the band Black Chalice were there, and they were each trying to act so cool and unaffected, but we practically had a triple fratricide on our hands as they savagely knocked each other out of the way in the race to sit next to Angel at the table. I sus-pect that Merlin and Selwyn felt pretty disappointed when they found out their father had already put place cards around the table and that Damien was on one side of Angel and Oliver's daughter Olivia was on the other. Then it was Damien's turn to be disappointed when his father came out of the kitchen and bellowed, "Who changed the place cards around?" and Damien didn't even bother to argue; he just slunk around to the other side of the table. Mind you, it was just as bad having them sit opposite Angel; none of them blinked for two hours. They looked like zombies, able to participate in conversation but never even glanc-ing at their plates, just staring blankly at Angel the entire time as they shovelled their grub into their faces. I kept praying that God would strike them blind, after which they'd each pass out and suffocate in their cat food, but no such luck.

God, what a weird family! "The War of the League of Augsburg, 1688, and the effects of the decision of Louis Quatorze to impose direct taxes on the French nobility – Damien, discuss!" is Oliver Black's conception of normal conversation. Maybe if his wife had been there it would have been less like a cross-examination and more like your average dinner party – but this was un-tempered, unrestrained Oliver Black, and it was entirely *his* party. Around *his* table you'd better be prepared to have informed opinions (preferably accompanied by written footnotes, primary source documents, and a panel of experts) and to defend them with the zeal of a brigadier general plotting his next attack around a topographical map of enemy territory. How do they manage to eat under those conditions? It's like being a mouse who's just trying to mind his own business and eat his cheese, but he's doing it right beside this enormous cat who might pounce at any moment and gleefully rip his head off – after which he smiles magnanimously as if nothing had happened. And you can never tell for certain whether the cat's being deadly serious or just having you on, given that when he's wagging his finger in your face, he's also pulling your leg (off). He's even like this with the Black Chalice boys, who've learned to give as good as they get by baiting their own traps for their dad to tumble into (which rarely happens, but when it does, no one could look more delighted than Oliver – in fact, *no one* seems to take *anything* personally), or by teasing him – "The museum phoned, Dad – they finally have enough space in their prehistory section to exhibit your suits" (at which point he beams and strikes back – "Champion! Will it be next to the live exhibit of you three, entitled Atavistic Mutant Yahoos?"), or by whipping a little Latin on him (*Sicut pater, sic filius* or some damn thing). And oh yeah, that's right – don't even bother going if you haven't recently brushed up on your ancient languages. You'll miss half the conversation.

You studied Latin in school, didn't you? See, I needed you

with me, Suzanne – I needed you in a way that old Bones McCoy never could. Okay, so enough about that lunatic Oliver Black and his weirdo sons and a dinner party that had all the atmosphere of a Gestapo interrogation hosted in a locked white cell under a single swinging light bulb. That's not important now. What *is* important is the answer to the question I asked you before, and which you seem unable to answer, probably because there *is* no possible answer. But this isn't supposed to be a rhetorical question, Suzanne. I absolutely need to know: Why are you still going out with that major aortic loser? What has he got that I don't? (And if you answered "a vibrating bed," then you're wrong because mine arrived this morning. Ha!) Honestly, Babe, I don't know what you see in a guy who spends his days staring at people's chests and pondering where he's going to stick the knife in, a guy whose profession is re-enacting the shower scene from *Psycho* on a daily basis. Come on, you know what I'm getting at here – it's just so *creepy*. I mean, when I'm staring at your breasts I'm having *normal*, basically incoherent, and slobbery guy thoughts, sanctified by God and Mother Nature – how do you know that when he's looking at your breasts he's not thinking, "Hmm, where would I make an incision?" Aren't you afraid that when he's resting his head on your chest, he's going to say, "Whoa, wait a second, what was *that*? We'd better take a look." Yuk! How can you let a guy touch you who's just been sliding around the OR soaked in blood, flinging people's vital organs around like a circus juggler? You're dating Norman Bates, Suzanne, a guy who likes to butcher people, and for the best possible reasons I admit, although I just wonder how fine the line is between butchering do-gooder and butchering mass murderer. Ask yourself this: *What if he goes bad?* I mean, if *I* go bad, what's the worst that can happen? I'll write a good review about Neil Diamond. Big deal. If *he* goes bad, you've got Hannibal Lecter on your hands.

You know that you should be with me, don't you? Let's do a little comparison: I have a total glam-job that involves great music, fascinating famous people, parties – at the end of which I whip my opinions into an article and get paid tons of money for it. There's no blood to scrub off at the end of it (usually), no bone dust on my shoes, no internal organs in my pocket. My job is hip, it's cool, it's *sexy* from beginning to end. What does Dr. R. Ventricle wear at work, hmm? A baggy light green dress that ties at the back. A little hat with a headlight strapped around his head. Latex gloves (okay, I admit that's pretty sexy, but that's the only thing). And what do I wear? Tight jeans that reveal my fantastic butt, a white pirate shirt open to the waist, black leather boots, *the gold chain you gave me when we were first going out.* Come on, Suzanne. Do you think I'm not serious just because I'm still seeing Angel? Don't believe it. She's just temping. And here's another thing, a secret, which you can never tell anyone or I will be forced to withdraw in shame from society and become a hermit on a different planet in a remote galaxy. I haven't actually slept with her. Not even close. *And it's not because she's too young or too religious either.* No way. It's because I'm not trying very hard. It's because I don't really want to. It's because I want you back in my life.

Ditch the butcher, Suzanne.

Your destiny,

Rafe

PS: Like I said, I got rid of that stupidly shaped round bed and got me one of those vibrating rectangular numbers, the kind that massages every muscle in your body so you wake up feeling like you've been done over by a Swedish masseuse. So do you want to get together tonight and experience Helga's Hands first hand? Come on, Baby, it'll feel so good to vibrate together, especially on my feather tic and my brand new black satin sheets.

First I'll turn the bed on;

Then I'll turn *you* on.

(You're not going to come over, are you? You're going to play doctor again with your medicine man, aren't you? Well, it's your loss. I guess I'll just have to ask Angel, but never let it be said I didn't give you dibs on Helga.)

PPS: "Scald parrot, remove feathers, place in slow cooker with 1 cup water, 2 teaspoons salt, dash of vinegar, and medium onion (diced). Let stew; it deserves it. Cool completely; parrot is a dish that, like revenge, is best serve cold. With crackers."

From: rafe.wilde@thedawnpost.com
To: oliver.black@thedawnpost.com
Subject: I'm Pickin' up Good Vibrations

Hey Oliver:

I'll keep this short because I've dddecided to try writomg from my laptop on my new vibrating bbbed and it's nnnot easy to kkkeep my fingersss ssttteady and in the ppproper pppositionnn. So, just three tjingss, rrreally. 1) Thanks for dddinner and for the cccopy og the book *The FFForgotten Quince – A TTTragedy of Our TTTimesss* 2) No, I couldm't pppossiblu accrpt the return og Starsky and HHHutchh. I've already mmmailed them bacj to you with ny cccomplinentsss and 3) My rrrelationshimp with Angel is nnnone of your damn bbbeeswax. She's nnnot too yyyoung, or tttoo rrrelingious, and she bbbegs mmme to dddo it with her every mmmoment GGGod ssssends.

RRRafe

From: rafe.wilde@thedawnpost.com
To: angel.day@agape.org
Subject: She's Givin' Me Excitations

Hey There, Angel:

Wow. First of all, never try typing from a laptop on a vvvibrating bed. And second of all, please – whoa, how do you shut this thing off? Okay, there we go. Oh great, now I forgot what I was going to say. No, wait a second. Please, please, please (et cetera) come out with me tonight on what I promise will be *the* absolute greatest, most explosively fucking marvellous date of your entire life. Seriously, Baby, this date's going to be out of this world, only better – more exciting than space walking (yawn) or moon landing (snore) or blasting off in a rocket to Mars for humanity's first alien encounter (Zzz). This is going to be the Mount Everest of dates, the winning lottery ticket of dates, the Olympic gold medal of dates, the Big Bang of dates (note the double entendre, pant, pant). After this date you'll nod off during your next bungee jump. You'll have to joy ride with jet fighter pilots just to put you to sleep. *Staying* asleep will require breaking the sound barrier riding naked on the wing of a Concorde. This is the date you'll tell your grandchildren about, Angel, the date that will be the title of your autobiography, the date that will have its own holy altar, pews, hymn books, the works.

Okay, so here's the plan: I'll arrive at your door wearing blue jeans the exact right shade of stone-washed blue for this fashion season, a classy understated white T-shirt of precisely the right tightness to reveal my perfectly defined pecs and widely coveted biceps, a pair of black designer shades concealing the limpid pools which are my eyes and into which you will inevitably fall when I finally remove the glasses at the perfectly timed moment just before our first kiss, and my luxurious mane of shoulder-length, black wavy hair, which I will tie back carelessly with a simple elastic band. I will be carrying an entire meadow of flowers in my arms for you, a box of chocolates, or if models don't eat chocolate, then maybe something they do eat, like broccoli, and a bottle of something appropriate – if not champagne then something else – maybe a bottle of Flintstones because I know you like them even though you're too young to know who the characters are and, for some mysterious reason, can't seem to wrap your head around the whole "modern stone age family" concept (what's the problem?) – although weirdly, because of your wacky religious beliefs, you have no trouble believing in Dino and his life as a pet in the Late Bodacious Period. Then I'll escort you to my 1974 red Ford Torino and drive you in aggressive young male fashion (remembering to rev the engine at stop lights, for example) to the best restaurant in the city – which is *not* La Jonquille, by the way, despite what Oliver Black thinks. Personally, I don't like to age significantly in the time it takes to eat a meal, thanks very much. No, I'll find some other, more intimate spot where we can expect to be finished eating long before we die from the blood clots that have formed in our legs from sitting so long waiting for the next course. Then, after a sumptuous dinner, I'll take you to a concert, since I have to write a review for this band called Kick My Ass (a sort of masochistic/karate/heavy metal/anti-ungulate/Equus asinus fusion thing), and afterward I'll take you to a bar – a juice bar, that is, for a low-cal but naturally sweetened nonalcoholic beverage, or maybe to an oxygen bar where we can get a buzz off nature, you know, get high off a piece of the periodic table, Baby. And then, after the flowers, the broccoli, the Flintstones, the meal, the music, the O_2, I'm going to drive you in my sexiest manner (with your hand under mine on the knob of the stick shift) back to my tastefully decorated pad, where you and I are going to connect in ways you've never connected with anybody before, and we're going to do it on Helga, my brand-new bed. That's where the real thrills begin, believe me. Come on, Angel. I just want to show you how much I love you, and the best place (the only place, really) to do that is on a vibrating bed, which I just happen to have. I got rid of that malfunctioning, heatable, adjustable thingy on which we spent an hour slowly roasting as if in a Dutch oven, playing a few chaste rounds of Catch the Giggling Girlfriend. And I chucked that wretched round bed out of which I kept falling, and on which we once had a painfully platonic pillow fight. Now I finally have Helga, a bed that's perfect for games of other kinds, games that should only be taught by a qualified instructor such as myself. Games like Bouncy-bouncy, Boff and Bonk, Jiggery-pokery, and Crudge Pummel and Thump.

Okay, so what do you say? Will you make the obviously superior choice and come with me on the date of a lifetime? Hey, feel free to add your own suggestions – I'm totally open to the idea of reversing the order of the above events, if that's what you want. Of course, if you don't want to come out with me I'll understand completely – what girl wouldn't rather draw the curtains and sit at home with her mother, growing old and senile in the dark, and reading the New Testament by candlelight while rocking quietly by the fire and thinking about the Apocalypse?

Oh yeah, one final thing: tell your mom that she is, respectfully, but definitely, *not* invited, even if she does pay for everything like she did last time. (Why do I feel like submitting a field trip permission form every time you come out with me?) And the other guy you hang around with – you know, your personal bodyguard – should also stay home for a change, given that his continual presence is playing absolute havoc with my love life. What's his name again? Oh yeah, that's right. *God Almighty*. Jesus, Angel, how can we get Mr. Almighty and his two sidekicks (Sonny and Boo) to just leave us alone and mind their own business for a change? I doubt if making reservations at one restaurant but then showing up at another would fool them for long. What do you think? Maybe we could set fire to heaven. That would give those pesky celestial Nosey Parkers something to do.

Hopefully, desperately, almost suicidally,

Your Rafey Wafey

From: oliver.black@thedawnpost.com
To: rafe.wilde@thedawnpost.com
Subject: You Scratch My Back, I'll Scratch Your Tattoo

Dear Rafe:

I'm afraid you may have got the wrong end of the stick. It was not my intention to insult the lovely Angel, who as I said is a deity. I was merely interested in *your* reaction to some of her behaviours (incessant hair-twirling, forever peering into small hand mirrors, removing her nail polish at the dinner table, and so on). And as for her age, I suppose it's all relative, isn't it? In base 4 she's already one hundred for heaven's sake, and in Mercurian years she's a ripe old sixty-seven! And I never suggested that Angel was not as sexually precocious as you claim her to be (dost thou protest too much?); I merely wondered why such a one as she would have a permanent reminder of God's wrath against fornicators tattooed on her perfect breast, that's all. Honestly, Rafe, what does it matter? Do you imagine that I will think less of you as a man if you haven't yet managed to seduce a healthy reproductive partner? Don't be ridiculous. Sex may indeed be the most important thing in the whole world, but an important thing is not necessarily an urgent thing, nor need it require an obsessive investment of all our time and energy. How refreshing to imagine a world in which the general public is as interested in intellectual arousal as in sexual arousal, in which individuals are more intrigued by science, for example, than by sex! What if the swimsuit issue of a sports magazine was regularly outsold by the swim bladder issue of a nature magazine? What if lab coats outsold edible underwear? Would not every evil thing in this world have been controlled, cured, and conquered? But, no – science could never compete with sex, not even with all its suggestively lewd talk of bare charm states, naked singularities, screw axes, excitons, classic hot bodies, rigid bodies, many-body theory, coupling schemes, vibration curves, magnetism, lab dancing, and stripping (i.e., the removal of the most volatile constituent from a mixture of liquids by boiling, evaporation, or distillation – you see? – it has nothing to do with leopard skin brassieres and feather boas.)

But never mind, Young Rafe. You have my forgiveness for your needlessly sharp tone. Now, I must needs address an item of business that I believe will be of considerable reciprocal benefit. As you must already be aware, my three sons, a.k.a. Black Chalice, will be staging their first substantial hometown concert at the Dome in a mere few days (if they can recover from their Angel-induced stupor, that is). I note that on the same evening there is another concert of equal – some might say greater – importance (some people are sadly mistaken). I trust that you will choose wisely, and review Black Chalice. I, in exchange, will happily review a particular eating establishment which is, so my sources have informed me, owned and operated by your uncle, a man with the Christian name of Billy-Bob and with no apparent surname, unless he is actually Mr. Bob? Dr. Bob? Perhaps Sir Billy-Bob, OBE? (One cannot assume that just because a man is named Billy-Bob and owns a bistro of Lilliputian dimensions in a squalid part of town that he has not, at some point in his life, been knighted by the Queen.) I trust that this arrangement will prove to be mutually agreeable; please let me know in good time so that I may prepare accordingly.

Have you contacted Ms. Savage yet? I sincerely hope so. I note that ere long, and as I mentioned previously, the New Works Ensemble will be performing the music of one of the most ingenious composers of the twentieth century, Mr. John Cage, and naturally our most esteemed editor will be expecting a review of the highest quality. I've no doubt that you are digging and deliberating, planning and preparing for the actual writing of your article, but the guidance of a devout Cage enthusiast (which I happen to know Gabriella to be) would be invaluable. Nota bene, my dear friend: the pitfalls of autodidacticism are many as so often one misses the tone and emphasis of the subject under scrutiny and picks up instead on that which is of self-interest, but of no real historical import. This can easily lead to one looking like an untutored and uncultivated prat – which, in addition to appearing suspiciously like a corrupting cradle-snatching deviant (I agree, pervert is too strong a word), would in no way be beneficial to your image.

Sincerely,

Oliver

The Dream Post
Popular Naturalist Gives Lecture at Sky Dome

Toronto, Ontario – Fifty-seven-year-old Doctor Reginald Dewey, a professor in the Biology Department at the University of Lethbridge, gave a rousing lecture entitled "Chordates and Hemichordates of the Western World" to an enthusiastic audience of 73,000 at the Sky Dome on Monday at 9:00 AM sharp.

The lecture was introduced by warm-up naturalist Doctor Cleavage Truffles, a shapely young female naturalist whose lecture, "Sexual Habits of Nymphomaniac Homo Sapiens" was booed off the stage after ten minutes of relentless demonstration.

Finally, Dr. Dewey, a slight man in a lab coat and wearing aviator glasses, flood pants, and an unconvincing comb-over, arrived on stage to the deafening cheers of his loyal fans. His opening words, "All right, people, settle down," followed by the dramatic switching on of the overhead projector, caused many of the hysterical women in the crowd to faint with excitement. Dr. Dewey periodically had to wipe his overheads free of the underwear and phone numbers that the screaming hordes of female fans kept throwing onto the stage.

When Dr. Dewey announced, "The fact is that Cephalochordates evolved from the urochordate tadpole larva through pædogenesis," fans erupted into a spontaneous wave, roaring and waving their lighters in riotous appreciation. "I haven't felt this much love in one place since last week," commented science reporter Phylum Newt, "when Doctor Dolores Dumpling opened up her lab to the public, and 175,000 eager fans were totally blown away by her climactic antibody stain."

From: rafe.wilde@thedawnpost.com
To: oliver.black@thedawnpost.com
Subject: Re: Back Scratching

Oliver:

Whoa, wait just a second. I am *not* a "corrupting cradle-snatching deviant." For one thing, Angel is just shy of *nineteen,* and for another thing *she's* the one who's chasing *me,* all right? The girl – I mean woman – throws herself at me with the force and enthusiasm of a three-hundred-pound defensive halfback. What am I supposed to do? Refusing isn't really an option, especially when she's got her tongue down my throat and halfway to my intestines – I couldn't scream for help even if I wanted to. And there are times I wish I could scream, believe me, times when I just want to say, "No, Angel! Bad Angel! At least leave me my dignity!" But there's nothing I can do, short of being less sexy and attractive than I am, which just isn't humanly possible. Be thankful that you don't suffer like I do, with women constantly throwing themselves at you like flies against a windshield.

So, on to other things. Your sources are right – my Uncle does own an "eating establishment," but it's what's technically called a greasy spoon, and it's in the slummiest, sleaziest part of town. I'm not saying that Uncle Bill isn't a first-rate chef, and he didn't have to go to some poncey, milksop, molly-coddling institution to get his credentials, either. He has a PhD with a thirty-year post-doc from the University of Hard Knocks. The bush, the army, the slammer – these were his teachers, and let me tell you, nobody can do a fry-up for five hundred like Uncle Bill. He knows grub better than a beetle larva. But understand, we're not talking about La Jonquille, with its courses and dainties and wine list the size of the yellow pages. We're talking victuals, provisions, fodder, rations. As long as you understand that my uncle is the kind of guy who wears laundry and cooks groceries, I think a review of the Burger and Bun would be a good idea.

For my part, I'd be more than happy to ignore the fact that you're essentially blackmailing me to review Black Chalice; their hit single, "Dog Almighty," is rising up the charts like a rocket. (What's with the lyrics anyway? "Are we fleas on the back of Almighty Dog? Does a sheep dog shepherd the lamb of God?") What I need is a little more background info on the band. You mentioned that Selwyn and Merlin quit taking music lessons when they were about twelve – obviously Ms. Savage had nothing whatsoever to do with their musical development, otherwise they'd still be playing the *Minuet in G*, badly, and wandering aimlessly in the interminable hell of elementary piano classics. What about the drummer? The guy's like a human jackhammer with a voice like a satin buzz-saw.

And, no, I have not contacted Ms. Savage.

And again, no, I do not protest too much. It's not my fault that Angel's so hot for me I have to drive to the emergency ward every night to be treated for first-degree burns.

Maybe somebody's jealous?

Lucky, lucky me,

Rafe

From: oliver.black@thedawnpost.com
To: rafe.wilde@thedawnpost.com
Subject: Humph

Dear Rafe:

How dare you suggest that I am even capable of something as monstrous as blackmail; indeed, Sir, you do me a tremendous injury. I am merely suggesting an equitable arrangement, and in the spirit of friendship and generosity, I will even confide to you the details of my plan: I shall be dining at your uncle's restaurant at the unfashionable hour of 5:30 PM tomorrow evening, wearing stained overalls, steel-toed boots, and a hard hat. Feel free to pass this information on to your uncle so that he may prepare accordingly.

I can assure you, Dear Rafe, that jealousy is not a motivating emotion in my life. I freely acknowledge that the beauty of your Angel is a miracle comparable to the loaves and fishes; this cannot be disputed. What might be construed as somewhat odd is that a man of your age should be sexually attracted to a girl freshly out of training pants, a girl who appears only recently to have graduated from primary school, a girl who still has reason to put her milk teeth under her pillow. (I recommend that you try a relationship with an actual adult for a change; you may discover that your wine bill hits the roof, but the expense will be offset by a decrease in the amount spent on lollipops and saddle shoes.) And there is still the ever puzzling presence of God's Holy Writ emblazoned next to her heart, a text which under no circumstance can be understood to condone concupiscence. Perhaps you are taking a liberal reading of that provocative Bible verse with which we used to tease the girls in Sunday School: "If two lie together they have heat, but how can one be warm alone?" I wish you luck, of course; your personal satisfaction would be substantially increased if satisfying your girlfriend meant something other than trips to the mall to buy religious icons and packets of Barbie shoes.

As for background information about my three geniuses, they have asked me not to give too much away, as they want to maintain an aura of mystery surrounding their origins. No intelligent young artist wants to admit he has lived comfortably and contentedly in the suburbs; Black Chalice wants its fans to believe that they have crawled to the surface of the earth from the underworld (and judging by the amount of muck in their bedrooms, one can easily believe this is so). However, I can tell you that, yes, Ms. Savage failed to excite their musical ambitions. Selwyn and Merlin each took piano lessons for six years and, upon quitting, forgot everything they'd learned within six minutes. It's true that children soak up information like sponges, you know, but a child's brain is more like a sponge than you might suspect – a gentle wringing and the soppy sponge, be it filled with the nectar of the gods, obligingly drains away its contents like so much toxic waste.

("Then why," you might intelligently ask, "are you wasting another $120 a month on piano lessons for darling little Olivia?" An excellent question indeed. After all, I used to have to put a gun to the heads of my sons to make them practice. I wish I could say this was a figure of speech – how cruel they never knew it wasn't loaded – and I should hardly wish to repeat the experience. However, neither I nor my wife have ever had to nag our girl to practice. Olivia *likes* piano lessons, and although liking piano lessons is a contradiction comparable to Zeno's Paradox or the task of clapping with one hand, I swear on the Bible – how I wish it were the one tattooed on your beloved's breast – that it is the absolute truth. Olivia claims that Ms. Savage is the nicest teacher she's ever had, and in only two years my little girl has progressed from "Chopsticks" to the first variation of Mozart's *Sonata in A Major*. A miracle! My little girl is a wonder – but then, you know all about the wonder of little girls, don't you?)

But I digress. Back to the boys, and that one inspired day during a particularly boring summer vacation when they decided to form a band. (I recommend boredom for children, by the way; it is this, not necessity, that is the mother of invention.) Selwyn decided to learn the electric guitar, Merlin opted for keyboards (including the computer keyboard, which provides access to all instruments – I do not pretend to understand how); within three weeks each of them could play reasonably well, and within six months they had attained total mastery. I estimate that I could have saved $25,000 on piano lessons, and firearms, if I had paid more attention to the signs of their dislike of the piano – refusal to practice, tears, fits of hysteria, slashed wrists – the things that parents learn to ignore in order to push their children successfully through the public education system.

How is it that my two eldest sons, and my youngest for that matter, blossomed into musicians without (some might say despite) formal instruction? Perhaps the real question is this: why do private piano lessons fail so miserably and so often? Let us lift the veil and face the facts: the track record of music teachers is abominable. For every one child who learns the instrument and sticks with it to adulthood, there are ten thousand others who fail so to do, and thousands of those learn only to despise the very music they are supposed to be learning to revere. Formal instruction in music appears calculated to destroy any musical interest a child may have initially possessed. Why is this so? There is first of all the problem of practice – for one half hour a day, the sun shines on a world chock-a-block with happy children reading comic books in their tree houses, carefree children dangling from rope swings and plunging into watering holes, serene children licking ice cream and wrestling with the dog and playing hopscotch and marbles and sardines – while the unfortunate musical child sits straight-backed on a wooden bench in a gloomy parlour under a cloud of doom, little fingers stumbling over scales like brave little soldiers fleeing the enemy camp, wishing they could just play to the end of the keyboard and keep right on going out the door and into a land where the only music to be heard is the harmonious call of the Dickie Dee ice cream man. There is no sunshine, no dog, no ice cream for the pallid, prepubescent pianist – there is only an endless supply of minuets, in an infinite number of keys, providing ever greater opportunities for misery and suffering. How many years was it until I realized that Bach was the name of a composer, and not an acronym for Banishing Altogether Children's Happiness? But of even greater importance than the problem of practice is the music lesson itself, an institution that has not evolved from times prehistoric when, for half an hour a week, a respectable woman in a cheetah-print dress and bejewelled cat's-eye glasses dangling from a chain around her neck – a woman unavoidably named Mrs. Kowalski – would instruct hairy-backed children on the subject of how to bang rocks together in the manner dictated by the certified syllabus of the Royal Conservatory of Rock Music. It is this sort of lesson, I am sorry to say, that has no reason to exist. Only rarely is a musician produced because, in general, the lesson dwells outside of every social context, except the student-teacher relationship, which is itself created only for the perpetuation of the lesson. The argument is a circular one, you see. It's chilling to ponder the total number of potential pianists who have been forever ruined by music teachers. There are exceptions of course: my Olivia, Horowitz, Ben Folds, Fats Waller. And teachers do serve a useful function if you simply require them to spout information at you (once again, I urge you to contact Ms. Savage).

Be on the lookout for my review in tomorrow morning's *Dawn Post*. And if you have any doubts about my ability to write a review about an establishment like your uncle's, I need only refer you to my review of a café known as The Mad Cow (January 7), and you can judge for yourself whether or not my talents extend to the ghetto.

Sincerely,

Oliver

A Blast from the Past
by Oliver Black

It was with good reason that I felt like Robert Falcon Scott embarking upon his adventure to the South Pole – a hostile, undesirable place from which he wondered if he would ever return alive. (He didn't.) It was with this very same sense of high adventure that I donned the garb of a common trades-man and drove in a rusty half-ton truck to a squat, dilapidated building on the corner of Fifth and Centre in the heart of what is unkindly (and accurately) referred to as skid row. After skillfully parallel parking my mammoth vehicle, I eased my-self out and jauntily proceeded to the premises of the most popular greasy spoon within several blocks, an establishment unpretentiously named Billy-Bob's Burger and Bun. It was a forbidding sight, especially since the doorway was sur-rounded by men who were clearly concerned with the quantity, not the quality, of the alcoholic beverages in their cir-culatory systems, and I won-dered, as Scott had, whether or not I would ever return alive. (I did.)

But oh, Gentle Reader, how wrong first impressions can be!

I entered Billy-Bob's and was immediately overwhelmed by the exceptionally astute inte-rior design; clearly, no detail had gone unnoticed, no expense had been spared, to recreate the look of a 1950s diner that has been neglected for half a cen-tury. One noticed immediately the gouged Formica tabletops, the cleverly placed rips in the red plastic upholstery on each chair, their aluminum frames artificially bruised to give them the appearance of many years' use. A thick film of grease had been allowed to accumulate upon the window sills, and in the name of authenticity, the red and white checked curtains had never been allowed to see the inside of a washing machine. The menus, laminated so that they could be easily wiped, had not been. Even a lifelike, apparently mechanical mouse and artificial droppings had been carefully placed behind the glass counter with the desserts. Undoubtedly, even the finest movie set director could not have so successfully cultivated the impression of poverty and poor hygiene.

There was no hostess to guide me to a table, no non-smoking section. I chose to seat myself by the window, though not in order to enjoy the view outside (such enjoyment was impossible given the opaque quality of the glass). It was not long before a gum-chewing, sensibly shoed, beehived woman in a floral-print dress (whose nametag said, incredibly, "Flo") approached me, and retrieving a notepad from her pocket and a pencil from her ear, asked, "Whaddya want?" in a successful gambit to avoid nonessentials and move directly to the business of satisfying my culinary desires. I boldly ordered the egg-salad sandwich but was informed that they did-n't have it; apparently Chef Billy-Bob cooks only with the freshest ingredients, and Flo wryly informed me that "Eggs is outta season." I decided to try the vegetable soup and complimentary saltines, the grilled cheese bunwich, followed by coffee and apple pie. Flo nodded, relieved me of my menu, and wordlessly retreated to the kitchen.

The table was bare in front of me, like a canvas waiting for the master's stroke. As I prepared for the masterpiece to appear before my eyes, I reflected upon the "real people" I saw around me; the bikers, the women of ill repute, the orphans, even the drunk ingeniously placed in front of the doorway to remind us of our own good fortune (access to medical attention, food, shaving kits, showers, cologne, homes) and also to imbibe wisely.

Flo delivered my order with timeliness and precision, sliding the plates across the table like stones at a curling rink. I began by removing my saltines from their plastic wrapper, an act that resulted in one unfortunate cracker being tragically catapulted onto the floor; I might have been embarrassed, but conveniently a stray dog sensitive to the situation immediately removed the evidence of my clumsiness. I crushed the crackers in my hands and dumped them into the soup (when in Rome) and then took a sip with a spoon (the spoon moving away from one and toward the opposite side of the bowl), and noted with delight that my spoon was, literally, greasy. (It's these satirical little touches that add so much to the overall impression of carefully cultivated grunge.) The soup concentrated on salt as its major spice and was not spoiled by being overrun with vegetables, with vegetables running amuck and dominating the broth. There was no mistaking this graceful soup for some stodgy, viscous stew (we all know too well the popular canned soups guilty of this obvious mislabelling); it was a celebration of clarity, of translucence, of bouillon, and served to tease the appetite rather than quash it.

I then proceeded to my grilled cheese bunwich and was delighted to find not Gouda or Edam or some other pretentious cheese, but the very cheese that this nation was founded upon, the cornerstone, the backbone of cheeses – none other than cheddar itself. The cheese was melted to the perfect consistency, and one could not help, nor did one feel any compulsion to prevent, the formation of long gooey strings from the bun to the mouth. (Some foods are more inherently comical to eat than others, but for the appropriately unselfconscious consumer, dining well means never having to say you're sorry. For example, one must never apologize for the shreds hanging from one's teeth when one has been eating a whole, ripe mango – an experience that can only be compared to sucking a wet cat. Some things cannot be helped.)

A masterfully executed piece of apple pie followed, accompanied by a mercifully uncomplicated medium-roast cup of coffee (no foam, no cinnamon sprinkles, no vanilla curds). I paid my bill (all this for under $10!), and deftly popping my complimentary mint into my mouth, idled over the drunk in the doorway and out to my vehicle. I felt well and truly satisfied, and even being approached by two drug dealers and subsequently mugged could not spoil the feeling of fullness in my belly.

Chef Billy-Bob has clearly done his research; he knows, as I do, the historical importance of the sandwich (created by John Montagu, the 4th Earl of Sandwich, in the late eighteenth century), and his menu reflects his commitment to the preser-vation of its survival in popular cuisine. His sandwiches range from grilled cheese to ham-and-Swiss to the ever popular BLT. What would a diner be without pie? Without instant pudding? Without crispy rice squares? Billy-Bob has all of these. In decor, in ambience, and in the actual menu selections, Billy-Bob's Burger and Bun is a masterpiece of retro-dining.

I end, then, with a poem in celebration of the second course, entitled:

O Humble Bunwich!

O Humble Bunwich! The grumbling tums which
Invoke thy name know naught of Montagu.
The unworthy Philistine on thee doth dumbly dine,
Unaware of the descent of noble You.

O Humble Bunwich! The bumbling Huns wish
That paradise was jam betwixt some bread!
An eternity they'd be, happ'ly sandwiched within thee,
Always jolly, always jammy, always fed.

O Humble Bunwich! The stumbling bums squish
Thy bread as they kerplunk in plonk-fuelled strife.
Rotting teeth and boozy breath, spells for thee a certain death,
But in death, O crumbling bun, thou givest life.

O Humble Bunwich! The Earl of Sandwich
Gave birth to thee whilst on a gambling fling.
The simple bun, which simpletons have et to clothe their
    skeletons,
Is food for gamblers, food for bastards, *food for kings!*

Billy-Bob's Burger and Bun is open from 7:00 AM to midnight, seven days a week, and is located at 522 Centre Street, roughly between Scylla and Charybdis. Reservations are not required. Dress is recommended.

From: rafe.wilde@thedawnpost.com
To: angel.day@agape.org
Subject: Moping

Hey There, Angel:

What do you mean you can't go on a date because you have to go on a photo shoot out of town? For two whole days? And you expect me to be sane when you return? I suppose it's a good thing you're leaving because right now just the slightest glimpse of your succulent flesh would be enough to make me suicidal with lust. Come on, Baby. Can't we come to some agreement about this? I admit that I was being a bit tactless the other night after dinner when I agreed to bow my head before the Heavenly Father and accept the Lord Jesus Christ as my personal saviour if you'd just let me put my hand down your pants. That was very wrong of me. And I agree that I was being needlessly crass when you said to me, "Get thee behind me, Satan," and I said, "Sure, we can do it doggie style, whatever." That was very naughty. I'm sorry. But, listen, if I was born again or saved or whatever, would you let me sleep with you then? Pleeeeeease? Come on, Angel – you've already convinced me that there's a God, okay? When you walk away from me with that perfect ass packed into those faded jeans,

I don't just believe, I *know; only* God Almighty could have created a caboose like that. Listen – do you want me to spend an eternity in hell? No? Well, it's too late. Every moment you won't sleep with me is an eternity in hell.

Think of the words of that song "Salvation" by Black Chalice:

Thoughts of his damnation were taking their toll,
    (their toll, their toll, their toll toll toll)
She cried, "What can I do to rescue his soul?"
    (his soul, his soul, his soul soul soul)
God said "Preach the gospel, do not be wary,
Go in the position of a missionary!"
So in order to save his soul from perdition,
    (perdition, perdition, perdition, ition, ition)
She naturally assumed missionary position.
    (position, position, position, ition, ition)

Don't just think about it; *call me* and I'll be on the next flight out of here (after I check out Oliver Black's review of Uncle Bill's, that is).

Lustfully yours,

Rafe

From: oliver.black@thedawnpost.com
To: merlin.black@freenet.org
Subject: Tongue-lashing

Oh Merlin:

Not you too! I was under the impression that Selwyn was the one obsessed with puncturing bits of his flesh and sticking various objects through the wound. Now I find that you too are on a piercing binge and that even your tongue is not immune! Good God, Son! Are you insane? If the eyes are the window of the soul, then surely the mouth is the door, and the tongue is – what? The watchman? The welcome mat? The cat flap? *The omnipotent master of the entire body?* So it would seem! Many a man lives wholly in the shadow of his own tongue; he waits upon it as a vassal waits upon his lord, he orbits it like a gas giant orbits a diminutive sun. I, however, harnessed my tongue to my will years ago, and it has been in the loyal service of the Black Family ever since. Do you realize that it is my tongue, and my tongue alone, that has supported you your entire life? My tongue has paid for every pet hamster, every skateboard, every musical instrument, and inadvertently, every piercing and tattoo, not to mention every banana (of which you and your brothers yesterday consumed a record twenty-one, by the way, a quantity of which any orangutan would be proud). Dear God, Merlin! Without my tongue you would never even have been conceived! (See your mother for details.) Hack off my legs, sever my ears, rip off my foreskin, gouge out my eyes – but leave me my tongue! How could you even think of so cavalierly toying with the sense organ that is at the very heart of such a vast array of pleasures and occupations? I do hope you realize that by permanently mutilating your taste buds, you're slamming the door on the noble career of professional taster with its jet-set life and its easy days spent in fragrant bakeries and picturesque vineyards, days filled with cheese, with chocolate, and with white wine in fluted glasses served on silver trays by buxom maids. And ask yourself this, Lad – after the tongue, then what? Where will it all end? With ritual facial scarring? Circumcision? Amputation? Decapitation? Self-trepanning? Double orchidectomy? A tummy tuck? And here's another thought: What if having your tongue pierced causes you to lisp? Horrors! You'll thound about ath thexy ath a prethchooler. Do you want to be found adorable by women older than the age of eight? And what about your flowering career as a vocalist? Are you not just a little worried that your impending speech impediment will cause you to be ousted from your position as lead singer in a rock band and replaced by someone only slightly less comic – say, Daffy Duck?

My dear foolish and deluded boy: In days of old I might have been able to convince you not to mutilate and defile yourself by virtue of the fact that your body is the alleged temple of the Holy Ghost and ought therefore to be treated as a tax-exempt charitable organization (presumably) and ought also to remain in a pristine state of newborn-babe purity. Nowadays, in these modern secular times when we rely on scientists rather than professional tilters-at-windmills for reliable information, we know that the body is not inhabited by ghosts but, rather, by trillions of single and multicellular life forms that outnumber our own cells by at least ten to one. Isn't this a rude and astonishing fact? The mites, the bacteria, the viruses, the nematodes – your living corpse is their copse. In fact, nematodes are so ubiquitous that if all other life forms were suddenly sucked off the Earth, there would still be ghostly shadows of every living thing – trees, animals, you – shadows that are the nematodes who live everywhere on the planet. Is now a good time to emphasize that nematodes are minute, unsegmented worms? Can you ever feel clean, or even happy, ever again? My point is this, Merlin: Even though you believe your body to be your own, it isn't, and you ought to thank your lucky stars that it's not run by the majority, or by committee, or by democratic elections. If it were, I'm afraid that without some serious campaigning and inevitable gerrymandering, your nematodes would vote against the half-baked, fat-headed, harebrained decision to drill a hole in your tongue and ram a metal rod through it. Even a creature lacking a brain can see the obvious foolhardiness of such a venture. Am I getting through to you, Boy? Have you placed your hands on your head as you back slowly away from the hole punch? I do hope so. I mean, why go out of your way to seek opportunities for unnecessary suffering? Does your school life not provide enough? Evidently your teachers are not doing their jobs.

Anyway, I won't go on at you. As you say, it's your body (fine), and as I say, you're welcome to it. Now, the important thing, and the real reason for this message from the Ancestor, is this: I've written a review of Billy-Bob's Burger and Bun as a favour to Mr. Rafe Wilde; he, in turn, will be writing a review of your big hometown debut. I did inform you and your brothers of this arrangement the other day, but I'm not sure it sunk into your collective consciousness because, at the time of my announcement, the three of you were wearing the Vacant Stare of Youth. How well parents and educators know this phenomenon, in which it appears as if an adolescent's brain has suddenly discharged its contents, and all of its convolutions have flattened so that it becomes as a perfect sphere, a Platonic form, and any bits of information simply slip off it. At such times I often think that a flashing neon vacancy sign would be amusing but redundant. Ought I to report you as truant, I wonder? Ought I even to file a missing persons report? Ought I to whisk what's left of your mindless form to the ER on suspicion of banana poisoning? Who knows. However, just in case your mind had gone AWOL, let me reiterate the importance of this development and my hope that the implications of the situation are beginning to emerge from the fog of consciousness. It would, of course, be ridiculous for me to order you to practise – nevertheless, it is my inalienable right as your father to issue insultingly obvious commandments, a practice that begins in infancy and continues to the grave. This is because it's hardwired into the brains of parents to believe that, although their children are geniuses, they have no common sense whatsoever. Be careful! Don't slip! Drive safely! Keep your pants on! And, of course, practise! But in all seriousness, Merlin, *do* practise; this could be the big break for which you and the other boys have been pining. One mustn't take Mr. Wilde's attention for granted; what he writes, *everyone* reads.

So – how can you prepare for this great event in order to ensure an optimal performance? Perhaps you might take your cue from the habits of more established performers. I understand that the pianist Glenn Gould used to soak his hands in a basin of warm water for at least half an hour before performing. You could do the same, and in order to warm up your voice, you might also include your head. (Find a mask and snorkel in the downstairs closet.) Ask yourself this: How did the great Farinelli prepare for a concert? What about Michael Jackson? No, on second thought, perhaps not Mr. Jackson. I understand that he obtains a new nose before each event, and given your recent fascination for radical bodily alterations, I think this might suit you only too well. I suppose I need to strike Farinelli from the list for similar reasons; although I believe in making every effort to prepare for a concert, nevertheless I think it wise to stop short of castration. Well, you know what I mean, surely. I'd advise you to investigate fully the preconcert warm-up habits of some of The Greats and imitate accordingly – and note well the absence of tongue piercing from the list of favourite preconcert rituals, in particular from the lists of vocalists of all kinds and, indeed, any other individuals who have not just recently come down from the trees. (Note to self: Perhaps this explains the bananas.)

Now, in light of your tendency to stuff yourselves like starving lions around a carcass, please note that on the day of the concert, I will personally be overseeing the preparation of all of your meals. The three tenors always ate lightly on the day of a perfor-mance, Pavarotti and Carreras consuming a little pasta with olive oil, Domingo drinking only some clear soup. I'll take my cue from them, taking into account that you are teenage males with meta-bolisms like gas-guzzling sport-utility vehicles, and thus adding a few thousand extra calories so that you won't be reduced to skeletons by nightfall.

Sincerely,

Dad

PS: It's not too late to take a few singing lessons. Oh, and lyrics, Merlin, lyrics! Remember, a thesaurus is not a dinosaur; there's still time and opportunity to add novel lyrics that have never before occurred in the history of popular song! Think of the fame that awaits by using original words such as humblebee, besmirch, scrofulous, gird! Use polished speech such as this, my son, and I guarantee you success when you and your brothers go a-wenching after the concert.

The Dream Post
New Survey of Performers Reveals
Interesting Preconcert Rituals

Nashville, Tennessee – Exclusive interviews with rock and roll performers from around the globe have revealed interesting preconcert rituals hitherto unknown to the general public.

"No performer just walks on stage cold without, like, performing some kind of ritual," explained head-banging superstar sensation Maia Graine. When asked what her preconcert ritual is, Ms. Graine explained, "I put my head in a cast iron pot and bang it again and again with a metal spoon until I'm in the right, you know – whatever that word is. Mood. Yeah, mood."

Another rocker, Minxie Mouse, explained, "My preconcert ritual is that I'm careful not to have sex voluntarily for several days before a show."

Preconcert rituals are as individual as the performers themselves. Sensitive new-age rocker Karmax says, "Some of my bandmates perform random acts of kindness before the show, hoping to improve their karma and reap the rewards during the performance. But I think that since we have to work off our bad karma in this lifetime through suffering, I improve my own karma by causing suffering to others – and I do this by performing what I call 'chaotic acts of compassion.'"

Self-professed Catholic band Mortal Sin explains, "We like to self-flagellate, of course, but before a show we usually get a little hyper, eating and drinking a lot more of the body and blood of Christ than is probably good for us. And one time, for extreme holiness, one of the guys got a priest to bless the wine and then attached himself to a "blood of Christ" IV. Mistake! Turns out Christ's blood type was totally incompatible. Actually, the doctor said it was wine in the IV bag, which sort of knocked the stuffing out of the whole transubstantiation thing. No big deal – we're a faith-based band, so stubbornly clinging to dogmatic assertions is our thing."

Other preconcert rituals include the stroking of a lucky rabbit's foot (though one could argue that the rabbit who previously owned the foot was spectacularly unlucky), consulting a Ouija board for last-minute messages from beyond the veil, and reciting all of Shakespeare's 151 sonnets, in reverse order, line by line, backward – *while eating soup.*

From: oliver.black@thedawnpost.com
To: wendell.mullet@agricorps.org
Subject: Extortion

Cutthroat:

You cause so many others to bleed, Mr. Mullet; must you bleed me dry too? You cannot get blood from a stone, it's said, no matter how hard you squeeze. I realize that you're disappointed with my latest review and that you want some sort of compensation; nevertheless, the simple truth is that I can't pay what you're asking. I do not have it. There is no way for me to get it.

Perhaps my hope that an extortionist such as yourself might play by the rules was in vain. However, *I* intend, at least, to keep my end of the bargain. I shall pay the amount, in full, to which I was forced to agree when you and your thugs initially began harassing me.

Now leave me alone.

O.B.

My Only True Love,

How very strange that you seem not to have received my latest love notes. In case you missed them, here is the text one last time: One hand upon your breast, the other upon your thigh and inching ever closer to heaven. Have mercy. Twenty-five years is surely long enough to wait for consummation.

Awaiting your reply,

Oliver

From: oliver.black@thedawnpost.com
To: branksome.black@rebel.net
Subject: Confidential!

Feast of D. H. Lawrence

Dearest Branksome:

All right, that's enough. Last I heard you were lying in your underwear on a beach, toasting yourself under a flaming sun and drinking draught after draught of spirits for "medicinal purposes," in order to thaw out frigid appendages. Come come now, Branksome; this is no time for you to take up residence at the bottom of a whiskey bottle. It's time to put down the shot glass, to pick the coconut out from between your teeth, to put away the bucket and shovel, to arise from the deck chair, to shake the sand out of your pants and to put them on – if you're not too entirely crapulent to locate your legs, that is. You've loafed long enough in Shangri-la-la-land, Dear Brother, and I do worry, especially given your weakness for ripe tomatoes, and I do not mean the kind that you find in a ketchup bottle either. I mean, of course, the weaker sex, weaker in this case meaning "exercising godlike powers over the other." Or am I misjudging the situation? Should I expect an indignant reply in which you insist that you are continuing to wrestle heroically with the enemies of freedom? I do hope so. It isn't easy to usher in a new era singlehandedly, you know; I am relying on you to be both my right and left hands, working for good from without, while I act as the Mighty Encephalon, toiling away in the hopes of effecting reform from within.

I trust that you received my latest e-mail, Dear Brother. You may remember that I asked you for advice, advice which I'm afraid I need more than ever given that I continue to be harassed and bullied by an individual who is less like a human being and more like a remote ancestor of a human being – perhaps like a Neanderthal, recovered and revived from his frosty grave, sent to agricultural college, and thence allowed to club his way to the upper echelons of local political power. The skull ridge and jutting brow, the hairy back and gaping mouth, the forward-leaning posture and dangling arms – all are evidence of a politician. But he's a politician of the worst kind, of the corrupt and money-grubbing kind, of the kind that rightfully belongs behind bars – though in his case whether they should be the bars of a cell in a prison, or the bars of a cage in a zoo, is up for debate.

You have always had a talent for thugs just as, admittedly, you have always had a talent for the ladies (especially ladythugs), and it is to the subject of the ladies, and one lady in particular, that I now turn my attention. Of course I'm referring to my darling Lucy, who has obviously been avoiding me as one avoids something sticky and brown, and has taken to behaving *not* like her normal enticing self, but more like someone who's seen something very nasty indeed in the woodshed. Oh, Branksome! I'm taking you fully into my confidence, and trust that as I bare my soul to you, you will remember the knightly virtue of secrecy in love. Nota bene: This is sensitive information of the highest order, so be forewarned – if you should dare to respond with brutish taunts or jeering mockery, I shall not stop short of personally exhuming Mother and telling. Just see if I don't.

So – the story I'm about to tell begins during the electrifying days of our courtship when I vowed in a moment of pious insanity that I would not make love with Lucy until she was my wife. Noting her evident bewilderment and disappointment, I decided to attempt an erotic letter as a substitute, but was terrified at giving offense or having her think I was a practised hand at such things, and so it was short and utterly tame. To my delight she replied immediately and picked up the theme, moving the action a little nearer to the fireworks. We carried along in this vein, both of us assuming that the letters would end with the climactic moment at some decent interval into the writing (a few weeks? a few months?). But no, it became a sort of joke between us to string the other one along, to linger, to dally, to savour, to move at a pace and with a sort of thoughtfulness and erotic genius that is not permitted in real life. Imagine a twenty-five-year carnal aria with only the occasional brief recitative to inch the action forward. Good God, but the suspense has been unbearable! After trailing a burning path of kisses up her neck for three years, it took that long again just to arrive at our first sustained osculation! It took an additional six years to finally get her supine! My right hand has been inching toward its target up the inside of her left thigh for the better part of a decade. I *had* been working one-handed at the clasp of her bra for most of our marriage; thankfully her breasts finally sprang free just last summer. One of us wrote a swollen member into the action early on, and it has been with me ever since (and surely, after twenty-five years I am entitled to some sort of award; Lucille herself suggests a Piece Prize, if you take her regrettably crude meaning). We agreed from the beginning that it would be frightfully amusing to sustain a creeping pace until very near the end, at which point the letters would arrive faster and faster, in a flurry, from one a month, to one a

week, to one a day, to one an hour, at which point we would
finally come together in the flesh and act out all we had written in
the letters. Fortunately not a one has been lost, and we have the
entire saga of seduction from the very beginning – which is essential for reference purposes, since it is impossible to keep the
action straight from year to year, and even now there are occasional glitches. Last year, for example, we realized that I had been
resting all of my weight on her arm for the better part of a decade, and surely the circulation would have been cut off by now.
And hilariously, after twenty-five years I am absolutely naked –
except for my socks. (In vainglorious moments I remember this
indignity and am humbled.) Of course there have been times
when out of sheer desperation I have tried to speed up the action
and attempt a coup – "Finally the moment had arrived," that sort
of thing, only to be met with something like, "But not yet – it was
much too soon!" Ah! The torment continues.

Why do I share with you in detail this shockingly personal
aspect of my relationship with my darling wife? It is because,
Branksome, last month, for the first time in twenty-five years,
there was *no letter* from Lucille, and no explanation from her
either. Was it forgotten? Deliberately not written? Written but
mislaid? Certainly it's not the latter of these three options, given
that after five-year-old Selwyn got his little apple-sauced fists on a
letter from me to Lucille that only read, thank heavens, "Ever
advancing over the curve," we realized precautions were imperative and therefore had specially large, locked letter boxes installed
just outside our individual studies for the specific purpose of
erotic postal delivery and storage. (This in turn led to the development of a "special" relationship with our respective postal
carriers, but that is another story and so, in order to prevent the
possibility of a vulgar, vicarious thrill by my own brother – ugh! –
the veil of decency shall be drawn *here*.) Perhaps she intentionally
neglected to compose the letter, but I've no idea why she would
do such a thing, and I've not the heart to ask.

There are other troubling symptoms as well, Branksome,

searching questions that require solid answers, such as where does she spend most of her time these days? Why did she deliberately miss an important dinner the other evening? *Why is the door to her studio locked?* I do realize that she's working like an ant before the frost, and of late she's been asked to deliver scores of lectures on the speculative subject of art as religion (and there is more urgent talk of her being offered a professorship in the salt mines at the University – I explode with pride at the thought of it!) but my petal has *always* had a voracious appetite for artistic, intellectual work, and I cannot understand how work alone could explain her frequent absences, nor her failure to pen a simple love(making) note. I continue to be hounded by the notion that it's some lack in myself, something that I have done or, worse, something that I have forgotten to do. But what is it? What have I done, I ask you, Branksome?

I'm counting on you for an answer, and trust that I shall receive a thorough reply immediately, if not sooner. In less rational, but more poetic moments, I pray to Saint Dwynwen for guidance – if only I could visit Ffynnon Dwynwen, the freshwater wishing well wherein lives a magical fish who can predict the future for lovers – if only, if only – but it's a place I can visit only in my dreams, Branksome, because in real life the magical powers, and indeed the very existence of such a fish, is, of course, a giant load of hooey. Ah well. At least all else is as always for the Family Black. Olivia continues to charm the birds out of the trees; the boys continue to eat them.

With brotherly affection,

Oliver

From: rafe.wilde@thedawnpost.com
To: oliver.black@thedawnpost.com
Subject: Sabotage

Oliver:

I read your review of my uncle's restaurant and was incredibly impressed with it, totally blown away by it even, up until, oh, I'd say about the second paragraph. Somewhere just after the introduction I began to feel a bit uneasy. By the end of the review I didn't feel uneasy anymore. I felt homicidal. I felt like tearing you apart with my bare hands, ripping out your intestines and shoving them down your throat. *There! Eat* that, *food critic*!

Bloody fucking hell! In the spirit of what you call friendship, you offer to write a review of my uncle's diner, and I assume, naturally, that the review will be a decent one, given that you've asked me for a big favour in return. You make good on the deal and write the review, and I think all is rosy until I actually pick up a paper and read the thing. Then I discover that the entire review is obviously a send-up, a farce, a mockery, and absolutely dripping with sarcasm from beginning to end. "Cleverly placed rips in the red plastic upholstery," "the drunk ingeniously placed in front of the doorway," "the historical importance of the sandwich," et cetera, an archaic reference to *orphans* for God's sake, and to top it all off, that utterly moronic poem. Was it your intention to make mincemeat of my uncle's business? I mean, who's going to go there after reading your review (other than the police, that is) now that you've made it clear that the place is populated by drunks, bikers, drug-dealing muggers, and whores?

I should have known you were losing your touch after reading that off-the-mark review of yours of The Mad Cow. What the hell did you mean when you wrote, "the meat dishes are not the true story here?" *What?* Didn't you notice that The Mad Cow *specializes* in wild game and exotic meats? That you have to go out of your way to order something that *doesn't* contain an ostrich or a bison? That there are moose and deer heads littering the walls? That the place looks like the wood-panelled recreation room of a trophy hunter? And besides all that, the salad bar is an absolute dump with the usual greens (wilting lettuce, rubberized celery sticks, petrified broccoli), boring cheese (presliced and weeping oil, dry, curled up at the edges), tasteless melon balls, bland cottage cheese, and chilled carrot coins. The desserts are mucilage-inspired travesties; lardy, cardboard-crust pies topped with anonymous sickly sweet gunk, puddings that taste like they've already been through a dog's digestive tract, and fruit forever trapped in jelly, like flies in amber. The cakes stand out from the rest because they're so dry you'd swear they got "dessert" and "desert" mixed up and just went with it. I'm telling you, the celebration of every possible carnivorous act, short of cannibalism and stewing our own pets, is the entire reason for the existence of this restaurant. The meat dishes are not only the *true* story – they're the *only* story.

Obviously you're losing your touch, Mr. Black. In addition to which you are a pompous, pretentious pain in the ass. And you can bloody well forget about Black Chalice's review because there isn't going to be one.

Rafe

From: rafe.wilde@thedawnpost.com
To: alma.wilde@command.net
Subject: Oops

Dear Mom:

Okay, I've really done it this time. I just wrote a scathing e-mail to that colossal twit, Oliver Black – you know, the guy who could gleefully lay waste my career with the merest twitch of a pinkie finger. But I couldn't help it, honestly. As you used to say, enough is enough, which is an excellent example of airtight parental logic a kid just can*not* argue with. Enough *is* enough, no question about it, just as A is A – the A in this case standing for ass, which is what Oliver Black absolutely is.

He's irritating me beyond belief, Mom, with his talk of Ms. Savage; his disapproval of my relationship with Angel, as if it's any of his business (oh, and you asked me how old she is – she's just a few months – about thirty-five – shy of nineteen); and especially with his recent review of Uncle Bill's café. You would not believe the utter crap he wrote in that article (I'm attaching a copy of it so you can see for yourself), but every word was calculated to wreak as much havoc as possible. You can bet that within the week, Mr. Clean and his band of health and safety inspectors are going to conduct a SWAT-style raid and swoop down on Uncle Bill like a ton of Ajax. Not to mention the social workers, the prison wardens, the police officers, and everybody else who's interested in the kind of clientele attracted by the Burger and Bun. I admit we had an informal deal – he writes an article for me, I write an article for him – but I've called the whole thing off given that what he wrote wasn't so much a review as it was a warrant for Billy-Bob's arrest.

Anyway, thanks for sending another box of my old stuff, especially for Quackers, my inflatable duck, and for my old bedtime stuffie, Loppity Lamb (I must be a genius – who would have thought to look for the drugs *in there*?). Thanks for my old electronic keyboard, too – I'd forgotten how useful it is to be able to play up to one note at a time on an instrument with a full ten seconds of memory. (I think I'll donate it to the band Mousetrap, and they can use it in their own special way during their next concert.) However, although it was fun to unwrap my old copy of *The Feathered Back Hair Manual*, and jeans that are so tight they require their occupant to be jeanetically modified in order to fit, it was *no fun at all* to discover *my old metronome*. How could you possibly even imagine that I might want it? It's like sending a former concentration camp victim a canister of gas as a nostalgic reminder of the good old days. How about a little striped hat? Maybe a meat hook? I still have nightmares about it – either I'm hopelessly trying to catch up to it, or it's running after me, faster and faster, from largo to allegro to prestissimo, trying to knock me senseless with its little triangular fist on that rigid arm of chilled steel. I can still hear its aggressive, unforgiving, unnaturally regular ticking in my sleep, and Ms. Savage's voice saying, "Let's try it one more time, but this time let's count, shall we? With the metronome and here we go – one and two and three and four, and one and two and three and four, and . . ." Jesus, Mom, I hate that tool of judgment, that ticking irritant, that robotic wagging finger. Even as I write, that cursed clockwork is sitting on the table beside me, and I just want to smash it, to have the satisfaction of hearing the wood splinter and the metal twang, to watch that diabolical spring launch itself into the depths of space. Oh, all right – I'm not really going to pulverize it. I'll just calmly dismember it and store it under the floorboards in my bedroom (The Tell-Tale Metronome), and let's hope I'm not driven mad even then by its incessant ticking and that I don't break down and wind up confessing my crime to the police.

"It's beating, it's beating, it's beating under the floorboards!"

"This is a metronome, Mr. Wilde."

"Oh, yeah, right. So, should I contact my lawyer?"

"No, Sir – your piano teacher."

So, anyway, I'll probably be out of a job within the next few hours, in which case I reserve the right to pawn the damn metronome for cash. Meanwhile, I've got some unfinished business with Helga, my vibrating bed, who is the only woman in my life who lets me crawl all over her and do whatever I want. Angel is out of town, besides which her guardian angel is a winged Sumo wrestler, and Suzanne continues to brush me off for some trivial reason, like maybe the time she came home early and found me dressed up like a (fabulously attractive) drag queen in her best dress and high heels. It was all a stupid misunderstanding, as I've explained to her a million times. I mean, I was only kidding, Mom – I did it for a laugh. I just whipped it all on a few minutes before she arrived as a sort of a joke. Besides, how can you women wear those clothes for any amount of time? Some of that haute couture stuff was definitely designed by a misogynist on a bad trip; it's about as comfortable as a burlap straightjacket with jute underwear and asbestos pants. And those shoes! After a couple of hours, those stiletto heels were killing me! (Not that I didn't love wearing her flannelette nightie the few times she let me. Now I know why every woman, no matter how stylish and sexy, owns at least one of those essentially shapeless bags and wears it as often as possible. God those things are cozy! I still wear the green-plaid flannel nightshirt she bought me as a replacement, but it's not the same as that ruffly pink dream.) And talk about confusing! The buttons are on the wrong side of all her shirts, her pantyhose always feels like it's on backward no matter what the orientation, and her bras should be the subject of either an investigative documentary or a horror film. Anyway, Mom, my point is that any normal heterosexual male should not be shunned for life just because of one teensy little cross-dressing episode. And how was I supposed to know that lipstick doesn't come out of silk?

Your boy,

Rafe

From: oliver.black@thedawnpost.com
To: selwyn.black@freenet.org
          merlin.black@freenet.org
          damien.black@freenet.org
Subject: Glitch

Hello Boys:

I regret to inform you that things appear to have gone rather badly wrong between Mr. Wilde and myself. Naturally I anticipated this event, just as I am expecting him to issue a profound

apology and offer contrite words of reconciliation in only a matter of days. Perhaps you read the review that I wrote about his
uncle's ridiculous café – probably the most vile eating establishment in which I have ever had the misfortune to set foot. I attempted to be as generous as possible, without actually being
dishonest, but Mr. Wilde misinterpreted my attempt as an exercise in sarcasm (and also had the gall to put the boot to my excellent verse "O Humble Bunwich!").

Don't fret, my boys – all is not lost. You shall indeed have
your review. I think we'll find that, within a very few days, Mr.
Wilde will not only issue a profound apology, but also that the
review of Black Chalice's concert will go ahead as scheduled.

Nil Desperandum!

Dad

From: oliver.black@thedawnpost.com
To: rafe.wilde@thedawnpost.com
Subject: "Blow, blow thou winter wind,
           Thou art not so unkind as man's ingratitude."
           -Shakespeare
                                        Feast of Ralph Nader

Mr. Wilde:

Let us be completely frank. Your uncle's eating establishment
is an abomination, as well you know. It is nothing short of a miracle that the Health and Safety people have not declared it a contaminated site of Chernobyl-like proportions and called in both
city officials, and the armed forces, to wrap it in impenetrable
polyester and raze it to the ground with bulldozers and tanks, or
perhaps shoot it off to Alpha Centauri where it can do no harm
(though this would be no favour to the Alpha Centaurians). We

both know that eating at Billy-Bob's is like eating in a landfill. It has all the atmosphere of a septic tank, a germ warfare laboratory, a human waste management plant. It is wholly and unalterably disgusting, from the sweat stains around the armpits of your uncle's undershirt to the inverted mountains of old gum hanging like stalactites under the tables. Am I to blame for the fact that people may not care to eat with a mangy dog sitting in their laps and drooling voraciously into their bunwiches? Is it my fault that, at Billy-Bob's, people actually *request* that flies be put into their soup, just to give it a little flavour? Ought I to be condemned because people may not want to pay for a case of stomach cramps and a head full of lice?

Mr. Wilde: I would like you to put yourself in my shoes (size eleven) just for a moment and then imagine *you yourself* attempting to write a charitable review of your uncle's café. How would *you* report positively on a restaurant in which there are more appetizing morsels, and fewer bacteria, in the proprietor's large intestine? "Impossible!" I hear you cry, "A miracle!" That's right, Mr. Wilde – a miracle, and that *I* somehow managed this journalistic wonder is a feat for which I expect gratitude, not insults.

We are both men of honour, are we not, Mr. Wilde? Therefore, I expect you to comply with our arrangement and write a review of Black Chalice's upcoming concert. Visiting the punishment for the (alleged) sins of the father upon the sons is just another of those irritating Judeo-Christian inventions that all men of reason must surely reject. It is a tiresome example of sloppy, primitive, BC thinking for which all theologians and many pre-enlightenment philosophers are famous. But we are men of the twenty-first century; the winds of reason have cleared the cobwebs from our minds, and we no longer see as through a glass darkly. Thus I know I can count on you to do the right thing, the reasonable thing, and pay off your debt to me by writing a review for my boys.

Sincerely,

Oliver Black

PS: In addition, I take offense at your characterization of my review of The Mad Cow. You are, of course, entitled to your opinions, as ridiculous and incomprehensible as they may be; however, just because you eat, do not therefore assume that you know even the first thing about the complex nature of restaurant reviewing.

From: rafe.wilde@thedawnpost.com
To: oliver.black@thedawnpost.com
Subject: Talk to the Hand, Mr. Black

Opening one of your e-mails is like opening the door at the far end of a wind tunnel – I find myself gripping the arms of my chair while my eyes water and squint and my skin flaps in the gale until my face is a skeletal grimace. Getting blasted with the full force of your infernal observations and opinions makes me feel irritated, makes me feel annoyed, but mostly makes me feel like dismembering you and shoving you under my floorboards where you can slowly rot beside the gruesome remains of my metronome.

Rafe

From: oliver.black@thedawnpost.com
To: rafe.wilde@thedawnpost.com
Subject: You've Made Your Bed . . .

Dear Rafe:

You're blubbering again, I'm afraid. How like a wave of the

sea you are, "driven with the wind and tossed." I feel this, and I feel that. You needn't feel obligated to favour the world with a play-by-play update of your every feeling-state, you know; life isn't like one of those slice-of-life novels, essentially medical in tone, in which the author takes the emotional temperature, feels the emotional pulse, of each of the characters every five minutes. In real life there is no omniscient narrator who cares about your every palpitation of feeling, your every fluttering response to the ever-changing winds of circumstance. Do you feel rapturous? Gloomy? Testy? Who cares? Only in novels in which the author treats his characters in essentially the same way that a garage mechanic treats a car engine (the overarching question being, "What's wrong with this thing?") are we expected to feel such all-encompassing fascination with the emotions of others (poor Mrs. Dalloway is depressed! Dear God, no!), and then human emotion, in all its subtlety and all its grossness, trumps all other concerns. I offer this insight as one of the many gleaned in that boot camp known as parenthood – the insight that your feelings are, essentially, irrelevant. One cannot delay changing the baby, for example, because one is feeling a little drowsy or peckish, nor indeed because one has a raging case of the flu, nor even because one has suddenly sprouted an extra limb or a full suit of fur. Has an alien spacecraft landed in the neighbour's garden? Are the tanks of a hostile nation rolling down Oak Street? Is an asteroid the size of Manhattan slated to impact the earth, with your house in the middle of the bull's-eye? So what? The baby is crying. What's required is action, not bellyaching. As further proof of my point, I offer the case of my darling Lucy, who had an amusing habit of faking her own death in order to avoid making supper, but even though our boys would regularly find her in a pool of her own blood (ketchup) sprawled in the middle of the kitchen floor, this would not deter them from demanding cookies and juice (not to mention trying to steal her rings and hawk them for cash) until she was forced to come back from the dead just to make them stop whining. And this is a good thing! What a relief to forget about how *you* feel for once and just to get on with it. What a lesson is this, to learn that love is something you do and not necessarily something you feel.

So buck up, Rafe, and stop imagining that the universe gives a hoot. Do you still imagine that your feelings are Mother Nature's chief concern? Think on. There is a greater mass of living organisms under the surface of the earth than above it. Bacteria, single-celled organisms – they're the real story. But what about God? After all, His eye is always on the sparrow. This is true, but sadly, He only does birds. Dress like a chicken and you'll have his attention full-time, and a lot of other people's besides. The point is you must forget about what you want, and do what you know is right. For example, my young Merlin cried "But I don't even *want* to go to school!" on his first day of Grade One, as if what he wanted even entered the equation. Naturally I sympathized with the lad, but I also explained that a boy has two choices in life – he can go to school or he can go to jail. You see, it didn't matter how the poor chappy felt; *feeling* didn't enter into the equation at all. Though it should mean twelve bleak years of being bullied alternating with meaningless busywork, still he did his duty – he knew he had simply to make the right choice and then follow it through.

Just as you must, Mr. Wilde. Remember – your emotional state doesn't matter a jot or tittle. What *does* matter a jot or tittle is doing the right thing, and that thing is fulfilling your obligation to the Family Black and writing the review that you have solemnly promised.

Ethically,

Oliver

From: rafe.wilde@thedawnpost.com
To: alma.wilde@command.net
Subject: Blankie Is *Not* Happy

Mom:

Oh, come on! You can't be serious. Yeah, I know that I promised a review for a review, but you can't possibly believe that I'm still obligated to write the Black Chalice article after Oliver's silver-tongued hatchet job on Uncle Bill's café. Did you actually read the article? And, if so, did you do like I did and print out a thousand copies to use as emergency toilet paper? Filth, rot, contamination, disease, vermin – of what infraction is Uncle Bill *not* guilty? Why doesn't he just change the name of the Burger and Bun to The Tongue and Dung, or maybe something quaint like The Midden, or how about The Mickey Mousecateria? Christ Almighty. I think it's colossally unfair of you to expect me to do Oliver Black *any* favours, and it's especially evil of you to take the entire Star Ship *Enterprise* hostage and threaten to dismember and discard all of my *Star Trek* action figures (is *nothing* sacred?). So, just to get you off my back, and because I value Nurse Chapel more than my honour, I'll do it. I'll write the stinking review – under one condition. And that condition is that you've got to get off my back about Angel, okay? I keep telling you, she is *not* too young for me, okay? Girls mature way faster these days – it's got something to do with the hormones they inject into the chickens they eat or something. Girls are moulting these days by twelve, roosting by sixteen. Angel is *my* age, Mom – at least, she's the age I feel inside, and that's good enough for me.

I suppose I'd better write to Oliver Black right away and tell him the bloody wonderful news.

Resentfully,

Rafe

From: rafe.wilde@thedawnpost.com
To: oliver.black@thedawnpost.com
Subject: For the Love of Spock

Yeah, yeah, all right. Forget all that stuff I said before. You win, Mr. Black. I'll write that review, but understand that I'm not doing it because of anything *you* said. I'm doing it because Black Chalice is a great band, and to ignore their hometown debut would be detrimental to *my* career.

I still contend that you're a pompous, pretentious twit, but your boys have managed to survive you unscathed, it seems, and so I'm willing to help them out – out of your house, that is, away from you and into the limousines and jet planes which will rocket them to stardom.

Rafe

From: oliver.black@thedawnpost.com
To: rafe.wilde@thedawnpost.com
Subject: Imperfect Contrition

My Dear Rafe:

This is excellent news indeed! How relieved I am that you've seen the light and are going to write the Black Chalice review after all! Of course I shall ignore the hostile tone of your e-mail; you'll find I am a fair man, Rafe, and make allowances for youth, for immaturity, for poor judgment, for drunkenness. And just to prove that you have my forgiveness and my blessing, I've sent back your delightful Starsky and Hutch mugs. Think of them as a peace offering.

Toodle-oo,

Oliver

From: oliver.black@thedawnpost.com
To: selwyn.black@freenet.org
merlin.black@freenet.org
damien.black@freenet.org
Subject: It's a Go!

Hello Boys:

As I predicted, the scales fell from Rafe's eyes just in the nick of time, so the scurvy young rogue will be writing a review of your upcoming concert after all. Oh, joy! I can hardly believe that your official live debut is only a day away; I feel as excited as I did on the occasion of your initial debuts in this world, each of you thrashing about and screaming your little heads off in the hope of making contact with a couple of breasts – and, after listening to your rehearsal yesterday, I see we're in for more of the same. Well, go to it, I say! If that's what it takes to rake in the dough, I'm all for it, especially since it means you'll eventually be keeping your mother and me in the style which we deserve. (Please note that, upon officially achieving glamorous-rock-star status, you are obliged by decades of tradition to buy me a ridiculously overpriced boat and a country house for your mother.) However, I was alarmed when you, Merlin, informed me that yesterday's performance was a *dress* rehearsal, implying that you were wearing the clothes which you intend to wear on stage tomorrow evening. But surely not, Boys! I admit that it is clever to have all of the Black boys *dressed* in black, but, again, I think you might consider how some of the truly great performers have dressed in order to grab the attention of the audience. Consider the mature Elvis, Liberace, Elton John. Would the latter have achieved such astronomical fame without five-inch heels and the extensive use of feathers? I'm thinking sequins here, Boys, or perhaps some amusingly large glasses. What about a bow tie? Compared to such inventive garb, you have to admit that plain black trench coats are seriously underwhelming.

Still, I have to believe that you know your business, in the same way that I know mine. So, remember – no unsanctioned meals tomorrow before the concert! The consumption of any food item not specified on the list in the kitchen will result in the application of some heinous penalty worthy of the most inspired of Spanish inquisitors. I'm thinking of installing a piranha-stocked moat around the kitchen, just to be sure. And don't think I'm above booby-trapping the fridge, or installing trap doors with alligator pits below, just in front of the pantry.

I want my boat.

Dad

From: rafe.wilde@thedawnpost.com
To: angel.day@agape.org
Subject: On My Knees

Hey There, Angel:

Thank God you're home again, and just in time for me to show you off at the Black Chalice concert tomorrow night – which I still can't believe I'm reviewing, but that's the power of Almighty Mom for you. (Hey, why don't you wear that mind-bogglingly tight, thigh-length, leopard-print skirt with the zipper that works both ways, up *and* down the back, and that sheer, gravity-defying halter top? And a burka, of course, because it's a waste of my time having to gouge out the eyes of every rival male who gawks at you in a stadium of thousands.) Since you left I've done nothing but fantasize about our reunion, about that moment when I'll place you gently upon my bed, pull your exquisite body under mine, and slowly, relentlessly, inevitably – respectfully – pound you into the mattress with my mighty sledgehammer of love.

Listen. After the concert I'll have to whip together a review, but after that I want you to come back to my place where your Rafey Wafey can perform his particular brand of carnal magic. Please, Angel, don't make me beg anymore. I'd drag my body over a bed of hot coals, of crushed ice, of cut glass, of live wires, just to get to your luscious body (and what a mess *I'd* be then). I'd give you everything I own, I'd buy you a star, I'd marry you – hell, I'd even *pay* you – if you'd just let me fondle *one* breast. Just one. *Please.* You can even choose which breast. I'm not fussy. Left or right, it doesn't matter. And then, if we can work out the breast issue, maybe I can negotiate my way to your thighs (inner or outer, again your choice), and to the other parts of your body that are driving me crazy with sheer animal lust.

You've got to understand that a man has needs, Angel. I *have* to ravish you, and not just for my sake, but for the sake of the planet. I mean, the heat between us is already the primary cause of global warming. Do you want to be responsible for turning the earth into some sort of hostile, toxic, scorching inferno with a Venusian atmosphere drenched in sulphuric acid? I didn't think so.

I know what you're really worried about. You're really worried about hell, aren't you? You're worried about going down on some antediluvian fornication charge and roasting on Satan's spit for all of eternity, right? Trust me, Angel, it ain't gonna happen. God is *not* going to send his most perfect creation to hell; it's much more likely that He'll whisk you off to heaven prematurely, just so He can fix you up on a date with his son – which, by the way, you should avoid at all costs. Face the facts, Angel. As much as you say you love Jesus Christ (sometimes, I think, even more than you love *me*), *He* wouldn't exactly be your dream date,

would He? I mean, does Jesus Christ have a 1974 red Ford
Torino, a fashionable apartment in a trendy part of town, and a
vibrating bed? No, Angel. The guy doesn't even have a *job* for
Christ's sake – the market bottomed out on personal saviours a
long time ago. It's so last millennium. And what would you two
talk about? You'd want to talk about fashion and your favourite
bands, and he'd want to talk about the poor, and the meek, and
the blessed (i.e., *losers*). Plus there would be the endless questions.
"Tell me again about the Pope, and telephones," He'd say with
that hugely uncool and embarrassing ancient Aramaic accent. *Bor-
innnngggg*! And what would you do? Go out for pizza? A movie?
Dancing? Afraid not. How about a baptism! And then an exor-
cism where you get to watch him cast demons into swine and
raise dead people (eww) and just generally go around making
everybody feel guilty. I hate guys like Him, guys who think
they're so special they can wash away everybody's sin with their
own blood. They're so preachy and serious – does Jesus say even
one remotely funny thing in the whole Bible? (Does *anybody* ever
say *anything* funny in the Bible?) Plus they always think they're
God's gift, and they only like girls who think so too, girls who are
so deferential and obedient they think that a good time on a
Saturday night is washing their date's feet with their hair. And
piercing your nipples is one thing, but it would just be incredibly
spooky holding hands with a guy with spike-sized holes through
them. Plus you hate Middle Eastern food. And what if you married Him? Do you want the guy who came up with the Ten
Commandments for a father-in-law? (Think about it – no more
shopping on Sundays!) Do you want a mother-in-law who's in
such denial that she actually believes she was still a virgin even
after she gave birth? You'll end up on some trashy American talk
show for sure. Trust me, Angel, you don't want to deal with any
of this. And besides, *if He so much as lays a finger on you, I'll
crucify Him* – got that?

Okay, where was I? Sorry, but I just get a little jealous when I
think of another guy anywhere near you. So, I guess my point

was, don't worry about going to hell. And, even if I'm dead wrong and you do end up toasting on the coals, it will have been worth it – even just one sexual encounter with the Great Rafe would compensate for an eternity of being squashed between the metal plates of Satan's waffle iron.

Think about it, Angel – maybe Jesus can take you to heaven after you die, *but I can take you to heaven while you're still alive.* Let me prove it tomorrow night after the concert.

Seductively yours,

Rafe

The Dream Post
Experts Prove Not One
Even Remotely Amusing Thing in Entire Bible

Mount Sinai, Egypt – A government-appointed committee of humourologists from around the globe claim to have proven that, as a work of comedy, *The Holy Bible* is a catastrophic failure.

"There are 791,328 words and not a gag, a pun, or a wisecrack among them," commented Rabbi Henny Whoopeecushion of the Holy Land. "Who could write that much material and not even accidentally say something that might produce a chuckle? The odds are against it, which, of course, adds further proof of His existence – only a divine entity could be that unremittingly *not* funny."

"God wrote the Holy Scriptures after the Fall – but before the summer," explains Biblical expert Eleazar Funstein. "Ha! A little joke! Actually, in all seriousness here, folks, God wrote the Bible before the invention of humour. If God were writing the scriptures today, the Bible would be a very different book. Sort of like, 'In the beginning was the word, and the word was followed by ba-dum bum.'"

Other experts disagree with the findings of the committee. "Let's face it – the whole Bible is just a joke from beginning to end," says dogmatic atheist Rex Schnauzer, "especially when you take into account the fact that the tall tale genre was the highest form of humour before the Enlightenment. Noah's Ark, Jonah and the Whale, Joshua and the Battle of Jericho, David and Goliath – these were the sort of yarns that kept the comedy clubs of Nineveh hopping in 3 BC."

"Actually the Bible is a masterpiece of satire and is without a doubt the funniest book ever written," continues Mr. Schnauzer. "You can't read a verse like, say, Judges 4:21 without ending up with tears streaming down your face, pounding the floor with your fists and gasping for air – it's that goddamn funny."

Other experts contend that the humour issue is impossible to resolve because the Hebrews are a preternaturally patient people and are used to waiting centuries, even millennia, for a punch line. As if to emphasize the point, Rabbi Whoopee-cushion vows that a Pentateuchical Comedyfest will be held next year in Jerusalem.

Chapter Four

From: oliver.black@thedawnpost.com
To: rafe.wilde@thedawnpost.com
Subject: Sore as a Gum Boil

Feast of Saint Expeditus

Mr. Wilde:

I was like an excited little puppy this morning, arising at an indecently early hour, padding around the kitchen for a while and then hovering about the front door, waiting, waiting, for our tardy, juvenile-offender/paper boy to toss the newspaper from a moving vehicle (bike, scooter, get-away car) in the general direction of the house. When the great moment finally arrived, I was armed and ready with my customary cup of embalming fluid (coffee), my croissant, my bowl of fresh fruit, and my reading glasses. Ah, the suspense, the thrill of the unknown. What penetrating comments, I wondered, would the insightful and discerning Mr. Rafe Wilde have to offer about the brilliant debut performance of the band Black Chalice?

I spread the paper out onto the table before me and turned immediately to the Entertainment section. How surprised I was to discover that the first page was dedicated to a discussion of the release of some trivial multimillion-dollar Hollywood epic, and not to a review of the Black Chalice concert. I thought this a bizarre and mysterious oversight, but became increasingly bewildered when I found no mention whatsoever of my boys on page two, page three, page four; in fact, the entire Entertainment section was perplexingly devoid of Black Chalice–related material. Ah ha, I thought to myself. It must be because the concert was of such major importance to both the local and international scene that the review has been printed in section A, perhaps even on the front page of *The Dawn Post* itself. But no, Mr. Wilde. There was nothing in section A. There was nothing in the Business section, nothing in the Sports section, nothing in the classifieds – although tomorrow there will definitely be a notice in the Lost and Found section which will read thus: "Lost – one music review. If found, please print immediately on page one of the Entertainment section in *The Dawn Post*, only after which please call off the hired assassins sicced on the critic."

All right, Mr. Wilde. *Where is it?* Why is there no review of the concert in this morning's paper? What possible excuse could you have for not submitting your article? Oh, I know. You must be dead. What a shame. Still, that review has to be in your laptop somewhere. Perhaps I ought to visit your apartment personally and shake it out of there.

I hope you're not reneging on our deal, Mr. Wilde. Do *not* forget that I wrote a laudatory review, a review in which I might have mentioned that your Uncle's café has all the flair and atmosphere of a proctologist's waiting room – but I did not. I might have said that, instead of a restaurant critic, the food really ought to have been examined by a scatologist – but I did not. I held my tongue (and, after eating at your uncle's, gave it a hand-written letter of apology) and produced a critique that put Billy-Bob's in the best light possible. To deny my boys a review simply because of the unfortunate fact that your uncle owns and operates a sewage farm masquerading as a restaurant (clearly, not my fault) is enormously unfair.

I demand an immediate response. And until such time as I receive one, I wish, sincerely,

A pox on your house,

Oliver Black

PS: Saint Expeditus: Patronage – *against procrastination.*

From: rafe.wilde@thedawnpost.com
To: oliver.black@thedawnpost.com
Subject: Get Knotted

You want to know why there's no review in this morning's paper? Two words, Mr. Black: *Ask Selwyn.*

Rafe

From: oliver.black@thedawnpost.com
To: selwyn.black@freenet.org
              merlin.black@freenet.org
              damien.black@freenet.org
Subject: In Knots

Good Morning, Boys:

Due to your late night/early morning postconcert revelry, I shan't disturb your well-deserved slumber. (Not that I could wake you anyway. Even as babies you were all such preternaturally heavy sleepers that your mother and I would strap mirrors under your noses just so we could be sure you were still breathing. Nowadays, as you know, you don't so much sleep as hibernate, and it normally takes an escalating series of events – alarm clocks ringing, cymbals crashing, cannon firing – just to rouse you to semiconsciousness.) Still, I find I cannot contain my jubilation. Not since Jesus Christ rose from the dead has a father felt as proud of his son as I feel of you three. I've often felt proud of you before, of course; I remember with great pleasure Damien's first (and, I believe, only) A, Merlin's extraordinary conquest of the potty, and Selwyn's starring role as a rutabaga in the eleventh-grade play (or was it first grade? It's all a blur to me now. *Tempus fugit.*). Triumphant moments all, but last night's performance was the moment when I knew that your mother and I definitely made the

right choice every time by not terminating you or putting you up
for adoption, by not donating you to the circus or selling you off
for scientific experiments – though at times the temptation was
almost overwhelming. Lucky for you I am made of stern stuff, and
when your mother begged me to sell you to the gypsies, or to replace you with life-sized cardboard replicas, or to send you to
boarding school in Antarctica, I forbade it – though I admit that
at times I was thinking primarily of the tax break.

Your performances last night were truly first-rate. I should just
mention, however, that the one part of the concert that disturbed
me was when the three of you, in a strip-tease manoeuvre like
that of the most accomplished exotic dancer, unbuttoned your
trench coats and flung them off your bodies, revealing the three
naked torsos beneath. It was not the synchronized stripping that
bothered me, nor was it your corporeal forms; actually, I was
rather pleased to see that after a lifetime of potato chips and bean
bag chairs, all of you have been taking the idea of fitness seriously
for once and, like torture victims on the rack, have evidently been
spending a fair amount of time strapped to various machines at a
gym. No, it was a shock for three reasons: 1) Selwyn, because
those were the diamond earrings I gave your mother for her birthday stuck in your nipples; 2) Merlin, because those were definitely claw marks down your back, and we don't own a pet; and
3) Damien, because you actually heeded my command and chose
not to have a naked woman tattooed on your back. For this I
thank you. That you chose, instead, to have the naked woman
tattooed on your front, though not technically a criminal offense,
is nonetheless a criminally stupid one. (And tattooed *upside down,*
no less – have you no shame?) It's for this reason that I will be
contacting a dermatologist who specializes in tattoo removal (I
believe they use a red-hot laser these days, and anaesthetic is
generally viewed with contempt) and financing the prompt removal of said tattoo with your early inheritance money. If any
extra money is required, please note that I will be foreclosing on
your room.

But never mind. Let's not spoil this moment of triumph. I must mention just one more thing, however, which is that I noted with alarm and dismay that there was *no review* of your brilliant debut by Rafe Wilde in this morning's paper. Upon detecting this unconscionable lapse, I immediately fired off an irate e-mail to the man himself, and he responded only moments later with this cryptic message: Ask Selwyn. I find this commandment bewildering. However, in the hopes of achieving understanding, I shall do as Mr. Wilde asks. I can't even begin to imagine what the answer might be. It can't be that Mr. Wilde was indifferent to your performance and thought it unworthy of a review; I myself watched him typing notes vigorously into his laptop computer for a great deal of the concert. It can't be due to illness; Mr. Wilde looked in fine form with the hypnotically enchanting Angel by his side. (Did you happen to notice her, Boys? Ha, silly me. I suddenly realize that this is the most rhetorical of all possible questions. How could you *not* notice a girl who is the ultimate embodiment of girly perfection, the princess of pulchritude, the supreme avatar of contemporary fashion, the essential archetype of seductive innocence? In addition to which the total amount of material on her body would not have been enough upon which to blow my nose.) And it most certainly cannot be due to your performance last night, which was exceptionally good and made it easy for me to imagine, as I gazed rapturously at the stage from my seat in the first balcony, that I was actually gazing at the sea off the prow of my luxuriously appointed seventy-foot catamaran.

So then, Selwyn, tell me: Why is there no review in the paper?

Con curioso,

Dad

From: oliver.black@thedawnpost.com
To: branksome.black@rebel.net
Subject: Sundries

Dearest Branksome:

I just now received a letter from you specially hand-delivered
by our mail carrier, since it was so badly abused it looked as if it
had been attacked by a pack of mail-starved wolverines shortly
before they trod upon a land mine. No matter – the contents appear to have arrived more or less in one piece. I note that it was
written from within the shuddering bowels of the Georg Philipp
Telemann express somewhere around the region of Berlin. I also
note, with deep satisfaction, that your efforts on behalf of the
unofficial left wing of Amnesty International (our little joke, eh
Branky?) have gone exceptionally well. Seventy-five freed from
their shackles in only three days! How could I ever have doubted
you? You impress me a great deal, you know, although your
reasons for leaving your south sea refuge sound suspect. I had
difficulty making sense of your convoluted tale – something about
a gambling incident intended to raise funds gone askew, an ancient crop-spraying plane converted to drop propaganda on behalf of the cause, an accidental marriage, a vengeful father, annoyed officials, irate farmers, extradition papers, the merchant
marines, a rescue, a sword fight, a narrow escape . . . good God,
Branky, but you do make 007 look like a bit of a girl's blouse,
don't you? Still, bravery and heroic exploits aside, I suggest you
concentrate on high efficiency rather than high adventure. I am
happy to provide funds for the cause, but please note that my
"Bail for Branksome" bank account is rather short of cash at present. Be careful, Old Chap! We don't want you to end up incarcerated in an overcrowded East German prison where you are
picked on by your cell mates, forbidden to see the sun, and fed a
steady diet of substandard grain for the rest of your life, like some
unfortunate fryer chicken.

Now, I note that you do not respond to my concerns about my beloved Lucille (your letter would have been posted before receiving my latest e-mail), but about your response to my concerns over my ailing Weltanschauung, I'm afraid that I don't quite understand how quoting Dickinson ("Hope is the thing with feathers . . .") pertains directly to my predicament, although I'll be the first to admit that it makes a damn fine slogan. I'm afraid you haven't quite got the gist of the situation – that your misunderstanding of the situation is so comprehensive that I can only react with red-hot hostility toward you. Be thankful that you are not currently in my presence, otherwise I should demand that we draw swords and fight to the death. Dear God, Branksome! Major world wars have begun over less! *How could you even suggest that I might be having an affair with another woman?* You imagine that an illicit liaison with another woman explains why I am being blackmailed? Ugh! The very thought of another woman is unthinkable! It is like trying to imagine the boundaries of the universe or an infinite number! And not only is it unthinkable but also appalling! Grotesque! Revolting! How could you even begin to imagine such a monstrous thing when you know very well that I love my Lucille with the white-hot intensity of a universe of stars? I could *never* be unfaithful to my dearest love, though I be strapped naked to an enormous bed and vigorously licked from head to foot by a thousand, no, *ten thousand* beautiful virgins, all of whom desired me and assured me that I, naturally, was the only man in the universe who could truly satisfy them. How I would loathe such an event as this! To even imagine a planet populated only by throngs of pliant, succulent females and me, its sole male inhabitant, is totally abhorrent! No, I assure you I would feel nothing, Branksome, nothing but pity. You are on the wrong track, though what the right track is I am unwilling to state plainly – both because I know you love a mystery, and just in case our correspondence is intercepted by my oppressors (unlikely, I admit, but given the ease with which they wield their instruments of extermination, I think I am wise to be cautious).

Try again.

In family news, I am pleased to report that your three nephews took The Dome by storm yesterday evening in their hometown debut concert. I *would* send you a copy of the review that was to have appeared in this morning's paper, but for some inexplicable reason, it was nowhere to be found. I shot off an incendiary e-mail to its ostensible author, Rafe Wilde, first thing this morning, and he replied immediately with a vexatious and utterly preposterous e-mail attempting to blame the immaculate *Selwyn*, it seems, for the absence of *his* article. Imagine! It reminds me of the time that Selwyn's pretty little kindergarten teacher attempted to suggest that it was *he* who was pulling various pranks around the classroom (whoopee cushions, misplaced amphibians, obscene pictorial graffiti); "I shall be contacting my lawyers," I wrote, "and we shall see what the Supreme Court has to say on the matter." Her baseless accusations ceased forthwith. But what ought I to do about Mr. Wilde? I suppose I shall wait for an explanation from my golden child (really, Branky, I wish you could have heard him yesterday – I've no doubt there's a boat in the works), and then I shall take the appropriate action.

That's all for now. Write again posthaste, both to let me know how the work is proceeding, and also to offer your normally invaluable advice, once you have successfully decoded my situation. (*Cogito bestiae.*) You're a hero, you know, Branksome, though clearly not everyone would think so (one man's freedom fighter being another man's terrorist, blah blah blah).

Your loyal brother in arms,

Oliver

From: rafe.wilde@thedawnpost.com
To: sales@bedsbedsbeds.cybersleep.net
Subject: Bed Head

To the Pinhead Inbred Quadrupeds at Beds Beds Beds:

Fucking hell! I can't believe you people! After dealing with you dunderheads for the last few weeks, I absolutely cannot understand how it is possible that your company is celebrating over *thirty* years in business and claiming *thousands* of satisfied customers. What is it those angels sing in that commercial of yours? "No more pills or counting sheep/We *guarantee* that you will sleep." Ha! What rubbish! What fatuous propaganda! Your advertising manager obviously took a page out of Goebbels' best-seller *Schwarz ist Weiß* to have come up with such a cunning, perverse, fraudulent advertising campaign. And who are these satisfied customers of yours anyway? People who have fallen off the wagon (who have deliberately thrown themselves off the wagon – oh, yeah baby, that feels good) at Masochists Anonymous? Whipping and Bondage enthusiasts? The Great Undead? And dare I ask who your product development manager is? Hermann Goering? Genghis Khan? The Marquis de Sade? I say you're all a bunch of sickos. And, by the way, I've noticed that Beds Beds Beds (BBB) is on the same page in the phone book as the Better Business Bureau (BBB), which I will definitely be contacting if I can't get some somnambulant satisfaction pretty damn soon.

Last night – possibly the worst night of my life by the way – I went to sleep in the palm of Helga's Hands hoping to get a desperately needed decent night's rest for a change. I was awakened not long after I had dozed off by a tremendous thump and wondered, in a confused and startled way, what had made such a huge noise. A burglar? A meteor? The sound of Helga's warranty expiring? No, it was none of these. The huge thump I heard was the sound of *me, my body*, hitting the floor, as Helga shimmied me to the edge of the bed and danced me right off my satin sheets. After the same thing happened at least a dozen more times, I decided that the problem was the sheets, and so I took off the satin ones and exchanged them for my old rubber ones in order to get a little more traction. Happily, I didn't fall out of bed again and I was dead to the world for six full hours; not even my own underpants catching fire could have roused me given the extreme nature of my sleep-deprivation. (I was also forced to take a largish handful of sleeping pills, further proving the spurious nature of your advertising.) However, when I finally awakened this morning, I discovered to my horror that I had *abrasions all over my entire body* from the friction between me and my bedding. Bloody hell! I look like I've been *sanded* for God's sake, like my pajama bottoms accidentally got snagged in the axle of a half-ton truck while I was asleep, and I spent the entire night being dragged through the outback on a gravel road. And what's happened to the hair on the left side of my head? It's fucking gone, that's what's happened! I have a gigantic bald spot above my left ear thanks to Helga massaging my hair right out of its follicles.

So you can take Helga and goose-step her back to the antiquated Nazi torture chamber where you found her. ("Ve haf vays of making you sleep!") And I'm giving you brainless boneheads just one more chance. I don't care what it is, just send me the bed of my dreams, or I'll report you to the relevant authorities and take my business elsewhere.

Abrasively,

Rafe Wilde

PS: Please note my change of address: Rafe Wilde – Poste Restante – Hell.

From: oliver.black@thedawnpost.com
To: rafe.wilde@thedawnpost.com
Subject: Ah

My Dear, Dear Rafe:

It was Selwyn himself who came to me this afternoon with
astounding tales of postconcert events that, at least in part, explain why there was no review in the paper this morning. How
shocked I was to discover that it was due to *Selwyn's* consummate
performance that you neglected to write a review of the concert.
As you know, however, I am not referring to his handiwork *on*
the stage but, rather, his handiwork *behind* the stage after the
curtain had fallen.

My dear friend and colleague. I see the scene so clearly before
me. There you were after the last *encore*, the last *bravo*, sitting
alone in the empty concert hall and furiously typing your review
into your laptop computer, when suddenly you realized that a
short interview with the eldest Black would provide just the right
finishing touch to your article. What a shock it must have been
for you to walk into Selwyn's dressing room and catch him *in
flagrante delicto*, on a makeshift bed of spare clothes and coats,
with a naked young lady writhing beneath him. This in itself
would not normally cause embarrassment or discomfort, I'm sure;
it would not be the first time that the passionate Rafe Wilde had
seen the pretzel-like entwining of limbs, the claw marks, the love
bites, and heard the profane demands for satisfaction emanating
from the lips of a beautiful woman. You have undoubtedly seen it
all – indeed, done it all (I do not intend mere flattery) – in your
thirty-eight years. Alas. All would have been well, if only the
young woman moaning with delight underneath my Selwyn was
none other than that hitherto virginal creature of unparalleled
nubile innocence – your girlfriend, the enchantingly beautiful
Angel.

Oh dear, oh dear. That Angel did not appear to realize that

the crucifix around Selwyn's neck was inverted, and therefore mistook him for some sort of Christian bad boy, does not speak well of her powers of perception, does it? And that my cunning knave of a son achieved in fifteen minutes what you have been campaigning for (*unsuccessfully*, according to Angel) for the last fifteen weeks must be an enormous blow to your manhood. Certainly nobody likes to be cuckolded.

Still, Mr. Wilde, you are a man of honour, and we do have a deal. I fully acknowledge that my son pitched the woo with the wrong girl, and I gave him the sort of tongue-lashing that would have brought Il Duce to his knees. So, given that my boy has been fiercely scolded, even right to the very edge of consciousness itself, could you not overlook this one indiscretion and submit your article? It would not be the first time a review was submitted late, and though your fingers would be rapped by our punctilious editor, it would be you who would have the moral victory.

Hopefully,

Oliver Black

From: rafe.wilde@thedawnpost.com
To: oliver.black@thedawnpost.com
Subject: Fuck Off

Are you out of your flipping mind? The answer is no – NO! NO! *NO!* You should be falling on your knees, kissing my feet, and thanking me profusely for not disembowelling that traitorous son of yours. Do you honestly think I'd write anything for that putrescent ball of slime except, maybe, his obituary? No, I don't think so. Christ Almighty, don't you get it? Maybe I should bang your wife sometime, hey Mister Black? Maybe then you'd begin to dimly understand what I'm feeling here.

So, in light of the fact that a) you laid waste my uncle's business and b) your son laid my girlfriend, I think I have every right to declare the deal *off*, don't you?

Rafe

From: oliver.black@thedawnpost.com
To: rafe.wilde@thedawnpost.com
Subject: Let's Not Be Hasty

My Valued Friend and Colleague:

You're upset. I suppose you're bound to be feeling unbalanced (this often happens to men who, like you, are denied sexual release), but I still think you need to consider more fully the facts of the matter. I can understand that you are upset about the whole world seeming to know about your fruitless wooing, your demoralizing celibacy, your supreme sexual defeat; to be ousted from your position of Sex God by a mere boy of nineteen must be the ultimate humiliation. One feels one's advancing age at such times; it is the old man in you, beating his chest in a futile attempt to scare away younger, superior rivals. But time creeps along, does it not, Mr. Wilde, and expecting to be able to compete with a suitor twenty years your junior is like expecting an antiquated biplane to outmanoeuvre an F-16.

Don't blame Selwyn, Mr. Wilde. I claim total and absolute responsibility for the fact that his charms are irresistible to the opposite sex. He is my offspring, bred of my loins, and has obviously inherited the almighty Black magnetism; evolution has been good to us, doling out spectacularly unfair amounts of charisma, appetite, and sexual omnipotence. Selwyn cannot be blamed for the fact that he stands at the apex of evolution; it is my fault entirely. After all, the acorn does not fall far from the tree.

Even though your life must currently seem like a living hell (one does not lose the opportunity to deflower the most desirable virgin in human history every day), still I trust that your honour, your integrity, and your conscience are all still intact. I still believe in you, Mr. Wilde, even if others may not. I believe that you will ultimately do the right thing, the thing that will ensure that you will not receive any more exasperating e-mails from me. I believe that you will finish your review of the Black Chalice debut and submit it for publication immediately.

Sincerely,

Oliver Black

PS: Don't forget to get in touch with the divine Gabriella; it is truly *she* who is the angel, just as her name would suggest.

PPS: Losing Angel is all for the best, anyway. You do see that, don't you?

PPPS: And if you ever so much as imagine the idea of physical intimacy with my wife again, I will cut off your testicles. If I can find them. (Note to self: remember microscope and teeny tiny sewing scissors.)

From: rafe.wilde@thedawnpost.com
To: suzanne@heartmail.com
Subject: Help!

Dear Suzanne:

You've just got to rally around this time – *please*. First of all, my entire epidermis has virtually disappeared after last night's extended session with Helga's Hands on my old rubber sheets. My whole body has been rubbed raw, and I'm all bald and pink and scabby – think of a baby eagle with a hideous skin disease.

Second of all, and even more importantly, I believe I may be in serious danger of Losing It, Suzanne, the "It" in question being my ability to prevent myself from committing some really atrocious and violent act. And the sad thing is that it wouldn't even be a crime of *passion*. It would be a crime of *irritation*.

Oliver Black is trying to drive me insane, I'm convinced of it. First of all he won't stop bringing up (and I use this term in a vomitlike sense) my old piano teacher, the woman who made every Friday evening of my childhood a misery. (Did I ever mention that my parents made me take lessons on *Fridays?* Fridays! The very day when all normal children with normal parents are celebrating the *release* from the week's mental grind, not revelling in its continuation, I had to go to my piano lesson to be tormented by that virago, Ms. Savage, with her flashcards and her metrognome and her other instruments of torture.) He wrongly thinks that I need some sort of teacher to guide me through the stinking cesspool of contemporary music, and even more wrongly thinks that it's Ms. Savage who should be my instructor. Fucking hell! *He just – doesn't – get – it.*

And, in addition to hounding me about that rabid shrew, he's got the nerve to insist that I write a piece about the Black Chalice concert after he attempted to singlehandedly shut down my uncle's café by writing that fetid review of his. The audacity of this guy is unbelievable! He even accused me of having microscopic balls! Oh, please! My balls are small in the same way that a basketball is small! In the same way that *Jupiter* is small! In the same way that Oliver Black's arrogance and stupidity are small! Do you think I should sue the guy for slander? I'm telling you, Suzanne, I'd pull down my pants in any courtroom in the nation just to make Oliver Black look like an idiot.

And besides all this, it's over between Angel and me, and not because of age or religion or another guy. Ha! As if! No, it's over because I decided to let her go, Suzanne. I decided that a young girl of only nineteen (more or less) shouldn't be tied down to her first and (let's face it) best lover. It's actually cruel to condition

her to the ultimate in male perfection before she's had the chance
to experience other guys. She could only be disappointed after
fully experiencing me (which is a feeling I'm sure you know all
too well). If you love her, I thought to myself, set her free. If she
comes back, she's yours. If she doesn't, she's obviously become a
nun. Actually, I'm the one who's bound to be nominated for
sainthood, given this recent act of sheer selfless martyrdom. I
think it would be rather cool to be Saint Rafe, actually. I wonder
how I can find out if the Catholic Church has an opening for a
patron saint of rock musicians and wayward virgins?

And speaking of setting things free – in a fit of rage I tore
open the cage door and threw Petey out the window this morning. God that felt good! Finally, after five years, to be free of the
little bugger – ah, it was beautiful. Flinging Petey out the window
belongs on the list of my top ten greatest moments – I may have
to bump #1 (first date with you) down the list in order to make
room.

Hey, I could really use a little sympathy right now you know.
I'm enraged, I'm in pain, plus I don't have a bed to sleep on
(again) since Helga turned on me in the night like an abusive
lover. Bloody hell. How was I supposed to know I was sleeping
on the enemy? Anyway, I want to come over tonight, Suzanne,
and I want to sleep in your bed curled around you like a vine
around a tree. Curled around your arms, your legs, your chest, my
tendrils feeling their way around you, tasting, probing, exploring.
Gee. Do you think your boyfriend will mind? I hope he doesn't
snore. Is he a heavy sleeper? Can we count on him not to take up
the whole bed? Wait a minute, I think I've got it. *Maybe you
could break up with him before tonight*, hmm? Come on, Suzanne.
I can't believe how slow you are at realizing how right we are
together. Forget Doctor Infundibulum, would you? You don't
want to be with the sort of incredibly uncool guy who sings stuff
like, "You've gotta have heart! Miles and miles and miles of
heart!" in the shower every morning. That's not for you. You
want to be with a guy who knows the way to your heart, and

that's me.

Rafe

PS: It was too good to last, of course. I have no idea how the little bastard did it, but it wasn't ten minutes before I heard a knock at the door, I opened it, and in marched Petey across the apartment and right back into his cage, slamming the door behind him.

From: rafe.wilde@thedawnpost.com
To: angel.day@agape.org
Subject: Giving My Notice

Angel:

You've smashed my heart.

Rafe

The Dream Post Book Review
New Scholarship Shows Best Way
to End Bad Relationships

Harvard, Massachusetts – They say there are no atheists in foxholes; now experts have discovered that there are no atheists in bad relationships either. "Oh, God! Oh God, oh God, oh God! I'll do anything! Just get – me – out – of – here!" is the common cry among those stuck in unsatisfactory love relationships.

But how ought one to ditch an unwanted suitor? This is the topic of a new book directed at a female audience and entitled *The Ocean of Love: Drowning Prevention Theory and Technique* by Harvard professor and relationship scholar Dr. U. Woo.

"It turns out that breaking up *is*, in fact, hard to do," explains Dr. Woo. "Nice young women, trained from the moment of conception to be polite and to avoid hurting anyone's feelings, find breaking up to be specially vexatious. Many of them simply can't do it and instead shrug unwanted suitors off their backs covertly using inferior techniques such as the cold shoulder (including, but not limited to, feigned ignorance of e-mail and voice mail messages and hiding behind the curtains); flaunting another sexual relationship with a man, a football team, a unicorn; gaining 350 pounds; refusing to shave any part of the body except the tonsure; killing; and faking a fatal, nondisfiguring illness. "None of these options is optimal, especially the last, as it only encourages needy men to ask the inevitable question, 'Could I date you posthumously?'"

How then ought one to go about the tricky business of ending a relationship? "Be direct, concise, and use appropri-ate language," advises breakup linguist Professor L. Franca. "A ski instructor should speak of the relationship going downhill, a metalworker should speak of rust and rot, a cat should speak of the relationship going to the dogs, an economist of recession, a biologist of extinction, a trophy maker of atrophy, an alien of qxzzqrx. Also," adds the professor, "don't be too obscure. Lines like 'Our love is nought but gall and wormwood' are likely to be answered with a confused 'What, now? Right here on the desk?'"

"Also, a lady always takes into account that even total jerks have feelings," says Dr. Woo, "so the secret to no one getting hurt is to take all the blame for the end of the relationship yourself. Try saying something like, 'No, no, it's not you. It's me, honestly. I just don't like gross things.'"

Also popular are relationship demolition and annihilation services, in which experts come to your home and terminate the relationship on your behalf. "We do whatever it takes to get rid of unwanted VERMIN (Vapid Engorged Redundant Males In Need),” says demolition expert Abel Squelch, “and because if you’ve got one unwanted man you’ve probably got more, we take extra care to flush out every last one and then, as humanely as possible, find other relationships for them far from civilization, where they won’t spread their diseases.”

From: oliver.black@thedawnpost.com
To: rafe.wilde@thedawnpost.com
Subject: Still in My Black Books

My Dear Rafe:

I felt a moment’s panic this morning when I surveyed the breakfast table and found there were only *two* young men at it stuffing themselves as if for slaughter. Where was my eldest child? Where was Selwyn? He is, after all, still a teenaged male and therefore rarely misses an opportunity to gorge himself as if in training for an especially demanding pie-eating contest. Suddenly alarmed, I imagined that you might actually have done him bodily harm in a fit of vengeful passion. I raced to his bedroom and threw open the door, thinking I would find him gagged and bound to a chair, a note in your handwriting tied to his lifeless body and reading “I, Rafe Wilde, slew Selwyn Black.” But no. May the heavens be praised, my dear boy was *not* bound to a chair. The little silly was bound to his bedposts and his new girlfriend, the stark naked Angel, was doing the sort of things to him that one rarely sees except in the most inventive of pornographic movies. “Help, Dad!” he cried in mock horror. “She’s got no off switch!” I myself fairly swooned in the presence of the disrobed Angel, as even a glimpse of her flesh causes an immediate overdose of Beauty, Liberty, and Truth so severe that one feels one’s eyeballs at risk of exploding; it is as if one has been staring at a ten-thousand-watt bulb at a distance of about four inches, such is the grandeur of your former girlfriend's naked form. This is an experience which you, of course, would know all about. But alas! Forgive me, Dear Rafe, and damn my eyes! You would know absolutely nothing whatsoever about the physical perfection of the divine Angel! Ah, curses! Short of a major global catastrophe, I cannot think of anything more tragic.

My Melancholy Comrade: does *quid pro quo* mean *nothing* to you? Allow me then to remind you once again of your professional obligation and also of our arrangement – an eye for an eye, a review for a review. I must also, once again, urge you *not* to blame the unimpeachable and indefectible Selwyn for *your* botches and blunders. Is it Selwyn's fault that Angel apparently found you about as attractive as a mouldy old pair of socks? Come on, Man – let's be realistic! Selwyn is a rock and roll star, and there is no known creature sexier and more appealing to a woman than this (a fact to which the bizarre phenomenon of the groupie speaks). It is not pulverized shark fin or powdered caribou antler but, rather, music that is the ultimate aphrodisiac. The keyboard, the electric guitar, the drum kit – they ought all to be marketed for what they are: sexual aids. Good God, how many women does the average male rock star sleep with in a lifetime? A number beyond which the average rock star can count, certainly (i.e., more than ten.) So if it was birds you wanted to pull, Mr. Wilde, why didn't you study crotchets and breves, a discipline well-known to lead to intimate experience with crotches and briefs? If it was the female of the species you wanted to impress, why on earth did you become a critic, especially the kind who cannot actually play a note of the music he reviews? A critic who can't tell Shütz from Shinola? A critic who knows that, in order to score, the puck has to go in the net but who, tragically, cannot himself handle a stick? This was astonishingly poor planning on your part, and Selwyn is no more responsible for your non-teleological approach to life than he is for the passage of time! (And, with the passage of time, its cruel decay, and the reduction of brain cells on the order of approximately a million a day, meaning, sadly, that since you are twice my son's age, you possess a brain approximately half the size of his. Again, not his fault.)

Now, Mr. Wilde, evidently you did not receive my latest e-mail, otherwise I've no doubt you would have replied promptly with a good-natured apology and perhaps with an appended copy of the review which you have submitted for publication. In the unlikely event that you *did* receive my e-mail and have unwisely chosen not to respond or to surrender your article, please be advised that you have now officially incurred the wrath of Oliver Black (no small matter, I assure you) and that I shall be taking the matter up with our editor, an honourable man known for his impartiality and, as it happens, for the long and fruitful working relationship he has had with a certain restaurant reviewer. But, no pressure, Dear Rafe. You do what you think is best.

Unwaveringly yours,

Oliver Black

From: oliver.black@thedawnpost.com
To: lucy.black@artnet.org
Subject: Lovebirds

Dearest Lucy:

I just finished composing another e-mail to Mr. Rafe Wilde in hopes that he will see sense and submit his review of our son's performance for publication. Say, did you realize that Angel spent the night in Selwyn's bedroom? I was shocked to find them together this morning, engaged in a sexual act so lewd it quite put me off my breakfast. Good God, I didn't know such a thing was possible! I could do nothing but stare dumbly at them in utter disbelief, like an animal behaviourist stumbling upon deviant behaviour in a mutant species. I do hope that's not how it's supposed to be done. My word, Lucille! How we managed to conceive four children I've no idea.

How do we feel about young ladies, and other females for that matter, spending the night in our sons' rooms? I don't remember laying out a specific policy, but it strikes me as a monstrous idea, at least where Selwyn and Merlin are concerned (no need to worry about Stringbean yet, I think; his spaghettilike physique and unruly mop have so far proven to be entirely resistible to the opposite sex). I think we can expect an irate phone call from Angel's parents, and perhaps a visit from an older, protective brother who will warn Selwyn to keep away from his sister or risk receiving a foot-long, a glass of punch, and a knuckle sandwich. They *have* fully comprehended the implications of the facts of life, have they not? I know I meant to speak with each of them about it many years ago when our now deceased, but then hugely fecund, Siamese cat Poohsee was giving birth to her kittens, but I'm not sure that I actually did it, or specifically delivered the message, "*Don't* be like Poohsee." Did you, perchance? Perhaps a reminder is in order; I just don't want to discover little foundlings dropped off at our back door, one after another, with notes like "Ask Selwyn" attached to them.

Now I know very well that it's an old-codgerish sort of thing to say, but good heavens, Lucille – haven't these young people ever heard of courtship? I realize that the whole concept has been obsolete for decades now, but I would like to campaign for its reinstatement, especially before our little Olivia reaches the time of life at which I will permit her to date (the time of *my* life that is, which will be the day that I can no longer load and fire a shotgun). I ask you, must unsuccessful attempts at reproduction be the ultimate conclusion of every date? Do not such attempts merely create a false sense of intimacy? What's left after the deed is done? And is there not something far more satisfying about a seduction that builds up over a period of months rather than minutes? Truly legendary sexual encounters are like a fruit or a cheese – they must ripen, age. They require the passing of time;

excellence must never be rushed, unless one is, say, a mayfly, and then I agree that it's best to get on with things. Perhaps this haste is only natural for the video generation; they're used to fast-forwarding through the preliminaries in order to get to the climax, and then watching the tidal wave, the explosion, the alien encounter a thousand times, ignorant of the demands of plot and only truly interested in the special effects.

Darling Lucy: How well I remember when you agreed to marry me, and I vowed that I would never make love with you until you were properly my wife! Of course, I couldn't help but notice the look of disappointment on your face, and when you then suggested we elope immediately I was positively enchanted. Nevertheless, we almost made it, did we not? (Though, admittedly, I spent the entire twelve months before our wedding day submerged in an icy bath and frantically occupying myself with impossibly difficult mathematical problems. I became expert at square roots, long division, finding derivatives; that I can now recite pi to five hundred decimal places I owe entirely to our courtship.) If only it hadn't been for that excellent bottle of bubbly, that astonishing halter top (admit it – you made it fall off on purpose, didn't you?), and the air simply disappearing out of the tires of my car in a secluded woodland just three days before the nuptials! (After which we couldn't help ourselves and barely made it out of the back seat in time to actually exchange vows.) It was all so right, so worth the wait that I can't help thinking that these young people are missing out given that they seem to have everything backward. They're practically shedding their clothing piece by piece as they rush out the door toward some stranger and the ultimate intimacy – making conversation being just too much trouble, apparently – and yet they feel mortally embarrassed to find themselves tucking into the toast and jam together the next morning. The thought of masticating together on a first date – how perverse! They treat human sexuality as if it were little more than flashing, than streaking – as if it were little more than a naked sprint through an unfamiliar parking lot, rather than a leisurely and luxurious amble through a much-loved woodland valley.

Don't I just sound like an old married man! So unlike Branksome – from whom, by the way, I received an e-mail and who, having just come from Germany, appears to be having a whirlwind sightseeing tour of Denmark. Branky says that he visited the Tuborg Beer Factory, and then after the copious free drinks, he wove his way to the Danish Resistance Museum, where he crawled around for a couple of hours, wondering why there were two of every exhibit and also what other pastries were involved in the war. Afterward he paid his respects to The Little Mermaid, who was much smaller than he had imagined, and he was disappointed to discover that there is not, in fact, a revolving restaurant in her head. Anyway, he sends you his love, my dearest.

As do I. It is bewildering to me how separate our lives have become, my darling, as if we are now travelling on parallel paths which rarely intersect. You do still love me, I hope. I admit that loving the young, virile, handsome, and dashing me was probably far easier than loving this older and even more overbearing and crotchety version (version 5.6), but I am still the same Oliver you married, more or less, and I am still quite desperately in love with you. Has there ever been such a crush as this, one that has lasted more than twenty-five years and only increased in intensity with each passing day? I think not. It almost makes me believe in the gods, for surely on that fateful day a quarter of a century ago, I was struck by Cupid's arrow, and so has it remained, lodged firmly and forever, in my helpless heart! (Maybe it is this, and not job-related indigestion, that explains the chest pains.)

Love, love, adoration, joy,

Oliver

PS: Dear, dear, I seem to have lost track. Is it *I* who owes *you* a love letter, Darling, or is it *you* who owes *me*?

PPS: The more I consider the matter, the more I think I ought to phone Angel's parents and attempt to explain the situation to them. Ought I to fear for my life, do you suppose? Yes – I think so too. Nevertheless, I promise to call them later this morning, after I've checked our life insurance policy to be absolutely certain that it covers crucifixion, defenestration, asphyxiation, and the like.

From: oliver.black@thedawnpost.com
To: selwyn.black@freenet.org
merlin.black@freenet.org
damien.black@freenet.org
Subject: The Straight Goods

Feast of Margaret Sanger

Dear Sons:

There comes a moment in every father's life when he must finally remove his deerstalker, put down his beer can, turn off the sports channel, spurn his golfing chums, ignore the wax and chamois, and sit his son down on the closest mossy log around the nearest blazing campfire and talk directly, openly, bluntly, and forthrightly about the great mystery of the Stork, and why he occasionally brings his pink and blue bundles from heaven to his great friends, Mr. Bird and Mrs. Bee. Fortunately for us, that sacred moment between father and son that was scheduled to happen at least a decade ago was inexplicably overlooked, thus saving us all from insurmountable embarrassment and irreversible psychological trauma. Hoorah! Thus far you have navigated your way successfully through the uncharted fluids of puberty without The Talk and you are now mature young men (chronologically at least) who are well-acquainted with the rude mechanics of human sexuality either through textual accounts, illustrations, moving pictures, or personal experience. The sheer amount of time and energy you spend slobbering over naughty magazines, gawking with pop eyes and slack jaws, and crooning about nubile females and romantic liaisons, attests to your boundless enthusiasm, and your responses are ripe and well-informed – not surprisingly, a picture of a naked young woman is to you as a red cape is to a bull. But have you ever stopped to consider this, my boys – if, suddenly, the red cape were yanked away, what exactly would you discover behind it? You don't know, do you? I thought not; hence the subject of this e-missive.

I suspect that each of you in turn will find that your eyes begin to glaze over at this point, and that as you read further, the words on the page will slowly disintegrate into an incomprehensible mumbo jumbo. Do not be alarmed, Dear Children! It is not that your eyesight is failing! It is simply the way of Mother Nature. It is in her best interests to keep you shrouded in clouds of ignorance, to make that which is obvious to the old unintelligible to the young, and only after she is done with you and you have unwittingly served her purposes does she blow the clouds of ignorance away, and you realize to your astonishment that, no matter what else may be true, this much is certain – *you've been hoodwinked.*

Isn't that amusing? Even as I write this, I find myself chuckling maniacally just as I do when you parade one of your pouty, pubescent girlfriends about – forgive me for snickering behind my hand and finally bolting from the room in raucous fits of laughter, but every time you introduce me to another of your fertile female friends, it's as though I've just heard the punch line of the funniest joke ever told. How hilarious it is when you boys stick out your chins in defiance and hold your pretty girlfriends around the waist just a little more tightly and ask, "What? What's so funny?" And what's even more amusing is when you actually use sex as a means of rebellion, believing that copulation is a daring, triumphant, defiant act when, in every respect, it is the most deeply conventional behaviour in the entire universe. Nothing could be more normal, more predictable, more profoundly status quo. Sex is, quite possibly, the least rebellious, the least subversive, of all human activities. I'll let you in on a little secret, shall I? Having sex is a tradition in our family. It goes back a *long* way.

Allow me to wipe the tears from my eyes and then I'll explain, briefly, what's so funny, even though I might as well write it in a foreign tongue for all the sense it will make to you. You see, Boys, a photograph of a tantalizing woman is simply advertising, nothing more. But it's not advertising what you *think* it's advertising. *That's* Mother Nature's big joke! Myopic young men such as yourselves imagine that the enticing model with the inviting gaze is posing for *their* benefit, that such an advertisement is about *their* sexual pleasure and the ultimate gratification. Nothing could be further from the truth! Such a picture ought just as well to contain a speech bubble in which our panting, rapacious female is crying "Fresh eggs! Fresh eggs!" Why do you suppose that nubile young females are called chicks? Think, Boys, think! What do chicks become? And what do hens do best, hmm? Exactly. Do you understand what I'm telling you, Boys? Photographs of sexy, naked women and commercials for diapers are virtually interchangeable. Not in their intended effect upon the consumer, of course, but in the sense that they are about *exactly* the same subject. The scantily clad female model doesn't belong draped over the sports car. She belongs draped over the family minivan with the booster seats and the child safety locks. When you say, "Wow, she's sexy," what you're really saying is, "Wow, she's a desirable reproductive candidate." Are you beginning to see what a tremendous kidder Mother Nature is? What an astonishing impractical joker? The sex act itself could not be more different from the ultimate consequence; she has disconnected the one from the other so completely that it is wicked and perverse even to *think* of a child during any attempt actually to *make* one. But behind every alluring female there is always a squalling infant. "Not behind my girlfriend!" you might protest. Ah, my poor boys. Nature bides her time. It may take a few hundred, even a few thousand sexual encounters before the production of an offspring, but Nature doesn't mind – she waits patiently, all the time urging you to go ahead and enjoy yourselves – rest up, she says, because when the babies finally come, *you're going to need it.*

You see, the great irony is that you actually believe that your sexuality has something even remotely to do with you – that love, if you will, is all about *your* emotions and physical desires when, I'm sorry to say, love doesn't give a hoot. "There has never been a love like this!" you think when, from the point of view of Mother Nature herself, there have been countless billions of loves exactly like yours, that is, the kind of love that will eventually result in progeny, the critical event. "Oh, come on, Old Man!" I hear you protest. "There's more to it than that!" No, Boys, there isn't. That's what I'm telling you. From Mother Nature's point of view, reproduction is the whole point. Sex is merely the carrot; it is the hypnotic device swinging like a pendulum in front of you, obscuring all that lies beyond. Lust is a drug, an illusion, and a jolly effective way of occupying you until, someday, you are so addled and habitually improvident that you find yourself wanting a baby, of all things, to "prove your love," after which you will want nothing more than to care for this little miracle, which your wife will wisely insist on dressing in comically idiotic outfits and wrapping in yards of flannel in order to disguise the fact that this little miracle is, essentially, a parasite. And all of this is foreordained! It is part of the great code etched into your very flesh! Let us face the facts: Mother Nature is a programmer, and you are mere threads in the great runtime environment of the universe.

Are you finally beginning to understand that when you're on stage singing about romance, you are, strictly speaking, singing about reproduction? Is it finally clear that as you strut about in front of your adoring fans acting sexy and cool, you are actually singing about the least sexy, most disgusting things possible – i.e., spit-up and poop? Say, here's a thought: Why doesn't Black

Chalice begin composing lyrics that reflect the reality of the situation as outlined above, instead of the standard romantic drivel that has thus far been the cornerstone of the popular song? What about songs with titles such as "Evolution's Got Me in Its Grasp," "Let's Avoid Extinction Together," "I'm Not in Estrus so Just Forget It," "Just an Old-Fashioned Reproduction Song," or the classic "I Love You Because Your Pheromones Are Exactly the Ones That Hook into the Appropriate Cells on My Nasal Receptors." Well, why not, now that you know that romance is not about the individual and his or her inconsequential emotions, but about the species, about the biological imperative to reproduce, about evolution, DNA, genes, heredity. Is this a terribly unromantic observation? Does it belittle your Love to observe that you are predestined to lust, to love, and thence to reproduce, and that Nature knows every trick in the book to get you right where she wants you, that is, in the sack? Not in the least! After all, it couldn't really be any other way, could it? And we still freely choose our partners, in the same way that when we're hungry we choose the restaurant. So Mother Nature gets what she wants and we get what we want. Everybody's happy!

Now, Boys, what you absolutely must not do is attempt to avoid the inevitable and spurn the advances of your nubile beauties or, worse yet, blame them for attempting to trick you into premature fatherhood. They are merely obeying their nature, just as you are obeying yours. Do not abandon real women who offer real relationships in favour of an unnatural celibacy or, worse yet, begin frequenting establishments such as strip clubs, for what could be more tragic than the sight of a group of rowdy males having to pay for the privilege of watching some young woman do to a pole what a dog does to your leg, and having to share this one woman with a bunch of reproductive competitors – and nobody even gets to touch her! These sad specimens are surely life's big losers. Nor must you become jaded and promiscuous like that well known sports hero who once claimed to have slept with over twenty thousand women, since this is exactly like saying, "I have very little grasp of probability and quantity, plus I am the shallowest man who ever lived," all in one go. There is only one noble course open to you, and it is this: with Beauty, Liberty, and Truth as your guides, and without clinging to hollow illusions, you must accept your fate and march steadfastly into the future, all the while preparing yourselves for the inevitable – though by "prepare" I do not mean that you ought to devote yourselves to the reading of books on fatherhood (have you noticed that these are almost exclusively written by comedians? This ought to tell you something), or books on sexual technique like the *Kama Sutra* – especially not the *Kama Sutra!* Unlike every other technical manual ever published, there is no version "for Dummies," and upon actually reading the book, the reason becomes embarrassingly obvious – the *Kama Sutra* is already written for dummies. (Unless you want to woo your beloved with ancient techniques such as "finding the middle finger, hide and seek, and hiding things in several small heaps of wheat and looking for them," I would suggest you avoid it.) And do be careful, Boys! Just because the diaper pail is your ultimate destiny does not mean you ought to needlessly hasten your delivery into its unspeakable depths. Use protection! Follow the precise directions on the package with as much care as you would if you were following the instructions for dismantling a bomb! Use every available backup method! Swaddle yourselves in latex, be awash in foam and jelly!

In short: Don't be like Poohsee.

Well. There it is. The essence of the prescribed father-son chat. I think it went rather well, don't you? You may now return your eyes to the normal from the crossed orientation; place your bodies in the upright position and store any unused information in your overhead racks; fasten your belt buckles; extinguish all erotic materials. And if you've any questions, Boys, absolutely any questions at all, please feel free, at any hour of the day or night, to ask your mother.

Paternally,

Dad

From: rafe.wilde@thedawnpost.com
To: alma.wilde@command.net
Subject: Sluffing Off

Mother:

You'll be happy to know that I've finally figured out what's wrong with my life, even without or, more accurately, *despite* the help of my therapist. Obviously part of what's wrong with my life is that this quack doctor of mine is slowly bleeding me dry; he doesn't even bother to put the leeches on my skin anymore, he just puts them directly on my wallet to save time. I mean, I don't even have a bed to sleep on, for God's sake, and *his* biggest worry is whether or not they'll run out of lemon-soaked napkins and chicken bunwiches on the flight to his resort in Maui. What's wrong with me? What's wrong with me is that I didn't have the foresight to become a therapist myself. Obviously I have all the qualifications, including the capacity to nod off during the most gripping human narratives, and a criminal ability to keep outrageous overbilling from troubling my conscience (if I even have one).

Okay, so that isn't what's wrong with my life. Do you want to know what the real difficulty is? Yes, of course you do; you're my mom, so everything I say and do is totally fascinating to you. Okay, here's what's wrong with my life. It's not *life* at all. That's the big joke. Actually I'm dead, and this is purgatory. Look at the evidence! I had a freak accident with a vibrating bed, and now I look like a creature from a horror film called *The Return of Mr. Scab*. I look disgusting, like my body's covered with fungus – though even another fungus would reject me, and you know you must be looking pretty bad when you can't get a date with your own kind, especially when your own kind is a nonsentient organism. *Nobody* loves me; Angel and I are finished (she was just way too immature), Suzanne's ignoring me (the opposite problem), and I can't get a date, even though I am such a fun-gi, to quote a punch line. It's not only women who aren't paying attention to me, either – even Blankie has been spectacularly uncommunicative lately, and all Petey does is mutter to himself and rock and bang his head against his jingle bell. And, to top it all off, Oliver Black is continuing his onslaught against my mental health. He continues to toy with me, to tease me, to irritate the bejesus out of me; the guy wants a sparring partner, but somehow I just don't feel like exchanging punches with the fiend who wasted Uncle Bill (not yet, but disaster's looming I'm sure), not to mention the guy who fathered Selwyn Black – a back-stabber, a poacher, and a guy who ought to be locked up for, among other crimes, Grand Theft Angel.

Oh all right. I might as well tell you what really happened – I sense the radar you hide in your bun rising slowly upward and the dish turning in my direction. So here's the deal, Mom – Angel smashed your little boy's heart. After all the Shirley Temples, after all the figurines and stuffed animals and lip gloss, after all the revival meetings and gospel concerts – even Disney on Ice, for Christ's sake – after all that she shoots me with emotional mustard gas, rips out my heart with her perfect pink nails, and dumps my corpse in a mass grave for jilted lovers. I would have done anything for that girl, you know. I was even considering joining that nutty fundamentalist church she goes to just to make her happy. I would have tithed for her, spoken in tongues, sung in the spirit, tended the lepers, drunk the grape juice, eaten the wafers, raised the dead, whatever. All I wanted was a little laying on of hands, a little sexual healing to quote Marvin Gaye, but oh no. What was all that crap she told me about saving herself for marriage? Silly me, I thought she meant *her* marriage. Well, I guess I just won't ask Jesus Christ to be my personal saviour after all. I guess I'll just rot in hell. But I'll save a couple of places for Angel and Selwyn – after what they did to me, they're both going to be there.

The thing is, I always thought that if Jesus had a little sister, Angel would be it, you know? Now I feel like the whole innocent virgin thing was just an act, and maybe all that time I was actually dating a whore in a witness protection program. Okay, so maybe she really was an innocent virgin – in the end, though, she was still just a common skank who would drop her drawers for any affected trench-coated freak with fake canines, but who refused to undo even just the top button of her blouse for her boyfriend. And *she* called herself a *Christian*.

Yeah, yeah, I hear you. You're always telling me not to cover up my true emotions with smart-ass remarks and to be genuine, so here's the real deal – I'm really, really upset. I'm hurt, Mom, blown away by Angel's cruelty and Suzanne's savage indifference. It's made me feel – old, you know? *Old.* Okay, I know I'm not really old, certainly not compared to you – what are you now? Sixty? Eighty? Jesus, Mom. I thought I felt bad; you must feel like complete shit all the time. Anyway, I haven't been able to stop cleaning the apartment since this whole thing happened, but to be honest, I'm running out of domestic chores – I mean, you can only defrost a freezer so many times a day.

Anyway, the upshot of all this is: not only have I been skinned, I've also been gutted. About the only thing I feel good about right now is my career, which I was actually pretty worried about for awhile but which I now understand is not going to be a big deal. Who's afraid of modern music? Not Rafe Wilde. Music is music, Mom, and music is my business. Writing about this avant-garde garbage isn't going to be any different than reviewing Alpha Male or Fuzzy Pink Pizza Train or Add Water and Stir or some other really shitty band – I just have to be totally authentic and call it as I see it. Get this: I've already scooped the program for my first concert review! And I've been doing a little research (i.e., using some gargantuan music textbook as a doorstop and pumping barflies for info), so I'm pretty up on this classical music thingy (although I don't want to do *too* much research – I want my approach to be fresh, honest, and unsullied by cultural conditioning). I realize that half the time my informants are just having me on – there's no way that funding for the arts has been cut so drastically that now orchestral musicians are just mannequins, dressed up like formal-wear Barbie and Ken, holding cardboard instruments while a recording plays over the sound system – and that if you really listen carefully you can actually hear the pops on the record. That's pretty obvious bullshit. I mean, they'd use a CD player, not a record. Hey, but did you know that classical pieces are in sections called "movements," and if you clap in between them, you're a bumbling, uncultured, know-nothing jerk? It's like clapping at a funeral, only worse. Seriously. Some guy told me that if you clap between movements, the conductor will hold up a "Throw the Bum Out" sign (I think I've even seen that on TV), at which point you can hear the thugs in the brass section crack their knuckles and start pulling on their chains, and then you just better get the hell out of the hall, unless you want to find yourself looking out from the inside of a tuba. And another thing is that if you hear the Hallelujah chorus, it's like a law or something that you have to stand up (which is why it's so dangerous to listen to those classical stations while you're driving). Probably the seats in those classical music halls have eject buttons for stupid people who don't know what they're supposed to do. Anyway, I expect that John Cage didn't write the Hallelujah Chorus, but if he did, I'll be the first one out of my chair (if only to avoid getting a ticket).

Anyway, I hope you're okay. I'm not, but who cares?

Your son,

Rafe

From: oliver.black@thedawnpost.com
To: branksome.black@rebel.net
Subject: Strike Two

Hello Branksome:

I received your e-mail from Denmark only a day after your letter from Germany arrived by post. It seems to me that sheer speed is the biggest change brought about by all this newfangled technology. When one uses a combination of technologies, old and new, it leads to the impression of time travel; how often you have sent a letter from one hemisphere, but before it can arrive we receive e-mail from the other hemisphere, and when the letter finally arrives, it appears, prima facie, that you have travelled back in time to the original location. Perhaps I ought not to blame technology, of course; perhaps you actually *have* acquired some sort of mysterious ability to travel back and forth in time at will, in which case could you *please* project yourself back about thirty-five thousand years and give those rude, hairy folk some decent crystal and proper linens. The correct place setting makes all the difference to a meal – cupped hands can never compete with crystal goblets, nor fingers with forks, nor incisors with knives, nor tongues with spoons – and there can be no excuse for woolly mammoth juice drooling down one's chin when one has access to Lady Windermere's Fan. Always remember this, Branksome: If the masses refuse to come and drink at the well of Elegance, which itself is fed by the ground waters of Beauty, Liberty, and Truth, then it is our bounden duty to lead them gently to it and, one by one, heave them in.

Of course, you might go after bigger prey and attempt to radically transform the course of world history; although innumerable dreary science fiction stories suggest that tampering with the past can only result in disaster, I find I cannot share this opinion and am compelled to ask the question, "Disaster for whom?" I believe there would be worldwide hoots of joy and enthusiastic clapping of fins, of paws, of flagella, if human beings had never evolved at all or, at least, had evolved into beasts that have an honest regard for Beauty, Liberty, and Truth, as opposed to creatures who glorify mediocrity and outright cruelty, and then have the nerve to call it tradition. *Caveat Humanum*! We are all of us barbarians, Branksome, and I fear that no amount of education concerning the correct way to eat soup or crusty rolls can ever alter that sad fact (although one has to begin *somewhere*). Yes, change the course of history, and I think you'll find that the entire animal kingdom rises up as one and gives you a standing ovation – after which it will tear you limb from limb and eat you, of course, but that is nature's way.

Thank you for responding, no matter how crassly, to my concerns about my relations with my darling Lucille. Honestly, Branksome, do you think I was born yesterday? *Of course* the appalling idea that my only love is having an affair with another man had crossed my mind, you insensitive oaf! I am not so comprehensively naïve as to imagine that a catastrophically awful situation such as this could never arise; she's only human, after all, and therefore subject to the same mad impulses as the rest of us. Nevertheless, though I should one day come home unannounced and stumble across my beloved in our bed in the arms of a rival male, I should sooner believe that I had gone insane and was hallucinating, rather than believe that She Who Means All could ever be unfaithful to He Who Provides All Means. I'm afraid you must guess again, for Lucille and I are as two geese, Branksome, two angel fish, two swift foxes, two rhizocephalans – we are mated for life, and I refuse, on principle, to believe that my trustworthy wife could so cunningly morph into a trystworthy adulteress. Any such vulgar suspicions are an insult to her all-encompassing goodness. Besides which, on a practical level, when on earth would she have the time? Any woman with a demanding career and *four* children who also has time for a passionate love affair either has a doppelganger, absolutely no inner life whatsoever, or an ability to multitask that, if he were telepathic, would be an outrage to her lover. (Imagine: all the while he's thinking, "O Sweet Rapture! Bliss Beyond Compare!" she's thinking, "pigs in blanket w/xtra cheese @ 6 . . ." I believe that this is the whole problem with the recent multitasking craze: one can no longer be confident of having anyone's full attention.)

I admit that the superficial facts can be accounted for by the claim that she's being seduced by the glittering tinsel charms of some fornicating Fabio; nevertheless I steadfastly believe that there is some other excuse for her erratic behaviour, but what that excuse might be I cannot imagine – unless, of course, she suspects *me* of being less than honest with *her*, even unconsciously, and is therefore rightfully recoiling from me in disgust and disappointment. You suggest that I put an end to doubt and break the lock on her studio door, shamelessly invading her sacred space in order to search for the clues to her withdrawal within. No, Branksome, no! How could you even suggest it? Invading my sons' privacy is one thing (one has to break into their bedrooms occasionally, if only to take out the compost), but invading my wife's is quite another, and I will not do it, I tell you, though I be tortured by incomprehension and suspicion for the rest of my days.

Now – I told Lucy that you're on a sightseeing expedition, which is not exactly untrue given that you've undoubtedly seen some extraordinary sights. Still, you won't get sidetracked, will you, Branky? I realize that you proved yourself in the south seas, but I understand that Denmark is a pastoral country populated by shapely, alluring blondes, and that after agriculture and furniture making, pornography is their largest and most successful industry. It would be wrong of you, while there is still so much work to be done, to waste your time lounging on Danish Modern whilst plying some ample-bosomed and double-plaited Danish confection, inevitably named Ingrid, with Aquavit and those irresistible brown-sugar pastries. Happily, you do mention several more victims freed from bondage, and to that I say a hearty bravo, my confrère and confidant. I trust that you are making certain that you have safe houses for all; remember, it is pointless to liberate all of those unfortunate souls if they are only going to be recaptured and incarcerated immediately upon release. Let nothing else but the elimination of unnecessary suffering be your creed, Branksome! Free the slaves! Protect the innocent! *Ignore the women!*

And do remember that I'm still relying on you to provide me with advice concerning the other matter that I spoke of in my previous e-mail. I've not received any further threats lately, but it's only a matter of time before my tormentor makes further demands – demands that are becoming increasingly unreasonable and, indeed, impossible. I implore you to reply posthaste, Brother. Mother Carey's chickens have flown the coop, so to speak, and they are scratching those ominous words of doom (*mene, mene, tekel, upharsin*) on the walls of the eating nook in my kitchen. Here I am speaking metaphorically, of course. In real life, the ability of a flock of chickens to write convincing Hebrew would be severely compromised given that, even as a unit, they're not much more intelligent than a single bowl of porridge (always with raisins, brown sugar, and a hint of cinnamon, Brother). Unlike a bowl of porridge, however, they are each the subject of a life; every chicken is a creature with its own individual history and biography, and is therefore deserving of our deepest respect.

Onward ho, Branky.

Oliver

From: oliver.black@thedawnpost.com
To: rafe.wilde@thedawnpost.com
Subject: Black Bile

My Dear Rafe:

As you well know, there is nothing worse than a reluctant lover, although I must say that a reluctant correspondent isn't much fun either. Sigh. Are we to be forever estranged, Mr. Wilde? Am I to spend the rest of my life chastising and goading you? This suits *me* naturally. Chastising and goading are entertainments I find hugely satisfying, but sadly my considerable talents are generally wasted on my sons. However, Mr. Wilde, as much as I enjoy admonishing and hounding you, I feel it's only reasonable to expect the occasional irate e-mail in return. It's simply a matter of etiquette. If you're having trouble getting started, may I suggest "How dare you . . ." as a useful beginning, as in the following paragraph:

How dare you remind me of the truth, Mr. Black, and so accurately pinpoint my deficiencies of character and temperament. That my uncle's café is a dump of unprecedented and unrivalled proportions is in no way your fault, nor is the fact that my former girlfriend wisely spurned all of my inexpert sexual advances and symbolically castrated me by so easily succumbing to the seductive charms of a much younger and far superior rival. These facts I acknowledge wholeheartedly. In addition, I apologize profusely for not submitting my article and for reneging on my part of the bargain. Not since Benedict Arnold has the world seen such a traitor. Death is too good for me. Only an eternity of perpetual torment is a suitable end for an unworthy, pigheaded Judas such as myself. Et cetera.

Feel free to cut, paste, and post. And for heaven's sake stop pulling on the skirts of blind ignorance for a cuddle, Mr. Wilde! Remove your head from the sand at once! Put up your dukes, as they say, and fight like a man!

Expectantly,

Oliver Black

From: rafe.wilde@thedawnpost.com
To: suzanne@heartmail.com
Subject: Grunt

Suzanne:

Oliver Black is turning me into a homicidal maniac, I'm ooz-ing pus, and you decide that *now's* a good time to totally avoid me? Come on, Suzanne, give a guy a break. You don't answer the phone, you don't respond to my messages, you don't text me, you don't write e-mails, you don't come to the door when I ring the bell for twenty minutes straight and then kick it in only to find you're not even home. Come on, Suzanne. It's impolite women like you who make stalkers out of nice guys like me. Would it kill you to pick up the phone and give me a call?

Hmm. I think I know how to entice you to dial my number. Get this – I'm getting my new mystery bed delivered in a couple of days, and you always did love a good mystery! I don't even know what kind of a bed it is, and I don't really care as long as it's flat, oblong, and completely motionless. Beware of beds like Helga with a Richter scale built right into the headboard. I'm thinking of installing a seismometer in this new bed just to be sure – any hint of vibration and I'm jumping ship. On the other hand, I don't mind those rolling wave type movements that happen when you and I set sail on the Love Boat. Come on, Baby. Why don't you help me take my new bed out on her maiden voyage? Just ignore my bald, patchy crusts. Why don't we break a bottle of champagne over the headboard (I declare this vessel officially open!) and christen her *The Rascally Rafe* or *The Saucy Sue*? And then we could play captain and first mate, or captain and naughty stowaway, or captain and sea wench, or captain and inflatable doll he just happened to stumble across in the tackle box. I don't care, really. Just as long as I get to say, in my most commanding sea captain voice, "Do you read me? *Over*," and you reply,

"*Roger,*" not as a statement but as a command.

Please, Suzanne – indulge me a little for once, would you? Your icy indifference is bringing me down, plus I could use a little relief from the rigours of preparing for my first big nonpopular music review – which I'm doing not only by casually shooting the breeze with the locals in bar bands but also, on the advice of my mother, reading some music history textbook recommended to me by a certified music person at the *university* (just call me Professor Wilde), some hugely famous tome called Grunt or Grope or something. God Almighty, you wouldn't believe this book! First the bloody thing almost bankrupted me, coming in at over *$75 a pound;* second, it has more pages than an Iraqi Arms Report; and, third, it isn't that music history is impossible to understand (well, it is, actually), but the real trouble is that I start reading, and about thirty seconds later I notice that my eyelids are glued shut, and I have to force them open with my thumb and index finger. This works for about another half a minute, at which point I lapse into unconsciousness and wake up several hours later with my forehead plastered against the book and with chapped, flaky eyeballs. Bloody hell! Why is it that I get a better sleep on a textbook than I do on a bed? I suppose that's because it fulfills all my requirements – it's flat, it's oblong, and it doesn't move. Anyway, they should label this thing as what it is – a sedative:

Warning: Common side effects of reading Grouse include drowsiness, headache, confusion, coma, bad hair, bookworms, the inability to find a willing reproductive partner, and terminal nerdiness.

So anyway, when I finally come to, what do I find? I find myself staring at the same page I was staring at when I passed out, a page with a headline like "Exciting Developments in Franco-Flemish Music of 1385." What? Where the hell is Franco-Flem anyway? *"Exciting developments?"* Yeah, right! Like what? Like finally making the first instrument that *doesn't* sound like a kazoo? Like that climactic moment when that famous composer,

Anonymous, finally reached organum? (Whoa! That last word's a real attention grabber, isn't it? I thought it must refer to some hugely sexy/obscene bodily event, but I swear to god *it doesn't*.) Who the hell cares? I don't care what Grump says – I say that nothing interesting happened in music history until the Council of Woodstock, New York, 1969.

So, to sum up my entire life situation at present: "I Can't Get No Satisfaction." No wonder this great hymn to the human condition was once voted the best song ever written in recorded history; truer words have never been spoken.

Have a little pity, Suzanne. Forget about the Petey situation and just call me. *Please.*

I love you.

Rafe

From: oliver.black@thedawnpost.com
To: rafe.wilde@thedawnpost.com
Subject: Disannul

Dear Rafe:

Well, well. It's too late now, isn't it? The time for publication of your article has come and gone. I am well aware that there were mitigating circumstances (the fallen Angel leaps to mind), but these most assuredly do not exonerate you from the crime of being a traitor, a knave, and a scallywag of immense proportions. Ought one's personal life ever to interfere with one's professional obligations? No, indeed not, Sir! What if we all behaved as you have done, Mr. Wilde, and begged off work every time there was a little glitch in our private lives? Civilization would come to a complete halt! Imagine what would happen if every broken love affair and failed sexual advance was the cause of work stoppage;

no one, from the humblest gas station attendant to the Pope himself, would ever get anything done! You have broken our contract, Sir, and in so doing, you have betrayed me and my sons. How I want to complain loudly and vociferously to our editor about your native deficiency of judgement, your dishonourable conduct, and your consummate lack of professionalism! I tell you that my finger is twitching madly on the big red button – the one which leads directly to the detonation of your entire career!

However, although I want desperately to push that button, I have decided, upon deep reflection, that I will not. The issue is a hotbed of intricate ethical dilemmas, complicated by professional loyalty and filial devotion, but in the end it comes down to the mutually exclusive concepts of mercy and justice and the reality that, in this case, there must be a triumph of one over the other. I am chagrined that any moral compromise is necessary. However, it seems that in the case of Black vs. Wilde there is little choice. I have determined, therefore, that the administration of mercy over justice is the superior and most noble course; but understand that I am offering you a pardon, Mr. Wilde, only with the understanding that justice for my sons will not be forever wanting, but merely delayed.

Rejoice, Mr. Wilde, and put away the noose and razor, the sabre and truncheon, the rack and boot. I've no doubt that you are overwhelmed with feelings of gratitude and are anxious to thank Him who has absolved you of your sins; nevertheless, please read on in order that I might fully explain the reason for my decision to allow you, essentially, to continue living.

As you well know, Mr. Wilde, the job of critic cannot be underestimated in either importance or potency. The critic is God Almighty – his subject, Job. The critic holds the destiny of those he critiques in his hands; one negative review is often enough to annihilate the subject and lay waste the lives of those around him. We all know that it's not uncommon for a French chef, for example, whose restaurant has suffered a blow from a critic and thus fallen from grace by two or three points, to do himself in; indeed, one expects any self-respecting French chef to blow his brains out immediately over a mere critical slight. It's a simple fact that bad reviews are the leading cause of death amongst three-star French chefs, and in Paris you read of two or three a month splattering their brains all over their gleaming chrome kitchens. These people are national heroes, martyrs if you will, individuals who have the courage of their convictuals, so to speak, and who would rather die than serve an undercooked carrot. This is how it is done over there, how it must be done, in a country where the entire population takes gustatory pleasure far more seriously than death, which seems to be viewed as a minor inconvenience in *Le Grand Repas de la Vie*.

"I am so sorry, Monsieur et Madame, but our chef has just this moment committed suicide due to a slightly scalded Bearnaise sauce."

"Mon Dieu! Does this mean that our dessert might be delayed?"

"No, never! Only, it might be slightly lukewarm."

"Aargh! Non!" (Exit stage left – a gunshot is heard in the distance.) The message is by all means, hang yourself over a defective sauce – but, by God, don't let it interfere with my crème brûlée.

Yes, Mr. Wilde, heads roll in the wake of a bad review; in this sense it is very like a public execution. Coleridge neatly summed it up in two words: "Critics – murderers!" It is for this very reason that I have always gone out of my way in my reviews to find the Beautiful and the True and comment upon *that*, often while offering a few friendly words of advice in private about how things might be improved. My reviews are always honest and I never mislead, but short of putting rat poison in the soup, I see no reason to categorically condemn. (Remember the old adage – what doesn't kill me makes me stronger – a good rule of thumb for the adventurous diner.) Just imagine the Vietnamese family – grandparents, parents, endless children, all with heads bowed, shuffling, dejected, their one rickshaw loaded with their meagre worldly possessions, returning defeated to the homeland, their sad little Noodle House boarded up behind them – and all because *I* found the spring rolls a little on the salty side! How could I live with myself if I should carelessly cause such human misery?

How ludicrously easy it is to obliterate another by outright ambush or by more subversive means – say, by damning with faint praise. Of course, *no review at all* also makes a profound statement: one is clearly saying that the subject is of no consequence, going absolutely nowhere professionally, and a waste of the reviewer's precious time. Often those under critical scrutiny enjoy throwing brickbats at the critics themselves (Christopher Hampton's famous insight, "Asking a working writer what he thinks about critics is like asking a lamppost what it thinks about dogs," leaps to mind), but ask if the individual under scrutiny would rather have *no review at all* and the truth will quickly out. Creative artists (fine and culinary) *need* critics in a way that a lamppost does not, in fact, need a dog. Attention from an established critic is especially important for a fledgling artist, but it's only the most preternaturally perceptive critic who is able to pick out those individuals who will be of lasting consequence. Would Chopin be a household name if not for Schumann's insightful and authoritative review and his definitive remark, "Hats off, gentlemen, a genius?" Maybe, maybe not. I have no doubt that Chef Octavio praises the heavens daily for Acumenical Me, as do many other chefs to whom I have given (and who have deserved) the Black stamp of approval. I ask you this, Mr. Wilde: How many artists owe their success to the critics? Here is my answer, as controversial as it may be: They *all* do.

Now, pretending to ignore the hometown debut of Black Chalice was an alarming professional mistake, but by some miracle even more impressive than the parting of the Red Sea (which itself is not as great a miracle as the parting of Merlin's hair), it seems not to have harmed either you, or Black Chalice, unduly. This was merely my boys' virgin appearance (at least, they were all virgins *before* the concert), and although it was a first, it will by no means be the only time they play live to the home crowd. I note also that there are other music critics besides you working in this city, and that there were write-ups by a lesser critic in our rival paper, as well as by several amateur critics in the blogosphere. Nevertheless, no matter what I may think of you on a personal level, *I fully acknowledge that there is not a critic of the popular music scene who is as fine or as influential as you yourself, Mr. Wilde.* And the truth of the matter is that, to ensure their success, my boys need you on their side. You are indeed the prince of the pop music scene, ruling over a mighty empire that stretches far beyond political borders and geographical boundaries. The masses bow to your judgment, and I too must humble myself and submit to your sagacity in all things pop musical.

Therefore, Good Sir, I suggest we bury the hatchet, not in each other's skulls, but in some mutually agreeable third location. Do you agree? I shall take the flickering of your eyes across this page as a *yes.* Thus we begin again.

It is in this renewed spirit of friendship and professional symbiosis, then, that I wish you luck with your first venture outside of the world of rock and roll. I understand that you will be covering the John Cage concert this evening and that all of your readers can look forward to an intelligent summation and consideration in tomorrow morning's *Dawn Post.* If I was a religious man, you would most assuredly be in my prayers. As it is, I shall keep your name highlighted in bold within my impeccably ordered thoughts, somewhere between rabid and rake, between Wilberforce and Wiltshire.

Godspeed, Rafe Wilde.

Yours sincerely,

Oliver Black, Esq.

Rattling My Cage
By Rafe Wilde

WARNING: Tonight's review will be radically unlike what Rafe Wilde's faithful devotees have come to expect from the High Priest of the Pop Music scene. Even those fortunate enough to be allowed within the Inner Sanctum have been unaware that, for many years now, the Great Rafe has been struggling to get a panoramic view of the music scene in this city, and now, happily, that very opportunity has come knocking at his door. Not only will Rafe Wilde be writing about rock music (which will always be his greatest passion – sorry, girls), but finally he'll be able to include the other little, less significant concerts that happen all around this great city. Popular music fans have come to trust Rafe Wilde implicitly to be the final word on popular music, and they can continue to trust him as he informs his public about the contemporary music scene in its entirety.

Hey there, fans of serious new music (and I do mean all ten of you)! For months now we've been anticipating the latest concert of this absolutely terrific music, and finally the New Music Ensemble staged a concert of works by one of the most serious new musicians of them all – the composer John Cage. Sadly, there was no mosh pit (just kidding!), but even worse, the euphemistically named New Music Ensemble (new? *music?*) was not up to the task of providing solid performances of the master's great works. It was a shame that Mr. Cage was not in attendance, as I think he might have had something to say about the nutty performances given by this under-rehearsed, overambitious bunch. We all know that Mr. Cage is a top-notch composer, but carelessness and even willful destruction of musical intent by the performers (I can't even really call them musicians) butchered a program that might otherwise have been slightly less boring.

I entered the seventy-five-seat Enid Kowalski Concert Hall (whoa – who knew they made 'em that small?) and had no trouble finding a front-row seat in between a middle-aged librarian with a severe head cold and an embalmed professor of musicology. The audience was totally hyped before the concert, in the same way that adult students are hyped on the first night of a continuing-education course on will preparation, or a congregation is hyped before church, or corpses are hyped in a mass grave. Their zombielike eyes were riveted to their programs, and only two or three audience members conversed in reverential, hushed tones. I suppose you could say it was a party atmosphere, as long as the party you had in mind was a wake. I slipped my Frisbee into my bag, deflated my giant beach ball, and proceeded to wait.

At exactly 8:00 PM the concert began, accompanied by the librarian's first major phlegm-clearing event of the evening. Onto the stage tottered a sort of ancient church lady with a blue rinse, and without even so much as a boo to the audience (hello, Miles Davis), she went directly to the piano in order to play the first piece, which my program informed me was called *The Wonderful Widow of Eighteen Springs* (boing, boing, boing – ha, kidding again!) and was written by Mr. Cage in 1942 (so not exactly *brand-new*). Now, I assume that all of my readers know what a piano looks like and remember roughly how it's supposed to be played – that is, by pushing down the little black and white keys with your fingers (unless you're a rock musician, in which case fists, heads, piano stools, or even fifty-pound sledgehammers are all totally kosher). I think we can all agree that every pianist, no matter how incompetent, should know at least this much. However, at the beginning of *The Wonderful Widow*, Grandma actually *forgot* to raise the lid thingy that covers the keys, and *she didn't even notice that she was playing on solid wood* and not on the actual keyboard. Was this grotesque pantomime of piano playing intentional? Was it supposed to be funny? If so, it failed catastrophically. Absolutely no one was laughing – our mummified musicologist didn't even applaud the performance, only twitched, grim-faced –

who knows what our librarian felt as she appeared to be having some sort of mucus malfunction – but all *I* felt was embarrassment. I believe there are three possible explanations for this bizarre oversight: our superannuated pianist was senile, or deaf as a post, or maybe there are even more drugs floating around at classical music concerts than is commonly reported. Take your pick.

After the applause, an eerie silence descended upon the concert hall, which was interrupted only by the sound of our librarian noisily snorting a line of medicated nasal mist. I noted that the next bit of new music was a piece hot off the press (in 1945) called *Three Dances*, and it was written for not just one, but *two* pianos, by the absent Mr. Cage. Thankfully two different pianists (clean-shaven men in tuxedos, always a good sign at this sort of event) arrived on stage, and even better, they remembered to lift the lids covering their respective keyboards. We would not suffer that sort of torment again; however, as it turned out, these two fellows had a different sort

of punishment in mind, and after experiencing about fifteen seconds of this alleged music, I realized it would have been far better if they'd left the lids closed. Now, I assume that all of you know not only what a piano looks like and how it ought to be played, but even more important, how it ought to sound. At first I thought I wasn't hearing properly over the cacophony of cough drops being twisted out of their cellophane wrappers – but, no. These pianos were not only out of tune, but it actually sounded like there was a bunch of stuff sitting on the strings (I swear to God I saw a ping-pong ball bouncing around in there), and again, nobody seemed to notice. And, once again, our musicologist didn't even applaud, just dropped his head to his chest where it wagged back and forth in disapproval. And no wonder! I mean, bloody hell! Haven't they heard of piano technicians around here?

Silence, like a thick black cloak of doom, once again enveloped the concert hall as our librarian (who, I should have mentioned, resembles most a tonsured monk – I'm thinking Brother Cadfael here) frantically sucked away at her inhaler, wheezing like the victim of a splintered chicken bone up the windpipe. I was starting to get a bit worried actually – I mean, what exactly did this woman have anyway? How contagious was she? Had our inert musicologist, God rest his soul, already succumbed to the plague she was carrying? Plus the stench was starting to get to me – from one side a heady mix of menthol, eucalyptus, and ginkgo biloba; from the other the unmistakable odour of formaldehyde. I thought of moving to another seat, preferably the one behind the steering wheel of my car, but the next piece on the program was about to begin, and suddenly I was riveted to the spot.

For out onto the stage walked two of the hottest babes I had seen in hours, both blonde, with faces as sweet as sugar and figures as curvaceous as sine waves. Hello – what's this then? Suddenly I saw the rest of the evening laid out before me – or, rather, I saw the two of them laid out before me

for the rest of the evening – until it dawned on me that they were dressed as sexily as nuns at a virginity rally. Starched white blouses and opaque black skirts hung like pleated curtains and concealed every interesting bit of flesh from ankle to wrist to chin. What century were these girls from anyway? Were they time travellers from a super-repressed Victorian English village? Employees at Ye Olde Funeral Parlour? Was their dress maker the Queen Mum? The whole thing was a mystery to me. Anyway, I glanced at the program (Oh god! Their names are Tiffany and Candy! Don't give up yet, Rafe!) and noted that the next piece was called *Litany for the Whale* and was, thankfully, devoid of pianos entirely. As our librarian with the bowl cut horked into a tissue, our two fashion-impaired sweethearts positioned themselves at opposite ends of the stage, and another punishing silence of about a minute blanketed the concert hall like a layer of thick black snow. Finally, Tiffany sang a pretty little five-note tune in a high-pitched, clear, vibratoless voice. Very nice. Then Candy imitated exactly the tune that Tiffany had just sung. Again, very nice. No harmony, no rhythm, no change of pitch or dynamics, but at this point I took what I could get, and at least it sounded dimly like actual music. Then Tiffany sang exactly the same melody in exactly the same way, and, after that, Candy sang exactly the same melody in exactly the same way *again*. Okay, I thought to myself, I get the idea. But I had no idea at all, not really, because twenty frigging minutes later they were still at it, still singing *exactly* the same tune in *exactly* the same way! I couldn't believe it! Was this another of the New Music Ensemble's little jokes, like the crap-stuffed piano and the lid-banging old bat? I began to hate Tiffany and Candy – the only way I could get through the ordeal was to imagine an elaborate sexual fantasy, but after half an hour had passed, forty-five minutes, fifty, fifty-five minutes, I just couldn't take it anymore – I walked out of my own sexual fantasy and left Tiffany and Candy to finish it off themselves. Tiffany and Candy *forced me out of my own sexual fantasy*! How sick is that? And, unbelievably, it was almost *one entire hour later* when they finally, *finally* stopped singing. Oh, God! I could have gone out to La Jonquille and had a five-course meal in the amount of time it took them to get that trite little five-note melody out of their system! I could've read a novel, *written* a novel, impregnated some women, gotten pissed *and* sobered up, done time, *done almost anything*, in the time it took Tiffany and Candy to perfect their torture routine. In a different time, in a different place, those two little sadists would definitely have been awarded Inquisition Employees of the Month.

More insanity followed, including the ugliest piece I have ever heard for, get this, twelve *radios,* and as I sat wedged between our phlegmatic musicologist and our phlegm-matic librarian, the thought struck me: so this is hell. And it's worse than I thought. Jesus. Isn't there some kind of armistice I can sign? But the torture wasn't to last forever – finally, we arrived at the last piece on the program, called 4'33", which my program notes informed me was Mr. Cage's most important work, the piece which summed up his entire philosophy of music. Great, I'm thinking, this at least will be good. And it got off to a fine start with the whole New Music Ensemble assembling on the stage with their violins and flutes, their cellos and bassoons, and with an actual conductor on the podium ready to direct this bunch of lunatics. I waited for the piece to start and figured it was like the silence before the *Litany for the Whale* – unpleasant, but now to be expected. After about half a minute, I noticed the conductor turn one of the pages of the music on the stand and, being off to the left a bit and in the front row, I could see what was on the page of music he had just turned. And do you want to know what I saw on that music? *Nothing! Nothing at all!* No musical staff, no treble or bass clef, no notes whatsoever! And do you want to know what I heard? *Nothing!* Nothing at all for four minutes and thirty-

three seconds. It was four minutes and thirty-three seconds of total *silence*. Christ almighty! It was like being in a sensory deprivation tank during a silent movie being shown in a vacuum in deep space. I kept imagining that I'd gone deaf (too bad it hadn't happened an hour sooner), or that invisible aliens had lobotomized my temporal lobes, or maybe that I really *had* joined the choir invisible and shot straight to hell (though the absence of accordions and bagpipes suggested otherwise).

Call me crazy, but I think of music as something played by instruments that has some sort of melody and/or harmony and/or rhythm, and in this I think any decent dictionary will back me up. I suppose there was a grim irony in ending a concert of nonmusic with no music whatsoever. But tell me this: why did the audience give the New Music Ensemble a standing ovation? There is only one possible explanation – they were overjoyed that the whole thing was finally over.

Noting that the program exhorted the audience to "perform 4'33" No. 2 at their leisure, a piece which is a solo to be performed anywhere by anyone," I turned to our professor of musicology for an impromptu interview. The man had barely moved for two hours, and I was beginning to imagine that maybe he was just a prop. Noting that rigor mortis hadn't quite set in yet, I gave him a little poke with my elbow but got no response except that his head lolled a bit to one side. I gave him another elbow jab, and this time he slowly keeled over sideways, his head coming to rest with a hollow *thunk* in the empty seat beside him – and I suddenly realized – he was *actually dead!* For real! So help me God, *I'd been sitting beside a corpse the entire evening!* Jesus! How many other people had this new music taken out? I suddenly felt like a clay pigeon in a shooting gallery. Calling not for a doctor (obviously too late) but for a mortician, I found myself sprinting over our librarian (now with a tissue dangling out of each nostril)

and over the seats of the concert hall, like an Olympic hurdler with a firecracker in his underpants. I got the hell out of Enid Kowalski and back to the womblike safety of my 1974 red Ford Torino in which, while driving like a bat out of hell, I blasted the Stones so loud it could have caused a major rock slide. It was the first real music I had heard all evening.

This is the first concert I've ever been to where I didn't need earplugs, but I sure as hell wanted them, and I lost count of the number of times I feigned the chewing off of one of my own limbs as if stuck in a leg-hold trap. How can a critic sum up such a concert? I suppose to say this: Thousands of dollars worth of instruments on the stage, and not a note of music out of any of them.

Next time I'm bringing my iPod and headphones.

I give this concert some astronomically high negative number out of 7.

Chapter Five

From: oliver.black@thedawnpost.com
To: merlin.black@freenet.org
Subject: Give a Little Whistle

Feast of Timothy Leary

Hello, Merlin:

It's a fact that all boys, upon reaching that embarrassing age known as puberty (and you know it well – the exploding fluids, the chicklike downy facial hair, the demoralizing and uncontrollable yodelling), believe that their parents are ignorant nincompoops and as competent as newborn lambkins at detecting deception. Some boys are right, of course; my own parents, for example, had no idea that I was selling boxes of grapefruit on the side in order to raise money for the blind. In your case, however, you have underestimated my powers of detection considerably. Your sins have found you out, my boy, and so has Oliver Black.

Did you think I would be oblivious to the illegal odours wafting out of your bedroom window after every decent human being has been tucked up for the night? Did you really believe that I wouldn't notice the exotic plants in your south-facing window, and that I wouldn't recognize the characteristic look of the hemp plant, the peyote cactus, the magic mushroom? I notice that you have labelled them all incorrectly with ridiculous names such as False Aralia in order to throw your mother and me off the scent. This was particularly naughty of you, though it was nothing less than diabolical when bits of these same plants mysteriously ended up in the spinach-stuffed mushrooms yesterday evening. Let us be clear on this point: that although I desire to bond with my children, I do not care to do it over psychedelics and hallucinogens.

I do hope that you are not officially rebelling against authority, another one of those culturally constructed practices that I find particularly tiresome. It's a simple truth that most revolting young people (and I don't insist upon the double entendre, but there it is) express their independence of mind and body by following precisely, to the letter, what popular advertisements tell them to do. They do not pause to wonder, "Which gigantic multinational corporation's pockets am I lining with this particular rebellion?" They drink, they smoke, they drive gas-guzzling vehicles, and they engage in various behaviours that couldn't make corporate America any happier ("corporate America" consisting largely of men wearing suits, the very people against which the young are rebelling). Rushing headlong into the adult vices is only good for the corporations who want to use you, Merlin, and use you they do. You may care deeply for, say, Jack Daniels, but what does it care about you? A human being is only a bottle of Jack Daniels' way of producing another bottle of Jack Daniels. Oh, lift the veil, Merlin! Lift it before it's too late and tell me this: what do you see behind what is, literally, a smokescreen? You're a bright chap; I shall therefore leave you to figure out the answer for yourself. Meanwhile, if you must rebel, could you please find ways of doing it that set you in ever sharper relief against your peers, rather than ways that make you appear ever more like a lowing ungulate in a herd of millions.

But perhaps you're not rebelling at all, and given that you are a son of Oliver Black, bone of my bone, flesh of my flesh, you ought to be given the benefit of the doubt. Let's assume that your motives for these misguided experiments with illegal substances spring from an essentially chaste heart. Perhaps you have some innocent dream of shamanistic revelation or of flying like the legendary birdmen of Peru. Nevertheless, the jig's up, my boy. You have twelve hours to eradicate all traces of these injurious plants from your bedroom, to issue a formal apology to both your mother and me, and to reform your entire personality so thoroughly that we can expect news of your canonization by sometime early next week. "Wherefore lay apart all filthiness and superfluity of naughtiness," proposes the epistle of James, and I hereby second the motion.

Sharply,

Dad

From: rafe.wilde@thedawnpost.com
To: suzanne@heartmail.com
Subject: Still Can't Get None of It

Dear Suzanne:

Oh, come on. When you finally decided to end your chastening silence and write me an e-mail, I expected more than one short paragraph, and I expected it to be on a topic other than the elementary rules of logic and the English language. You want to quibble about grammar? Fine. I suppose that "I can't get no satisfaction" uses a double negative and therefore means "I *can* get some satisfaction," but what kind of a song would that have been? "I can get some . . . satisfaction . . . I can get some! I can get some! I can get some! Some some some!" It would've been an asinine song, that's what. Besides, a guy who's getting some satisfaction isn't going to write a song about it – he's too busy doing it. And a man who can't get no satisfaction isn't remotely concerned about grammar or coherence. "I can't get no satisfaction" is the inner cry of a tortured soul, Suzanne, not the title of an essay for a high school English teacher. It's not a request for grammatical assistance or a plea for reparation or compensation for wrongs received. It's not a song about the performance of a penance by a repentant sinner, or a revelation about the IQ of the singer. I admit that the song was written by a man who gets very little else *other* than satisfaction – as much as he wants, with anyone he wants, anytime he wants – a man for whom there are no limits to satisfaction – no restrictions, no restraints, no conditions – a man whose supply of satisfaction is immeasurable, inexhaustible, and unbounded. Which is a bit of a piss off, isn't it, and I don't feel like writing about this anymore.

So – I'm going to ignore the fact that I can't get no satisfaction out of your e-mail, because I absolutely have to tell you about the insane concert thingy I had to review last night. It was my first contemporary art music concert, and I've got to tell you – if all new music concerts are like that one, I think I just might be able to get out of my contract after all, given that, at these new music events, *there isn't actually any music*. Oh, there are *sounds* all right, but it's like these people asked themselves, "Is it ugly? Is it boring? Unmemorable? Undanceable? Unsingable? Does it serve no human purpose whatsoever? Great! Let's play it!" Honestly, Suzanne, I felt like my ears had been raped. There ought to be a law, but apparently these concerts are totally legal. I think I *would* be justified in demanding my money back, though, especially given that there were only a handful of pieces on the program (what kind of rip-off is that?), and one of them was – get this – four minutes and thirty-three seconds of *total silence!* I paid to sit *in silence,* for God's sake! Can you believe it? I wonder why they stopped at aural deprivation – I mean, why didn't they turn out the lights too so that I could pay to experience the art of darkness? Why didn't they sand off my taste buds? Hack off my nose? Unplug my nervous system? And then call it high art and charge me twenty bucks for the privilege! These new music people are a weird bunch, all right – but you already know that, since you must have read my very first *un*popular music review. (You *do* still read my reviews, I hope.) Can you believe I was sitting next to a *dead* guy the entire time? I was freaked out at first, but then I realized – what a perfect metaphor for the whole concert! A dead musicologist listening to absolute silence. It's like poetry, isn't it? Anyway, Suzanne, the Emperor of the Avant-Garde was buck naked, and I thoroughly enjoyed being the one to give him a good kick up his royal backside. Not that it was the composer's fault – the problem was those incompetent nincompoop nonmusicians and their idiotic interpretations. Hey, I wonder how I can get John Cage's e-mail address and tell him the good news, that the

Great Rafe is standing up for the little guy?

So, I'm feeling a bajillion times better now that I've got that Cage article out of the way and proved my competence as a contemporary "music" (ha!) reviewer. Even the fact that I loathe Oliver Black even more than I loathe contemporary art music is not enough to wreck my good mood. Obviously my feelings have gone way beyond irritation, but who wouldn't feel justified murdering in cold blood the sort of fathead who ends his e-mails with a word like "Godspeed?" *Godspeed!* What kind of lunatic uses a word like Godspeed? The kind who deserves to be locked up in a home for the criminally pretentious. And he actually wants to re-establish contact, but only because he wants me to write a good review for his boys in future. He says he's forgiven me. *He's* forgiven *me!* That's rich! I'm telling you, Suzanne, never have I wanted revenge as badly as I want it now. I want to see Mr. Black turn white with horror as I dangle him helplessly over the bottomless precipice, the crocodile's yawning jaws, the contemporary music collection at the university. I want to impale him on the sword of vengeance, to make him feel just a tiny fraction of what I've felt over these last few weeks. Do you think I should seduce his wife? I could, you know (and I'd do it before we got back together again, honest). Maybe that and something else. What I want to do is expose him, to get a hold of his deep, dark secret and reveal it to the world. And what deep, dark secret would that be, you ask? Damned if I know, but there's got to be something. Everybody has a skeleton in the closet, something ugly and embarrassing that they want to keep hidden at all costs. Even me (though I'd rather not discuss my little fabric-softener habit here, thanks very much, besides which I *am* down to one bottle a week).

The trouble is, though, that unless I hire a private detective (and Sherlock's first job will be to detect any funds at all in my bank account, what with all these beds I've been buying), it's going to be almost impossible for me to nail that scum from a distance. So, as much as it torments me even to imagine it, I think

I'm going to have to re-establish contact and cozy on up to him, so that I can eventually get him on the rack, slip on the thumbscrews, shove the bamboo under his fingernails, and whip him into the old iron maiden. (Wait a second – you have an iron maiden, don't you? Oh, no – that's the name of the company that makes your bras. Ha!) I've just got to take some sort of positive action, Suzanne, like maybe writing him a treacly epistle of repentance (all fake, of course) and then inviting him out for dinner or something – though the thought of dining with Oliver Black is enough to put anyone off his feed. Still, I've got to do it. My therapist says I'm always just *reacting* to other people (I reacted by agreeing completely), and this leaves me feeling helpless (he said, handing me a bill so large I can only dream of paying it). He says I need to be more proactive, to take charge of my life and make things happen (at which point I ripped up the bill) and to start taking full responsibility for my own destiny (he said, handing me the card of the collection agency that will be handling my account). And that's exactly what I'm going to do. I'm going to send Oliver Black an e-mail in which *I* will *apologize* to *him* (grrrr) for overreacting to his review of my Uncle Bill's café, and for the thing his son did to me (don't ask) that only adds fuel to the fires glowing deep within the engine of revenge. (Spite is so poetic, isn't it?) And then I'll invite him out for dinner, even though I'd rather have dinner with that colossal bore Madonna (not the rock star – I mean Jesus's mom, a Jewish mother whose son really *is* God's gift – and you just know how *that* conversation's going to go), and then I'll cleverly trick him into revealing the information that's going to give me the leverage to catapult Mr. Black into a place even more foul than the avant-garde orchestra pits of hell. I want my pound of flesh, Suzanne. Preferably packaged in plastic and presented on a Styrofoam tray, but I'll take it any way I can get it.

So then, that's settled. You know, the Hatfields and McCoys knew a thing or two – I never realized that a simple vendetta could give life so much positive direction. I feel fantastic! Even the fact that I'm still waiting for a response to the question of why you don't want to go out with the Famous Music Critic, and prefer instead to waste your time with Marcus Welby, MD isn't enough to wreck my positive groove. Even the fact that my skin is falling off in great scabby chunks and I'm doing this elaborate comb-over thing to cover up my bald spot can't wreck this good vibration. You'll come back to me, I know you will. After all, you loved me once, and I'm still the same guy I always was, except that now I'm oozing pus, but I mean besides that. It's only a matter of time before you come around, before you get tired of playing *General Hospital* with Chad Everett and want nothing more than to play *Thrill of a Lifetime* with Rafe Wilde. Come on, Suzanne. I'm wearing my heart on my sleeve. Let's just hope your boyfriend doesn't have a heart on *his* sleeve. (Yuk.)

Lustfully yours,

Rafe

PS: I see that an e-mail just arrived from Oliver Black. What perfect timing! This is my chance to feign contrition (and God knows I'm an expert at that, having had regular practice for six interminable years at my weekly piano lesson) and to begin re-building bridges in the hopes of luring Oliver Black onto one of them and then tossing him over the side.

From: oliver.black@thedawnpost.com
To: rafe.wilde@thedawnpost.com
Subject: Galimatias, Noun.

My Dear Rafe:

I praise the heavens daily for the fact that we are friends yet again! (At least, I assume that we are friends, given that I have heard nothing to the contrary.) And are we, or are we not, the sort of friends who feel the maladaptive imperative to tiptoe gingerly around each other's feelings for fear of giving offense? Would you fain point out a blinking oil light, a leaking hull, a dangling jet engine? Indeed, Sir, I hope you would. A true friend is one who will not pussyfoot around when the bridge is out up ahead, but who will tell his comrade clearly and decisively without undue regard for superfluous emotion. It is in this renewed spirit of confidence and trust, then, tempered with the spirit of complete incredulity, that I offer an analysis of your fantastic (I use this word in five of its nine senses) and excessively entertaining article on the recent concert staged by the New Works Ensemble.

I confess that I read yesterday's review of the John Cage concert with a sort of bemused horror, the kind of emotion that one might experience, for example, when watching a falling anvil pulverize an unfortunate cartoon character; it's so awful and yet so amusing at the same time. Can this be real? one asks oneself. Is Rafe Wilde playing an amusing little joke on his unsuspecting readers? Is he having us on? Or can it be, perhaps, that Mr. Wilde has unwittingly exposed himself as a simpleton of colossal proportions, displaying an ignorance so vast that to house it in a single entity is a feat of metaphysical engineering not unlike stuffing the entire contents of heaven and hell into an object the size of a melon?

Was it your intention to sabotage your career in a burst of stupidity so spectacular that one feels as if one is looking at an especially dazzling display of fireworks? If so, you succeeded and ought to be commended for your thoroughness. It is rare that one has the opportunity to witness tsunamis, planet-threatening meteorites, earthquakes that shake entire hemispheres; but I feel now, after reading your review of the John Cage concert, that I have witnessed a disaster of comparable magnitude, and from the comfort of my own armchair no less.

Good God, Man, what on earth were you thinking? It's clearly evident that, beyond a cursory glance at the program notes, you did no research whatsoever – not even enough to know that Mr. Cage is, I'm sorry to report, *dead!* I most assuredly do not pretend to be any sort of expert on John Cage myself, but at least I know this much. I also know that you missed the point so completely that you and it (the point, that is) are as two north poles, oil and water, Diana and Camilla, matter and antimatter. You have not even the slightest intellectual grasp of the nature of experimental music, nor do you understand that every aspect of the performance was intentional, that the music was performed in exactly the way Mr. Cage himself intended it to be performed. The keyboard was supposed to be covered. The ping-pong ball was supposed to be on the strings. The silence was supposed to be lengthy. *The music critic was supposed to understand this.* That you did not is a testament to your carelessness, your smugness, your consummate unworthiness.

How on earth did such an atrocious pile of poop manage to get published? There can be only one explanation – Mr. Midge. While our illustrious editor is sick or vacationing, Mr. Midge is inevitably in charge, a desperate state of affairs given that he is a pedant of pyrotechnical proportions – true, the pages under his pen end up covered in a veritable fireworks of ink, but none of his splatters and splotches relate in any way to the actual content, which Midge ignores as so much background noise. To Midge, ideas are like fruit flies (dare I say like midges?): their only purpose is to annoy. Midge is a margin maniac, a spelling zealot, an i-dotting, t-crossing menace. While our own primitive ancestors were emerging from the primordial broth, Midge's were arising directly from the alphabet soup, and it wasn't long before there was a scourge of Midges punctuating the landscape. Nathaniel Midge is a direct descendant of Homo Correctus – how else to explain why he speaks with filial tenderness not only of grammar, but of his great grammar? Honestly, I have no idea why he hasn't been fired, or even set on fire by now, especially given that the last time this happened, he let an article get past him on the subject of an air show featuring the Harrier Pigeon, "a British multipurpose pigeon capable of vertical takeoff and landing by means of vectoring its engine thrust." Extremely silly stuff, and Midge had his knuckles rapped, I can tell you.

Nothing could be more pointless than offering up advice in order that you might avoid the same mistakes in future, given that it is wildly improbable that you have a future. Nevertheless, I am compelled to ask at least this: Have you any feeling at all for the unwritten – but I should have thought dazzlingly obvious rules – that govern the coverage of the local scene? Rules such as: you must never insult a defenceless antiquarian. Say what you like about popular musicians working the international scene, but under no circumstances insult your grandmother (who has certainly popped off by now after the shock of being shred to bits by your sardonic critic fangs). Rules such as: you must never make comments of a deeply personal nature. (Poor Candy and Tiffany, your new music trollops, will never be able to show their faces on stage again, unless it's a stage with a pole and a python.) Rules such as (and this above all): you must never, under any circumstances whatsoever, speak ill of the Queen Mother! Dear God, Rafe! You insulted the Queen Mum and, therefore, an entire nation and its diaspora; I shan't be surprised to hear that hordes of men in large bearskin hats have taken you away to chain you forever within the bowels of the Tower of London, where you shall be fed a diet of limp, overcooked vegetables and then beheaded (beheading being a blessed relief after the torture of an English diet). Should I mention that the Queen Mum is also dead, a fact that could not have escaped you if you had been reading anything in the paper other than your own reviews? Dear, dear boy. I'd advise you to fake your own death or at the very least go into permanent hiding forthwith; contact your new best friend and mentor, Salman Rushdie, for details.

In short, Mr. Wilde – you are an ignoramus.

Sincerely,

Oliver

PS: Clearly, you need help. You *need* Ms. Gabriella Savage. Contact her without delay.

From: oliver.black@thedawnpost.com
To: lucy.black@artnet.org
Subject: *Rafe Reviews*

My Dearest Lucille:

As I sit here at my desk wearing the lovely (though increasingly blimp-shaped) Amelia like a fox-fur stole, I find myself wondering if you happened to read Rafe Wilde's colourful review of last evening's performance of the music of John Cage. I highly recommend it, my love, as it is probably *the* most amusing music review I have ever read in *The Dawn Post*. Poor Rafe gets it all so right – and all so wrong – at the same time. It's an absolute travesty but jolly good fun at the same time, and all morning I have found myself suddenly bursting into great sobs of laughter: the diseased librarian, the deceased musicologist, and the descriptions of pieces of music that might as well have been written by a reactionary, irascible Martian with no real interest in understanding anything about the planet upon which he finds himself stranded. I understand that John Cage wanted his music to "change people's minds" – I'm afraid that in the case of Rafe Wilde, music just isn't going to do it; I believe the only way of changing the mind of Mr. Wilde is through surgical excision. Would it be too extreme to say that, given the supreme shallowness of Mr. Wilde's thinking, even a full frontal lobotomy would be nothing but cosmetic surgery? Perhaps. I think it *would* be fair to say, however, that Rafe Wilde is not interested in deep-sea diving in the great ocean of cultural life but, rather, in merely snorkelling, floundering blind and directionless, close to the surface and near to the shoreline. What seems to interest him are entertainments – pleasant distractions that do nothing to enlarge his mental capacities or expand his consciousness, and that merely confirm his experience of life, after which they are discarded in favour of other, similar entertainments. Rafe Wilde's attention seems to flit over the surface of music, setting up an essentially superficial, anti-intellectual, purely emotional relationship that does not require his full mental participation and that, lacking depth, yields fewer rewards. Am I being a cultural snob, my love? Do let me know. Certainly the boys think so and call me a hypocrite to boot, because while I condemn what is the worst in popular music, I actively encourage their participation in it. I don't deny it, but I'm not crazy either – I know a good opportunity when I see it. Suppose our boys decided to become, not rock stars, but lute players or madrigal singers or orchestral musicians or piano teachers? Horrors! I could cancel my subscription to *Boating Monthly* and kiss my hopes for a catamaran goodbye, that's for certain.

As well, my treasure, I phoned Angel's mother – it seems as though Angel has no earthly father – although she does have an extraordinary number of siblings, all of whom she is supporting singlehandedly through her modelling career. Does this seem right to you? No, nor does it to me. I had an excessively odd conversation with her mother, or rather, not so much with her mother but with Micah, Nahum, Habakkuk, and various other Biblical prophets whom she appears to be channelling. The conversation revolved around the twin concepts of good and evil, and why the former is preferable to the latter, and what God will do to those who may be operating under any misapprehensions. What Angel's mother thinks of the Almighty is as clear as a bell – but one can't help but wonder what the Almighty might think of her. (Or, to be fair, of any of us. Poor old God. It can never be easy for *any* father to watch his children squander their inheritance.) At any rate, after much cajoling, Mrs. Day agreed to meet with me at the café of her choice, though a firm date for our meeting has not yet been set. I'll attempt to sort something out posthaste, and we'll see if she won't agree to help shepherd her little lambkin of God back into the holy sheep paddock.

Love,

Oliver

The Dream Post
God the Father Hopping Mad Over Behaviour of Earthly Children

St. Cloud, Minnesota – God the Father, who has been out of the universe on business, returned unexpectedly yesterday to the surprise of all his earthly children. "I leave the universe to run by itself for a few thousand years, and what happens?" God asked, striking his forehead with the palm of his hand. "*I* didn't invite all *these* people – what are they doing on *my* planet drinking all *my* booze? And where the hell are the rainforests? Where did you put all those whales I made? What do you mean you ate *all the woolly mammoths?*"

Faced with the Almighty's wrath, God's children could do nothing but stare sheepishly at the ground and scuff their feet in the dirt. "I leave you alone for the geological equivalent of *five minutes* because I think you're mature enough to handle a little responsibility, and *this* is what happens," God thundered, pointing to the oil spills, beer cans, and empty potato chip bags littering the planet from one end to the other. "I even leave a few basic rules behind to guide you, but what good does it do? I mean, what part of *"Do Not Kill"* don't you people understand?"

When God's children tried to explain how word had gotten around, and how one thing had sort of just led to another until the whole thing had somehow gotten way out of hand, God wouldn't have any of it. "Talk to the hand, people," He said, shooing them away from His Almighty presence. "You're supposed to be made in my image! Ha! *That's* the joke of the epoch! I'm creative, I'm interesting, I'm funny as hell – but what do you people think interests me? Holiness! Oh, please! As if I give a rat's ass! Being holy was *your* idea, *not* mine. What I care about are my Great Auks – where in blazes are they anyway? And don't try telling me I must have left them in my other pants!"

When God's children point-ed to scripture and mumbled, "But we thought you said –", God picked it up and swatted them on the head with it. "You call this journalism? Where did your reporter get his quotes? I never said *any* of this. And what is *this*?" an irate heavenly Father asked, pointing to His favourite continent. "What the hell did you do to *Africa*?"

In response to their unacceptable behaviour, God has grounded His earthly children ("There'll be no trip to the moon for *you* this summer!") and has taken away their celestial TV privileges, blacking out the heavens until further notice.

From: rafe.wilde@thedawnpost.com
To: sales@bedsbedsbeds.cybersleep.net
Subject: Bedsore

To the Bungling Moronic Manager at Beds Beds Beds:

Fucking h-e-double hockey sticks! What exactly is it that's wrong with you? I mean besides the fact that your ancestors are chimps. Besides the fact that you don't know a goddamn thing about beds because your owners put you out every night. Besides the fact that you've never actually slept in a bed – only in a coffin. Besides the fact that what you really need is the phone number that will connect you to tech support for your own brains.

I have absolutely had it with your heatable beds, your adjust-

able beds, your round beds, your vibrating beds, your beds of
nails, your oyster beds, your flower beds, your ocean beds, and
especially this last one quaintly named Triton's Reward Water
Bed. You claimed, once again, that this bed would finally be the
one, that it would be the bed of my dreams. *It's the bed of my
nightmares, more like.* Do you know what it's like to try to sleep
on a bed *made* of water, for God's sake? It's fucking impossible,
that's what it's like, because a sheet of plastic that looks to be
about the thickness of a trash bag is the only thing separating me
from death by drowning. How restful for someone who never
learned to swim – because every time I went in the water about
ten buxom lifeguards insisted on carrying me back out again, and
I'd emerge on a tidal wave of girls. But there are no girls anymore
thanks to Helga from the gulag in Algolagnia, whose massage
technique culminates in flaying, in skinning, in savage epidermal
stripping. There won't be any more sex for the Great Rafe now
that I look like an experimental life form bobbing along at sea.
Besides, there isn't any room for a woman since I have to sleep
spread-eagle, hanging onto the edge of the bed for dear life. Plus I
have to get up every five minutes to pee because sleeping on fluids
is like trying to sleep with your wrist in a bowl of warm water
with a tap running beside Niagara Falls. Oh yeah, I'm having wet
dreams, all right. But that's all I'm having since I started sleeping,
not with women, but with water wings and my inflatable duck
Quackers. Flaming hell! The damn thing never stops moving; it's
like a living thing, a gigantic, one-celled organism. It's like I have
a pet instead of a bed – just me and my amoeba. It's like lying on
the smooth underbelly of a gigantic slug. What made you think I
was an aquatic mammal, anyway? I realize that sometime in the
distant past my ancestors crawled out of the primordial swamp,
but I've moved on from there, all right?

You'll find your fucking bed, drained and quartered, sliced
and splintered, in the alley outside of my apartment building. If
you dare to charge me for it, I will take you to court and will
offer, as evidence of your incompetence, the tranquillizer gun

with which I have had to shoot myself every night for the last six months just to get a little shut-eye. I will offer, as evidence of your bungling, the fact that I've gotten out of the wrong side of the bed every morning for the last six months. This is because your beds don't have a right side – you cut your beds in half, throw the right sides in the trash, and glue the wrong sides together. And finally, I will offer as evidence of your ineptitude six months of nightly flow charts outlining the complicated series of moves from the bed, to the floor, back to the bed, back to the floor, to the love-seat, to the bath tub, to the table, to the hallway, to the top of the deep freeze, and finally to my ancient rock-hard futon, which is now so compacted that, unlike all other objects in the universe, it has absolutely no space whatsoever between its atoms. It's a degenerate matter mattress that deviates freakishly from the classical laws of physics. Neutrinos hit it and ping right off in the other direction. But I better not give those quacks in your re-search and development department any ideas! What's to stop you from manufacturing a line of futons and adding it to your stock of novelty beds with a catchy advertising jingle that prom-ises "It's like sleeping among the stars," which is true except they're all white dwarf stars. (Look it up, moron.)

I've had better sleeps on railway tracks, in graveyards, during a scrum, bound and gagged in the trunk of my car. Tuck me up for the night inside an active volcano, or tied to the tail of a tiger, or strapped to a nuclear warhead set to whiz through the strato-sphere – I'd get a more satisfying sleep *anywhere* other than on one of those purgatorial contraptions you call a bed. They're not beds. They're abominations against nature, every one.

I'm finished with you people.

Rafe Wilde

From: rafe.wilde@thedawnpost.com
To: alma.wilde@command.net
Subject: Enough Already

Mom:

Oh, very nice. What do you mean I never loved Angel and that I'm just sulking because I didn't get to be the one to corrupt her? What a thing to say to your little guy! Mothers are supposed to be advocates for their kids, to stand up for them, to believe in them no matter what, to love them unconditionally. You're not my shrink, you know – you're my *mom*. Why don't you start acting like it?

Okay, so listen up. I don't mean to seem ungrateful or anything, but please don't send me any more of my old stuff, all right? It was fun for awhile, and I admit that my science notes from high school just came in handy (who knew I'd need to know about white dwarf stars, apparently one of the densest things in the universe, in order to write another mad-as-hell letter to a bed company), but all these reminders of my lost youth are really bringing me down. The piano arrived this morning, and rather than allowing it to stink up my living room, I made the movers put it up on the roof of the apartment building. Geez, that thing gives me the creeps! I'd forgotten the bloody thing's so macabre looking, like you bought it from a funeral parlour or the Addams Family, or that one day you answered the door, and the piano slid silently past you and just sort of *moved in.* How come when I look at that thing all I have is this nightmarish vision of the skeletal corpse of an old lady crumbling to dust all over the keyboard? Why does it feel like Halloween wherever *it* is? And what is it about *one* piano that makes it feel like an infestation? I've just never seen anything more *black*, you know? It's like an Azkaban guard, just sucking up every little bit of light and happiness around it. It looks hungry, hungry for piano students, scrubbed clean and ritually offered, fresh and raw.

Anyway, thanks for faithfully reading the review I wrote of the John Cage concert. So are you going to say anything more about it, or do you still want a son to support you in your dotage? I could use less of your lip, you know, Mom, fewer of your "What kind of drugs were you on?" remarks. I made a mistake, all right? I wanted to prove that you shouldn't have to do a whole mountain of research in order to understand music. I was wrong, okay? Nothing short of a PhD in new musicology with a double major in Plink and Plonk, a skull the size of an orchestra pit housing a brain as powerful as the engine in my vacuum cleaner, and a music dictionary – and I mean a good music dictionary, not one of those dictionaries you can actually lift – is enough to make sense of this stuff. It's a whole different world, Mom. All these musical concepts, categories, ideas – mostly they sound like diseases. "I'm sorry, Mr. Jones, you've got tropes." What can be done for hockets? For hemioliacs? And the terms that don't sound like diseases are just this weird double-speak. Actually I made a list, which I'm thinking of having printed up as a poster or a novelty tea towel – are you ready for this? Okay, so – don't get excited about Passion music – it's not what you think it is. Neither is organum, a sextet, or a virginal. Neither is a Fagott for that matter. Tonguing in public is not indecent. And don't be afraid to remark on a musician's Sagbut. Shofars do not drive people around in limos. Pasticcios are not nuts. Phrygians don't keep food cold. Polonaise does not go in a sandwich. You don't find portamentos in olives. There is no such thing as a Psalter shaker. An organ grinder does not make ground bass. Sordinos do not come in a tin. Don't order a Seguidilla in a Mexican restaurant. Tapiola is not a pudding. You can't drink a cup of rococo before bed. You can't wear a tie around your neck. You may not dock a boat at the Tromba marina. There is no such thing as a tuning spoon. If the antiphone rings, don't answer it. The Supertonic does not wear a cape and tights. No one has ever been tried and convicted for serial composition. See? Do you see what I mean?

It's just gobbledygook. Einstein played the violin, you know – but why do you think he went into theoretical physics rather than become a professional musician? Exactly. And who can blame him for choosing the easy path?

So Oliver Black practically wet himself, he was so happy about the whole thing. Please let me kill him, Mom, please! I'd be doing the world a huge favour! Trust me on this one: If it would've been morally right to kill Hitler in 1939, it's morally imperative to kill Oliver Black now. He's hoarding the world's whole supply of smugness. He's cornered the bloody-minded bastard market. He's got a monopoly on affectation, on sanctimony, on self-righteousness. There's nothing left for the rest of us! Oh, don't panic – as much as I'd like to, I'm obviously not really going to do him in. And you can put away that list of group homes you used to keep taped to the fridge. I'm too old now – ha! I'm just mad, that's all, but I'm sure I'll get over it. And I'll get over Angel. And Suzanne. And the humiliation of a botched review, a bald patch, and a face that looks like a freshly skinned knee.

Your son (for now, anyway),

Rafe

PS: And yeah, of course it's okay that you gave Uncle Bill my e-mail address. (Since when has *he* been able to afford a *computer*?)

From: oliver.black@thedawnpost.com
To: nathaniel.midge@thedawnpost.com
Subject: Rescue Mission

Dear Mr. Midge:

I note that the Letters to the Editor column in this morning's

Dawn Post is a positive onslaught of communications expressing bewilderment and disgust at Rafe Wilde's ludicrous review of the John Cage concert, with the exception of that one outstanding letter of praise and admiration, so obviously and heartbreakingly written by Mr. Wilde himself. It's easy to imagine that, due to Mr. Wilde's immense and frankly hilarious miscalculation, you are now on the verge of shooting off a letter of reprimand and dismissal; however, might I be so bold as to suggest an alternative course of action? I agree that it was as bad a piece of journalism as ever there was, that essentially it is only good for a laugh – and this is, I think, the key to handling the whole affair. Personally, I think it best to pass the whole thing off as a joke, as an exercise in irony, in lampoonery, in satire. Menippus, Lucilius, Aristophanes, Seneca, Swift, Molière – all amateurs compared to Rafe Wilde! Or, if this solution won't wash, perhaps you might present it in the spirit of those publications that deliberately include spelling errors to give those more pedantic readers the satisfaction of discovery and disclosure – perhaps you might suggest that it was an ill-conceived experiment, presented in order to discover if our readers are still paying attention by the time they get to the arts and entertainment subdivision (which I have always argued should be the opening section of any newspaper), after being lulled into slumber (as I so often am) by engaging in the study of the morning news: the predictable acts of criminal minds, of random meteorological events, of international gossip, and the repetitive trivia of intransient, mundane existence scrounged from all four corners of the globe and ever laid before us in mind-numbing detail. What is G. K. Chesterton's observation? Ah, yes: "Journalism largely consists of saying 'Lord Jones is dead' to people who never knew Lord Jones was alive." It's no surprise, then, that the morning newspaper must always be accompanied by a Herculean cup of caffeinated coffee – one requires what is essentially potable dynamite in order to keep one conscious after reading the identical news article on the subject of, say, peace in the Middle East, which one seems to have been reading every day for the last thirty years. This represents a perversion of the natural order, a fact that can be demonstrated by leaving a container of food in the fridge for several months; note that the content gradually changes while the date on the top of the container remains the same. Where the news is concerned, the reverse is true; it is the content that remains the same – only the date ever changes. *Plus ça change pas, plus c'est les nouvelles.*

But I digress. Whatever tack you take, Mr. Midge, I do believe that Rafe Wilde deserves another chance to prove himself, and that our regular editor, were he not languishing on his sickbed, would command a characteristic display of compassionate understanding and forgiveness. It's obvious that Mr. Wilde made a colossal blunder, stumbling into the common error of condemning in order to look superior (wrongly imagining that to agree is merely a demonstration of weakness, and that to pooh-pooh is more powerful than to praise) but, sadly, condemning from a place of comprehensive ignorance. It was the always risky "man-on-the-street" approach, but alas, the man-on-the-street that Rafe chose to emulate was not the pipe-smoking music scholar but, rather, the uneducated, inebriated bum in the gutter. Still it was only one mistake, wasn't it, and it was a mistake that surely will not be repeated (and if I'm wrong I should be more than happy to take Mr. Wilde behind the woodshed and shoot him myself).

Why do I find myself defending the very scoundrel who broke our covenant (I was to write a review for him, which I did – he was to write a review for me, which he did not), thereby proving himself unworthy of any future consideration? I suppose it is in part a situation of *noblesse oblige*, but the real truth is that I have a bit of a soft spot for poor Rafe Wilde, given that he reminds me so acutely of my own green and tender striplings. I have a fatherly feeling toward him which causes me to be naturally protective, while at the same time wanting to crush within him all that is plainly stupid and misguided, and to provide some basic instruction in how to be a decent human being, given that he seems to be so badly in need of it. In the forlorn hope of modifying maladaptive behaviour, I find myself goading him ruthlessly, just as I do my own much-beloved sons. I'm afraid, however, that Mr. Wilde misunderstands me – it's true that I hound him like one of my own pups, but I do so with affection and good humour, not with rancour and hostility. My sons understand this and reply in kind; Mr. Wilde, I believe, does not quite catch my tone. I suppose I ought to go a little easier on him, given that he's had a stormy time of late (overcome by a sort of sexual tsunami) – and given that it was one of my own sons who captivated the heart of the girl he was wooing, perhaps I feel just a trifle responsible for his current *melancholia dementia.*

So, given that Mr. Wilde is a smidge *non compos mentis* at present, perhaps we ought not to mention to him the subject of this communication, Mr. Midge. Not that I intend to refrain permanently from telling him so when the spirit moves, but at present he has a bewildered public to do the job for me, and I'll leave them to it.

Many thanks for your kind attention.

Oliver Black

From: rafe.wilde@thedawnpost.com
To: billy-bob@hellion.net
Subject: Whoa!

Hey Uncle Bill:

Thanks for the e-mail, but *do not*, under any circumstances, tell Oliver Black what you told me. *This is of critical importance,* all right? He's insufferable enough as it is – I don't need him crowing about this too.

Rafe

From: rafe.wilde@thedawnpost.com
To: billy-bob@hellion.net
Subject: Oh Thanks Very Much

Great bloody fucking hell! What do you mean it's too late?

Rafe

From: oliver.black@thedawnpost.com
To: billy-bob@hellion.net
Subject: Joy Unbounded

Dear Mr. Billy-Bob:

I was thrilled beyond measure to discover your e-mail in my in-basket this morning. Oh happy day! What extraordinary news! Not that I'm in the least bit surprised, you understand, as my review was carefully constructed and calculated to draw as much positive attention as possible to that little anachronistic gem of yours; but still I find myself turning cartwheels at these glad tidings.

You tell me that your business has skyrocketed since the writing of my review, and that now there is a constant line-up of people around the corner and down the street, waiting to get a table. How extraordinary that most of these are adventurers and fortune-hunters, who flock in droves from the sterility and chilling predictability of the suburbs just to catch a glimpse of the Dickensian conditions which you have preserved with such care. Oh what delightful news! I find it amazing that you've had to hire another two cooks in addition to four new full-time waitresses, and that you have even expanded your menu (which is, you say, an unprecedented event) to include macaroni and cheese. Good show! And is it really true that some young man, who is marrying his bride whilst astride a Harley Davidson motorcycle, even asked if he could have his wedding reception at your fine establishment? But how marvellous! You must be over the moon!

Your insistence that I dine daily, for the rest of my life, at your excellent little bistro as a way of expressing your gratitude is most generous indeed; sadly, however, it is an offer I must decline. Might I be so bold as to suggest an alternative? I do just happen to have three sons who might be very interested in your offer indeed, three fine young men who, as a unit, constitute the band Black Chalice. Imagine what business would be like if your café was haunted daily by three members of a band that is already locally famous and manifestly destined for international stardom. Shall I suggest to my boys that they treat your café as a kind of clubhouse? Shall I suggest that they pop 'round on a regular basis in order to add even more sparkle, more pizzazz shall we say, to the splendour of your business, to attract the young and the glamorous, the famous and the rich, in exchange for a bit of free nosh? I tell you in all sincerity, Mr. Billy-Bob, that though you bake me a cake the size of a planet and write my name across the stars in letters of icing a million light years high, still you could not find a better way of thanking me than this.

Now, I trust that you have written to your nephew, Rafe Wilde, and told him the excellent news. I assure you that nothing could make him happier than the knowledge that *my* review has been the direct cause of the flourishing of *your* business – and, in addition, that all of my boys, including Selwyn, of whom he is especially fond, are more than welcome at your café anytime. Oh joy! I think I just may write and break the happy news to Mr. Wilde myself.

Sincerely,

Oliver Black

From: oliver.black@thedawnpost.com
To: selwyn.black@freenet.org
             merlin.black@freenet.org
             damien.black@freenet.org
Subject: Jammy Beggars

Hello Boys:

You will be ecstatic, as I am, to know that I've located the ideal hang-out for you, a place that has free food and more atmosphere than the planet Venus. As long as it doesn't interfere with your schooling (Merlin and Damien – you do still go to school, I trust), and as long as you promise not to imitate the unseemly habits and lifestyle of some of the locals (alcoholism, drug-abuse, pimping, breeding), I suggest that you hang out *there* with your friends, rather than having the lot of you in our kitchen, clustered around the open refrigerator, worshipping it as if it were a holy relic. Promise me that you will dine daily at Billy-Bob's Burger and Bun (522 Centre Street); nothing could make me happier than the knowledge that you're doing your very best to ruin your appetites before every meal.

Prosit,

Dad

From: oliver.black@thedawnpost.com
To: rafe.wilde@thedawnpost.com
Subject: Telling You So

My Dearest Rafe:

Behold, I bring you good tidings of great joy that shall be to all people but, especially, to me. Have you heard the wonderful news, my dear boy? If not, let me be the first to relate the rags-to-riches tale – and why should I not, given that it is none other than Oliver Black himself who is the author?

Now, you'll never guess who sent me an e-mail just this morning! It was your Uncle Billy-Bob writing to thank me, in the way that a man rescued from the jaws of a crocodile might thank his rescuer, for my adroit critique of his previously inconsequential café and the astonishing impact my review has had on both his personal and professional life. Actually, it was less of a letter and more of a prayer, really, a sort of extended psalm with me as the object of worship. How embarrassed I would be by such abject veneration if I hadn't, *de facto*, rescued the Burger and Bun *de profundis!* Yet one cannot deny that the publication of my review was the occasion of your uncle's blossoming prosperity; he, himself, summed it up beautifully when he wrote, "I owes [sic] you bigtime [sic] Mister and you sure as hell [have] done more fer [sic] me than my own flesh and blood ever did." Isn't that heart-warming?

There is so very much upon which to expound that it's hard to know where to begin! Rogers and Hammerstein might suggest that we begin at "doh," a very good place to start indeed, given that "d'oh!" is quite possibly the involuntary exclamation you will make upon hearing of the triumph of my review, but also conveniently suggestive of both your uncle's much-coveted "dough" recipe, and the fact that he is now rolling in it – in dough, that is. Perhaps I ought to begin with the fact that there is now a line-up of patrons around the block at every hour waiting patiently for a sacred piece of raisin pie and cup of coffee with whitener, not unlike that served in the Bible for dessert at the wedding feast of Cana; or with the fact that the mayor of our city will be holding weekly open-mike discussions on issues of social neglect, to be broadcast on television and radio live from your uncle's café, with your uncle acting as the rough-and-ready, *enfant terrible*, reality-check co-host; or with the fact that your uncle has been paid several exorbitant sums of money to appear in a documentary on feeding the poor and the downtrodden (with your uncle cast as a character more or less like the offspring of the Incredible Hulk and Mother Theresa), a TV special called "Burgers and Buns for Orphans and Bums," and a television commercial – a sort of before-and-after affair – for a popular brand of underarm deodorant. The most wonderful thing of all, of course, is that your uncle has welcomed my three sons into the fold as one would welcome three princes of Egypt, and every evening my boys are destined to return home stuffed and positively reeking of free jelly donuts and banana cream pie. Oh joy! Once again I'll have a disposable income, since not every last penny will be squandered on victuals, continually shovelled into their cavernous bellies as one would shovel coal into the glowing furnaces of three appallingly inefficient train engines.

Isn't it marvellous, Rafe? What a relief it must be to be assured that your uncle has not been liquidated by indignant health inspectors, as you had so sourly predicted with all the accuracy of a newspaper psychic, but instead was vindicated by patrons, politicians, social workers, newspaper columnists, and others who understand your uncle's essential service to the community. As it turns out, the only problem of grave concern to health inspectors involved the multitudinous vermin – mice as thick as fleas, fleas the size of mice, and rats hanging off your uncle's pant leg that were so monstrous he had long assumed they were just grisly little Chihuahuas (hence the collars). But the problem of pestilence proved to be a minor one and was greatly improved inside of a weekend with the assistance of a few lean cats from the local animal shelter, whose campaign of terror, led by an enormous ginger Bolshevik nicknamed Kitler, resulted both in an unholy pogrom, and a dozen satisfied cats with just a touch of indigestion. Those few smug mice who did not meet their Maker in the jaws of a ferocious, blood-lusting wittle kittums will most certainly be set to rights in one of the whopping number of traps hidden around the café; in fact, during the course of a meal one can often hear two or three traps *SNAP!* and this lends itself nicely to the overall impression of the café as a hard-knock, un-sentimental, no-nonsense kind of place.

With the glorious success of my review and, as a direct result, the flowering of your uncle's fortunes, it becomes glaringly obvious that you erred grievously in your decision not to publish your review of the Black Chalice concert. There's nothing to be done about it now, no way to right the wrong, nor even any way of assuaging your guilty conscience – though I suppose you might try the confessional, even though any priest worth his salt would only shake his head in disbelief and condemn you immediately to the everlasting inferno. Perhaps the best we can do is to draw up a contract written in blood, and here I'm sure you would enjoy personally extracting Selwyn's blood (sorry, not an option) in which you assure me that, when next my boys play a hometown concert, you will ungrudgingly write a review and submit it for publication *tout de suite*. We'll have no more of these unprofessional little shenanigans, Mr. Wilde. From now on let us deal with each other honestly and openly, as colleagues and comrades. Let us begin again, secure in the knowledge that, in your role as a critic of the rock and roll scene, I hold you in the highest esteem; you are a fine writer with a vocabulary and a command of the language that is the envy of many a music journalist. Erudite, expressive, and ever on the lookout for the *mot juste*. I can give you no higher praise than this; let us hope it is enough to grease the wheels of friendship, and that I'll hear that all is well with you, and between us, sometime in the very near future.

Expansively,

Oliver Black

From: rafe.wilde@thedawnpost.com
To: suzanne@heartmail.com
Subject: Le Mot Juste

Fuck!

From: rafe.wilde@thedawnpost.com
To: sales@comfortfirstmedical.cybersleep.net
Subject: Can I Order an IV Pole Dancer?

To Whom It May Concern at the Comfort First Medical
Supply Company:

Bloody bloody fucking hell! What is it about the people who
manufacture and sell beds anyway? Are your heads stuffed full of
the same pink fluff that you put in your mattresses? Does being in
a warehouse full of beds make you drunk with the suggestion of
sleep? Or are you in cahoots with the Dementors at Beds Beds
Beds, salespeople who are hell-bent on seeing that my quest for
comfort ends with the purchase of a single, upturned spike, which
they advertise as "a super new sleep solution providing terrific
lower back support, at the same time allowing you to swivel 360
degrees!"

Okay. You promised that the bed I ordered would arrive
promptly, and guess what? You were wrong. Surprise, surprise. A
bed arrived all right, but it's the *wrong model*. Given that I am an
SSM (single scabby male) whose chances of getting laid ever again
are nil and that the odds of reproducing are therefore not great, it
is no surprise that *I did not order the water-birthing model*. Water
and beds do not go together, my friend, and I have come to the
conclusion that the whole birth thing, the whole creating another
human being thing, is an incredibly bad idea. Just ask my mother.
Anyway, I specifically ordered Nurse Mary's Delight, the "ultimate comfort" bed with the motorized as opposed to manual

crank system for hi-lo back elevation, no-roll mattress, collapsible safety rails, bumper guards, swivel castors, detachable tray, head/footboard flipdown, and IV pole mount. And don't forget that I ordered a bed that conforms to "stringent European standards" like it says in your advertisement. I don't have a fucking clue what European standards are, but I sure as hell want them (because the implication is that North American standards are a joke – and I don't want to end up sleeping on a bed with two short legs across the diagonal, with its collapse-function on a timer, and with sloping sides to ensure that patients roll like sausages out of their beds and into the hallways all night long).

Currently I'm sleeping on a slab of concrete, which used to be a futon, with a piece of corrugated cardboard over me for effect. Basically I'm living like a homeless panhandler in my own apartment.

Hurry the fuck up,

Rafe Wilde

From: oliver.black@thedawnpost.com
To: branksome.black@rebel.net
Subject: Wampum

Mon Cher Frère:

I received your message just now and am responding immediately to your plea for assistance with a whopping foreign money order – and just when I finally had a little extra cash due to the boys eating gratis at the Burger and Bun! Sigh. This is invariably the way, isn't it? It's why I'm always reluctant to accept an increase in salary, since it is as if the very *act* of accepting extra funds is the direct *cause* of, for example, a hitherto unnoticed but astonishingly pronounced, lower-lip-eclipsing overbite in a child who will suddenly require major orthodontics, or risk chewing his own head off. Do you want to see your car, your computer, and your favourite internal organ break down on the same day? Now you know how to do it. And speaking of favourite internal organs, parting with money is about as much fun as parting with one; and yet, I understand the imperative for funds in order that you might find some unconventional means of shuffling undetected past various authorities and getting yourself out of Australia, pronto. Your behaviour, though profoundly moral, is also deeply criminal; feeding the downtrodden and the innocent lambs of this world is usually considered to be a good thing, but I'm afraid the police won't see it that way considering what you've actually been feeding the flock. You are truly the good shepherd, Branky, leading the sheep away from the precipice – how unfair it is, then, that the shepherd should find himself unwittingly backing into a police cruiser. Jesus himself had the same sort of trouble with the law, but note that, although he came to a sticky end, his stock has only risen since; so clearly, being on the right side of the law isn't everything. But that makes no odds now. The point is that you have to get out of there, and fast. Though Australia be a continent made of sand, still the sands are running out; I therefore sanction any method of escape, short of trying to swim for it. It's one thing to be a symbolic fish in troubled waters swimming against the tide, but to be an actual fish in Australian waters is merely to bear the aspect of a formal dinner invitation.

I should tell you that your request for funds was only one of two blows to the old pocket book. The other is that we seem to have acquired another daughter, a young lady named Angel, who appears to be living over the brush with Selwyn, having taken up permanent residence in his boyhood room. Lucy and I find ourselves *in loco parentis* to a lass whose twin passions appear to be 1) Selwyn Black and 2) Jesus Christ. (Twice in one letter He appears – a sort of Second Coming, in miniature.) There has not been such a confused young lass as Angel since Syrinx found herself changed from a nymph into a bunch of reeds and Pan playing upon her as a musical instrument day and night. "Why am I suddenly a bunch of reeds?" is clearly the look on Angel's face, and for answers she seems to be turning *not* to the conventional sources (self-help books, friends, gardening manuals) but, unbelievably, to the Holy Bible – and if one can be certain of nothing else, at least one can be certain of this: that the authors of the Bible did *not* sit around a curvaceous, pink, Formica table surrounded by the latest in makeup and fashion, consulting teen focus groups and asking themselves, "How can we make this book maximally helpful and relevant to the troubled adolescent girl reading our publication in several thousand years time?" Honestly, Branksome, I don't see how an ancient book in which reeds figure only as symbols of fickleness, weakness, or uncertain support can help the pubescent Angel, especially an ancient book cobbled together *by men* (because *all* scriptures are written by men, a fact of which Lucy reminds Angel daily). Still, when she isn't making beautiful music, so to speak, with Selwyn, you'll usually find her holed up with the Holy Bible, red pencil sharpened to a deadly point, looking cross and circling the controversial bits. And she won't go home – she claims her mother is clinically insane, although to me she merely sounds clinically Christian. You know, Branksome, I might have said that there has not been such a confused young lass since poor Io found herself changed from a nymph to a heifer, but comparing Angel to a heifer might imply that she's not the most dazzlingly beautiful creature ever to have walked the earth, with more natural sex appeal than a thousand salacious supermodels compressed into one. Ah! Down, Branksome! Down! And don't you dare even think of catching the next flight home! Besides, you wouldn't see much of Angel anyway; I rarely even catch so much as a glimpse of either her or Selwyn anymore, but we appear to be going through even more bananas than ever, which is irrefutable proof that we have yet another teenager living under our roof. Did you know that the Victorians were scandalized by the practice of eating bananas right out of the skin? There's a good reason for this, believe me. Even if I'm not in the kitchen, I always know when Angel is about to place one between her lips. Conversation can be flowing freely, but then suddenly – a gripping silence. One can hear only panting and occasional drool splattering on the kitchen table, three zippers spontaneously splitting open from the terrible pressure, Selwyn dragging Angel by the hair to his room Merlin, and Stringbean weeping piteously. And then, naturally, there's the sound of Lucy suddenly stomping about and banging pots in a fury, invoking the hallowed name of Gloria Steinem and threatening to ban bananas, cucumbers, zucchinis, and all other even remotely phallic food from the premises. "Is that a banana in your pocket, or are you just glad to see me?" is no longer a line that is tolerated in the Black household. How did Lucy put it? Ah yes. Sometimes a banana is *just* a banana.

My keyboard suddenly feels hot to the touch, Branksome, so that's quite enough for now. Please let me know the minute you've evaded capture and are on terra secura once again. Until that time I shall be, not just on tenterhooks, but . . .

On eleventerhooks,

Oliver

From: rafe.wilde@thedawnpost.com
To: suzanne@heartmail.com
Subject: Your Mistake

Suzanne:

Okay, listen. This is insane. I know you're just trying to get my goat here. Either that or there's been some sort of breakdown in communication – probably some rogue tree roots growing through the lines, or maybe some gigantic mutant computer particles plugging up the wires in cyberspace. It's like when we were kids and we used to play that telephone game – you know, the one where you sit in a circle and whisper something into the ear of the kid beside you, and that kid whispers it into the ear of the kid beside him, and by the time it makes it around the whole circle whatever was said initially is transformed into something totally unintelligible. That's obviously what's happened here. I'm guessing that what you wrote was something like "I'm pretty harried" (yeah, Baby, aren't we all), but somewhere along the cyber-line it mutated and, after several nonsensical variations, ended up with the nuttiest one of all – laughably, "I'm getting married."

Which is a mix-up, right? Or is it a joke? I mean, what exactly *do* you mean by "I'm getting married?" It makes no sense. I haven't even asked you yet! It *is* customary for the groom to propose first, you know. I didn't even know you were *that* kind of girl, you know, the marrying kind, otherwise I would have asked you to get hitched years ago. Honest, I would have! I can just imagine you with flowers in your hair and dressed in a gown of white organdy (whatever organdy is), and me in skin-tight blue jeans, a black leather jacket, and cool shades, making love in the back seat of a limousine with pink and white plastic flowers plastered all over it and tin cans with a "Just Married" sign stuck on the back. We could be married by tonight if you wanted, and by next week we could be arguing over finances, making mother-in-law jokes, and having our first extramarital flings – just like a proper couple. *That could be us.*

Yeah, okay, I know. You're actually thinking of shackling yourself for all eternity to that gruesome heart surgeon, the guy who uses a scalpel to cut his steak, who puts extra ketchup on his fries and then washes it all down with a Bloody Mary. I can't believe you're even considering something like this, Suzanne! I mean, look at my diary. "Had lunch with celebrity rock band, went to yet another kick-ass concert, partied into the night with abandon" – compared to his – "Sliced open some people, accidentally killed a guy. Good golf game. Had boring evening at home, exactly the kind I like." Come on, Suzanne, wake up! When are you going to clue in to the fact that there might be something a bit off about a guy who begs you to put extra giblets in the gravy? And a doctor would never have any time for you; just as he's about to get all romantic he'll get distracted ("I love you, Suzanne, with all my . . . ocardial infarction"), and his pager will suddenly play "I Left My Heart in San Francisco," and off he'll go in his ambulance, leaving you alone and frustrated and unable to think of anything except what a mistake you made by not marrying *me*.

Please, Suzanne, I beg of you – give me one more chance! I promise you won't have to sort my groceries or iron my towels – you can even have my Guatemalan foster child, all right? Please, just tell me what I'm supposed to say. Tell me what you want me to do. And then do this for me – *just think about it.* *We* could be the ones accidentally chipping our teeth on one of those enormous Styrofoam wedding cakes with the plaster icing and a little plastic bride and groom on the top! *We* could be the ones to have bridesmaids stuffed like sausages into taffeta casings! *We* could be the ones hopping into the marriage bed, which brings me to the other reason for this e-mail which is – I need a bed to sleep on again. The blockheads at Beds Beds Beds sent me the wrong mystery bed – I evidently got the one intended for Captain Highliner. Then I ordered a new one off the 'net, but they mistakenly sent me a water-birthing tub, which Quackers and I did make use of once, even though the only thing I gave birth to was a desire to drown some bed company employees. I felt the urge to push, all right, and to make those bedheads do some serious postpartum bleeding. Anyway, my replacement bed won't be here for a few days, so in the meantime – can I sleep over? Come on, Suzanne. Just tell Mr. Heartthrob Hearty Pants that when you said "Okay" you meant "No way," and I'll be over with a ring, a marriage certificate, and a minister faster than you can say, "I do."

Love,

Rafe

PS: I threw Petey out the window again, and this time he didn't come back. Good riddance, I say!

The Dream Post
New Book Reveals Men
Clueless about Relationships

New York, New York – A new self-help book to be released today finally offers men the advice they need in order to successfully woo a woman of any race, religion, or social class. Authored by legendary ladies' man Studley Mannix III, *Never Be Dumped Again – What Women Want and How to Give It to Them in Order to Achieve Your Own Sick Ends* is destined to be a number-one bestseller. "I know women like a hand knows a glove – having dated, and often married, women of all types," said Mr. Mannix in a recent interview. "Men think they can use the same seduction techniques every time, but women are not all the same – besides which they need more than food, shelter, warmth, and

adequate phosphates. You need to know what your individual woman wants and then . . . give it to her," explained the author while making rude pelvic motions.

"Take the rural lady, for example. Now the hutterite woman likes to be plied with live chickens and bolts of polka dot fabric, whereas the Amish lady in your life still tends to go for the man with the biggest plow. A pair of hand-carved wooden clogs also brings a blush to her cheek. But all rural ladies can be won over by Country Living's line of fine, farm-fresh fragrances and cosmetics – 'For a Whole Gnu Ewe,' as the advertising says."

"On the other hand," Mr. Mannix continued, "The suburban woman wants mass-produced consumer goods for which you've paid an atrocious sum but in themselves are worth essentially nothing. The suburban female becomes as mad as a wet hen if you don't give her a consumer item like millions of others, purchased from a bona fide mall on every single artificially manufactured occasion. The only way she can define herself – and you – is through consumer choice, so take my advice: don't even think of crafting a unique gift item with your own hands for your sophisticated suburban sweetheart. Even though women are obsessed with shoes, for example, forget the hand-made clogs, even if you are a cobbler by trade – though if you are a cobbler, you don't really have a hope in hell, do you? Your suburban gal wants a man in a bleeding-edge, twenty-first century profession, so unless you've been described in Fortune 500 as 'The Bill Gates of the Cobbling World,' I'd avoid cobbling altogether, as well as the miller, cooper, and shepherd professions."

When asked about women of various faiths, Mr. Mannix replied, "Don't try to impress the Christian gal by saying that you know Jesus personally – they all know Him personally – but saying that you've stared down the devil and made him dance is sure to impress, especially if you're wearing a cheap suit and slick hair, and toting a Bible the size of an occasional table. However," he continued, tapping his nose, "some girls, especially those who believe Christ's blood covers all their sins – past, present, *and* future – like a whiff of danger, if you know what I mean." What does the Hindu woman want? "Eau de Ganges, without fail." The Sufi woman? "A dervish and a couple of wool socks." The Palestinian woman? "Real estate, every time." Mr. Mannix's final advice is this: "Remember, men – don't overlook the homeless bag lady in your life. Happily, all *she* wants is food, shelter, warmth, and adequate phosphates."

From: rafe.wilde@thedawnpost.com
To: alma.wilde@command.net
Subject: Jilted

Dear Mom:

What was the big idea anyway, giving me life? What were you thinking? Life isn't a *gift* – it's a *sentence*. A *life* sentence, by definition. So here's the most recent hammer blow, the latest in a long series: not only is Angel gone for good, but I just got a note from Suzanne announcing the fact that she's getting married – and not to me! What a bitch! She sent me an aggressively hostile e-mail suggesting that I treat her place as no more than a flophouse, and that I treat her as nothing but a sex object. As if! I just can't figure women out, Mom. I mean, if I compliment Suzanne on her body, she gets offended and makes some crack about me not appreciating her mind. So then I'm smothering her naked body with kisses and I say, "Oh yeah, Baby. What a great mind you have. What a cerebellum. Mmm. So big and soft." And then she slaps my face because I said it was big. Ouch! I didn't mean overweight, for Christ's sake! Just tell me what to say to her, Mom, and I'll say it! I've just got to win Suzanne back because, no matter what she claims, I don't just appreciate her for her body. She's got really great hair too. (That's a joke, all right?)

So you got an e-mail from Uncle Bill telling you the big news. Yeah, that's right. Oliver Black is the big hero, the saviour of the world, Jesus Christ returned to earth as exactly what he was the last time – i.e., a critic. Still, I can't believe you think I should apologize to him for my "surly tone," as you put it, and that I should make a big effort to mend fences. "Given that Oliver Black practically saved your Uncle's life," you write – and that's a colossal overstatement, but anyway – "I think that buying him a cup of coffee isn't too much to ask." Oh, hello! Are you in there, Mom? When we talk on the phone, do you ever actually wear your hearing aid? With a battery in it? Switched on? In the correct orifice?

When you read my e-mails, do you ever think to actually wear those enormous reading glasses? You know, the ones for your bad eye that make you look exactly like a Borg with a couple of balloons shoved down the front of a flower-print dress? Then you may have noticed that I can't stand Oliver Black. I *hate* him, Mom! Why can't you understand this simple concept? Oliver Black is a stuffy, puffed-up, chain-thinking killjoy, and right about now I'd like to rip the boards right out of the fence and beat him senseless with them, rather than mend the bloody thing.

But, all right. Fine. I'll ask Oliver Black out, just for you, and certainly not because I have any sinister plans of my own. Maybe I'll invite him to La Jonquille and drop three hundred bucks on a meal so tender and delicate you could chew it with your eyelashes. Or maybe I should take Uncle Bill's Number One Fan to the Burger and Bun, since it would be so much more meaningful to surprise him with food that, though less elaborate, is infinitely more chewy.

Your little guy,

Waif Wilde

From: rafe.wilde@thedawnpost.com
To: oliver.black@thedawnpost.com
Subject: Repentance

Dear Oliver:

I deserve to have a humble cream pie thrown in my face, to eat crow until I puke my guts out, to be thrown face-down into the mud and backed over again and again by a semi filled to overflowing with a load of your weighty opinions. I can't believe how wrong I've been about everything! You were right about my uncle's café, my review of the Cage concert, Angel, even my microscopic balls. *I* can't even find them half the time, and the other half I'm not looking. I'm just sorry it's taken me this long to fully understand the depth of my incomprehension, but in my defence, I'm a bit of an idiot.

So, would you care to have dinner with me sometime? Maybe somewhere that serves crow stew and humble-berry pie for dessert?

Your lowly servant,

Rafe

PS: Hey, how are Angel and Selwyn anyway? I just hope they're so happy.

From: oliver.black@thedawnpost.com
To: rafe.wilde@thedawnpost.com
Subject: "Tell me what you like, I'll tell you what you are."
              —Ruskin

Dear Rafe:

Don't be absurd! After all, it took the Pope three hundred years to pardon Galileo, to admit, finally, that the great scientist had been right all along and that he himself had been a complete ass. That it took you a mere month to acknowledge a similar situation is a credit to you. Rest assured that I accept your apology and know this: that the review I wrote for you was *not* intended to be a mockery; it was carefully crafted to attract the maximum amount of attention to your uncle's diner, which as you readily admit, it has done. (I have to say, however, that it's difficult for me to forget your description of my poem "O Humble Bunwich!" as "utterly moronic." I admit it's not as fine a poem as "The Lady of Shallots," or "Shall I Compare Thee to a Cheese Soufflé," or even the semierotic "Slather My Bun," which is loosely based on what I once naïvely understood to be an early example of gustatory verse – John Donne's fine poem "Batter My Heart;" nevertheless, it is a decent example of the genre in which I am something of an expert. But never mind.) Perhaps I was a little harsh in my criticism of your review of the John Cage concert – it was, after all, your first time at bat. That you swung with impudence and wild abandon, and succeeded only in clubbing yourself over the head with it, is not unexpected or unforgivable, nor is it sufficient reason to dismiss you entirely from the team – provided that you are taking steps to make sure that a revolting abortion such as that Cage review never appears in print again.

To that end, have you contacted Ms. Savage yet? Trust me, my boy, you need that woman as much as you need food and shelter, because without her you'll soon find you don't have either. Gabriella Savage will be your salvation! It is she who is the great shifter of paradigms, and believe me, Dear Rafe, you sorely need your paradigms shifted – either that or blown up and replaced entirely. I do not mean to say that the best of popular music is not worthy of attention, even reverence – for surely the greatest popular music ought to be classified with the greatest music on Earth, regardless of genre. However, a steady diet of it is not only addictive but, quite simply, corrupting. All your life you've devoted yourself to that great workhorse, the Popular Song (not to be confused with the Advertising Jingle, though they are often identical) with its three chords, its four beats to the bar, its predictable form (verse, chorus, verse, chorus, instrumental solo, chorus – or some slight and insignificant variation), its backup singers and their doo-wop doo-wops and their hey nonny nonnies. And just look at you! Because of the popular song you now have an attention span of exactly three minutes and twenty-eight seconds. A piece of music without a back beat startles you and leaves you feeling confused and agitated. Five beats to the bar makes you weep. The prescribed electric guitar or saxophone solo is essential in every piece – without it, you feel as if you are in a vast and hostile wilderness, a musical no man's land, orphaned and utterly alone. You've become an unabashed cultural philistine, Rafe, which is only to be expected after a lifetime of living safely within the bounds of unyielding tonality, of rhythmic regularity, of metrical predictability, of structural invariability, of rigid cultural conformity. Brevity, simplicity, familiarity, repetition! These are the mighty concepts that have spawned two of the most colossal and successful industries of our time, two titans which are far more alike than different – the fast food industry, with its burgers and shakes, and the music industry, with its ballads and bellyaches. These are the quintessential lowest common denominator industries, devoted to telling us what we want and, therefore, what we value (brevity, simplicity, familiarity, repetition), reminding us at every opportunity what it is that we want and then, happily, almost miraculously, giving us precisely what we want! But lift the veil – and you must yank it aside quickly and catch a glimpse before anything skitters away – and what will you find behind it? Behind the veil of popular music, as behind the veil of the fast food industry, what you will find is one thing, and one thing only: the boardroom of a marketing department.

And to think that it is the young with their popular music who believe they are staging some grand insurrection! Such little rebellions! How amusing it is to see groups of young people, mostly males I'm afraid, still forming rock and roll bands and jumping about upon a stage in front of their peers exactly as their fathers *and grandfathers* did before them! Can you imagine young people of the 1960s behaving exactly as their forebears did in the 1920s? And yet this is precisely the situation in which we find ourselves in modern times! It is quite fantastic to think that what was considered to be cool, to be hip, to be daring and seditious forty years ago is still considered to be all these things today! And yet popular music continues to be so paradoxically tame! Do you want *real* musical rebellion, defiance, even violence? You won't find it in the world of conventional rock and roll, I'm sorry to say, given that most rock bands are little more than corporations that specialize in the manufacture of a homogenous product whose function is to elicit pleasant herd responses. You see, Rafe, you've been at the wrong party all these years; the *real* party with the musical risk-takers, the experimenters, the gamblers – the actual interesting people – is somewhere else entirely. Forget about all those prepackaged, ready-to-assemble bands that come as a kit! Forget about these old-time rock and rollers and their never-ending Medical Mystery Tours (I read that Keith Richards is now 95 percent dermawax – true?). Forget about heavy metal, grunge, glitter, hip hop, disco, reggae, punk – and by all means abandon rap, for it is surely the rap musician who is the most hilarious of all; with his drum machine on one side and his rhyming diction-ary on the other, he's a sort of freakish cross between Mike Tyson and Dr Seuss. Elvis has left the building, Rafe, and you ought to leave too. Let the enchanting Gabriella guide you through the magic land of atonality, polytonality, pandiatonicism, indeterminacy, serialism – and once you acquire a basic understanding of the music of our time and have given it a fair chance (by listening to each new work at least six times, no less) only then will you be prepared to do the job for which *The Dawn Post* is so handsomely rewarding you.

But enough watertight, unimpeachable, ex cathedra insights about the world of music for one day! Let us turn our attention to the world of human relations for a moment and allow me to tell you that I thought it so very kind of you, so expansive – so unexpected – to ask after Selwyn and Angel. For the longest time I knew not myself how they were, given that they seemed to be aiming at carving out a spot for themselves in the *Guinness Book of World Records*, or perhaps making a scientific attempt at per-manent tissue fusion through continual contact, or proving that it was possible to create (in actual fact, to *be*) a perpetual motion machine. Perhaps they're stuck, I kept thinking, as happens sometimes in the animal kingdom, and I wondered if I ought to break into Selwyn's room and throw a bucket of cold water over them. But even if they are stuck, I thought to myself, they might not thank me for it. Why should it be up to me anyway? I thought. Why do I always have to solve the world's problems? Let them figure it out for once.

Eventually Selwyn emerged from his chamber looking for all the world like Theseus after a tough week of conquering Amazons: both exhausted and deliriously happy. How ecstatic my boy was – ecstatic being from the Latin "ex" (out of) and "static" (to stand), meaning to stand erect out of one's own body and, in this case, to be erect in someone else's. Selwyn was in bed day in and day out cavorting with his enchanting mistress, oblivious to events on the world stage, rarely even coming up for air it seems. How happy he was when Angel agreed to live with him in his hamster-cage of a room, and to cleave to him between the sheets of his boyhood bed! (Which they gleefully wore out, by the way – you wouldn't happen to know the name of a reputable bed company, would you?)

Aye me. Life so rarely turns out as we expect, don't you find, Mr. Wilde? Sadly, the whole thing underwent a catastrophic collapse; after staring at Angel's perfect breasts unremittingly for days on end, Selwyn suddenly came down with an acute case of Stendhal's Syndrome from which he has not yet recovered. He's no good to Angel anymore; mostly he just lies around in bed staring cross-eyed at the ceiling, muttering, "It's too good, it's too good," and looking indecently happy, the poor boy. In the meantime, Merlin is filling in for him since, as Selwyn informed me previously, the girl has no "off" switch, though he diligently searched every inch of her body looking for it. It's been about a week since I've seen Merlin, actually – I believe he's in his room and, from the sounds of it, Angel is too. Such a racket! Relentless banging day and night. Have they never heard of putting a pillow behind the headboard? Must we all be subjected to Merlin's thump thump thumping as he plows mercilessly into his insatiable tigress accompanied by Angel's periodic cries for divine intervention ("Oh God, oh God!")? Surely they can't keep it up much longer, which is what I told Damien and which is why you will now find him posted outside Merlin's door "just waiting in line," as he put it.

Ah, my dear Rafe. It's a funny old life, isn't it? I'm just glad that a man of your age and maturity can see that, as far as Angel is concerned, he's well out of it. This excessive copulation – orgasm after orgasm after orgasm – is nothing more than Mother Nature's way of tricking the young and fit into reproducing the species. Sex is merely the veil! The naked woman is the great illusion – the booby trap, if you will. I try to tell my boys this, but they won't listen. They see as through a glass darkly and thus give not the slightest toss about Mother Nature's point of view. Sadly, they have rejected my sage advice, so don't expect to find them composing bleeding-edge tunes with titles such as "I Naturally Select You," "Pleased Gamete You," or "My DNA All the Way." Ah well. We'll just let them go on believing that they have some sort of choice in the matter, that they are imbued with free will, and we'll rely on Mother Nature to take care of the rest. She'll get them in the end; she always does.

And finally – yes, my dear old friend, let's make up, shall we? Let us break bread together, and I don't mean by jousting with baguettes either. Just name the restaurant and I shall be there with bells on! Well, not only bells. I wouldn't want to cause a stampede.

Sincerely,

Oliver Black

PS: My daughter Olivia, who as you know runs her own animal rescue service, has recently rescued a parrot whom we believe might be yours. He's a curious little thing, forever autistically rocking on his little swing and uttering only one sentence, over and over. "Rafe is an idiot. Rafe is an idiot. Rafe is an idiot." Any ideas?

From: rafe.wilde@thedawnpost.com
To: alma.wilde@command.net
Subject: Waving the White Flag

Dear Mom,

Oh God, help me! Give me air! Give me air! Oliver Black just tried to asphyxiate me again with another one of his imperious, bombastic, maximalist e-mails! The man is a monster, Mom, a madman, a nutcase – he's the sort of psychopath who attempts to render his victims senseless by hitting them with a barrage of deranged observations, ever shovelling upon them his ponderous convictions, suffocating them under the weight of his demented ruminations. The man is a total sicko! Reading his e-mails is like being trapped in a fucking Edgar Allan Poe story – like being chained to a wall in his basement as he bricks you up behind a solid wall of his own opinions. And you should hear what he has to say about popular music! It's a desecration, Mom! The man hasn't got a clue about what makes rock and roll great! The power, the energy, the texture, the volume, the girls, the leather – oh, don't get me started!

So, I've asked him out for dinner. That's right. Just for you, Mom, to get you to stop whining and hitting me with lines like, "Don't make me come over there," but mostly because you still have Nurse Chapel hostage, and I don't want her shaved and severed head to arrive with your next care package.

And, because spending an evening with Oliver Black probably isn't quite enough tedium and irritation to actually stop the flow of blood to my heart, and because I can't take both you *and* Oliver Black hassling me about it anymore, I finally called Ms. Savage today and arranged to take modern music history lessons from her.

Hearing her voice was like hearing a thousand nails on a thousand blackboards.

My first new music lesson is next Friday.

Your little guy,

Rafe

Chapter Six

From: oliver.black@thedawnpost.com
To: selwyn.black@freenet.org
Subject: Tsk Tsk

Feast of the Amazing Randi

Hello Selwyn:

It is not enough that you have pierced your own scrotum (and it is with every ounce of my might that I prevent myself from projectile vomiting at the very thought of it), but now I find that you have also, perhaps unwittingly, pierced my heart. I had predicted that all of these bodily mutilations would end in various septic infections leading to multiple amputations so that you would eventually end your life as a torso, able only to find work propped up in front of doorways as a draft-stopper or as a poster boy for the War Amps, but I see now that the effects are far worse than I had at first thought. Who could have imagined that the end result of punching all those holes in your body would be that your brains would slowly ooze out of them?

Consider the evidence: yesterday evening as you sat in the kitchen with your roguish chums, huddled around a pot of baked beans simmering on the stove and strumming your guitars like cowboys around a campfire, I happened, by chance, to overhear your conversation in its entirety. (I don't make a habit of eavesdropping, by the way; however, a father must have uncommon hearing.) Your discussion of music, sports, vehicles, and young women was predictable if slightly fantastic, given that much of what you described is impossible unless you and your beloved happen to be contortionists in zero gravity. But no matter; the point is that I was stunned by the direction the conversation took after that horrible boy with the dreadlocks, dressed from head to foot in some sort of handmade hemp monstrosity (not Merlin – the other lily white Rastaman), pulled from his saddle bags one of those dreadful supermarket tabloids and read the imaginative headline "Hunters Shoot Cherub," complete with a doctored (we may assume) photograph of a woman dressed as an angel, in a costume evidently borrowed from a kindergarten Nativity pageant, lying face down in a puddle. This seemed to me like just a bit of jolly fun until the gullible youth dared to suggest that there are stranger things in heaven and earth (my words) and that, therefore, it was not impossible that the photograph was authentic and that the journalist who had penned the article had done so without malice or prevarication. Perhaps the writer had even stumbled across a conspiracy of silence regarding the supernatural, the dim youth suggested, presenting the alleged evidence, gleaned from the same tabloid and undoubtedly written by a team of humorists in top form, while you and your friends sat dumbly without offering any resistance to this onslaught of irrationality. And then my disbelieving ears heard my very own son, bone of my bone, flesh of my flesh, say, "Yeah, I guess there might be something to it." Ah! My heart!

How can this be, Selwyn? Does the ice water of skepticism not flow through your veins as it does my own? Did you not spend hours as a baby poring over your copy of *Introduction to Critical Thinking*, specially made with those puffy plastic pages that squeak so that you could also chew on it philosophically and snuggle it in the bath? Did you not sit at my knee as a mere tot and recite carefully chosen selections from the writings of Bertrand Russell? I have tried always to steer you away from harmful superstitions and irrational ideas, to prevent the formation of debilitating mental scotoma; in fact, any hint of wayward thinking in you boys has always been treated like a cold coming on, the cure being to dose the infected subject with a powerful antimemetic. The great atheist philosophers, the skeptics and debunkers, are particularly good in this regard; how often I have prescribed two pages to be downed before bed with the transparent and uncontaminated waters of eternal vigilance. And when the philosophers themselves seemed to be unable to reach you with their austere, unornamented words, I called upon the philosopher-poets to shake you to the depths and rid you of harmful, parasitic memes. "I accept Reality and dare not question it," writes the admittedly inconsistent Whitman. "Materialism first and last imbuing. / Hurrah for positive science! long live exact demonstration!" Not to mention the many fine philosophical verses I wrote myself for your edification, there being an inexplicable lack of such poetry in children's literature. Do you recall this one?

> Believing in Santa, his reindeer and sleigh,
> Means an empty stocking on Christmas day.
> But to doubting, disbelieving boys,
> Santa brings sweets and treats and toys.

This short verse kept you paralysed by indecision for months – should you send your Christmas list to the North Pole or not? How well I recall you racing to your mother in tears, waving the offending document like a flag of surrender; and how well I recall also the subsequent lump of coal I found in my own stocking on Christmas morn. Ah well. Your mother, a skilled critical thinker in her own right, always frowned upon my attempts to create topnotch philosophers still in diapers. "Boys should *not* be expected to recite selected passages from the works of Aristotle if they first have to spit their soothers out to do it," she would gently chide as she whisked away your child-friendly copies of *The Nichomachean Ethics* (lovingly handmade and bound by myself, with charming illustrations of woodland animals, each with a speech bubble reciting the words of Aristotle – naturally translated into English for ease of understanding by the preschool set). But why should a responsible father not pass his values on to the young as soon as the young can, let's say, sit without support? The practice of "getting 'em while they're young" is the modus operandi of most religions, after all, and while mobs of somnambulant children stumble through recitations of the Ten Commandments, why should it be any more remarkable that others recite,

for example, the Top Ten Logical Fallacies? Is this any less useful
for the aspiring tot? I know it isn't, for how often I myself, as a
child, invoked the fallacy of *ignoratio elenchi* in order to counter
my mother's claims that, for instance, millions of people were
starving in Africa, and it was therefore my moral duty to eat her
sinister smoked tongue. "So send it to Africa, then!" I remember
suggesting emphatically, offering to wrap the hideous, rubbery,
spotted thing in brown paper myself, address it "To Occupant,"
and send it by post to Africa where, according to my mother,
children would dance with delight around a lovely little scrap of
tongue after the usual cheerless diet of accidental roots and watery gruel. Admittedly, my appeal to reason was often unsuccessful because my mother detested cleverness in the young and also
had a fixation with Crime and Punishment – not the book but,
rather, the actual detection and administration – and given that
she also acted as judge and jury in cases involving me, the accused
willful child, I usually had the despicable tongue shoved down my
throat regardless. (Not that the Ten Commandments would have
done me any good either, having absolutely nothing to offer in
my defence – all that advice about coveting, killing, theft, adultery
and so on was irrelevant, and the injunction to honour thy mother
was deliberately destructive to my case.) But the rich resource of
cool-headed, uncompromising logic was useful often enough that
it was worth having a solid grasp of the weapons of reason – deduction, induction, and all manner of premises, conclusions, and
the relationship between them – and, of course, the fallacies, to
which I contributed by inventing a few of my own. I found particularly useful the *argumentum ad maternum*, an umbrella term
that included all other commonly known fallacies, especially the
argumentum ad misericordium, which my mother employed with
all the expertise of a grieving Sicilian widow.

But look at where we are now, eh, Selwyn old boy. "There
might be something to it," he says. Oh dear, oh dear. Look sharp,
Son, and lift the veil. And consider the source, Selwyn, always
consider the source! One must be especially cautious of ideas that

arrive via flabby-minded tabloid readers, of whom I am reminded every hour, on the hour, by the clock I keep in my study. Cuckoo! Cuckoo! I recommend such a device to provide insightful editorial comment on the current state of the world and those who inhabit it. In thirty years of service, mine has yet to be in error.)

Trust your senses, Boy, and their technological extensions – and trust in reason as the honest broker, because the senses can, admittedly, be deceived. Demand evidence, and don't be taken in by those who claim you've not got the proper apparatus to perceive the supernatural. It may be true, of course, but it's also the oldest trick in the book, providing a convenient defence for anyone who might want to place himself in a position of power and advantage. There's no way for the unbeliever to argue the case, except to assert that he doesn't believe in the mysterious sense under question, given that there's no evidence for it, except an intuitive feeling of its existence in the mind of the believer – at which point the discussion degenerates into unproductive assertion and counter-assertion. How one tires of the "I know something you don't know" stance! Just show me, for heaven's sake. Show me the evidence and let's be done with it! Stop levitating in private! Quit forever suspending the laws of physics *behind* closed doors! Channel the spirits but forbid the usual dull platitudes – let them speak truths yet unknown and unknowable! Let us make water into wine and base metals into gold, but let it be done in the lab! Why hoard all the magic? Is scientific demonstration really too much to ask? And please, by all means, bring them to dinner – your shy angels, your timid powers and principalities, your bashful ghosts, your skittish aliens, your quivering succubus and incubus, your quailing Loch Ness Monster, your chicken-hearted Bigfoot – and let us put an end once and for all to this childish, melodramatic hocus pocus. Thus ends today's lesson. In the event that none of the above has moved you to a renewed commitment to sanity, let me at the very least offer some practical advice:

If there's a Cherub in a puddle,
Get not your noodle in a muddle.
Don't gawk and pray, nor spit and scoff,
Just help her up and dry her off.

With dogmatic nondogmatism (arf, arf),

Dad

From: oliver.black@thedawnpost.com
To: lucy.black@artnet.org
Subject: Greek to Me

Dearest Lucy:

I just finished composing a rather lengthy tract on the subject of Angelology and so, naturally, my thoughts turn to you, my dearest angel. I did so want to tell you about my evening out yesterday with Mr. Rafe Wilde, and to explain why I arrived home in the wee hours of the morning reeking of olive oil, retsina, and cheap perfume. I would have offered up an explanation upon my arrival home, but was surprised to find that you yourself were not *chez nous* and that, instead of your mother, you had put one of the boys in charge of babysitting Olivia. Forgive me for questioning your actions, my darling, but do you really think this is wise? You remember the last time the boys were put in charge of their sister, and we discovered only the next day that there had been a raucous bacchanalia in our absence, and that little Olivia had been put in charge of mixing drinks. Should an eight-year-old know how to assemble the perfect Manhattan, I wonder? Probably, yes, but I'm not sure the authorities at Child Welfare would agree. Nevertheless, all was peaceful when I arrived home last night, and I only wonder where you were, my treasure, and why you came home an hour after me smelling not of olive oil, retsina, and cheap perfume but, rather, of oil paints, turpentine, and a perfume of an unfamiliar vintage.

But never mind that now. I absolutely must tell you about my extraordinary dinner with Mr. Rafe Wilde (a man for whom we should spare a kind thought, Lucille, since he's sure to awaken this morning with the proverbial pickaxe in his skull and an agitator in his stomach). Since I'd been wanting to write a review of that new Greek restaurant, The Pythagorean Pub and Grill, I suggested to Mr. Wilde that we combine business with pleasure and dine there. Do you remember me telling you about it, love? It's an outlandish and high-spirited sort of a place, run by university students, and it caters to the rules laid out by Pythagoras for the running of the religious order he established. For the most part, these rules are a bunch of fatuous "Thou Shalt Nots" that make one wish Pythagoras had stuck to his triangles, as they include commandments such as: never pick up that which has fallen, never step over a crossbar, never stir the fire with iron, never touch a white cock, never pluck a garland, never sit on a quart measure, never break bread, never eat from a whole loaf, never eat the heart, never walk on highways, and the most famous injunction of all – never, under any circumstances, eat beans. One wonders what Pythagoras thought would happen to those who panted after the dreaded bean – perhaps soular wind. At any rate, these rules are posted outside the pub, and patrons are supposed to agree good-naturedly to follow them in order to keep up the spirit of the place, though I must say that Mr. Wilde never quite caught on, despite encyclopaedic instruction.

Upon entering the pub I immediately spotted Mr. Wilde sitting by the window at a table shaped like a triangle. All of the tables are triangular, by the way, which I discovered is the worst shape possible for a table since, as a consequence, one is always seated too close to one's companion but never actually facing him, and this makes conversation frightfully awkward, whether or not one happens to be seated along the hypotenuse. Mr. Wilde stood up to greet me, and after shaking hands I opened the conversation by asking if he was short one parrot. He practically tripped over his tongue, adamantly denying any knowledge whatsoever. "I don't know anything about Petey!" he exclaimed. I merely raised an eyebrow as we sat down together (avoiding the quart measures placed nearby to tempt us), and a spotty youth identical to the one at that revolting adult video store approached our table. (Are they everywhere?)

"Hi," he said, pulling out a pad of paper and a pen from the pockets of his apron. "My name is Isosceles. I'll be your waiter this evening."

Isosceles indeed. Upon hearing his ill-modulated, adolescent voice, I knew for a fact that it was young Fabio from Zippers but decided, due to the inauspicious circumstances of our first meeting, to keep silent. Before settling in, I excused myself in order to fulfill the custom of some traditional Greek restaurants where one inspects the dishes available right from the kitchen and orders directly from the chef. Sadly, by the time I returned to our table, Mr. Wilde was already downing glasses of ouzo as if downing pints of beer, no one having explained to him that ouzo is about 40 percent alcohol and ought to be sipped slowly, watering it down as the evening progresses, and eating generous quantities of mezedes in order to ameliorate the effects of the alcohol. "Steady on!" I urged, but I think my warning came too late because Mr. Wilde was already acting strangely and, if the truth be told, downright shiftily. Honestly, Lucy, it was not so much like a meeting between friends as it was like a job interview for a spy agency. Did I have a criminal record? Had I ever committed what I perceived to be the perfect crime, and could I supply details? Did I love my wife? Had I ever paid for sexual favours? From someone other than my wife? Honestly, the questions were preposterous, Lucille, and each time I tried to change the subject, Mr. Wilde would find some way to bring the topic back to some abhorrent indiscretion or other. Our conversation went something like this:

"And so there I was in Mexico, on holiday with my wife –"

"Your first wife?"

"My *only* wife."

"Are you sure it was your wife? Not some bean-eating, cross-bar stepping, loaf-gnawing tart?"

"I think I know my own wife, man!"

"Not your mistress? Maybe a heart-devouring highway walker? And I think you know what I'm saying here, Oliver."

"I haven't a clue what you're saying. What mistress?"

"You mean you've got more than one?"

"Of course I haven't got more than one!"

"So you admit to having one? A garland-plucking, bread-breaking chippy? Eh?"

"No!"

"No? Okay then, Oliver. I'll buy it. But what about sheep? Do you like sheep? Maybe a sheep who likes to eat a bean now and then, if you see what I mean."

"Dear God! Are you mad?"

"Just asking. Baa. Baa. Bring back any memories?"

"Barking mad."

"It's dogs then, is it? You like dogs, do you? The kind of dog who's not shy about sitting on a quart measure, eh Ollie?"

And so on. His dipsomaniacal fascination with deviant behaviour knew no bounds. It was tiresome and silly, and more than once I tried to order a smoking cup of hemlock, either for him or for myself, I cared not for whom. Still, I believe I managed to churn out an adequate review. Did you read it perchance? I praised the Empedocles Special, which was simply the classic Patate al Forno, which are potatoes roasted much like "Empedocles, that ardent soul" who "leapt into Etna and was roasted whole," as the poet tells us. Rafe Wilde ordered an entire, oddly carved chicken on what the menu explained was "a Procrustean bed of lettuce." ("What the hell's that?" Mr. Wilde asked incisively, and as I explained that a Procrustean bed is one that requires the individual to be stretched or to have bits lopped off so that he will fit into the bed properly, a sort of faraway look came over his face – talk of Procrustean beds seemed to have some sort of deep meaning for him, God knows why – he even muttered something amusing about knowing a fellow named Procrustes who apparently works at a bed shop.) I myself ordered the Plate O' Plato, a medley of classic Greek fare, and I was particularly effusive about the moussaka, which seemed only to be enhanced by a near-fatal overdose of cinnamon – one gets the feeling that the chef was carelessly measuring the cinnamon over the moussaka itself when the lid suddenly popped off and the entire contents plunged into the bowl in an explosion of reddish-brown dust; I imagine him weeping at his spill like the captain of the Exxon Valdez and recovering his spirits only upon tasting his marvellous invention.

At any rate the evening progressed, and as Rafe continued to drink ouzo like retsina and retsina like water, he became increasingly blotto and quite overcome by *Kefi* – that untranslatable Greek feeling of happiness that causes one to radiate goodwill, to dance, to sing, and essentially, to act like an unbridled imbecile. "I love you, Oliver man," he professed again and again. "You're like a father to me, man, even though all you ever do is kibitz. Kibitz, kibitz, kibitz." Not a very flattering portrait, I admit (I would hardly describe my insightful instruction as kibitzing); nevertheless I was interested to know his true feelings for me, which confirmed the fatherly feelings I have always had toward him. However, after a couple of hours of Rafe's genial effusing, I had had quite enough, and so I asked young Isosceles to bring the cheque, at the top of which was written Pythagoras's famous saying "All things are numbers." (Ah, so true! All things *are* numbers – so make with the drachmas.) Pythagoras also believed that the body and soul can be in two separate places at once. Certainly Rafe Wilde came apart, and Isosceles and I had a terrific time carrying him out of the pub, especially given the injunction not to pick up that which has fallen (down drunk). We managed to wrestle him into my car, and after getting his address off some ID in his wallet (when asked, he kept insisting that he lived in hell), I drove him home and then manhandled him up a flight of stairs and into his apartment.

What a terrible shock I received upon opening the door and lugging him in! I'm afraid Mr. Wilde was callously forgotten (I temporarily draped him around a coatrack) as I quickly surveyed his astonishing flat. I had expected it to be a typical bachelor pad, a sort of habitable Burger and Bun in the style of Billy-Bob. Instead I found tastefully decorated rooms that appeared to be so beautifully organized, clean, and sterile, it was easy to believe that I had stumbled into a wholesome French maid fantasy. The bed was made. Pillows fluffed. Food alphabetized in cupboards. Towels and sheets neatly folded and stacked logically in the linen closet. Not a speck of dust on the top of doorframes. Windows spotless. Birdcage immaculate. (Ha! The truth will out!) At first I thought I must have had the wrong apartment until I noticed a framed letter above the bathroom mirror, addressed to Mr. Wilde himself, extolling in detail his virtues as a lover (dated several years ago and signed by some lovesick girl named Suzanne, although I expect it was actually written by Mr. Wilde himself – we know he is not above such petty deception). The point is, Lucy, that we absolutely must get the name of his genius cleaning lady; she's an absolute marvel, and I would love to set her loose on the boy's rooms, cruel as that may be. (Perhaps she might be able to answer the question that has plagued us for so long – what's under all the muck? Did we install a sort of yellowish-brown carpet in their bedrooms? Or is it, as I fear, a slick of banana peels?)

After forcing Mr. Wilde to drink large amounts of liquid (to little end, I expect, since he drank ouzo like a man on a quest for the ultimate Katzenjammer), I got him into his flannel nightshirt, charged through the nightly routine as one would with Olivia, and then tucked him up in his bed – a bed that was by far the most extraordinary thing about his entire abode. It's a sort of gurney affair piled high with feather ticks – imagine what the princess troubled by the pea would have slept on should she have found herself in hospital. I elevated his head slightly, put a glass of orange juice, a little hair of the dog, and two pain killers on the tray, adjusted the bumper guards, put up the rails, and left him to his slumber. Mind you, seeing the empty birdcage on the way out filled me with pity, and so I quickly drove home and returned with Petey, who is again ensconced in what is obviously his rightful home. Rafe will be delighted, I'm sure.

So, that explains why I was so late coming home yesterday evening. Ah, it doesn't explain the cheap perfume, of course, but perhaps you have already guessed that it was Rafe Wilde's pungent cologne. Perhaps you would like, in turn, to favour me with a description of your own exploits of yesterday evening. I am all ears. Or, if you care to write, all eyes. In any case, I am all yours.

Love,

Oliver

PS: Oh, yes, one other thing. Branksome sends you his love all the way from the Strait of Belle Isle, where he appears to be taking a little holiday, whiling away the hours on a cruise ship whilst indulging his artistic nature. Though he's not an artist of your rank, my dearest, he always did like to paint, and it would appear that he has finally found the perfect medium.

PPS: And yet another thing. How could I have forgotten to mention it? I have secured a meeting with Angel's mother – at high noon tomorrow – and would obviously greatly value your presence. Can you arrange to be there on such short notice?

From: rafe.wilde@thedawnpost.com
To: suzanne@heartmail.com
Subject: Rafe Is an Idiot. Rafe Is an Idiot. Rafe Is an
              Idiot.

Dear Suzanne:

Sssssshhhhh! Do you mind? Just the sound of your eyeballs scanning this e-mail is ear-splitting at the moment. And I've banished Petey to the closet because I can't take his incessant yammering. (Petey. *Petey?* How the fuck did *Petey* get here?) I don't know what happened to me last night, but I have a feeling it involves an ancient Egyptian embalmer, my brain, and that tool they use to scoop it out through your nose. Holy headache, Batgirl! And how is it that I remember *almost nothing* about what happened last night? One moment I'm happily drinking what feels like velvet and tastes like liquid licorice – and the next thing you know I'm having my teeth brushed and flossed, my neck vigorously scrubbed, I'm in my underwear with my arms up like a toddler so my nightshirt can be put over my head (my kat'z pajamas?), the covers tucked up under my chin, and I'm listening to a bedtime story (*The Princess and the Pea*, if memory serves) told to me by Oliver Black.

Oliver Black. Oh God, Suzanne. Oh God. Oliver Black flossed my teeth. What kind of insane nightmare is that? How could I let my greatest enemy, my nemesis, my personal Lex Luthor – how could I let him wash behind my ears, for God's sake? What kind of a man finds himself standing happily in his underwear in front of his archenemy and then lets him tuck him into bed and sing him a lullaby? A lullaby! Christ almighty, that thing gave me nightmares – I spent the whole night trying to stop the wind from blowing my cradle right out of the fucking treetop. And if I wasn't plagued by the sound of boughs breaking, it was the damn bed bugs biting, or the sandman throwing dust in my face, or that psychotic Wynken, Blynken, and Nod trying to force me at knife-point into their fucking sky-sailing, wooden shoe-boat. Oh God, Suzanne. Oh God. How could I have let this happen? It couldn't have been my fault – somebody must have slipped something into my drink. Either that or *I* slipped into my drink, face first, and stayed there until I was so tanked I probably should have been thrown *in* the tank with those two fish – you know, the ones from that old joke who, when they find themselves together in a tank, one says to the other, "Do you know how to drive this thing?" Oh God, I'm rambling I know, but if I stop writing I'll start thinking, and I just can't bear the thought of Oliver Black buttoning up my nightshirt, fluffing my pillows, and reciting *Good Night, Moon* to me – especially *Good Night, Moon* with its comb and brush and, at least for me, that hugely upsetting bowl full of mush. (What *is* mush? And why the hell do they keep it on the night table? They've already got mice, for Christ's sake.) Oh God, Suzanne. Just tell me how 007 would have felt if Goldfinger had tucked *him* into bed with *his* Blankie. It doesn't do a whole lot for your manhood, let me tell you. Why didn't he just dress me in a tutu and make me sing "On the Good Ship Lollipop" while he was at it? That would have been too manly, I guess – it's far more humiliating to beg your nemesis to rub your back while reciting "Goosey Goosey Gander," believe me.

My first mistake was letting Oliver Black choose the restaurant (as if a food critic would have a clue), and he suggested that we go to this weird new Greek pub where the only good thing were the tables, all of which were triangular for some incomprehensible reason – which meant, at least, that I never had to look Oliver Black directly in the eye. The worst thing, though, was all of these asinine rules about avoiding beans, and crossbars, and bread, and highways, and hearts, and quart measures, and it was just so stupid and Oliver was so uptight about following every rule to the letter that I couldn't help goading him mercilessly – all the while trying to subtly wrangle information out of him about past indiscretions, of course. Our conversation went something like this:

"So there I was, Oliver, eating jelly beans . . ."

"No! Not beans!"

"And bread from a whole loaf . . ."

"What?"

"Which I was breaking off in pieces . . ."

"Ah!"

"While walking on a highway . . ."

"Surely not, Rafe!"

"When I stepped over a crossbar . . ."

"Please, no!"

"And came across a white cock . . ."

"SSSHHHHH!"

"Ever touched a white cock, Oliver?"

"Dear God! You mean a rooster?"

"Ah, no. I don't mean a rooster."

"Thank goodness! That's all right then."

"So you have, eh? Was it your own 'rooster' or someone else's? Hmm?"

Anyway, Oliver got increasingly pissed off, and I got increasingly pissed, and that's how the evening went until I found myself kneeling by my bedside, hands folded, and praying to Charles Darwin with Oliver Black. ("Bless the primordial slime that became the vertebrate that became the Neanderthal that became me.") Oh God, oh God, oh God! And I didn't even get anything on the guy, Suzanne, not a thing. There's more dirt in a vestal virgin's underpants than on Oliver Black. There's no law he's ever broken, no charity to which he doesn't contribute – there's no infidelity, no controversy, no enemies, not a whiff of dishonesty or scandal. He worships his wife, adores his kids, works hard at his job, pays his taxes – it would be inaccurate to say that it was like having dinner with Gandhi – it was more like having dinner with Gandhi's mentor, with the guy that Gandhi was always striving to be but just couldn't quite make it. He even kept insisting that I share the food right off his Plate O' Plato, especially this moussaka fantasy where the chef evidently had an accident with the cinnamon, but it only ended up tasting even more like spicy ground beef manna from heaven. I can just hear that booming voice of his urging me to indulge. "But I insist! I simply won't take no for an answer! You must try the Kreatopita, the Kalamarakia, the Sardeles, the Savridi! Eat and observe, Mr. Wilde. Eat and observe."

So I ate and observed, but mostly I drank and disgorged, heaved and hurled, and now I smell like something even the cat wouldn't drag in. My head is ringing off the hook. My stomach is a hydrochloric acid centrifuge. And my heart is a bombed-out smoking ruins, but that's not the fault of the drink, as well you know. Anyway, take my advice, Suzanne: Never step over a crossbar, sit on a quart measure, or pluck a garland, unless you want the DT's of a lifetime.

Spewingly yours,

Rafe

PS: So are you still getting married, or have you come to your senses? Hey, don't let the putrid stench of vomit fool you – I clean up well, as you know from experience.

From: oliver.black@thedawnpost.com
To: branksome.black@rebel.net
Subject: Ultima Thule

Feast of Paul Watson

Dearest Branksome:

What in the name of Neptune are you doing at sea, Bucko Me Lad? I told Lucy that you were living the life of a great painter and whiling away the hours on a cruise ship whilst indulging your artistic nature. Would this were so! That you are currently living on board the *Farley Mowat*, and leaving it only to totter precariously on ice floes whilst being shot at by the authorities, in order to spray paint furry white seal pups is, sadly, wholly misguided. Do I pay you to roam the seas? Do I pay you to prevent acts of savagery committed by human beings against the creatures of the ocean? No, Branksome, I do not. Don't misunderstand me; the seal hunt is devoid of the tiniest shred of Beauty, Liberty, and Truth, and that it perseveres to the present day is evidence of the stupidity of government, and the heartlessness of men. The seals must be harvested in order to restore the fisheries, they say, as if it's the *seals* who are responsible for the decimation of the fish stocks. Too right! And what about those flatulent cows who are the cause of global warming? And those clumsy elephants who knock over all the trees in our national parks? And those untidy racoons who strew about the litter we see on our urban streets? What a relief to know that it's not humans who are responsible for the collapse of the planet. It's the damned seals! Surely a pre-emptive first strike is in order; better to get them before they get us.

Nevertheless, Old Salt, you are thousands of nautical miles off track. Leave the life of the oceans to those intrepid defenders of Liberty who are the shepherds of the sea. The seals have their champions, Branksome, and a brave lot they are, willing to face incarceration and to risk life and limb, often over just a few silly fish. They are the incarnation of vigilant compassion, and my admiration for them, and for all who take action against those who cause unnecessary suffering for mere monetary gain, or even for no gain at all, is boundless. But, no, Branksome. It's time for you to leave the untamed world of nature and to come back to the savage world of human beings with their tin sheds and stinking cesspools and gruesome procedures. You know our mandate. You know that *here* is where our work lies.

And speaking of our work, I regret to say that I was forced to throw Wendell Mullet a bone in my last review. (Moussaka – ugh!) Congratulations, Brother, you finally figured out exactly why Mr. Mullet has been blackmailing me, but now threatening letters from him are arriving weekly, and at times I'm tempted to chuck the whole thing in, confess my deception, and simply throw my job overboard in order to put an end to the tyranny of that great ape. But how can I, Branksome? Funding our work is of utmost importance, in addition to which I have a family to support – five people who depend on me to provide all worldly goods and services, from apples to zwieback and everything in between. To let my family down is unthinkable, and has always been so. It is necessary that I continue to do the only thing for which I am qualified, and the one thing at which I can earn a living – I see no other possibility.

And what choice do I have but to finally take your advice and break into Lucy's studio in an attempt to discover her dark secret? She recently stayed out *almost all night*, Branksome, but when I invited her to tell me where she had been, she declined the invitation and pointed out that I didn't have a leg to stand on, given that I had arrived home not long before she did. This was grossly unfair, given that my work often keeps me occupied into the late evening (and thus has it been for the entire twenty-five years of our marriage), and she knew very well that I was with Mr. Stinko – a man so spifflicated by drink that if I'd not seen him home and directed him to his bedchamber, he would surely have kept downing ouzo, eventually drowning in ooze. No, directing the issue away from her behaviour was merely a ploy to avoid the *real* issue, which she is unable to confront; thus I've no choice but to force her hand.

Now, I know that you're really an old married man, Branksome, and that you've had many wives, some for as long as a week at a time. Still, I wonder if you can imagine what an agony this is to me, and if you fully realize just how wonderful a wife can be – especially a wife as talented and intelligent, as spirited and sensual, as my own Lucille. Have you any idea what it's like to live with a true artist, Branksome? Lucy's creations are everywhere – sculptures, paintings, furniture – as well as the children's art for which Lucy has crafted frames – and all arranged in a manner that is engaging and pleasing to the eye. I've never once been at a loss for something interesting and absorbing to look at. How wonderful to live with a woman whose godlike talent is creation, and not just shopping and then arranging various mass-produced purchases in order to create an environment as predictable and sterile as a furniture show room, in a house devoid of memories and empty of content.

Simply put, I want my wife back, Branksome.

Anyway, Brother, I shall end this missive, as is my wont, with news of the children. Olivia's pianistic prowess continues to astonish, although if her life was represented by a pie chart, the biggest slice would be all paws and whiskers. "There are two means of refuge from the miseries of life," says Albert Schweitzer. "Music – and cats," and my Olivia couldn't agree more. The domestic cat is the dominating theme of her life, and her attitude toward them continues to be positively Egyptian. Though I remain devoted to my Amelia (who has finally mastered the perfect landing and now spends much of her time draped around my shoulders like a boa), it is Queen Noor who is Olivia's particular favourite, and when I find her sitting in my favourite chair, I am always careful to bow low before her, put my hand over my heart, and cry, "Your Majesty!" before I respectfully toss her off. The boys are also well, and why should they not be given that they are as well fed as visiting royalty from Hungry. If only bananas were self-peeling, life would be perfect. (Ah, there's an invention for some mad food scientist – add to it carrots that can be plugged directly into electrical outlets for quick cooking.) Mind you, we had a bit of philosophical trouble with Selwyn; it seems that schooling our sons firmly in tolerance and broad-mindedness has unwittingly created a climate of credulity in which it is possible to believe almost anything. Selwyn shot back an impressive e-mail in response to mine – bright lad – in which he accused me of gross intolerance, to which I responded that tolerance does not mean respecting every individual's right to believe any blame fool thing that pops into his head. Infinite tolerance is no tolerance at all. He and I are still wrestling valiantly together on this issue, and each of us tries to score points whenever possible – he leaves knives sharpening under pyramids in the kitchen, I replace all the reading material in the bathrooms with back issues of *Skeptic Weekly*. Just typical father-son squabbling. Thankfully, all is now quiet with Merlin, our Rastafarian in residence, and you'll be stunned to know that young Stringbean, i.e., Damien, has actually acquired for himself a girlfriend – the beautiful and nymphomaniacal fundamentalist Christian Angel, who wore out Selwyn and Merlin in succession (and now neither of them can stop that infernal whistling) and is now putting Damien through his paces. Lucy is irate about it and feels our boys are taking advantage of her youth and (former) innocence; she pulls her aside at every opportunity and reads excerpts from the great feminists to her, while Damien bangs his head and fists repeatedly on the locked door, choking back tears, crying out frantically as a voice in the wilderness. "No! Don't listen to her! Please, God, don't listen to her! She's menopausal! She's demented! She's *old*!" So far Lucy appears to be fighting a losing battle with Mother Nature and can only hope to buy time before the inevitable happens. I don't know, Branksome; I would say that parenting is a thankless task, but that would be willfully disregarding the letters of thanks I receive almost weekly from the United Federation of Banana Growers.

Hoping you'll get back to the land, Branky.

Toodles,

Oliver

The Dream Post
NASA Sends Divining Rod to Mars

Cape Canaveral, Florida – In an effort to locate water on Mars, top NASA scientists today announced the launch of a rocket which will travel forty million miles from earth at a speed of twenty-five thousand mph in an effort to deliver traditional dowsing equipment to the planet.

"Our scientific equipment with all its fancy doodads and high-tech gizmos wasn't finding a dang thing," said top scientist and intuition technologist Dr. Corpus Callosum, "and we thought, hell, why not give a proven traditional method a chance? Our technology is only a few years old – why not rely on the wisdom of the ages to provide some solid answers for a change?"

The wisdom of spending several billion dollars in order to send a pointy stick to Mars has been questioned by some, but many are ready to leap to the scientists' defence. Respected Yeti hunter Harry Flake explains. "Historically, scientific equipment has been absolutely useless at detecting the presence of Big Foot, the Loch Ness Monster, extraterrestrials, and what have you. Not only that, but these guys can't seem to find hard evidence for simple, everyday notions that even a child can grasp such as telepathy, reincarnation, feng shui, and the power of celestial objects billions of light years away to regulate every aspect of your life. The question is not, 'Is there water on Mars?' The question is 'Why do we bother to pay these impotent bunglers?'"

Renowned master of levitation, Guru Abstemious Yeast, agrees. "No offence," said the little Indian man, adjusting his turban and loincloth, "but when it comes to finding things, these guys are rubbish. I can be floating three feet in the air right in front of them, and they cannot discover the real reason for my flotation. Trust me – these guys cannot see the forest for the strings – I mean trees. The point is, if you want to find answers, don't send scientists."

This is the second attempt to send dowsing apparatus to Mars; the first ended catastrophically when the divining rod, having not yet cleared the gravitational pull of the earth, began twitching wildly upon detecting water on its home planet, reversed the direction of the rocket, and plunged into the Sahara desert. Scientists guarantee this tragedy will not repeat itself as the rocket will be launched on an auspicious day, in the year of the Monkey, when the moon is in the seventh house and Jupiter aligned with Mars.

From: rafe.wilde@thedawnpost.com
To: suzanne@heartmail.com
Subject: Turning the Triangular Tables on Oliver Black

Hey There, Suzanne:

I just knew it! I knew by Blankie's smiling shape that this was going to be the happiest day of my life! Actually, this can't possibly be *the* happiest day of my life since, technically speaking, the happiest day will be when you finally dump Doctor Who (Cares), come to your senses (shortly after which *I'll* come to your senses, Baby – ooh la la), and go out with the Great Rafe once again. However, until the arrival of that glorious day, the best day of my life is happening *right now*, Baby, right this very second! I was too wasted to see it at first, but after reading his review of The Pythagorean Pub and Grill, it hit me like a ton of moussaka. I can't stop hugging *The Dawn Post*, I can't stop kissing his review. What's that old schoolyard taunt? "If you love it so much, why don't you marry it?" I would if I could, Baby, I would if I could. I just can't believe I didn't see it the first time – the evidence I need to annihilate that bastard Oliver Black! And just to make my case even stronger, I even went back over the last couple of years of his restaurant reviews and found more than enough proof, all the evidence I could ever possibly need, all there in black and white.

Look at his review of La Jonquille, of Billy-Bob's Burger and Bun, of The Mad Cow – it's all there, or, rather, it's not there – what Oliver Black *is* is obvious by what Oliver Black excludes! Oh, Suzanne! Ah! Oh don't you cry for me! 'Cause I'm goin' to ruin Ollie like a Hatfield on a spree! Whee!

Anyway, I'm just way too excited to give you the details now – I've got to write to Oliver Black immediately and gloat like a puffer fish. God, this feels good! I feel like shouting from the rooftops – actually, I feel like I'm on the rooftops already, specifically the roof of my apartment building, with my old piano, and I'm dangling it over the side and Oliver Black is down below and I'm about to yell, "Yo! Oliver! Look up! Rafe's got a little surprise for you!" And then I let go. No, wait! Rewind the tape! Let me put my old metronome inside the piano first! And my conservatory of music books! And let me get his wife on the roof with me! Oh, yeah. Now it's the perfect fantasy. I nail him *and* his old lady, if you get my drift.

Look up, Oliver, look up.

Here it comes.

Rafe's got a little surprise for you.

Yes!

Rancorously,

Rafe

PS: I chucked Petey out the window again, and just like the first time, he found his way back in. So I chucked him a second time – that time he found his way back in. But the third time I hurled him out, he didn't come back, and something tells me I've seen the last of him. This day just keeps on getting better and better!

From: oliver.black@thedawnpost.com
To: lucy.black@artnet.org
Subject: "Therefore hath hell enlarged herself, and opened
            her mouth without measure" —Isaiah 5:14

Dear Lucy:

Blessed are the peacemakers, the Good Book tells us, and I
should think that blessings are the *least* the peacemakers should
expect, given what we have to put up with. Yes, Lucy, I finally
gained an audience with Angel's mother (her adoptive mother, as
it turns out), and a more bizarre encounter I cannot imagine. It
comes on the heels of my recent meeting with Rafe Wilde, which
at the time I considered outrageous – but, in fact, it was as unremarkable as tea and toast compared to my interview with Angel's
mother. Mrs. Day (her first name is Agnes – Agnes Day – an old
joke-name that, in this case, is no joke) is the polar opposite of
her daughter in every way. Where Angel is appealing, Mrs. Day is
appalling. Where Angel is alluring, Mrs. Day is repelling. The
overall theme of her being, as manifest by her couture, says,
simply, "Grunge," and she resembles most a crumpled bag lady,
an anachronism from nineteenth century Industrial England. I do
not exaggerate when I tell you that she was dressed in tattered,
woollen, fingerless gloves; an oversized, shabby black coat; a
shapeless black hat, and dingy grey woollen stockings with black
lace-up boots. I swear that those were ashes on her face; she was
wearing a sackcloth shawl. There was a stuffed buzzard on her
shoulder. (Oh all right, there wasn't a buzzard, but there *ought to*
have been.) It was a get-up of which the costumier of any amateur
theatre company would have been envious. There was something
deeply fungal about the woman, Lucy, something mildewy, boggy,
dungy, and something that her perfume – Eau de Bilge – could
not conceal. However, her forbidding presence was nothing
compared to her grim personality, which can be compared favourably to a rabid fire-and-brimstone preacher who has a chip

on his shoulder, a bone to pick, and an axe to grind. Goodwife Day is a religious nutcase; she's on a spiritual toot, stoned on the prophets of the Old Testament, and as high as a kite on the opium of the people. Most astonishing of all, she refuses to converse in anything but Bible verses! I do *not* exaggerate, Lucille – she spoke not one original thought, but quoted scripture *the entire time,* guided as though by some celestial Cyrano. I thought I knew my Bible quite well, having been forced to recite it at my mother's knee, but I was no match for the formidable Mrs. Day. I wracked my brains coming up with verses as appropriate retorts, something that was second nature to Mrs. Day; quite soon she tired of this, however, and retrieved a battered KJV from her enormous carpetbag, which I understood I was to use as a reference. But it was no use, I couldn't keep up. Honestly, Lucy, the woman is quite mad, and I felt that I had to humour her or risk having her go off like a dirty bomb spiked with Biblical shrapnel.

How I wish you could have been with me, my darling, but I understand that your prior engagement was of superlative importance. (I don't mean to pry, but I can't help but wonder just who you had an appointment with yesterday? It must have been someone of great significance. I imagine your daily planner might have read: Appointment with Destiny, 12:00 noon. Coffee and croissants. May bring Fame and/or Obscurity.) Since you could not be present, however, and since I just happened to have tucked into the pocket of my Harris tweed the little tape recorder that I use for professional purposes, I decided to record the conversation word for word and simply play you the tape at a later time. But when will that be? It seems that we've had no time together for weeks (and you can take that as a little hint if you like, but no pressure); therefore, I thought I'd transcribe some of it for your amusement, and we'll listen to the conversation in its entirety together sometime, hopefully in the very near future, when we're both in the mood for a jolly good laugh. Thus we begin around a clumsily wiped table at The Mad Cow, which you will not be surprised to discover was the restaurant of *Mrs. Day's* choosing, and certainly not *my* choice, given that in ambience it ranks only slightly above a bovine feedlot. I'm given to understand that she picked The Mad Cow on the basis of the great significance of the cow in holy writ. (Cattle *are* mentioned in Genesis One after all, and even the Psalm states that "He owns the cattle on a thousand hills" – a verse that in modern times suggests not so much the wealth of the deity but rather busloads of placard-wielding environmentalists, contaminated ground water, and a colossal waste-management headache.)

"Won't you have something to eat, Mrs. Day?" I ventured, as yet unaware of the imperative to speak only as scripture dictates.

"Only the fool foldeth his hands together and eateth his own flesh!" she spat hastily.

"Indeed, only a great fool," I responded, thinking it a bit of an oddball remark, but trying to answer earnestly nonetheless. "In fact, probably only an insane, masochistic cannibal would actually *eat* his own flesh," I continued, "some poor chap, psycho to the bone and clearly in need of heavy medication and a good therapist. In any case he sounds a rare sort of fool indeed, and no bother to us, only a threat to himself. I should be afraid of feeling even just a little bit peckish if I were him. In any case, you must have a little something, Mrs. Day! My treat, naturally."

"Even unto this present hour we both hunger and thirst . . ."

"Well, then, all the more reason to chow down, as my sons would say. You *must* eat – I insist absolutely! Waiter!" I gestured to our food server, a gangly young man who approached our table with obvious reluctance. His name tag announced simply, "Tex," but when I looked at the nondescript, fuzzy, spotty face, the spindly limbs, and the enormous tennis shoes, I knew him at once.

"Good Lord. Are you *everywhere*?" I asked, staring incredulously at young Tex, alias Isosceles, alias Fabio.

"Oh, hello, Mr. Black," he said, his voice changing at every syllable from his chest register to falsetto, in the manner of the finest Swiss Alpine folk singers. "No, not really. This is just my day job. I work at the Pub in the evenings and Zippers on week-ends. College isn't free, you know."

"That's very true," I acknowledged, sympathetically. "But when on earth do you study?"

"I don't have to study," he yodelled. "I have an IQ of 180 . . ."

My estimation of young Tex rose –

". . . so I can hack into the system and cheat on all my exams."

– and fell. I imagined commenting at length but realized in time that now was not the right moment for an edifying monologue. Turning my attention again to the depressingly upholstered lump of humanity before me, I asked, "So, what about a nice sandwich, Mrs. Day?"

"Man shall not live by bread alone!" she replied, outraged. "Stay me with flagons! Comfort me with apples!"

I scanned the page before me. "No, I don't actually see apples on the menu, although I'm sure a flagon of something could be arranged," I said, catching Tex's eye and making a slight circular motion with my index finger beside my head and nodding in Mrs. Day's direction. "So you want something a little more substantial than a sandwich, eh? What about pasta then? I've eaten the linguini here before, and although it won't exactly cause one's heart to sing, it won't stop it outright either, something that cannot be said for the Mad Cow's 100 percent all-beef pats."

"Meats for the belly, and the belly for meats!" she exclaimed emphatically. I was beginning to catch on.

"Well, hmm, yes I suppose you could have a burger, then, and I don't want to throw my weight around of course, but, in the expert role of qualified food critic, I'd have to discourage the consumption of what I like to call Kreutzfeld-Jacob-On-A-Bun. Doodah, doo-dah."

"*Will I eat the flesh of bulls or drink the blood of goats?*" she exclaimed insanely.

"I wouldn't recommend it –"

"*And behold joy and gladness,*" she interrupted loudly, rising up in her chair – while I buried my face in one hand and thought,

"Thar she blows" – and shouting, *"slaying oxen and killing sheep, eating flesh and drinking wine! Let us eat and drink, for tomorrow we die!"*

There was a moment's pause as she settled herself back into her chair and gave me a sort of self-satisfied grimace. "Well, maybe you wouldn't die tomorrow," I said sotto voce, "if you'd lay off the beef, hmm? Now, let's get you that linguini, a flagon of root beer, and a piece of apple pie to finish off." I placed the order with the alarmed young Tex, who was relieved to be sent off to the kitchen. At this point, however, Mrs. Day began furiously brushing crumbs off the poorly cleaned table and muttering, "For all the tables are full of vomit and filthiness, so that there is no place clean."

"Good Lord, Mrs. Day. You do have a way with other people's words, don't you? Busboy!" I called, snapping my fingers. "Would you be so kind as to give our table another wipe? It isn't exactly spotless, as you can see."

"Yea, the lamb of God is spotless – "

"Well we won't trouble the busboy about *Him*, then, will we? Now, my good woman," I continued, deliberately speaking in hushed tones in the hopes that Mrs. Day would follow suit, "we must needs discuss *your* daughter and the curious fact that she is currently living under *my* roof. I do hope she's not being shunned or excommunicated or in any way cast from the flock."

Mrs. Day's eyes narrowed. "It is reported commonly that there is fornication among you."

"Indeed?" I replied, gratefully unsurprised at the direction the conversation was taking. "Yes, well, I suppose there is what is technically called 'fornication' among us, though I prefer the less judgmental and more scientific term, 'mating.' However," I continued, searching the deep recesses of my mind for an appropriate Biblical retort, "'I trust that ye shall know that we are not reprobates.' Ha! Second Corinthians 13:6."

Mrs. Day scowled. "Be not deceived!" she hissed, poking her stubby finger in my face. "Neither fornicators, nor idolaters, nor adulterers, nor effeminate, nor abusers of themselves with mankind, nor thieves, nor covetous, nor drunkards, nor revilers, nor extortioners, shall inherit the kingdom of God!"

"Well – naturally He'd want to keep the riffraff out, wouldn't He?" I replied pragmatically. "On the other hand, that's a rather exclusive list," I continued, respectfully giving the matter my genuine consideration. "I hope God wasn't planning a big afterlife, and that He hasn't overspent on the balloons and the party favours and the ice cream cake that says, 'Well Done, Thou Good and Faithful Servant,' because I'm afraid His caterer is only going to have to do dinner for a mere handful of people – and four of those will have the last name 'Flanders.' On the bright side," I added, "there'll be no interminable line-ups in heaven, will there, and one might reasonably expect same-day service.

"But I digress. The point is, Mrs. Day, that your Angel is a lovely young woman and –"

"*Woe to her that is filthy and polluted*!" the mouldy old nag yelled. "She obeyed not the voice! She received not the correction! She trusted not in the Lord!"

"She *obeyed her nature*, Mrs. Day, just as my son obeyed his –"

"*Yea*, also the heart of the sons of men is full of *evil*, and *madness* is in their heart while they live, and after that they go to the dead!" she observed.

"Well, now, I wouldn't say my boys are mad *as such*, at least, not in their hearts; if I had to pinpoint the exact location, I'd say the madness is in their pants, actually. But they are three robust teenage males, Mrs. Day, and this hormonally driven pubescent insanity is to be expected! It's *normal*, not to mention boringly predictable. Not to them, of course – young people always imagine that they *invented* sex – it's always cool, always the new thing – and so should it be, given that reproduction is for the young. And let us be fair, Mrs. Day – although they're responsible for everything they do, still, my poor boys' urges are not entirely under their own control. Mother Nature, perhaps obeying God's commandment to go forth and multiply, rather has them by the nuts, if you'll pardon the expression; and what is true of all mothers, in households the world over, is also true of Mother Nature. What is the exact expression? Ah yes: 'If *Mama* ain't happy, ain't *nobody* happy.'"

Mrs. Day shook her head in dismay. "If a man have a stubborn and rebellious son, that, when he has chastened him, will not hearken unto him, the man shall say unto the elders of his city, my son will not obey my voice; and all the men of his city shall stone him with stones that he die, so shalt thou put evil away from among you."

"Ah, well, I believe there are laws about that sort of thing nowadays –"

"*Woe* to the rebellious children, saith the Lord –"

"– but that's my *point*, Mrs. Day. Our children are *not* rebelling. They are *mating*, which is quite a different thing. It's natural, ordained of God. What does the Good Book tell us? Ah, yes. 'Birds do it – bees do it – even educated fleas do it!'"

Mrs. Day riffled the pages of her Bible and glowered.

I continued. "Does that mean we ought not to be concerned for their safety and well-being? Of course not! Exchanging diseases and breeding are not activities to be done at the drop of a hat. But frankly, Mrs. Day, I am more concerned for my sons' welfare when, for example, they cram themselves into a motor vehicle already packed to the rafters with their chums, and go charging off, tires squealing and rubber burning, to destinations unthinkable. At least when they're under my roof, snogging the girl of their dreams, I know they're not stealing apples, or setting things on fire, or sniffing adhesives. I know that they're safe from others, and, just as importantly, that others are safe from them.

"But back to the fact that Angel seems to have left the Day home and has taken up residence in the Black abode," I continued doggedly. "Please, be reasonable; what would convince you to welcome the lovely Angel back into the fold?"

Mrs. Day crossed her arms across her chest and scowled, her

face looking uncannily like Beethoven's death mask. "If thy right eye offend thee, pluck it out and cast it from thee! And if they right hand offend thee, cut it off and cast it from thee! For it is profitable that one of thy members should perish, and not that thy whole body should be cast into hell!"

"But Angel is not an eye to be plucked or a hand to be severed," I argued. "She's your *daughter*, Mrs. Day, your precious pink bundle from heaven. Surely you cannot just abandon her to the whims of fate!"

Mrs. Day looked coyly about and then announced, "It is good for a man not to touch a woman. But it is better to marry than to burn."

"Good God!" I exclaimed in alarm. "Are you suggesting that you'll have Angel back only on the condition that she *marry* one of my sons?"

She leaned back in her chair and replied thus: "If any man think that he behaveth himself uncomely toward his virgin, if she pass the flower of her age, and need so require, let him do what he will, he sinneth not. *Let them marry.*"

"Marriage! That seems a bit previous, don't you think?" I replied in a panicky tone. "They're only children, for heaven's sake! They can't possibly take a trip to the altar! They've barely made it past London Bridge and Pooh Corner! And what about I Corinthians 7:35, Mrs. Day? 'He that giveth her in marriage doeth well; but he that giveth her *not* in marriage *doeth better*.' What do you say to that? And, besides – which of my sons is your daughter supposed to marry? I'm afraid she's made rather a meal of them, partaking of all three in rapid succession."

I probably don't need to tell you, Lucy, that this last bit of information didn't go over too well with Mrs. Day. *"Eli, Eli, lama sabachthani!"* the old harridan cried as she slumped over the table, her head in her hands, a torrent of tears rushing from her eyes as water through twin drainpipes. As fate would have it, it was at that precise moment that the terrified young Tex chose to bring us our victuals.

"Is she – is she all right?" he asked, dropping our plates like hot potatoes and backing away in terror. "Should I – you know – should I bring her something?"

"A sponge sopping with vinegar might be appropriate," I replied, shooing the perplexed Tex away and turning my attention back to the distraught old hag. "Now, now, Mrs. Day. There, there. Calm yourself, Dear Lady," I said, reaching across the table to give her a reassuring pat on the shoulder. "Is this any way for a woman of faith to behave? Do not the scriptures tell us that 'All things work together for good to them that love God, to them who are the called according to his purpose?' Romans 8:28, I believe."

I was rather proud of myself for recalling this "It'll all work out in the end" bit of New Testament philosophy; however, although Mrs. Day may be a Christian, she's not a New Testament Christian. She's the type of Christian who could do without the wishy-washy, feel-good gospels, who profoundly regrets the overriding by Christ of the law and of sacrifice, and who wishes deep in her heart that Jesus could have been a bit less like his biological father (good with his hands, meek, willing to do his bit for mythology by blindly accepting alleged supernatural direction), and a bit more like his heavenly progenitor (good with a lightning bolt, insanely jealous, notoriously hot-tempered, and an eager proponent of smiting as sound foreign policy, and also as a solution to minor domestic problems). At any rate, Mrs. Day violently shrugged my hand off of her shoulder, leaned on her elbows across the table, and tore into me like an owl on a rat.

"*Are ye not children of transgression, a seed of falsehood, enflaming yourselves with idols under every green tree, slaying the children in the valleys under clifts of the rocks?*"

"Ah, no, I'm afraid that's not us, actually," I replied, more convinced than ever that I was conversing with a lunatic of the first water. "Wrong family –"

"*Therefore the lord will smite with a scab the crown of the head of the daughters of Zion, and the lord will discover their secret parts! And in that day the lord will take away the bonnets, and the ornaments of the legs, and the headbands, and the tablets, and the earrings, and the rings, and nose jewels, the changeable suits of apparel, and the mantles and the wimples and the crisping pins, the glasses and the fine linen, and the hoods, and the veils! And it shall come to pass, that instead of sweet smell there shall be stink! And instead of a girdle a rent! And instead of well set hair baldness! And instead of a stomacher a girding of sackcloth! And burning instead of beauty!"*

There was a pause as we stared at one another, and the other patrons of The Mad Cow stared at us. "Oh come now," I said, "you're having me on. The Bible doesn't really say that, does it?" She slid her Bible across the table, which she had opened to Isaiah, Chapter III. "Good Lord. It *does* say that. Forgive my ignorance, but what, precisely, is a crisping pin?"

But Mrs. Day had only been catching her breath and continued on as if crisping pins were of no theological relevance at all.

"Howl ye!" she continued, as I looked around at the other diners and shrugged a sort of helpless apology, *"for the day of the lord is at hand; it shall come as a destruction from the almighty! And they shall be afraid! Their faces shall be as flames! Every one that is found shall be thrust through! Their children also shall be dashed to pieces –"*

"Ah, now I think that's going a bit *too* far –"

"And their houses shall be spoiled, and their wives ravished! Their bows also shall dash the young men to pieces; and they shall have no pity on the fruit of the womb; their eye shall not spare the child!"

"Gosh, it's all good, clean fun with your deity, isn't it? You really are a marvel, Mrs. Day. No, no, I mean that. Your memory is astonishing. Have you considered writing a book on the subject?"

"Behold, I am against thee," she continued, ignoring my question and pointing to a school photo of Angel that she'd retrieved from her enormous sack, *"and I will discover thy skirts*

upon thy face, and I will shew the nations thy nakedness, and the *kingdoms thy shame! And I will cast abominable filth upon thee"* (here she made great scooping gestures) *"and make thee vile, and will set thee as a gazingstock!"*

"Of course everyone parents differently," I remarked; and on it went, Lucy, with Mrs. Day drawing upon the Old Testament wrath of Yahweh, and me, drawing upon empathy and common sense. You'd be astonished at how many verses in the Bible refer to fornication and vengeance all in one breath, and doubly astonished that Mrs. Day can quote them all from memory. I must say that she didn't take it at all well when I suggested that God's vision of the world seems to be little more than a school of rewards and whippings, and that God's total lack of interest in, say, intelligence and creativity, and his obsession with obedience to his bizarre whims, seems just a trifle one-dimensional, which is surprising in a cosmic being. Do you know, Lucy, that at one point she even inferred that Selwyn himself is the devil incarnate, which I gleefully told him the moment I arrived home. Can you imagine Selwyn's reaction? That's right – compliments don't come any bigger.

Sadly, our conversation concluded in a stalemate; if I refused to consent to a marriage between Angel and whichever boy is behind door number 1, 2, or 3 – and I did refuse, *absolument*, and I hope that *we* are in agreement on this point – then Mrs. Day will *not* allow Angel back under her roof, although she *will* continue to accept direct deposits into her bank account off Angel's modelling. I find it outrageous that Mrs. Day appears to be living off Angel's income, not to mention contradictory on the face of it; doesn't it seem odd to you that she allows Angel to display herself in such a wanton manner, considering the contempt she has for the human body? It seemed positively perverse to me, but then I realized that it made perfect sense given that Mrs. Day is a) as mad as a March hare and b) steeped in archaic Biblical notions, in which women are conceived of as mere chattel, and female subservience and absolutely ego-busting humility are taken to be the ideal. Her treatment of her daughter is not an illogical extension of Old Testament attitudes, in which females are treated at worst as slaves, and at best as pets. Angel herself says she was kept on a very short leash, which is an apt metaphor considering that Mrs. Day paraded her about like a dog after taking best in show. At any rate, the meeting with Mrs. Day ended when she informed me that the Almighty would "surely violently turn and toss [me] like a ball into a large country," and then, as she swept out the door, she cried, "Flee fornication!" which I assured her I would do right after I paid the cheque.

Now I know that Mrs. Day is an extreme example of the religious type, and I'm not saying that religious people have a monopoly on bizarre ideas – clearly not. I'm only saying that religious people believe a lot of kooky things. I don't mean to be uncharitable. It's just an observation, and a commonplace one at that, which can be backed up with an astonishing amount of evidence. As for Mrs. Day, I believe any further communication is pointless; if we wish to know her thoughts on any matter, we need only read Malachi, or Zephaniah, or any of the other blustering Old Testament prophets. Meanwhile, I believe it is our duty to provide warmth, shelter, and a continuous supply of bananas for the lovely Angel, and to treat her as we would one of our own. I shall purchase a Latin/English dictionary and a copy of *The Forgotten Quince* for her immediately.

Love,

Oliver

PS: By the way, in case you didn't know, that makes two "birds" we are currently housing under our roof. With the uncanny instincts of a homing pigeon, Rafe's parrot has returned to Olivia's animal sanctuary – and I do believe that, like Angel, he's far better off not having to deal with his nutcase caregiver. May we keep him? May we, may we? And because there isn't anything much more depressing than a caged bird, Olivia and I already have plans for a giant backyard aviary where Petey (we believe that's his name) can live out his days in cat-free splendour. Meanwhile, I've eagerly agreed to keep his cage in my study, both to be companionable, and because I find his chatter most agreeable, as his thoughts so closely mirror my own.

From: rafe.wilde@thedawnpost.com
To: oliver.black@thedawnpost.com
Subject: Humbug

Oi! Ollie!

You don't mind if I call you Ollie, do you? Good, good. The thing is, Ollie, this morning I was reading your review of The Pythagorean Pub and Grill in *The Dawn Post*, and as I was reading about the Kreatopita and Kalamarakia, the Sardeles and Savridi, a thought suddenly occurred to me. Can you guess what that thought was, Ollie? It's the same thought I had after reading your wonderful description of the moussaka – how did you put it? "Spicy ground beef manna from heaven," you said, "an accident with the cinnamon," you said. *You* said. "Eat and observe, Mr. Wilde. Eat and observe." That's what *you* said, Ollie, and eat and observe is what *I* did. Have you guessed what I was thinking, Ollie, after reading your fine review? Yes, that's right. What I was thinking was, and I quote – Oliver Black is a *fraud*. Mr. Morality himself – Mr. Beauty, Liberty, and Truth – is a *fake*. A mealy-mouthed, double-tongued, two-faced hypocrite. I was also thinking, Ollie, that I know exactly *why* you're a frigging no-good flimflamming bamboozler. No one else has figured it out, have they? That's because you've been doing this job for so many years, no one's paying close attention anymore – your reputation provides the perfect cover. But *I'm* paying attention, Ollie. *I've* figured it out and *I* know why. And soon everybody else is going

to know too, because I'm going to blow the whistle.
Have a nice day.

Vengefully,

Rafe Wilde

From: rafe.wilde@thedawnpost.com
To: nathaniel.midge@thedawnpost.com
Subject: Blacklisting

Mr. Midge:

Firstly, I have to thank you again for not sacking me after that whole John Cage fiasco – and thanks also for sending me a pay cheque regardless, even though, just to make the point, your smart-apple accountant made it out for a thousand bajillion dollars. Ha! You can just imagine how funny I found this. Secondly, I'd like to arrange a meeting with you to discuss something I really think you should know about your star employee, Oliver Black. I won't say too much here, only that I have reason to believe that "Mr. Beauty, Liberty, and Truth" is a hypocrite of titanic proportions. Do you think we could arrange to meet sometime next week? I'd make it sooner, but as you know I have an important musical event to attend – and I can't say how much I'm looking forward to reviewing a concert based exclusively on something those wacky new music people call *musique concrète*. (Ha! Even *they* admit that the experience of listening to new music is like wading through concrete.)
Till next week then.

Rafe Wilde

From: oliver.black@thedawnpost.com
To: wendell.mullet@agricorps.org
Subject: Turning A Deaf Ear

Mr. Mullet:

With each threat comes more evidence that you are as unworthy a chap as ever wielded a fork and walked upright. What do you mean the moussaka wasn't enough? There were other dishes upon which I commented at length and with unrestrained enthusiasm. Your threats are futile, Mr. Mullet, and your pressure tactics are a waste of your time and mine. I will not – I *cannot* – pay you another dime.

Give it a rest.

O.B.

From: oliver.black@thedawnpost.com
To: rafe.wilde@thedawnpost.com
Subject: *Veri amici sunt pauci*

Mr. Wilde:

I haven't a clue what you're talking about. I expect that you're still sozzled; instead of downing a little medicinal hair of the dog, you probably ate the entire pooch. It is undoubtedly this, and not just poor hygiene, that explains your furry tongue, hmm? You're obviously out of your mind, *non compos mentis extremis*, and you hotheadedly composed your e-mail in a moment of boozy delusion, of plastered madness, of inebriated barbarity. Actually, your insane ravings about the moussaka, for example, suggest psychosis; have you recklessly gone off your meds, my friend? There's no shame in admitting to mental illness. Paranoia, hysteria, delusion – it's enough to make any American talk show host salivate. Ah well, it's the chemicals, it's not you. Although, while we're on the subject, how *do* you feel about straitjackets and little striped hats?

Nevertheless, Mr. Wilde, even given your maniacal state, how is it that you could treat me with such disrespect, such loathing, such utter contempt? Considering all I have done for you, my friend, this seems horribly unfair. I championed your uncle's café, and because of me, he's now a local celebrity and his premises are more popular than Mecca, than the Ganges, than Graceland itself. Why bother going to the offices of Social Services, or the Red Cross, or Amnesty International? Everyone knows that their new unofficial headquarters are at Billy-Bob's Burger and Bun, where you will find journalists, aid workers, the destitute, all having a coffee together and solving the world's social evils. What is the difference between the Burger and Bun and the United Nations? Only the price of a cup of coffee. I shouldn't be surprised if world peace begins around one of those gum-encrusted tables. I wrote an eloquent letter to the editor *in your defence* after you wrote that abominable Cage review, for which you rightfully ought to have been sacked, preferably *with* a sack, possibly even *in* a sack, again and again and again. I gave you my only copy of *The Forgotten Quince*, a first edition no less, signed by the freelance, bow-tied historian who wrote it. I found you the best music history teacher in the city, the brainy and beautiful Ms. Gabriella Savage. I advised you, counselled you, helped you, each of my letters containing not just the usual idle chitchat but, rather, little pearls of wisdom, little gems of experience – I think of them, without hyperbole, as Baedekers for good living. They're rivalled in quantity of advice only by St. Paul's letters to the Ephesians and *Ladies' Home Journal*. I thought I was like a father to you, Rafe; you were certainly like a son to me.

What did I do to make you hate me so?

With deep bewilderment,

Oliver Black

PS: I have also given your Petey a home, by the way – a bird who has shaken my disbelief in telepathy, as he seems *always* to know *exactly* what I'm thinking.

From: oliver.black@thedawnpost.com
To: branksome.black@rebel.net
Subject: Shoving the Cat to the Bottom of the Bag

Dearest Brother:

Lies, lies, and more lies! Oh, Branksome! Of what is man capable when he feels himself cornered? Rafe Wilde just wrote me an e-mail in which he accused me, quite rightfully as it happens, of being a fraud; still, I felt forced to defend myself, but I did so with a sloppy *ad hominem* attack portraying him as some kind of hopelessly psychotic drunk with a bed just like the one at his flat waiting for him at the local rehab centre. I admit that it was a cheap attack on his character, but attempting to throw him off the scent by questioning his reliability as a witness was all I could think to do, given the surprise nature of his attack upon me. Honestly, Branksome, I can't understand it. One moment Mr. Wilde and I are getting on like a house on fire – the next moment Rafe Wilde has abandoned the house entirely and locked all the doors from the outside. I thought I was like a father to him, Branky – a bothersome father, perhaps, the kind that acts like an irritating grain of sand in the soul of his child in the hopes that a pearl will be created thereby – but a father nonetheless. The question is, what did *I* ever do to *him*? You don't suppose he's still cross about Selwyn, and then Merlin, and then Damien, nicking his best girl, do you? Oh, please! Rafe Wilde is *twenty-two years* her senior – quite old enough to be her father – and it's not *my* fault that he failed to grow up and is thus under the impression that he and Angel are essentially the same age. The fact that he's still chasing after giggling schoolgirls and continues to listen either to the music of his youth, or contemporary music which is indistinguishable from the music of his youth, is evidence that he got stuck somewhere in time, where girlfriends are perpetually sixteen years old, downbeats occur exclusively on two and four, and lyrics centre upon the wholly predictable, and therefore frightfully tedious, means by which the human race reproduces itself.

Anyway, Branksome, I do hope you are back on terra firma, having slung your hook off of the *Farley Mowat* (who, by the way, just happens to be basking in a ray of sunshine on my desk at this very moment – and a fine, grizzled old tom he is, stretched across the beam in flying super-hero position). Wherever you are, Branky old boy, do be careful. *Periculum est magnum!* This is a critical time, and you mustn't put a foot wrong. I've got enough on my plate as it is – a veritable feast, with crow for starters and ending with dessertion, if you see what I mean. I suppose it *is* still possible the whole business will blow over. After all, I do have a point – Rafe Wilde *was* pickled to the gills the night we had our dinner together, thus he cannot be certain who said what to whom, and why. Still I am uneasy, Branksome, and wonder if I shall end my days alone and penniless, my goose not only cooked but charred to ash, and my whole pitiful existence shrouded in disgrace and ruin.

Bother.

Tensely yours,

Oliver

From: rafe.wilde@thedawnpost.com
To: oliver.black@thedawnpost.com
Subject: Kiss Off

Oliver:

How do I hate thee? Let me count the ways. Jesus, Ollie. Can
you possibly be serious? You honestly don't know what you did to
make me hate you? What *didn't* you do to make me hate you?
You're *the* most affected, self-righteous, clinically uncool, pompous, hypocritical, know-it-all bastard I've ever met – isn't that
enough? You're a big Black *liar*, Ollie – you've lied to *everybody,*
your life is a farce, and yet you make it your *business* telling
everybody else what to do. This alone is enough reason to despise
you, but there's so much more! You *insist* on taking the credit for
the rejuvenation of Uncle Bill's café, even though your review
could easily have had the opposite effect; that your article resulted in an *increase* in business was just a happy accident, and
don't pretend you don't know it. I hate you because you're the
father of Black Chalice, the band that stole Angel – sixteen,
beautiful, mine – and for that I will *never* forgive them, or you. I
hate you, Ollie, because of your asinine opinions – especially your
opinions about music. I was forced to listen to you at that atrocious dinner party going on and on about classical music, especially defending the artistic merits of the music written in the last
hundred years, including all of that avant-garde crap. And you're
just so, *so* wrong. *All* of the art music of the last century is going
to be long forgotten, or if it is remembered, it's going to be remembered as what it is – a joke. A terrible idea. How many
people were at that Cage concert? A dozen. There were more
players on the stage than people in the audience. Why? Because
it's *dead music*, Ollie. It belongs in a museum under glass. It has
no energy, no purpose – it's all theory, and no passion. I'd rather
have no theory and all passion, thanks very much, and so would
billions of other people.

Christ, Ollie, you're more pathetic than I thought. I don't
need your damn book, your opinions, your letters of defence and
certainly not your letters of advice. So, nice try, Soy Boy, but let
me suggest you prepare for a veggie wedgie of major proportions,
because you know damn well what I'm talking about. You know
that *I'm* not *on* any medication. What I'm *on*, Ollie, is a quest,

and it's a quest for truth. And, as you once said to me, the truth will out.

With loathing,

Rafe

PS: It's *not* my fucking parrot, all right?

The Dream Post
Composers' Strike Hits Day 10,000

Vienna, Austria – It was 10,000 days ago today that composers of avant-garde music just got up and walked away from their computers, their keyboards, their trash can lids and rubber chickens, and voted against the composition of even one single note of music until their demands for more money and better working conditions are met.

"This job stinks!" cried composer of progressive danger music Fringy von Fibonacci. "What kind of bogus career is this anyway? Pushing the limits of what is considered to be music should be a noble occupation! I mean, I bust my butt coming up with great ideas, like my piece called "One Suicide Bomber Will Be Seated in the Audience," and absolutely nobody shows up for the performance! Yeah, okay, except for the guy who performed it, Ahmed 'Lucky Bastard' Husayn, but he was so totally unprofessional that he wouldn't even do a dress rehearsal. And do I get paid for my work? Ha! I have yet to see a dime of the royalties from my ballet for a hundred thousand troops and tanks entitled, 'America Declares War on Iraq!'"

Marching in front of the Vienna opera house with a placard stating "Avant-Garde Music Is Not a Thing of the Past," Fibonacci continued, "Jesus! Everybody hates my music, and they all believe I'm just some kind of attention-loving musio-psychopath! Oh, how wrong they are! Do you think I enjoy painting my naked body red and generating the notes for my piece by shooting up a Steinway grand with an AK-47? I'm just doing my job, and what do I get? Scorn! Ridicule! Jokes like 'How many avant-garde composers does it take to screw in a light bulb?' Answer – 'What a great idea for a performance piece!'"

After putting down his placard and attempting to collect more signatures on his petition (in ten thousand days he's collected only one, from fellow composer of progressive modern music, Mr. Spear Headly), Fibonacci made a large bonfire outside the opera house, in which he threw his *I Ching* and dice, his astronomy charts and rubber tubing, his ping-pong balls and slide whistles.

Headly joined Fibonacci with his own placard, which proclaimed simply, "I'm tired of being a social pest!" and continued the angry-musician tirade by feeding all of his compositions into a paper shredder. "Oh yeah. People are really going to start hurting now. I don't care – I say, if people want good old-fashioned avant-garde music, they're going to have to pay for it!"

The two composers were outraged when curious onlookers mistook the crackling of the fire and the buzzing of the paper shredder for an actual avant-garde performance piece. "No! This is *not* art!" a frustrated Fibonacci cried. "Jesus! Can't you people tell the difference between a piece of avant-garde music and random noise when you hear it?" Things got particularly ugly when some onlookers misunderstood the spirit of the act and began happily shredding and burning their own copies of manuscripts by composers of modern music.

Defeated, Fibonacci and Headly promised to return quietly to their desks on Monday morning, as long as the return to their desks will in no way be regarded as performance art.

From: oliver.black@thedawnpost.com
To: branksome.black@rebel.net
Subject: Botches and Blunders

My Dear Brother:

I must remain calm. No matter what else, I must remain calm. I don't know where to begin, Branksome – with my own dire situation or with yours, which you so briefly sketched on a piece of toilet paper and then had smuggled out of your cell by the besotted daughter of a prison guard. Dear God, Branksome – how do you do it? What's your secret? Most men can't connect with a woman during ladies' night at a crowded singles' bar – you, on the other hand, can pick up a woman in a maximum-security, all-male prison, and convince her to commit a criminal act on your behalf to boot. You are truly a marvel, Branksome, and I only wish you were as smooth with the authorities as you are with the ladies.

Didn't I say this was a critical time? Didn't I tell you not to put a foot wrong? Honestly, Branksome, I have enough on my plate without you committing acts of insanity, getting charged with public mischief, and thrown in the clink. As you say in your note, you didn't plan any of it; you were simply overcome by a crazy impulse and acted in contradiction to all reason. Clearly reason didn't enter into your actions in the least – and yet, I can at least understand how it happened. There you were, having recently come from the vast and beautiful expanse that is the frozen north, wandering in some infernal jungle town on some south Asian island, when you accidentally came across one of the local attractions – a zoo, advertising rare and exotic animals collected from the four corners of the globe. For some reason (perhaps aggravated by looming sunstroke) you strayed inside the gates, and the first thing that met your gaze was a tiny circular enclosure, with a concrete floor and metal bars, and inside – God help us – a majestic white bear, pacing around his thimble-sized,

concrete wading pool. You read the sign that noted that the polar
bear has only been called "polar" for the last two hundred years,
and that it used to be called, simply, the white bear, until humans
forced it increasingly northward and renamed it to fit its new environment. You looked around you – heard the chatter of the
local visitors who were interested, not so much in the beauty of
the incarcerated beasts but, rather, the best ways to cook them –
saw nothing but violations of Beauty, Liberty, and Truth – and
something inside you snapped. From there it wasn't hard to get
extremely chummy with the zookeeper's wife, to nick the keys,
and to return under the cover of darkness in order to carry out
your hastily devised and idealistic-to-the-point-of-madness plan,
which was, in essence, to commence returning the planet to its
original state; that is, as one gigantic and glorious wildlife pre-
serve.

Honestly, Branksome. Am I my brother's zoo keeper? I don't
recall that our mandate included anything about casually releasing
animals of *any* description into the *wild*. Good Lord! Think,
Branksome, think! Make use of the old Black bean for once! Did
you stop to consider, even for a moment, that releasing ungainly
and dangerous carnivorous animals to roam the crescents and
mews of Asian suburbia might have undesirable side effects such
as, let's say, the consumption of tasty children? Did you for a
moment consider the environmental impact, as if the native fauna
were bored with the same old ho-hum predators and would welcome the chance to be ripped limb from limb by something more
exotic for a change? How exactly *did* you plan to stop the animals
from eating each other? – a headache of animal husbandry that
dates back to the time of Noah. Kangaroos and panthers do not
traditionally make happy forest fellows. And just where did you
think you were going to hide, oh, the elephants for example?
Were you going to teach them to tweet and stick them in the
trees? (See *Horton Hatches the Egg*, Dr. Seuss, 1954.) And, lastly,
did you stop to consider your own safety? Did you imagine as you
made a run for it after opening the lion's cage, that the reason he

sprang toward you and opened his jaws was to say, "Thanks ever
so much, old chap?" Life is not an Aesop's fable, Branky – I'm
afraid that no matter how helpful the little mouse is, he gets eaten
by the lion *every time.*

I freely admit that the spirit of your actions was commend-
able; the act itself, however, was profoundly insane, and you
ought to have your head examined, and the other bits of you
besides, perhaps by a prison nurse – a male nurse, preferably, in
order to avoid the risk of true love blossoming during the colon-
oscopy. Nevertheless, what's done is done. Cool under fire,
Branky! Confess to nothing! How many weak individuals break
under the weight of their own petty transgressions! Yet all of us
must bear the weight of secret sins, most of which are laughably
trivial (or so I have learned – at least in a geological time-frame)
but which become monstrous when given an airing. How many
misguided fools divulge all in the name of honesty, when it's only
a pathetic and childish excuse to relieve oneself, to shift the
weight from one's own shoulders, to treat others as a dumping
ground for one's own psychic refuse? Why draw others into one's
own personal hell? Men especially are forever confessing things,
Branky, and always at the wrong time and to the wrong person;
this is because it is men who are the hysterical sex, and well we
know it. Always overreacting, always given to dramatic displays of
(mostly bad) temper. As I'm sure you know from recent firsthand
experience, our prisons are stuffed with men who, given the least
provocation, will attempt to beat you senseless. In some circles
this sort of thing is seen as a manly display of bravado. Of course
it's all just simply violence – and if violence isn't hysteria, I don't
know what is.

Your situation is a grave one, Branksome, but so, unfortunately, is my own – and so, at last, we turn to me. I do believe
that I made a momentous tactical error, that Rafe Wilde has
figured out my secret after all and therefore, for me, the end is
nigh. I'm afraid I underestimated Mr. Wilde, and I stand cor-
rected and humbled. He's an example to me, Branksome, an

example of something of enormous importance that I had to finally understand in this life; how grateful I am that I learned it directly from Mr. Wilde himself – the undisputed master, the supreme virtuoso, the unrivalled champ – and what I've finally learned is this: that just because one *acts* like a gibbering ignoramus, it doesn't actually mean that one *is* a gibbering ignoramus. This seems highly counterintuitive, but I assure you it is so; acting as if one is intelligent violates the unwritten rules of cool – and let us briefly examine, as a prime example, the rock and roll musician. He may *act* like a simpleton – strutting about the stage like a deranged peacock, warbling about sexual reproduction and picking relentlessly at the guitar positioned strategically at his genitals – but in sooth, Branksome, the CEO of any successful multinational corporation would give his right arm to have even a tenth of a rock star's business acumen. A million dollars means nothing to a rock star – it is the loose change he carries about in his pocket. Ask a rock star where he wants to go for breakfast, and he may well reply, "Venice." He owns a penthouse apartment in New York, a villa in Barcelona, a pensione in Florence, an island in the South Pacific, but he enjoys most his English country home, where he can live like the gentry and revel in luxuries that would embarrass even the Sun King, even Donald Trump, even the Pope himself. The rock star eats gold leaf on toast for breakfast, and drinks Dom Perignon from a pint mug. He enjoys football, cars, and being knighted. And the women! The turnstile installed at his bedside, and the little red box that instructs one to "Take a Number" say it all. Mind you, this is his compensation for having to act the part of the total buffoon his entire life, for the surely horrifying thought that he will be remembered merely as a sort of professional kangaroo, jumping about and singing the same little ditties of embarrassingly elementary construction, decade after decade, until he finally dies of liver failure or injuries sustained in a plane crash.

On the other hand, unlike me – a person who acts with deliberate intelligence, wit, and sophistication – he has never spent even a moment fretting about the price of bananas.

So who's the genius?

Sorry, Old Boy, I didn't mean to go on a rant. The point I wish to make, Branky, is that even in a drunken stupor, Mr. Wilde is, like the rock stars about whom he writes, far more astute than his behaviour would lead us to believe. Even while intoxicated, his powers of detection are supreme – one is reminded of Sherlock Holmes or Hercule Poirot. And, in warfare, make no mistake – Rafe Wilde takes no prisoners. When he claims that he's going to ruin me, I do believe he is sincere. I believe he has every intention of exposing me, of humiliating me, of revealing my true nature to the world; at which point I shall lose everything and end my life in shame, living a poor and wretched existence with Amelia Earhart in a dismal basement suite, eating chunky soup directly from a can and watching my sons on television as they make their living bounding about a stage like laboratory rats on an electrified grid, to a pounding 4/4 beat and a series of three wildly exciting chords in root position, whilst crooning about the joys – though not the consequences – of fornication.

If you've any last minute advice, do feel free to send it. As for your situation, I will do all I can for you, as always, whilst waiting patiently for the penny to drop on *me*. I wish it was only a penny, mind you, but in actual fact, Branksome, it feels more like a piano.

Stoically,

Oliver

From: rafe.wilde@thedawnpost.com
To: alma.wilde@command.net
Subject: Re: How Could You Embarrass Your Mother Like
             This?

Listen, You Old Crone:

For the love of your little guy, would you please, please, *please* stop spamming me with your infernal e-mails, and cramming my inbox with the same frigging letter? Jesus, Mom, you can be a major pain in the ass. And here's a newsflash for you – *I'm thirty-eight years old.* No, I don't know how it happened either. One minute I'm sitting in my sandbox, peacefully playing with G. I. Joe and his instruments of germ warfare – the modified tank with the feather duster that explodes out the front, that pumps out cleaning solution and lobs bits of agent orange peel – and the next minute I'm opening a box sent to me from my Mom *(even though I explicitly asked her not to send any more of my old stuff)* marked "Rafe's Old Toys. Some antique/collectibles." Oh, that's a cheery thought – my toys are now valuable because they're *antiquities.* Why couldn't the Great Rafe be more like Raphael himself, the immortal, celestial being you named me after? It's so right that he's the patron saint of lovers, mind you (no surprise that the name Rafe is linked with *amour*) and also the patron saint of the insane (same thing, really), but naming me after an *angel* was just wrong, unless it was a Hell's Angel, or Lucifer. You know, I always wondered about that plaque you nailed above my bed with a picture of the angel Raphael, who looked like a hippy in a nightie (*lucky bastard*) casually floating in between cloud banks; and I remember you were so pissed off when I drew a speech bubble with Raphael saying, "What's that roaring sound?" and the nose of a cruise missile zooming into the picture. Kaboom! It wasn't his picture, though, but his dates that always spooked me. "The archangel Raphael," the plaque said. "Born – wasn't. Died – hasn't." What kind of freak of nature is this, I used to wonder. I thought that maybe you named me *after* him because I was *like* him – eternally young, immortal, nightie-clad – and now, of course, I wish I was.

Anyway – all right, all right! You've made your point – you can stop with the electronic hen tracks already. I promise I won't embarrass you by cancelling my music lesson with Ms. Savage. Jesus, how is it that a grown man can be old enough to be the president of the most powerful nation on earth, but his mother still has to make him go to his music lesson? Hmm? Does this tell you something about piano teachers? Still, even though my inbox is jammed with a thousand e-mails from you hassling me, it isn't enough to wreck this great mood I've got happening here. I know you think Oliver Black is just the bee's knees, but I've got news for you, Mom – the man is a fraud of monumental dimensions, and it's Rafe Wilde who's gonna bring him down. That's right. I've got the goods, which is exactly how I'm feeling – good! You know, I don't think revenge gets enough press. Psychologists ought to recommend it as a form of therapy. I know forgiveness is the big thing these days, but I find that revenge brings a special feeling of deep satisfaction that forgiveness never could. Revenge is a noble goal, but what the hell is forgiveness? Forgiveness is just giving up, that's all. Vengeance is about justice, fairness, balance. And it comes packaged in so many colourful forms! Like, I may not have Angel anymore but, on the other hand, I also don't have to put up with the prophet of damnation that is Angel's mother. *And Oliver Black does.* Ha! Mind you, based on the fact that she herself speaks of little else, I'm sure Angel's mom would whole-heartedly endorse my revenge campaign. According to her, God Himself is pretty big on the whole vengeance thing, which, if God is good, is proof that vengeance is a good thing, right? (This *Thought for the Day* courtesy of Father Wilde – freelance theologian.) And what about the fact that God is consumed by revenge fantasies, and so am I? I'll let you work out the obvious conclusion.

Right. Time for my last meal before the long walk to the

Savage gibbet.

Your godlike son,

Raphael

Chapter Seven

From: oliver.black@thedawnpost.com
To: damien.black@freenet.org
Subject: Moral Outrage

Feast of the Father Almighty
(I mean *me*, knucklehead)

Hello Damien:

Although I've scrutinized my thesaurus from beginning to end, all the way from abandoned (immoral, shameless, corrupt, depraved) to zany (fool, imbecile, nitwit, dunce), I find that there exists no word in the English language strong enough to express my horror and my unmitigated disapproval of your recent behaviour. (There may be a word in another language, but I am simply too tired of being a father to look it up; perhaps I ought to fashion my own word to express the idea of bottomless disappointment. How about infinidisapprobodium? Yes. I like it. Please add it to your spell-checker forthwith.) And no, I'm not talking about Angel and your more-or-less continuous mating – although it might be decent of you to consider occasionally leaving the confines of your bedroom and treating Angel to an evening at the rollercade, or an amusement park, or a ball game, or some other location where young people traditionally go to eat corn dogs and quietly molest each other, on what we old-timers used to call "a date." No, this has nothing to do with Angel at all. It has to do with second-degree infanticide and your part in the downfall of the civilized world.

Where did your mother and I go wrong, Damien? I cannot understand it, especially considering that I personally took the task of shaping a civilized human male into my own masterful hands, since I could hardly rely on the public school system to create something other than an uncultivated ignoramus. Under my expert tutelage, you learned everything you needed to know in order to blossom into a well-bred, refined, and upright man about town. Good Lord, Damien! You could tie an ascot by the time you were three! You knew how to fold a cloth napkin into Lady Windermere's fan by the time you were five, and eleven other ways besides! After finishing your soup, it was nothing for you to place your spoon *not* on the table beside the underplate like some kind of wild animal, but in the soup plate itself in the 10:20 position. That you knew how to eat pie and ice cream in both the American *and* the Continental style by the time you were six was a credit to you. Your expertise in the area of cheeses was immense. How ought one to clean a top hat? How does one iron a newspaper, and why? When ought one to wear white gloves? And, for those later years, how ought one to remove rose petal stains from white cotton sheets? You knew all this and so much else besides; it is not every boy in nappies (and a bow tie) who knows precisely which kind of grapes are required to make a Beaujolais Nouveau!

And it wasn't just the rules of etiquette, nor an expertise concerning the finer things in life that I attempted to instill in you; it was your moral education that I took upon myself, knowing that the chances of you becoming a psychopath were just too great if I left it up to a society whose values had been shaped by television and Sunday School teachers. It was no surprise to anyone that your first word was "Plato" (although others in the room heard "Play Doh" and immediately brought you a colourful doughy substance, which you proceeded to mash with your tiny fist, no doubt in frustration; when I whisked it away and gave you a copy of *The Republic,* I knew only too well that those were tears of joy streaming down your apple-red cheeks). How you loved our Saturday morning philosophy drills when I would say to you and your brothers something like, "The first one who finds Kant's statement 'Act only according to a maxim by which you can at the same time *will* that it shall become general law' gets the sweet in my hand – go!" and you would flip wildly through your copies of *The Critique of Pure Reason* to find the right page and to be the first to stand up and read it aloud. So often it was you, Damien, who would notice my little joke (the categorical imperative is not in *The Critique of Pure Reason* but, rather, in Kant's *Groundwork of the Metaphysics of Morals* – ha!) and then it was you who was so often the fastest to find the correct passage, to leap to your feet, and to read it aloud with that engaging lisp.

Yes, all right; I hear your howls of protest. Perhaps I do exaggerate a little. Perhaps I am recalling my earliest dreams, when you were still just a gleam in my eye, and I thought to myself "John Stuart Mill could read Greek by the time he was three – why can't my boys?" Still, I gave you the best education in all matters of taste and morals, and I expected to produce a young man who was, if not saintly (and who wants to father an old-fashioned saint anyway – the world contains more than enough tedious dinner guests), at the very least a person worthy of the respect and admiration of his parents.

Nevertheless, I have failed. I have, unwittingly, sired a Nimrod.

It was yesterday evening when I came upon it, the *corpus delicti*, lurking among the ruins of your lunch; it was a small and unassuming morsel, but like a champion bloodhound whose exquisitely trained nose can detect misery a mile away, I knew by smell and by texture what it was in a twinkling. How on earth did such an abomination come to be in your lunch bag anyway? It certainly didn't come from the Black larder; evidently you've been trading provisions with one of the other inmates again – a case of Jack trading the beans for the cow if ever there was one. Ah, my heart! Better that I should find a syringe, a warrant for your arrest, a note from your principal explaining that you can't read, a tin of chewing tobacco, a severed nose, a prostitute – almost *anything* other than *that thing* I found in your lunch bag!

Now, I know very well that I'm *occasionally* guilty of cajoling you and your brothers about the most seemingly insignificant of matters. I bluster and rage about mere details – though given that life is actually nothing *but* details, I think it important to get them right. As Wilde once said (not *that* Wilde – the other one), "The world was my oyster, but I used the wrong fork." Let this be a lesson to us all. However, this particular matter exists on a different plane of importance entirely. Go ahead. Use the fork in your left hand with the tines up, wear your cufflinks fastened inside rather than outside the double cuff, wear your underpants on the outside of your trousers for all I care, but remember this:

The Blacks do not eat suffering. We do not feast upon the misery of the innocent.

Do you understand what I'm telling you, Damien? Then let me make myself plain. One can deprive a banana prematurely of its mother, feed it an unnatural liquid diet, stick its head through the bars of its cage so it's unable to move or to lie down with its legs fully extended, deprive it of all comforts in fact, and then slaughter it and eat it and, happily, it doesn't really mind. It had no other plans. Have you dissected a banana in biology class? If you have, you will remember that you found no evidence of a nervous system, no brain, no calendar of upcoming events. Nothing. Therefore, although we can say that a banana can come to harm, it cannot actually hurt; this is the great advantage of being a fruit, and it is the trade-off for a life devoid of sensual pleasure.

Animal life, however, is another manner. To do to an animal what was done to the above banana is an unconscionable act and a criminal one in my view. And do not think that because it was not you who mistreated the unfortunate creature that you are somehow not responsible for its abominable life and untimely demise. If there was no market for the torture of the innocent – if people like you, *you*, my own son, Damien Black, did not place gustatory satisfaction above the welfare of the children of the earth, there would be no unnecessary suffering at the hands of humanity. It was *you* who murdered a guileless creature as surely as if it had been your own hand that wielded the knife that slit its tender throat.

Ah, my heart! It was, unbelievably, veal that I found in your lunch bag! *Veal!* The body of a baby animal! Ah! Answer me this, Damien: Are you out of your mind, or did you just take a brief holiday from sanity, a little respite from ethics, a short recess in the long school day of the good life? Have you gone insane, and if so, did you have the courtesy to leave a note for your mother and me telling us when you would be back? Have you any shame left at all, or did you stuff it in your locker before you sat down at table to eat with your degenerate chums?

Veal. *Ugh*. I shall dry heave for all eternity.

With nausea,

Dad

From: oliver.black@thedawnpost.com
To: rafe.wilde@thedawnpost.com
Subject: Quivering Giblets

Mr. Wilde:

Well? Are you going to terminate my career, or not? I tell you the crick in my neck is becoming quite unbearable as I kneel upon the cold flagstones, my cheek against the granite chopping block, neck fully extended, waiting for the blade to fall. I find it most discourteous of you to needlessly prolong my suffering in this way, and I demand that you put me out of my misery *posthaste*.

Oliver

From: oliver.black@thedawnpost.com
To: branksome.black@rebel.net
Subject: This and That

Dearest Branksome:

Thank you for the roll of toilet paper with all the latest prison news, although next time you needn't use two-ply – I don't need an extra copy. I'm glad to hear you are well and thriving once again on gruel and hard labour. On the other hand, I don't quite believe you when you say that things between you and the prison guard's daughter are progressing in the right direction – i.e., courtship, marriage, children, oblivion. You know very well that you are not the marrying type, Branksome, that all of your experiments in this field have gone horribly awry; how many times do I have to tell you that you cannot base a marriage simply on a fatal weakness for peasant blouses? I hope that you're not leading her on, merely using the gullible young thing as a messenger and accomplice in the effort to smuggle you out of there, at which point you'll take to the hills, never to be seen by the poor lass again. Your positively Machiavellian approach to romance has always made me squeamish; on the other hand, if your young lady doesn't help you, I shouldn't think that your prospects of escaping from prison are particularly good, and we've simply got to get you out of there, Branksome. There is still much work to be done. I wish I could do something for you, but I believe I'm helpless to come to your aid. Mind you, if it's merely a matter of bribing some corrupt official, I can certainly provide funds for the cause – and I will begin by raiding Olivia's enormous piggy bank, which I recently discovered contained the fantastic sum of $976.37. When confronted, she explained that this war chest of hers was enlarged through "involuntary charitable donations" to her pet rescue centre. With further probing, I discovered the extent of her fund-raising commitment – recesses spent sifting the gravel under the monkey-bars for lunch-money fallen out of pockets, carefully feeling in between the seats on the bus and at the movie theatre for abandoned change, and various other subtle tactics, such as relieving her brothers of the great wads of cash left clumsily lying around in their wallets.

By the way, you'll be pleased to know, if you don't already, that your rampage was not all for nought. This morning I read on the first page of *The Dawn Post* that your escapade has attracted the attention of the world community, who are now up in arms over the cruel conditions in which many of the animals in the zoo were being kept. A few of the more massive animals have been reclaimed (and are now being pampered like Hollywood super-stars for the cameras), but all of the other wildlife you released is still at large, and hope of recapture is becoming slimmer every day. Being so near the waterfront, all of the sea life simply swam to freedom, including your polar bear, by the way, who has be-come something of a celebrity in his own right. Guided by some ancient instinct, he is bravely beginning his trek northward, and the eyes of the world are now upon him as he makes a beeline for the pole. Apparently he's being tracked twenty-four hours a day by military helicopters carrying media crews from fifty nations – classes of school children around the world stop their work and gather around the television to cheer him on – he is the new poster-bear for the World Wildlife Fund. I say, Branky – isn't it vexing that people are touched by *individual* tales of animal tri-umph and freedom, while *en masse* their plight is virtually ignor-ed? They trap them, shoot them, eat them, wear them – but as soon as the public hears of a straggler duck becoming frozen in a pond, or a whale washed up on a beach, or a penguin that has had an unfortunate encounter with an oil slick, then, suddenly, they can't do enough for them. Pockets are bottomless when public pity is adequately stirred. Undoubtedly this is because tragedy must take the form of an Event, not merely the form of an ongo-ing saga. In this way we are exactly like our feline friends, who also pay little attention to what isn't moving.

And so I say to you, Branksome, well done. I apologize for thinking you were a complete ass, and I only wish that I could tell Olivia of your heroism. She would be so proud of you, as am I, Dearest Brother.

As for me, all of this waiting-for-the-axe-to-fall business is driving me quite mad, and all I can do till then is steady myself by concentrating on my work and raising my children. (I try to avoid thinking about my wife, as it leads inevitably to the imperative to break into her studio, which I've not yet been bold enough to do – either because I'm a moralist who remains ever true to his lofty ideals, or a coward who wouldn't say boo to a goose – I know not which.) I just poured my whole heart into a rather inspired letter of condemnation after discovering veal in Damien's lunch bag (and why is it always *me* dealing with things like lunch bags these days? Where the hell is Lucy?); on the bright side, at least the fact that Damien uses a lunch bag at all means that he tears himself away from Angel at least occasionally, and leaves his bedroom to go to places such as, oh, school. This is more than Merlin appears to be doing, and I recently received a sympathy card on behalf of the entire school staff, consoling me on Merlin's death after his lengthy and courageous battle with polio. Six months my boy apparently spent in an iron lung, but he never complained, he only showed the rest of us the real meaning of the word courage. He's a fighter, is our Merlin – I tell you, Branksome, I was in tears at the end of it. Selwyn, who you may remember actually graduated from high school last June – not exactly with flying colours, but with colours flying at about half-mast – is continuing to torment me with public experiments in levitation, telekinesis, astral travel, mind reading, and, most hilariously, voodoo. He makes a big show of carrying about with him a little corn husk doll of me which he abuses in various ways – I make an equally big show of strutting past him in excellent health. Still, having a son who loudly advertises his belief that "natural laws were made to be broken" (as he once put it) comes in handy at times – when Merlin arrives hale and hearty at school on Monday morning, he can simply credit Selwyn with the miracle of raising him from the dead.

And to Olivia, who is not only drawing individual cats but is now producing whole comic books, something like the boys used to do when they were her age. Oh, how well I remember the boy's comics – the severed limbs, the exploding heads, the brutal torture devices and sinister weapons dedicated to eradicating the evil characters who had sprung fully formed from their own tender imaginations. Their comics were a classic celebration of good versus evil, though "good" and "evil" were more like team names and not so much like concepts, given that anything was permissible for the good, and they regularly pulverized evil in the most barbaric manner possible ("Well, they deserved it") in order to restore harmony to the universe. Yes, the boys' comics were violent and gruesome, but as shocking as they were, they were absolutely nothing compared to Olivia's, all of which are devoted to the harrowing theme of animal rights and liberation. A young boy's depiction of a superhero and an evil cyborg locked in mortal combat cannot even begin to compare to an eight-year-old girl's depiction of the imagined atrocities of the slaughterhouse: the stunning, the beheading, the skinning, the amputation of limbs and tail, the disembowelling, the boiling and plucking – and finally, the finished product, – the animal, restored to recognition, but now squawking in a stew or lowing in a bun. She even has little illustrations in the right-hand corner of all her comics, which make a flip book: when one riffles quickly through the pages, one can see an entire cow, looking gradually more unhappy, as the poor beast is squashed between two halves of a bun till its legs and head are sticking out at right angles. In fact, this seems to be Olivia's iconographic signature line, and now not only are individual pages unsafe if left around the house unattended, but even the corners of entire books are not immune from the cow-in-bun theme. Everything from Faulkner's *As I Lay Dying*, to Vonnegut's *Slaughterhouse Five*, to Hemingway's *A Farewell to Arms* (Olivia has added "and Legs"), now depict bovine suffering on its pages. The whole world of literature groans for the oppressed. I've tried to protect my most cherished works, but even my copy of Whitman is now graced with the cow-in-bun logo – and how could Olivia possibly resist a book named after a cow's favourite fodder, *Leaves of Grass*? I flipped through it, and found that she had also highlighted the following passage:

I think I could turn and live with animals, they are so placid
    and self-contain'd,
I stand and look at them long and long.
They do not sweat and whine about their condition,
They do not lie awake in the dark and weep for their sins,
They do not make me sick discussing their duty to God,
Not one is dissatisfied, not one is demented with the mania of
    owning things,
Not one kneels to another, nor to his kind that lived thou-
    sands of years ago,
Not one is respectable or unhappy over the whole earth.

It's true that animals do not sweat and whine about their condition, and so Olivia sweats and whines on their behalf. She has
conviction, Branksome, and a clear mission: to make everyone in
the whole world stop eating animals, before she turns blue and
passes out. She's a remarkable girl, Branksome, and an inspiration
to those of us on missions of our own. Think of Olivia, and take
heart.

Be well,

Oliver

From: rafe.wilde@thedawnpost.com
To: suzanne@heartmail.com
Subject: The Savage Beast

Hey There, Suzanne:

Whoa. Okay, the weirdest thing that has ever happened to me
happened last night – and for once, hallelujah, it didn't involve a
malfunctioning bed. Actually, I'm totally shook up about it,
Suzanne – so if you could possibly tear yourself away from that

wedding machine you're on for just five minutes and actually talk to me, I'd appreciate it. (I got the invitation, by the way – is it just me, or is it objectively weird that you're registered at a department store *and* at a medical supply company?)

Anyway, I found myself at the home of my old childhood piano teacher for my first ever lesson in music history – *me*, the Great Rafe, thoroughly established music critic genius, back at the scarred wooden table I used to sit at as a kid to be tortured *colla voce, assai adagio, furioso, agitato, con fuoco e con passione.* (All those music terms just came back in a rush – I swear they must have seeped out of that table through my elbows and into my brain.) That I was at *any* type of music lesson at all is an outrage in and of itself, and you can just imagine me sprawled in a chair, arms crossed, sneering, with a whole arsenal of rude comments at the ready for the splenetic Ms. Savage. Imagine the eye rolling, the lip curling, the head tossing, the snorts of disdain, the catcalls, the jeering, the mocking, and the tried-and-true withering stare of boredom drilling past her bifocals and into the beady little eyes beyond. Imagine the clever rejoinders, the scoffing, the arrogant derision – and then me verbally sticking the knife in with some hugely clever comment about how her piano lessons were about as interesting as watching pitch drip. Ha! I'm sure you can imagine all that – but if you imagined it that way, you'd be wrong, because that's not how it happened.

This is what happened:

I arrive at her house – late, on purpose – and from outside I can hear her thumping away on the piano, playing one of those fractious Bach fugues, the kind that sound like four old men constantly interrupting each other and engaged in one long domestic argument. I don't wait for her to finish (pieces like that don't come with double bar lines – you have to be careful not to accidentally start playing one of those things as a kid, or you'll finally get to the end just in time to fall headlong into the grave) – I just ring the doorbell and walk in, just like I was always supposed to do when I was a kid. Immediately I recognize the smell – musty, like the smell of her yellowed, dog-eared music books, books that in turn smell like the armpits of the guys who wrote the music. I note the row of brass coat hooks and begin to shrug my jacket off my shoulders, but then I remember Ms. Savage's three rules of conduct – no gum chewing, no yawning, no jacket wearing (it gives the impression that you can't wait to bolt) – and I decide to leave *my* jacket on, while fishing for a stick of gum – preferably a whole package – in the pocket, and lowering my jaw experimentally to see if I can work up a gaping yawn. I stroll slowly down the hallway (bright raspberry, like the colour of old-lady lipstick), and I see that it's decorated with tacky musical knickknacks – little identical white busts churned out of some bust factory in Berlin, each with a different name stamped on the base (Wagner, Beethoven, Mozart, Haydn, Schubert – you can tell him from the rest because he's got the John Lennon glasses – oh, and three Bachs), miniature china pianos, a music box orchestra – each with a different plastic insect playing a different plastic instrument – and a gallery of framed portraits of big-time celebrity pianists of whom nobody's ever heard and who've all snuffed it.

By now I'm chewing and yawning pretty furiously – jacket zipped to my neck – and so I enter the enormous, recital hall-like living room that's been her studio since the time of Victoria and Albert. Naturally, I fully expect to be greeted by the odious Ms. Savage herself – maybe sitting on her perch like a vulture, or chained to the floor like a Mastiff-Rottweiler cross, just like she was in the old days. But, as it turns out, Ms. Savage isn't there at all – having slid gracefully off the bench and now standing beside the piano at the other end of the living room is this shapely blonde Venus – leggy, svelte, a perfect 36-26-36 (unlike those pathetic lingerie salesmen you're forever reading about in porno magazines who have to check everything manually, I can round a woman up or down to the nearest half inch without so much as laying a finger on her), and she's dressed in faded jeans and this sassy little maroon velvet jacket with flared sleeves that shows off her adorable little pierced navel. She's wearing lots of gold bangles and these sexy little black boots, and as I walk toward her I'm flipping frantically through my mental Rolodex of the best come-on lines, and my heart's pounding in that primal way, you know, like a lion's heart pounds when it's about to bring down an impala. She's gorgeous, this woman, she's got style, presence, and I'm instantly on the make and hoping desperately that Ms. Savage doesn't suddenly show up and destroy the moment ("No, no, no, Rafe – we fondle a woman in 2/4 time"). All I can think as I saunter toward this total Babe in my most seductive manner is – please, if there's a God – please let it be thong underwear. Thong underwear or nothing, and suddenly there's this battle raging inside me – which would be best? Maybe no underwear at all – I mean, who's got the time? I know I've got to play it cool – and suddenly I'm like this little David trying to slay the Goliath of my passion with a rock in a slingshot – only it's not a sling shot – it's thong underwear and I'm fixated and horrified that I'm going to say something to this woman like, "Was that you playing that thong on the piano?"

And as I get closer to this bombshell, I become obsessed by the thought that this might not be one of Ms. Savage's students, but Ms. Savage's daughter – if she has a daughter – and she may already have ruined my chances by telling her about my antics as a kid. I knew every trick in the book, and invented some besides, to get out of the half-hour of misery that was my weekly piano lesson. All I needed was thirty seconds alone with the piano and a tube of Crazy Glue and I was home free. Of course I used more conventional methods, like forgetting to bring my piano books to my lesson for six years straight, feigning ignorance ("Duh, was I supposed to practice *that*?"), and claiming not just that my dog ate my homework but that my dog lived exclusively *on* homework, that he refused anything but homemade homework kibble. Then there were the aliens and the astonishing number of times I was abducted, coincidentally, just before my lesson; there were more flying saucers parked in our backyard than at Roswell. Not to mention the mafia blackmailers – "You wanna keep alla your fingers? You don't play no more piano, capiche?" There was also all the emotional upset – it was amazing over the years how many of my closest friends and favourite aunts unexpectedly dropped dead on my lesson day. And then there was the string of maladies – the old arm in a sling ploy, the sprained thumb trick, the white cane and sunglasses, the hangnails, the bloody noses, rabies, scurvy, leprosy, brain tumours, induced vomiting escalating to full-scale grand mal seizures – anything to get out of playing the fucking piano. And suddenly all this guilt just blasts me like acid wind and rain, as if somebody had just swung open the gates of hell, and I almost trip over my own feet as I continue to saunter sexily toward my Bach-thumping beauty. Suddenly I remember that Ms. Savage would always appear almost insanely happy to see me, always chipper, upbeat, solicitous. I used to try to keep her talking because I knew that, as soon as she stopped, I'd have to fake my way through some wretched minuet calculated to humiliate the uncoordinated as much as possible. I'd be sitting at this enormous glossy black piano – the very one my Venus was standing beside as I drew nearer – and she'd put some piece of music in front of me that I'd claimed I'd practised for several hours that week, and I'd hack my way through it with excruciating slowness and inaccuracy. All those awful moments, when I was fumbling hopelessly around and she was listening with rapt attention, lasted forever. My face burned, my hands sweat. The shame I felt was unbearable, and I felt like calling Amnesty International to report a torture.

And then, after this pitiful exercise in sight reading, after I'd butchered yet another piece (or the same one, again and again, week after week), after my practising sham had been brought to light yet again, then would come the inevitable, fanatically enthusiastic, "Good for you! It's really coming! Now we just have to work on a few things . . ." What? Was she deaf? Was she stupid? Did she really think I'd practised at all? Did she think that *I* was so stupefyingly untalented that, after a week of alleged practice, that was really was the best I could do? Christ, Suzanne – if there was ever anyone who knew how to kill with kindness, it was that woman. Did she know that every nice word was an insult? A humiliation? A dagger? I wanted to break her somehow, I wanted her to show genuine emotion, I wanted her to admit that she knew I hadn't practised. Why didn't she get mad? Why was she always so fucking pleasant? If only she'd been mean, if only she'd given me what I deserved. Instead, she insisted on taking me seriously, or, at least, she *pretended* to take me seriously – I could never tell which.

Anyway, even through my guilt trip I keep mentally undressing this woman – removing the little boots (red toenails!) unbuttoning the little jacket (no bra!) unzipping the jeans (thong underwear! – do I hear angels singing?), and still Ms. Savage doesn't swoop down from the ceiling or arise like an apparition from the floor to halt my progress toward sexual conquest. Closer, closer. And as I keep walking toward this beauty I notice, as I get nearer still, that she's got these little crinkly bits around the eyes behind the funky specs, and laugh lines around the mouth, and just a hint of silver streaked through the white-blond hair. I realize, with a start, that she's a middle-aged woman, *twice* the age that I feel, who by some miracle I can't get my head around, also happens to be a total peach.

I realize that the woman I'm walking toward, the woman who's as naked as a jay bird in my imagination, the woman who I want to badger, bodge, boff, bang, bonk, poke, stuff, stab, bash, grapple and thrub – that woman, Suzanne, is none other than Ms. Savage herself.

"*Nnnnnnnnnnnnooooooooooooooooooo!*" I scream in horror, dropping to my knees and clawing out my eyes with my bare hands, rather than look upon the hideous freak in my path. You want a premise for a horror movie? This is it. Piano-teaching funsucker from hell disguises herself as beautiful woman – lures unsuspecting former student into studio – torment ensues. I'm telling you, Suzanne, no woman has ever been mentally dressed by a man as fast as Ms. Savage was dressed by me.

"Oh, God, no!" I whimper, everything painfully deflating, withering, shrivelling, with the force of an imploding white dwarf star. "It's you!"

"You were expecting someone else?"

"Yes!" I sob, truthfully. Yes, I was expecting someone else. I was expecting the Ms. Savage of my childhood nightmares, the ten-foot, slimy, green-fanged monster who made my life a living hell –"

"Well, I'm afraid it's still just me, Rafe, and it's nice to see you too." She gestures for me to stop retching and get up, to spit out my gum and take off my jacket, and to follow her to the old table that speaks perfect Italian. I obey like a dog. Then she sits me down and gives me a cup of something a hell of a lot stronger than the lemonade she used to give me as a kid.

We talk. Well, she talks – I whimper pitifully, and the first thing I demand to know is how she can be younger *now* than when she was teaching me as a kid. I'm thinking a pact with the devil, but she just laughs and says it's all a matter of perspective. Kids are notoriously bad judges of age, she says, and since she started teaching at sixteen, and I was six at the time, she was almost *three times older* than me – hence my conviction that she ate dodo eggs and pooped coprolites. But still, that didn't explain the trail of slime, the rotating head, the eyes on stalks and the stench of death – where was all that now? In the old days she looked more like a coelacanth than a human, and plastic surgery can only do so much after all. So she pulls this photo off a shelf and hands it to me – it's a photo of a pretty young woman, a woman who looks like the younger sister of the woman in front of me, and I ask who it is, and she rolls her eyes and says, "It's me, you idiot" – and I look at it again and I realize it's absolutely true – I *am* an idiot.

How can this be, I ask, and as she takes the photo out of my hands and puts it back on the shelf, she says something like, "Maybe it wasn't *me* who was the monster, Rafe – maybe it was *your guilt* that was the monster."

"So that's your pat little explanation!" I snort, and she goes on to say that because I couldn't accept my own guilt, I made someone else responsible for my failings – I did it to myself, she says – it was *me* who turned *her* into a monstrosity. "A classic case of Freudian projection," she says, crossing her arms and leaning back in her chair. "As if!" I cleverly reply, and because I can't think of anything else to say, I change the subject and ask her why she agreed to teach me again, and she fires the question right back at me – why did I agree to be her student? And I can't think of anything but the truth – "My mom made me" – and she laughs because she thinks I'm trying to be funny. And then she says that she agreed to teach me because she was curious – she says it's because I've made such a big splash in the music world, and then she has the gall to say, "Which I must admit surprised me, given the attitude toward music you had when you were a kid."

It's at this point in the conversation that I totally flip out. "What the fuck are you talking about? I *loved* music!" And then I proceed to vent about how she tried to kill that love with all the wretched stuff she made me practice – all that fucking fairy music – those prissy minuets and sonatinas and inventions. They were so . . . they were so . . . and as I'm looking for exactly the right word to describe what a punishment these pieces were, she fills in the blank herself. "They were so complicated? And you didn't want to put in the intellectual effort necessary to understand them? You were lazy? And it was easier to think up excuses than to actually practice?" That really pissed me off, Suzanne – she was so *not* getting what I was trying to say – in other words, nothing had changed in twenty-five years, and it was then that something just snapped. I felt compelled, and completely qualified by the way, to be the spokesman for the music of *my* time, *my* genera-tion. You should have heard me, seething and hissing, snake-like, about how tedious those sissy pieces were, how irrelevant, how churchy, how grooveless, how *dead* – why had she tried so hard to force me to play music from the grave anyway? I'm practically foaming at the mouth now about how I wanted to play *my* music, the music of *my* youth, not all those snobby, poxy confections. On and on I rave, and after a good five minutes my (hugely inspired) diatribe finally ends with these words, spat out of my mouth like old vomit: "I wanted to *rock*, you know?"

And then? Silence. There's a few minutes of it while both of us revel in my triumph. At least, I imagine that's what's happening, until Ms. Savage says, "The problem isn't *classical music*, Rafe. The problem is *you*. Classical music *does* rock. *You* don't know how to listen."

You can imagine how well I took this particular pronouncement. "In case you'd forgotten," I hiss (and I add the words "you condescending bitch" in my mind), "*I make my living listening to music.*"

"But it's what you're listening *for* that's the problem, and what you're listening *to* is mostly manufactured crap," she retorts, and I feel insulted, I feel angry – I feel like I always felt, like maybe she knows something I don't – and then it's her turn to preach but I'm not paying attention – I'm too incensed to make sense of anything she's saying, and so I just wait until she's finished yammering (like I always did – don't listen, just wait, that was my motto), and then I bring up something that Oliver Black (of all people) once wrote to me. I ask her, if classical music is so wonderful, how come piano teachers have such lousy track records? I ask her how many students she's taught – and how many of them have ended up like me, unable to play a note of the crap music she was trying to teach them. She admits that she's taught hundreds of students, and has turned out maybe a dozen competent musicians. "My point!" I proclaim triumphantly, until she asks me how my algebra is, my knowledge of capital cities, Newton's laws of motion, the boiling point of nitrogen. Apparently it isn't just music teachers who fail – "Most seeds of knowledge fall on sterile ground, don't they, Rafe?" – and there she goes again, just like when I was a kid – making me feel like it's all *my* fault that I never learned a goddamn thing.

We keep on crossing swords for an hour, two, three – and I

feel like there's an earthquake rumbling away under my chair, and I'm on shifting sand, and I could go under any minute. Sometimes I feel desperate and pull some pretty low punches – like "You're *forty-eight* years old and still living at your parents' place?" (Turns out she's temporarily separated from the guy she's been with and is staying at her folks' house until she can figure things out – and even in my fury I feel like a total chump for having brought it up.) And after about four solid hours of conversation, she decides I need a lot more than just a few modern music appreciation lessons to fix me up. So we get in her car and drive to the slummiest, roughest part of town – in fact, we're within a block of Billy-Bob's – and it suddenly occurs to me that she's probably insane after all, and she's going to knife me right here and dump my body in the gutter with the rest. But instead we stop in front of this big ugly factory or warehouse or something, and I can't imagine why we're here – until I see the sign painted in big block letters on the side of the building, and do you know what the sign says? I swear to God I'm not kidding Suzanne – the sign says "Beds Beds Beds." Beds Beds Beds! It's the fucking Beds Beds Beds factory! I hadn't mentioned anything about my association with these people, and here she is taking me to their bloody factory! What kind of nightmare is this? And the irony of the whole thing is overwhelming, because the place is surrounded by homeless people sleeping under cardboard boxes in puddles on the street, and all around the top of the building there's advertising in gigantic neon letters – Pillows! Mattresses! Box-springs! Duvets! Comforters! Sheets! And in a moment of pure illumination, I realize that this situation is the absolutely perfect metaphor for my whole purgatorial existence.

Anyway, we park and walk to the entrance, but she's foiled because the sign on the door says "Closed."

"We can't go in there," I say, relieved.

"Oh yes we can," she says, taking out a key and putting it in the lock. And I'm thinking, what is it about this woman? Why is she so utterly nasty? And why is it that she's doomed to be forever associated with all the things in life that I find most unpleasant? I become increasingly flustered, paralysed by internal conflict – until Ms. Savage finally just grabs my arm and leads me through the doors of the Beds Beds Beds factory and – bingo – my whole life changes.

See, it's not a bed factory at all, Suzanne. It's had nothing even remotely to do with beds since they relocated years ago. The whole bed thing is just a cover for the fact that this factory is really a – I don't exactly know how to say what it is without you freaking out on me – I guess the best way to put it is that this factory is really a – temple. A temple thingy. And I don't know what to call their belief system because it's the craziest religion you've never heard of. I can't describe it here – technically I'm not even allowed to – the whole thing's hush-hush for now. Actually, the place itself isn't even finished yet – when we entered the building I immediately looked up and spotted this gorgeous woman up on a ladder painting these sort of angels on the ceiling – angels without faces yet, because she's still looking for exactly the right models. Actually, she's not looking anymore. As soon as she laid eyes on me she almost crashed to the floor – apparently, I have just the face she's been looking for (aw, shucks), and she's already started doing preliminary sketches before immortalizing my face in oils.

Anyway, I spend several mind-blowing hours at this temple thingy, just sitting and listening and staring. They do a lot of sitting and listening and staring actually – it's kind of a Zen thing, you know? Well, sort of. And when I finally end up back home, the first thing I do – the first thing I feel absolutely compelled to do – is to open up my old piano books, you know, the ones my mom sent me a few months back. So I'm looking through all these pieces – the preludes and the sonatinas and the rondos, and the little character pieces with goofy gay names like "Elfin Dance" and "To a Wild Rose" – and I get to the end of the book, to the inside of the back cover, and what do I find written there? I find these words, scrawled in my own twelve-year-old hand – "I love Miss Savage." What the fuck? I love Miss Savage? No! *I loathe*

Miss Savage! I loathe Miss Savage!

This is not the way it was supposed to be, Suzanne. This is *not* the way it was supposed to be.

Anyway, I'm going to be out of touch for a while because Ms. Savage invited me and Blankie to go on what she calls a retreat at this temple thingy for a few days. I'll still be writing *Rafe Reviews*, and Ms. Savage is going to help me with the whole new music thing. Don't worry – I'm not going to wind up with a shaved head handing out flowers at airports – it's not that kind of cult. It's more a culture, you know what I mean? No, you don't. Maybe someday I'll be able to explain it.

Until then –

Yatha bhutam, Baby,

Rafe

The Dream Post
Zen Spy Trashes Hope of Sartori

Tibet – A recent leak of top-secret Zen documents, which have been under wraps for thousands of years, and which have subsequently been published on the Internet under the title *Koans for Dummies*, is creating havoc among Zen practitioners worldwide.

"This has blown Zen Buddhism wide apart," said Sheriff Rock Braun of Hung Tich Thnang county. "Basically what we've got here is a koan master key, the answers to all the standard koans. What is the sound of one hand clapping? What was the appearance of your face before you were born? Does a dog have Buddha nature? Well, now we know."

Buddhist monks are working frantically to devise brand new koans (What is the sound of one tooth chewing, etc.) but the solutions are being leaked and published on the Internet as fast as the little men can make them up. "We've got a spook, no question," said the Sheriff, pausing to push back his Stetson and adjust his badge. "There's a mole in a monk's robe and it stinks. For thousands of years these good folk have relied on questions with irrational answers to boot them off the lower planes of existence. How the hell are they supposed to realize their Buddha nature now? The DA's office is just sick about this, I can tell you."

After receiving a call on his radio, the Sheriff abruptly excused himself, adjusted the gun in his holster, and jumped into his cruiser. "All hell's breaking loose, dammit! We've got monks believing in permanence, attachment, noncontingency, all kinds of crazy shit – somebody's got to get up to that monastery and stop the insanity!"

The Sheriff turned on the sirens and began the treacherous ascent on the narrow dirt road up the mountain, narrowly missing a goat and several novitiate monks doing the can-can.

The investigation will be given additional support tomorrow, at which time a supercomputer with Apple's new Soul Detection software will be installed in the monastery. "The monk with the soul – he's our spook," the Sheriff later confirmed.

From: oliver.black@thedawnpost.com
To: branksome.black@rebel.net
Subject: Beggar This for a Game of Soldiers

Dear Branksome:

I'm writing this e-mail with the brilliant Richard Dawkins curled up in a ball and purring contentedly on my lap. I shoo him off periodically, but he keeps returning to my side, either because he is psychically tuned in to my emotional state and senses my intensifying distress, or perhaps because I smell faintly like tuna. He's a sort of barometer of emotional pressure, actually, and I always know when the children are out of the house because it is then that he seeks out my lap and looks up at me as if to say, "Forget the other four. I am your true child. I will never leave you, if only because I have a brain the size of a walnut."

(Speaking of cats, my Amelia has been missing for almost twelve hours now, but I know I ought not to worry. Her passion for heights is boundless, and so any opportunity to sneak out of the house, climb a tree, and ambush life in all its variety is irresistible. Still, even though Richard Dawkins is always a comfort to me in both his human and feline form, the whole world feels wrong without my blue-and-amber-eyed beauty.)

So, Branky, this is really just a quick note to warn you that you shouldn't expect to hear from me for the next few days, since what I desperately need is to shake off the manacles, remove the black bag from my head, and leave my firing squad of one to his perverse little game of Blind Man's Bluff. As you well know, I have of late felt quite on the edge of hysteria, and I desperately need the peace that passeth all understanding, not to mention defies all logic. I therefore intend to take a busman's holiday, living for a few days at a virgin aquifer where I shall be pampered like a Turkish prince, whilst taking a course on the miracle of dihydrous oxide from Chef Octavio's water sommelier. Did you know that water is all the rage these days, Branksome? Everybody's drinking it, especially the rich and famous; in fact, the composition of the average human celebrity is now 65 percent sparkling water. But it isn't just the difference between a carbonated and noncarbonated beverage anymore; now there is glacier water, rain water, spring water, dew water, iceberg water, snow water – mere tap water is for philistines, even though when the veil is jerked aside, we discover that the tap is exactly where most bottled waters originate. So what, then, is the problem with ordinary tap water? It doesn't have a brand name (yet), that's the problem. Oh, if only we could all breathe brand-name Air™ and tread upon a brand-name Earth™, life would be complete! What do you suppose the ancients would think of this modern madness? Certainly Jesus™ wouldn't be happy; given that the mark-up on water is about five hundred times that of alcohol, turning water into wine in modern times would undoubtedly result in swift legal action.

So, farewell, Branksome. I shall return in approximately seven days' time in order to resume my long, slow dance with Fate, who, by the way, is a frightful dance partner – pushy, inflexible, capricious, uncaring – she waltzes you backward through your life, stomping gleefully upon your arches, slamming you casually against brick walls, and dipping you willy-nilly until one day she simply lets go, and you end up flat on your back with her bright red stiletto heel piercing your heart. That Fate-dipping day is fast approaching, but for now, I shall dip myself in the Waters™, being careful not to drown in them for fear of causing a legal and linguistic headache over what could only be construed as a brand-name death.

All best wishes,

Oliver

Chapter Eight

From: oliver.black@thedawnpost.com
To: damien.black@freenet.org
Subject: Pardon

Feast of Oliver Wendell Holmes, Jr.

Hello Damien:

I just returned home from a rather dizzying week of sampling H_2O in all its many advertised forms (Ah! Once again two hydrogen and one oxygen! The mind reels!), and the first thing I found was a note from you under my study door, a note that, I don't mind telling you, I received with a glad heart. Thank you, my son, for your official recantation. How marvellously crafted it was, too, reading as a sort of conjugation of the Latin *peccavum* (to sin) in the first person singular. Bravo, my young lad! Know that I accept your apology in full and that you are back in the will. Hoorah! Sadly, however, I've not reinstated your allowance, given that you're still in the habit of leaving the milk on the counter to spoil quotidianly. Good God, Damien! It's as if leaving the milk out to spoil were a matter of principle for you, a sort of mysterious moral imperative. You are devoted to milk spoiling in the same way that others might be devoted to social or political revolution. Above all else, this much must be so – the milk must be left out! And leave the refrigerator door gaping open while you're at it – the hot earth must be chilled! How tragic that you were not born four billion years earlier when, by leaving the fridge door permanently ajar, you might have played a pivotal role in the earth's original cooling.

With regard to the other matter of which you write, I must say that I find it *of no interest whatsoever* that you are pursuing an investigation of the ways in which other farm animals are raised and slaughtered. It is not only veal calves, you tell me, who are mistreated, but domestic animals in general who live lives of deprivation, and who die needlessly in filth and misery. Like your sister, you also see the evil in the dairy industry, based as it is on the tragic separation of mother and infant. (Perhaps your leaving the milk out to spoil, previously an act of carelessness, is now an act of defiance, hmm?) You seem suddenly to be a warehouse of information, quoting everyone from Gandhi to Brigitte Bardot. However, *I do not wish to speak about this subject with you, nor do I wish to disclose my reasons.* On this matter I am immovable. Whatever you find out you may share with anyone you like, with the exception of me. End of conversation.

And, end of e-mail.

Unalterably,

Dad

PS: I'm wondering about the whereabouts of a) Amelia and b) your mother. Where is my cat? Where is my wife?

From: oliver.black@thedawnpost.com
To: branksome.black@rebel.net
Subject: Slaves to Freedom

Dearest Branky:

Oh, well done, Old Chap! Congratulations on being at large once again, for what are Beauty and Truth without Liberty? Admittedly, I was disappointed concerning the particulars of your escape, as I have come to expect an account that reads like an action-adventure drama, and not like the plot of a Bugs Bunny cartoon. What an unoriginal jailbreak, as hackneyed and banal as the old file-in-the-cake trick; or the shovel, conveniently forgotten by a negligent maintenance worker and propped up against the wall of your cell, to use in tunnelling your way to freedom; or the droopy-eyed, loose-lipped old dog holding the keys in his mouth, enticed by the promise of a bone; or the inattentive prison guard, keys sticking out of his back pocket as he snoozes beside the cell, cap over his eyes and gun abandoned on the floor beside him. But no. In the end it was the prison guard's daughter who helped you escape in – of all things – a *laundry hamper!* Tut tut, Branksome. For shame, for shame. How disappointingly derivative and predictable! It's exactly like the musical *Annie*, isn't it, with you cast as the flaming-haired orphan herself. Did the other inmates burst into a gravelly baritone rendition of "It's a Hard Knock Life" as you were whisked out the front gates and into the waiting laundry truck? Did Miss Hannigan follow in hot pursuit? You *will* let me know if Daddy Warbucks adopts you, I hope. It would be a relief to know that our financial troubles are over – where are all the bald-as-a-billiard-ball billionaire philanthropists when you need them, eh Branksome? At any rate, I expected better of you, but at least you are free to continue the work, praise be to Dwynwen, and I suppose that's all that matters in the end.

Here is a remarkable fact for you, Branky: Rafe Wilde could have ended my career in my absence, but for some unknown reason, he has not. Undoubtedly there is ample satisfaction in simply keeping me waiting, a satisfaction apparently deeply rooted in the human psyche, to which the maladaptive idea of the "waiting room" will attest. Why should professionals not have welcoming rooms instead? Because those who make others wait are those who have all the power (were we not instructed to "wait upon the Lord" in Sunday school?), and the waiting room stands as a baleful reminder of this fact. I believe Mr. Wilde has discovered this for himself and is enjoying the luxurious sensation of rocking back and forth on his haunches in the tall grass, as I stand frozen to the spot like a skittish animal of prey – ears pricked, eyes wide, muscles taut – waiting for the unhappy sensation of fangs in flank.

Finally, to the headline news of the day. I did it, Branksome. Upon returning home yesterday evening after a week of taking the waters, I seized the opportunity to break into Lucy's studio and peruse its content for clues. And what did I find within? Ah,

Branksome. How right you were. You knew that when a wife suddenly looks more lovely than ever, when she starts keeping odd hours, and when she begins to avoid the knock at the bedroom door as one avoids the knock of the Watch Tower–toting octogenarian with nothing but time, time, time – then the reason is inevitably a rival male. Obviously I must confront her about it immediately, but I just don't want to, Branksome – it's all so unpleasant. (Is it a coincidence that Venus, the planet of love, is in sooth a raging hell?) The truth is that my wife has grown weary of me and is having an affair – and here was *I* accusing *you* of a hackneyed plot! I was going to write a letter to her, but I put it off by writing first to Damien, who, by the way, might be onto us. A bright lad is our Stringbean, you know. Selwyn's intelligence is temporarily eclipsed by a Ouija board, and I fear Merlin's dreadlocks may be ingrown and strangling the supply of oxygen to his higher faculties (this would explain so much), but young Stringbean seems to be all there, knock on wood. Now if he would only put the milk back in the fridge – but this is like asking the leopard to change his spots, or, indeed, like asking any creature to shed his primary defining characteristic.

Anyway – I have a letter to write, Branksome, and I mustn't put it off any longer.

Resolutely,

Oliver

From: oliver.black@thedawnpost.com
To: lucy.black@artnet.org
Subject: Brass Tacks

My Dearest Lucy:

I confess that I'm at a loss as to what to say or what to do. For months I've begged you to be straight with me, and for months you've brushed me aside. "Honestly, Oliver, I'm not hiding anything," you tell me, all the while spread-eagled against the closet doors, lunging at the trunk to close it before I can observe what's inside, always dodging from side to side so I can't quite see what's concealed behind your back (figuratively speaking of course). "I'm just a bit preoccupied," you say, in the same way that somebody with the SS on their doorstep and a closet full of Jews might be "a bit" preoccupied. Would it offend you terribly if I suggested you never seek work as a secret agent? Though the content is unknown, it's ludicrously obvious that you have a secret. Forgive my bitchiness, Darling, but the truth is that you are laughably inexpert in the art of deception.

Who was it who once observed that the two essentials for a woman are guineas and locks? It is these two things that I have always earnestly provided, knowing that you required my financial support until your career as an artist took flight (which it has done, and I tell you in all sincerity that nothing could give me greater satisfaction than this), and that you needed a private space to work, if only to keep the children from adding their own personal stamp to your masterpieces (*Sunset at Noon – with Little Red Hand Prints*). I know very well that your studio is your sanctum sanctorum, not to be invaded by anyone, not even me, and I have always accepted and respected this. You require absolute silence and privacy, an almost womblike atmosphere, in order to work well. Nevertheless, your continual absence from my life lately has caused me to miss you ferociously, and my motive for letting myself into your studio was an innocent one: I only wanted to feel close to you and to know what in heaven's name is going on. (I was also hoping to find Amelia in there, actually – she's been missing for days, as I assume you know, and I'm feeling more than just a little panicked about it. Losing my wife is one thing, but losing my wife *and* my cat – well, it's just too much for any man.)

Much was as I expected; there was the inevitable messiness of studio life – brushes, charcoal, sketchbooks, wood, miter saw, drawings – all strewn across the gigantic antique table. Finished canvases were stacked against the walls, a new painting was begun upon an easel. But there was much that shocked me, and convinced me more than ever that some event of colossal importance has occurred in your life, without me having an inkling of what it might be.

It was in a corner of your studio that I first glimpsed the unexpected. Placed upon a low table was a decorative red and gold box, lit from inside and open at the front. Incense, bells, and candles surrounded it. Inside the box there was a strange collection of objects, all of which relate in some way to the arts, and which included a framed portrait of someone whom I believe most resembles Oscar Wilde as a faunlike young man. Now I know that you are given to amassing curious objects, and I thought at first that this might be another of your bizarre collections. But then I noticed the abundance of fresh flowers placed carefully in front of the portrait, and it was suddenly easy to imagine that this was not a haphazard collection at all. It was easy to imagine that this was, incredibly, some sort of an altar.

I'd barely taken all of this in when the real punch to the gut came – my eye caught a number of charcoal sketches of a practically naked male on the table, evidently done from life. How startled I was that these were done in your own hand, especially given that I recognized the man immediately, though I had no idea that you and he had ever met. Suddenly I imagined that more had gone on than a little innocent life drawing, though it beggars belief that you might have been untrue to me, my darling (especially with *him*). Didn't I once say you that you were free to do whatever you wished so long as it did not involve other men, bizarre religious practices, or unnecessary saturated fats? I wasn't trying to be funny, you know. The attractive naked man, the altar – what will I find in your studio next? A greasy and half-eaten container of deep-fried onion rings? Dear God, *no!*

Lucy – every morning you disappear into your studio; every

afternoon you disappear I know not where. You are sometimes at home in the evenings, but it's obvious that your presence is due to Olivia and the boys, not to me. This is no longer mere speculation; clearly you're avoiding me, and you're involved in something that you wish to keep secret from me. What is it, my love? Where do you go? What are you doing there? You know I'm devoted to you, but I feel increasingly as if I'm devoted to a mental construct, to the memory of someone I once knew, and not to an actual person.

Is it me? Have you suddenly realized what I've known all along, that I am not worthy of you, and so you are gradually inching away? Am I too ancient? Too ridiculous? Too prickly? I try very hard not to repulse you, you know, and don't engage in half the disgusting behaviours of our sons. I'm not such a bad husband, am I? Certainly I can think of worse (Henry VIII, Onan, Peter Peter Pumpkin Eater, etc.). I am also trying very hard not to age, even going so far as to occasionally consider the possibility of voluntarily putting night cream on my face, which you have urged me to do for the last twenty years, always patiently explaining the benefits of a regular skin-care regimen; how I've enjoyed feigning ignorance, and then horror when you – used to – come at me nightly with that white goop in your cupped palm to spread all over my neck and face. "You don't want to get wrinkles," you would say. "I don't really give a toss," I would respond, intentionally goading you but loving the attention all the same. "Oh yes you do," you would assure me, attempting to smooth – crush, actually – the offending lines on my forehead with your flat hand. Rarely would this be the end of it, and once you had taken a good look at my imperfect visage, you would come at me with your fingernails, little sharp scissors, all manner of toners and masks and astringents. You were always the artist, weren't you, always trying to make the world a more beautiful place. "All right. Now, lie still and let me look at those nose hairs. Here come Mr. Tweezers! Oh, don't be such a baby. Come now, it's not that bad. Ow, you bit me! Bastard!" It was all good clean fun, was it not, my love?

Perhaps it isn't my appearance that has become increasingly objectionable but rather my persona, my me-ness, which, as I age, has become distilled into the Essence of Oliver. You of all people know best what I am, my love. You know that I'm really a sheep in wolf's clothing, and that I consist of a complicated amalgam of character traits – I am a romantic, a sensualist, a philosopher, a stage manager (in the sense that all the world's a stage, and *I* want to be in the director's chair), but above all, I am a moralist, and moralists – like crumhorn players, soothsayers, and alchemists – are obsolete. We are as fashionable and as welcome as a convention of nuns in a brothel. Is it this, the very thing I consider to be the best part of me, to which you have taken a scunner? Ah me! It's not easy to be rejected, but to be rejected by the person who knows you better than anyone, who has seen you at your worst but also at your glorious best, is an added kick in the teeth. It's a reminder of the unhappy fact that, sometimes, one's best just isn't good enough.

I do trust that you would let me know if there was some issue with the various goings-on in what is euphemistically known as "the bedroom department." Perhaps nature is playing another one of her nasty little practical jokes (colds, mosquitoes, winter) and has made what was once alluring and seductive (me) into something repulsive and grotesque. Does familiarity breed indifference? How cruel that making a baby is sexy, but having a family is not. Perhaps, after twenty-five years of making love with the same old reliably virile, sensitive, interested, potent, generous, romantic, sufficiently naughty, relatively fit, supremely well-endowed male, you want something else. Ah.

Anyway, my dearest, I do hope that your recent lack of interest in pair bonding has some insignificant and temporary cause. Need the words monogamy and monotony be interchangeable within the context of lifelong partnering? Are monogamy and celibacy really the same thing? My own experience suggests otherwise. Personally, I have always found the monotony of sex within marriage to be much like the monotony of eating chocolate – it is delicious every time.

My darling Lucy. What can I do to attract you to me once again?

Please explain yourself, I beg of you.

I am in despair, and in your hands.

Semper fidelis,

Oliver

The Dream Post
Disgruntled Housewife Finally Says
Enough Is Enough

Hollywood, California – After almost sixty years of marriage to the founder of the world's most successful soft porn magazine, Playguy, disgruntled and long-suffering suburban housewife, Mrs. Myrtle Frehen, finally declared that enough is enough.

"Fred's spent the last sixty years sitting around a pool in his pajamas smoking a pipe," explained Mrs. Frehen, a stocky woman with a poodle perm wearing support hose and sensible shoes. "Put down the martini! Get your pants on! Get a real job, I tell him, but does he listen? Nah! Life's just a big party for my good-for-nothing Mr. Bigshot husband."

The Frehens were married in the 1950s, but due to the fact that they are both committed Catholics, they must remain united for all eternity. (The Playguy Mansion, with its working cathedral extension, employs a certified Catholic Bishop named Trixie).

Mrs. Frehen, who has miraculously survived a long litany of accidents that almost appear calculated to bump her off, says of her husband, "He's a bum, plain and simple, just like I told him on our wedding day."

For his part, Fred Frehen

credits his wife with his success, claiming that it was Mrs. Frehen who inspired his ambitious drive to found his vast Empire of Pleasure. "You won't find a tuna casserole at the Playguy Mansion," Mr. Frehen quipped drily.

From: rafe.wilde@thedawnpost.com
To: alma.wilde@command.net
Subject: Extreme Bliss-Out

Dear Mom:

Oh Mom, Oh Mom, Oh Mom. Oh Mom Mom Mom Mom Mom. Your little guy's got something to tell you, and although nobody reads e-mail standing up, I'm advising you to sit down anyway, just to emphasize the importance of what I'm about to say. My wildest dream has finally come true, Mom, and I think you know what I'm talking about here. No, I'm not talking about getting back together with Suzanne, given that she's offered up her heart on permanent basis to a guy who just happens to be in the business. And no, I'm not talking about getting back together with Angel either, given that she's been forever Blackballed from my life, if you get my meaning. I'm not even talking about pounding you-know-who to a pulp, and then turning the pulp into the paper on which to write his obituary. I'm talking about my dream of floating through a world where the grass is so green, and the sky is so blue, and circles are so round, and sugar is so sweet, and beds are so soft – and, no, before you go making accusations, this has nothing to do with the contents of Loppity Lamb either. It's got to do with my big news – so are you ready? Here's what your little guy's got to tell you:

I – *finally* – got – rid – of – Petey!

Can you believe it? After five pointless years, the little shit's gone from my life – *forever*. Isn't that glorious? I feel like a new man now that I'm free of his constant editorializing. Actually, though, Petey's not my big news. I was just using Petey as a warm-up, to work up to the real thing, which is this: Are you ready? Okay:

I – am – in – *love.*

I'm in love! Oh Mom! Oh Mom, Mom, Mom. I've met the most amazing woman – she's blonde, she's beautiful, and she's an artist in so many senses of the word. I don't want to tell you who it is, though, because there are some nasty complications, and I just know you're going to flip out on me. The thing is, she's sort of already with somebody, a guy I call O.B. for short – S.O.B., if I want to take my time. He's the sort of bastard who has one thing on his mind – *food* – and frankly, she's tired of playing second strudel. So the upshot is, she's finally dumpling him once and for all, and she's doing it so she can be with *me*, which is another reason why I know you're going to freak. Considering what I just went through with Angel, I'm sure you're wondering how I could pinch someone's girl off him. I can do it, Mom, because they were practically estranged before I burst on the scene, and trust me – the guy she's with is a pretentious twit, and she deserves better. Okay, so if you haven't yet flipped like a pancake, you will when I tell you the age difference between me and this woman. Remember how old Angel was? Well, this woman's just a little older than Angel – about thirty-two years older, actually. I guess you could say that this woman's not exactly old enough to be my mother, but she is old enough to be my babysitter. But age doesn't matter, Mom, not with a woman like this. She's sort of timeless, you know? And it's the way she makes me feel that's so important here. And, oh God, how she makes me feel! Ooo la la! I swear on a stack of *FDA Drug Reference Manuals* that this woman is the best amphetamine I've ever had.

And Hallelujah! You sent me my vintage fake-Vietnamese Stratocaster just in time! I *had* borrowed a guitar from this place I've been going to lately (I'll explain in a minute), but no instrument could ever take the place of my white-and-black beauty. Remember when I used to play the opening of "Smoke on the

Water" – and absolutely nothing else – for months at a stretch?
Well, I've already mastered it again, but this time I'm going way
beyond the music of my fellow creators and making *my own*
music and finding *my own* voice. I think I've really discovered my
true art form, Mom! And I can't stop writing poetry lately, poetry
that is obviously the lyrics for my pieces. Here's an example of a
sort of cutesy bit of verse I wrote for the love of my life (to be
sung to the tune of "Smoke on the Water").

Bedding Bliss

I love you in the summer,
I love you in the fall,
But on my no-flip mattress,
I love you best of all.
I mould myself around your form,
You mould yourself 'round mine,
My mattress moulds 'round both of us,
Supporting both our spines.
You pull upon my heartstrings
As we bounce upon my bedsprings,
Motion transfer isolation,
For a tranquil nonsensation.
We slake our thirst for snugness,
We reach a cozy peak,
Let's be like John and Yoko,
And stay in bed all week.

Oh, and speaking of music, I went to my piano lesson by the
way – and, don't feel *too* guilty or anything, and don't blame
yourself *too* much, but because you made me go to my lesson, I'm
now heavily involved in this weird religious cult. Don't worry,
though, it's not one of those cults where you have to sacrifice
your mother or anything like that – at least, not at first. Mostly
we sit around on colourful little mats not meditating. That's

because meditation is a process where you blank out your mind, and the people at this temple thingy say blanking out my mind any more than I already do probably isn't a good idea.

Oh, and here's more good news. Remember how Helga tried to skin me alive, leaving my body covered in scabs and pus? Well, guess what? All the scabs have finally all fallen off, and do you know what was underneath all that mess? Skin like a little baby's butt, that's what. Smooth, soft, silky – I'm glowing, Mom, my entire epidermis is totally renewed. Christ, some people pay a dermatologist thousands of dollars for a treatment like this!

Sigh. I think I'll go pick some flowers now.

Your little guy,

Raphael

From: oliver.black@thedawnpost.com
To: rafe.wilde@thedawnpost.com
Subject: Fire And Brimstone

Mr. Wilde:

I demand an explanation. What in the name of all that is good and holy has been going on between you and my wife? You once threatened to seduce her – that you've managed to do it is a surprise on par with finding that a rat has been successful in mating with a swan. One shudders at the image, imitating the manner in which you will be shaking, you scrofulous cad, once I get my hands around your scrawny little neck.

Oliver Black

From: oliver.black@thedawnpost.com
To: branksome.black@rebel.net
Subject: The Road to Ruin

Branksome:

You advise against hysteria, do you? Too late for that, I'm afraid. I'm going to crack up, Old Boy, and not just because I've had it with this infernal waiting for Rafe Wilde to let the cat out of the bag. Ah! Can you believe that my Lucy has been having an affair with that menace? It's preposterous and disgusting in equal measure; do you know she even has charcoal sketches of him plastered all over her studio, and in some of those sketches he is almost stark naked?! Rafe Wilde! It's ridiculous! And yet, I feel it must be true. The man is a committed scoundrel (by "committed" I do not mean "institutionalized," sadly), though I've only myself to blame for falling asleep at the switch. I ought not to have dismissed his threats so lightly, Branksome. I ought to have defended my interests with tall stone towers, moats, drawbridges, catapults, cannon balls, flaming arrows – the works. I believe wholeheartedly in the concept of the butter slide, Branksome, and I don't suppose there's anything quite so entertaining as watching an unsuspecting arch-rival go shooting down one at top speed. How I would have loved to have set the dogs on him, just once. But I've missed my chance, and it's too late for all that now. The door of opportunity has been firmly shut – but what's the old saying? When God closes a door, He opens a window. Yes, that's it. Too bad it's the window of a speeding vehicle, say, or a window on the forty-seventh floor. But no, Branksome, I'm not having it. I'm not going to let Rafe Wilde get the best of me. I say that when God closes a door, Oliver Black kicks it right back open.

So, that's it, Branksome. Even whilst writing this e-mail, the path I must take has become obvious to me. I've been twiddling my thumbs under the sword of Damocles quite long enough, and I'll be damned if I'm going to give Rafe Wilde the satisfaction of laying prostrate both my wife *and* my career. I've made a deci-sion, Branksome. Rather than bend my knee to that worthless rapscallion, I'm going to end my own career on my own terms, thank you very much. It's better to push the big red button one-self than to have others do the job on one's behalf; therefore, my next review will be my last. It will be a not-so-very-veiled confes-sion that will undoubtedly set in motion a whole series of situa-tions that would make Job himself whistle, and wipe his brow with relief at having got off so dashed lightly. What are a few boils and some misplaced kine compared with my failing circum-stances? One imagines things exploding, erupting. The sound of things smashing, toppling, crumbling. The crunch of metal, the shattering of glass.

The plop of Oliver Black falling in the soup.

Ah, what a Snakes and Ladders game is life, eh Branksome? You spend your life toiling up the ladders, and just when you think you're on top of things, you step on the wrong square and down you go, snaking into the pit. Ah well, it will all be over soon. Before long I'll have lost everything, and then, perhaps, I shall join you in your rough-and-ready life, journeying around the globe together as knights errant, doing the good deeds that are a part of our sacred mission. It would be a change, anyway, and might even be fun as long as you remember that I do not sleep in tents, that I am accustomed to three square meals a day (two of which occur in fine restaurants), and that the iron, the espresso machine, and the toaster belong in *your* backpack. I don't suppose you still snore like a bloody great mastodon, do you, Branksome? I can't be having you inhaling the curtains, while the dresser drawers slide in and out, in and out, all night long. Oh well, not to worry. I'm sure we'll work something out between us – a con-crete wall springs to mind, the kind that fits nicely in a backpack, in between an iron and a toaster.

Farewell, Branksome. Wish me luck, Dear Brother, in this my darkest hour.

Decisively,

Oliver

From: oliver.black@thedawnpost.com
To: lucy.black@artnet.org
Subject: Enough

My Dearest Lucy:

Like a respectable married man caught *in flagrante delicto*
with his male lover, I find that I too have a closet to come out of
– or in my case, a pantry. You have your secrets, Lucille, but I
have mine, and I tell you now that for the last three years I have
been deceiving you – and not only you but also the rest of the
world (with the exception of Branksome, who has been my rock)
in a not entirely ignoble attempt to keep my position as restaurant
critic. My duty to you and the children has come first, and so I
have clung like a drowning man to *The Dawn Post*, as I'm qualified to do nothing else that would earn a decent income for our
immense family – which, as well you know, includes three perpetually starving teenage males, who might reasonably declare themselves a nation and apply for foreign aid in the form of food
rations. (Dear God! Have you seen the price of bananas lately?
No, don't get me started . . .) I've wrestled heroically with my
conscience lo these many years, always with the scales of justice
before me, with my duty to support my family on one side, and
the weight of my secret life on the other side, and have found
ways of rationalizing and justifying my position which would
boggle the mind of even the craftiest defence lawyer. I readily
admit that what I have done is unconscionable and unpardonable,
and although I do not ask for your forgiveness, I do at least ask
for your understanding. I had come to terms with my deception
and had therefore hoped that this moment might never come.

Nevertheless, it is upon me.

Read my review tomorrow morning in *The Dawn Post* and all will be revealed.

I await your judgment. All that I have done, I have done for you.

Oliver

Hey There, Baby:

Why aren't we allowed to talk during these sessions anyway? I feel like a naughty school boy writing notes in class. Okay, so just listen to me. Ditch him, once and for all. Just do it. You said you wanted to leave that obnoxious, food-obsessed blob O.B. before you even met me, right? So what's stopping you now that we're together? You've been avoiding the old man for months anyway and avoiding the real issues that have been plaguing you for years like a pesky swarm of flying butter tarts. Issue Number One: his suits. Old-fashioned isn't the word for them – they look like something the smilodon dragged in. Issue Number Two, almost as important as Number One: you told me you don't even really love him anymore, that the old spark is more like a snowflake. To mangle a common phrase, I'd say it's time to jump out of *his* frying pan and into *my* fire, wouldn't you? Issue Number Three: his obsession. *Food.* It's like you're locked in a prison cell, and your roommate is a cross between a full-time foraging animal and the Galloping Gourmet. But I'm here to bust you out, Baby, and I'm going to do it with music. With *my* music. I've written a bluesy number about it called "Oh My Lady," and it's based upon this total kick-ass guitar chord I figured out – you put your pointer on the second string, first fret, your tall man on the fourth string, second fret, and your ring finger on the fifth string, third fret – and then you strum it over and over again, nice and slow and sexy. "She's got Kevlar coils and a titanium spine / I'm gonna sleep in that bed and make her mine."

Anyway, I wonder if I can get out of posing this evening? Hmm? What do you think? I just want to spend some time with my hands roving around in your nightie – and not only my hands, but the rest of me too. God that thing is cozy! Thanks for letting me, you know – wear it. Oh, and sorry about the bed situation – at least with the guard rails up, there's no danger of either of us rolling out, but the fact that the thing's on wheels is a real pain in the ass. I hate it when we begin making love in the bedroom and end up on the other side of the apartment in the hall closet. It makes me feel like I'm a contestant in a four-legged race, you know? Call me old fashioned, say I lack vision – but I just think that sex shouldn't be a form of transportation – although, if it was, it would renew interest in public transit – or would that be pubic transit? Still, I say when you make love, you shouldn't need to pack a road map and passport, or have to worry about accidentally emigrating to a neighbouring country. Let's just remember in our eagerness not to leave the front door of the apartment open accidentally. We don't want to find ourselves doing the locomotion, if you know what I mean – humping into the hallway, bumping down three flights of stairs, banging out the door of the building, and bonking down the highway and across the nation. What a mistake that would be. I mean, there's no way to steer – but, on the bright side, O.B. would finally get the message loud and clear.

Right. Back to full lotus. Not that I'll be able to focus on anything, mind you, except the thought of giving you a totally transporting sexual experience (transporting as in ecstasy, rapture, bliss – not as in movement from A to B). Let me know about tonight ASAP, OK?

Movingly,

Rafe

Buddha's Veggie Delight Is Pure Nirvana
By Oliver Black

Faithful Reader: This review begins like dozens of others before it, with me mounting my rickety bicycle and pedalling in the manner of the typical oriental peasant (swaying from side to side over a dirt road as chickens scatter at my wheel) to a small, overcrowded Chinese restaurant. Predictably I have donned my classic black silk Kung Fu suit with the mandarin collar and frog closures, giving me a look of unaffected elegance and quiet authority. My exceptionally long Fu Manchu moustache, coolie hat with pigtail, and dragon slippers complete the ensemble. (Initially I had taped my eyes into the standard oriental orientation; however, I found that I could barely see out of them, and what I could see was blurry and double, making navigation all but impossi-ble. How do the Chinese manage it? Never mind. I took the kindly police officer's advice and still found that, even without the eyes, heads practically spun off necks as I passed by, and I was even greeted with a round of applause as diners stopped to admire my excellent taste.)

Prepare to embark on a journey, one which will take us well outside the province of the typical restaurant review, and into the domain of the philosopher and beyond, until we are no longer in the realm of the human at all, but somewhere entirely unexpected. Let us take the road less travelled, the steep and unpopular narrow path with its sheer sides and tangles of vegetation, with its maze of complexity requiring us to bear down with the full weight of our mental powers in order to extricate ourselves from the jumble. The narrow path is not the easy one, but fear not, my friend, for I have heroically marched with machete through the overgrown foliage, and I know what lies ahead. And what, exactly, *does* lie at the *end* of the road less travelled? Is it a rainbow? A leprechaun with a pot of gold? The Holiday Inn? An abstract concept (satisfaction, gratification, smugness?). No, it is none of these. At the end of the road less travelled by, Gentle Reader, is the Buddha's Veggie Delight Restaurant.

Now, I beg you to stay with me as we put China aside for a moment and imagine, instead, a standard North American dinner, the kind that you might have after church on Sunday at Grandma's house (think of the antimacassars on the chairs, the Blue Boy over the mantel, the grandfather clock in the corner sinisterly ticking away life's precious moments). Before eating you clasp hands, bow your heads, and say grace, remembering He who gave his life for you – and then you eagerly tuck into the crispy, light brown roast chicken nestled in a bed of roast vegetables (onion, carrots, garlic), with a tureen of buttery mashed potatoes, a delicate gar-

den salad, and a sumptuous apple pie for dessert. Ah, delicious! The Peckish Reader will undoubtedly find himself drooling like a stroke victim all over this review at the very thought of it! But, I ask you, at what cost does such a dinner come? "Under twenty dollars," you might well reply. But I am not speaking here of mere home economics; I am speaking, specifically, of *He who gave His life for you,* the individual you thoughtfully mentioned in the preceding grace. Do you know who that is, my friend? Yes, it doesn't take a PhD from a reputable Sunday School to know the answer to this one. Some call Him Jesus, others have no name at all. Personally, I prefer no name, since Jesus is an absurd name, especially for a chicken.

Yes, it is the chicken who gives its life or, rather, has its life, such as it is, taken away. (Of course there are cultures in which it is believed that every animal who is killed for human use has actually given its own life voluntarily, and the hunters are always careful to thank the beast before they drive the spear into its neck, which they usually do faster than you can say "convenient fiction.") Need I give a factual account of the conditions that the modern fryer chicken must endure in its mercifully brief seven week life span? Need I speak here of debeaked birds in cramped cages crammed into artificially lit warehouses, of animals filthy with their own excrement, of creatures who will never see the sun or feel a breeze and who are destined to be hung by their feet on a conveyor belt and have their heads mechanically sliced off by a clever machine? Need I speak here of cruelty, of misery, of fear?

Frankly, I would prefer not to speak of a world bathed in the blood of animals and other such stomach-churning horrors. Rather, I would like to imagine a world without the butcher, the charnel house, the meat-packing plant, the carving knife. How I would love to sing a song of Eden, before human beings were expelled from the garden,* a paradisiacal planet in which no animal – from the lowly grub to the majestic blue whale – ever suffers needless annihilation at the hands of a human being! A world in which all animals everywhere join the ranks of those who have been freed from their shackles! This, my friend, is the world in which I wish to live and this, happily, is also the world of the Buddha's Veggie Delight Restaurant.

The BVD (as I shall henceforth refer to it) is not located in anything even close to paradise; its home is an unremarkable little strip mall, surrounded by all of the predictable chain stores of which there are countless reproductions all over the western world. However, unlike the doors to the other establishments (which are made of dusty glass and rusting metal), the BVD's door is made of heavy, solid oak, and carved into the front of it is a fanciful

---

*And note that upon leaving, the Almighty's very first act was to clothe Adam and Eve in animal skins – that is, fur. This act implies the death of an animal, unless He created the skins *ex nihilo*, in which case it was, in actual fact, *faux* fur.

picture of a lion sleeping peace-fully with a calf nuzzled into his mighty mane. (One can't help but be reminded of Woody Allen's cautionary proverb, "The lion and the calf shall lie down together, but the calf won't get much sleep.") Upon entering, one is struck by the calm atmosphere that prevails – tasteful waterfall in the corner, greenery, candlelight, though still the vibrant reds and golds that are the trademark of any authentic Chinese restaurant. The walls are graced with prints of the great ethical vegetarians – Plato, da Vinci, Goodall, Gandhi, Shaw, Schweitzer, Singer, Simpson (Lisa). And at every table there is a framed plaque with a quotation in sup-port of vegetarian ideals. The plaque at my table, to which I was guided by my pleasantly round-faced oriental hostess wearing a white plum-blossom cheongsam, was Jeremy Bentham's famous quotation: "The question is not Can they reason? Nor Can they talk? But Can they suffer?" On the walls of the typical fast food restau-rant such a quotation might be taken to be referring to the din-ers (to which my reply would be probably not, possibly not, and, if they are actually eating the food, oh yes), but in the context of the BVD, the mean-ing is clear. Yes, animals can, and do, suffer and they suffer *unnecessarily*, which is a point that becomes increasingly obvi-ous as one samples the fare of the BVD. Why eat our way through the animal kingdom, like some sort of grotesque par-ody of a greedy fat person who is hell-bent on stuffing himself with every last crumb in a box of animal crackers, when there are so many other, even more delectable alternatives?

It may be impossible for the career carnivore to believe the above claim; how could any-thing be tastier than, say, a cow's bum? Or the leg of a lamb, the liver of a goose, the entrails of a pig, or – for those readers with tastes more exotic and, given that we share 98.5 percent of our DNA, all but cannibalistic – the brain of a chimp? (The delicate reader may be revolted by this last item on the list, but keep in mind the observation that "Cus-tom will reconcile people to any atrocity" (Shaw) the next time you dismember a corpse on the kitchen counter, ripping it limb from limb and serving the body parts to your hungry children. *Bon appétit.*) But I do not ask you to believe. I do not ask you, ever, to take anything on faith, Faithful Reader. The committed epicure approaches gastric matters armed with the same tools as the scientist: he demands exact demonstration, controlled conditions, reproducible results! Believing is not, in fact, seeing. Believing is wishing. It is merely hoping with your fingers crossed in a dark room. Faith is for those who have abdicated the responsibility of critical thinking, not for the committed gastronomer. "Oh taste and see," the psalmist commands, and I, too, ask you to experience the fullness of vegetarian cuisine at its finest firsthand.

I have not even begun to convey the subtle flavour and aroma of coconut, of ginger, of saffron, of the permutations and combinations of a thousand different seasonings and spices. Nor have I mentioned a specific entrée – but I say why bother, given that anything on this weighty, fifteen-page menu is guaranteed to satisfy and delight. (I will reveal only this: that although I am not a superstitious man, nevertheless I deliberately avoided the dish entitled Three-kind Mushroom on Udon, given that it was a poisonous mushroom that prematurely sent the Buddha himself home to be with Jesus.)

Yes, the prices were competitive, the presentation of each dish engaging and tantalizing, the service brisk and solicitous, Dear Pragmatic Reader – all of this is true; but in the context of this particular review, it is of secondary importance. Of far greater significance is the fact that I feasted without causing harm to any other living creature – I dined well, and also dined good, to make an important moral distinction, admittedly at great grammatical expense. Eating our fellow creatures may be what is natural – but what is natural is not always what is civilized and I, for one, am proud of being soft, of being unable to come to grips with the harsh realities of everyday existence. It's called having a conscience, by Jiminy.

Upon leaving the restaurant, I note that there is yet one final quotation above the door reputedly spoken by the Buddha himself, which reads, "To become vegetarian is to step into the stream which leads to nirvana." Those who have taken this step know that this is the highest truth. It is this quote, then, that is the inspiration behind today's poetic tribute.

The Five Noble Truths

O Buddha! Thy four noble truths to Mankind thou once gave.
All life is suffering, thou hast said, and is so for we crave.
Lose want – lose pain, and this achieved upon thy middle way,
'Tween abstinence and clover for the Arahant manqué.

O Buddha! Thy four noble truths do conjure up a riddle,
For we find our rude intestines and our tums within the middle,
Suggesting yet another way that craving can be beat;
Step off the Wheel of Samsara and have a bite to eat.

O Buddha! Thou wouldst cluck thy tongue at this ignoble truth,
That craving can be quashed by quashing craving with the tooth.
Yet, if the atman is anatman, we are process solely,
Ipso facto our digestion is inherent fact and holy.

O Buddha! How we hunger after dishes appetizing!
The chef, the pot, the flame, the soup contingently arising.
And karma ever with us whe'er we starve or whe'er we dine,
So let us slay our cravings with the blade, the spoon, the tine!

O Buddha! When we're empty we are full – want terminated,
But surely too when appetites are glutted we are sated.
Thy final fatal fungus an odd lesson doth convey,
Whether poisonous or safe, *Nirvana's just a bite away*!

The Buddha's Veggie Delight Restaurant is located in the Coral Springs Mall (not that coral can exist in a spring, nor is there any living coral within several thousand miles, but never mind) on the road which we who live here fondly call the Parkade (usually with added expletives) during rush hour. The BVD keeps highly civilized hours and is open for lunch from 11:00 to 2:00 and for dinner from 5:00 until midnight. Closed Tuesdays. Ah, and one last thing, Dear Reader – don't forget to bring your own reusable chopsticks with you. I make it a rule always to bring my own exquisitely detailed jade utensils, since the Chinese alone use forty-five billion pairs of disposable chopsticks each year, destroying twenty-five million trees in the process. At this rate, all of China's forests will be chopsticks in less than a decade, the forests of the world in under a century; the peoples of the world will be wading through waist-high chopsticks by the year 2100, totally submerged a hundred years later. The earth is destined to be known by future alien civilizations as the best planet to play Pick-up Sticks in the galaxy.

The Dream Post
God Still Hopping Mad Over
Behaviour of Earthly Children

St. Cloud, Minnesota – God the Father, who returned to earth several weeks ago after being out of the universe on business, is still hopping mad at His earthly children.

"How many times do I have to tell you Do Not Kill?" God said, jerking yet another chicken McBunwich out of the hands of one of his creations and throwing it to the floor. "Flaming hell! I told you to name them – not maim them! I mean, I create the niftiest animals this side of Alpha Centauri, I give you dominion over them all, and what do you do? You eat them! And it's not just the woolly mammoths, is it? Every time I turn around, another one of you has an appendage stuffed in his mouth, or a wing, or an internal organ or something. If it moves, you try to eat it! You people aren't just sinful – you're disgusting!"

When God's children pointed out that it's not fair because other animals get to eat each other all the time, God just rolled his eyes and snorted with derision. "Fine! We'll compromise. *You* get to eat all the animals you want – but *I* get to put you anywhere I want on the food chain! How does the bottom sound? I'll give you a thirty second head start before I release your predators."

When this suggestion was met with startled whining, God boxed the ears of his earthly children and ordered them to stand in the corner. "Eating animals loses its attraction when it's your name on the menu, doesn't it?" God thundered.

In order to wean His children off their revolting habit, God the Father intends to temporarily substitute stuffed animals for living ones. After they ingest enough Fun Fur and plastic pellets, God hopes that His children will lose their appetite for their fellow creatures, in addition to which people such as seal hunters will not suffer immediate economic hardship, and can continue their trade by clubbing to death stuffed-animal seal pups, skinning them, and selling their Fun Fur for car-seat covers, and their insides for cushions.

Chapter Nine

From: oliver.black@thedawnpost.com
To: lucy.black@artnet.org
Subject: Perfect Contrition

Feast of Olivia Black

My Dearest Lucy:

By now you have read my review of the Buddha's Veggie Delight Restaurant, the veil has been rent in twain, and what has been concealed will have been made manifest. I have apologized profusely to both editor and publisher at *The Dawn Post*, and will be composing my letter of resignation from the office of restaurant critic forthwith. Now it is time for me to apologize to you, Lucille, and to offer you a similar letter of resignation, before you have the chance to demand it from me yourself, as you've every right to do – because I'm afraid it's all true, Lucy. What did Rafe Wilde call me? Soy Boy. Gluten Glutton. There are many names for what I am, but the most straightforward one is this: vegetarian. I am, and have been for three years, a vegetarian. And I am a vegetarian of the worst sort, Lucille. I am not a vegetarian for reasons of health and wellness, though it is a happy thought for me that vegetarian men live, on average, six years longer than their carnivorous brethren. No, in this matter, I care not a jot for myself. So who is it that I do care about? I think my latest and last review makes it obvious. What I care about, Lucille, are the animals, specifically those domestic animals who are all too often raised in intolerable conditions, casually slaughtered, and turned, needlessly, into what we have traditionally thought of as food. I confess to you now, Lucille: I am a vegetarian for reasons of compassion. *I am an ethical vegetarian.*

Well, so what? Of what consequence could this piddling detail of my diet possibly be to anyone other than myself? There's no shame in being a vegetarian, after all. You don't find them lying in the gutter, their breath reeking of parsley, a telltale bit of V-8

juice dribbling down their chins. Our prisons are not stuffed full
of vegetarians. You don't find them stealing to support their habit
(Peter Rabbit being the exception). But you know very well, of
course. If I were anyone other than Oliver Black, this trivial fact
would be of no consequence. However, I am a vegetarian *restaurant critic* who lives in the heart of cattle country, an area of the
world in which it is commonplace for people to have bacon for
breakfast, a tuna fish sandwich for lunch, an afternoon snack of
beef jerky, and a rump roast for supper. Dear God! Do people
around here eat nothing that didn't have an anus? I exaggerate, of
course, but tell me this: exactly how many restaurants are there in
this vast city of ours that are exclusively devoted to a vegetarian
diet? There are *three*, Lucille, and here I am including the vegetarian kitchen at our local Hare Krishna temple. Obviously I do not
find myself at my wit's end, racing from one vegetarian restaurant
to the next, unable to keep up with the demand. The truth of the
matter is that I am obsolete. And so it is that I find myself, a vegetarian restaurant critic living in the heart of cattle country, a critic
who has a family of six to support (seven, including the lovely
Angel – twenty-two if you count the cats), who has a reputation
to uphold, who has a blackmailer to pay, and who knows nothing
except how to be a restaurant critic. In the heart of cattle country.
With a family of twenty-two to support. Do I make my dilemma
plain?

In circumstances such as these, it is only natural to cast about
frantically looking for someone to blame – and here we need look
no further than our very own daughter, the astonishing Olivia.
Yes, blame your brilliant last-born – a girl who *would* have to use
both her head and her heart – for my slide into this vegetarian
nightmare. Olivia, as you very well know, was instinctively re-
pulsed by the practice of eating our fellow creatures, and identified so heavily with cats that the notion of eating any animal at all
seemed transparently cannibalistic. It all seemed so silly and
divisive at first, not to mention damned inconvenient; how annoyed I would become, after slaving away over stuffed chicken

breasts, or a rather daring beef bourguignon, or even a lovely bit of turtle soup, to be met at table by an apprehensive Olivia who, at the first mention of what was for dinner, would go off like a police siren. Willful child! I was under the illusion that I could reason Olivia out of what was surely just a fanatical phase; instead, it was Olivia who reasoned me into what is surely the sanest lifestyle imaginable. After many a before-bed discussion with our live-in midget philosopher, I slowly awakened as if from a dream, a dream which gradually morphed into a sickening nightmare. I began to see the whole business through the eyes of a child, who in turn had the ability to see the whole business through the eyes of an animal.

How true it is that, so often, it is children who are the most imaginative and, therefore, the most insightful thinkers. I am reminded of an incident related by the pianist Glenn Gould who, at the age of six, was taken out in a little row boat by friends in order to have his very first experience of fishing. When a little perch was finally reeled in, and Gould witnessed firsthand a fellow creature struggling for its life, he declared that he was going to throw it back, but the fish was taken out of his reach. Little Glenn decided to protest in the time-honoured manner favoured by our own Olivia: he threw a temper tantrum, stamping his feet, jumping about, and rocking the boat, both literally and figuratively, and he refused to cease this hazardous behaviour until the vessel was brought back to shore. This is the end of the episode, but not the end of the story, because Gould immediately began his campaign against fishing, and for the next decade strove to persuade his father to abandon the practice. That he finally managed it seems a minor event in the life of a major artist; but what does Gould himself say about convincing his father not to fish? What he says about it is this, Lucille: "It took me ten years, but this is probably the greatest thing I have ever done."

Pah! The greatest thing that musical Titan ever did? How could saving a few meagre fish be considered a greater achievement than his recorded legacy – a gift to all humanity from one of the greatest artists of the twentieth century? The idea is preposterous! Mr. Gould was by all accounts an eccentric, but he wasn't delusional; why on earth would a rational being make such a fantastic claim? It's because, Lucille, at the age of six, Gould had the imagination to see the world *from the fish's point of view*, and he understood that fish don't give a tinker's cuss about music. What fish want – what all creatures want – *is to live.*

Slowly came illumination and then, suddenly, revelation. I was horrified, Lucy, and not just on behalf of the animals who become our food. I was crippled by my own conscience. I was like a fundamentalist preacher who, through a process of personal transformation brought about by specific events – the accidental-on-purpose candle-light dinner, the secretive hand-holding, the intimate confession, the tentative goodnight kiss leading to the ultimate satisfaction – realizes that he has a problem of biblical proportions. For the Bible is rather frosty on the subject of extramarital fun between the sheets (stoning being the recommended upshot), not to mention the Bible's surpassingly dim view of romantic dinners, hand-holding, kissing, and copulation between a man of the cloth and a person without cloth entirely, a person whom, we might imagine just to complicate matters further, is a rather fetching chap named Norman. Oh dear! How can such a one as he possibly continue to preach the gospel in good faith? He cannot. In the same way, it was only in bad faith, in the worst sort of faith possible, that I could partake of the flesh of animals. I turned a jaundiced tooth and gradually developed what would become a catastrophic substance nonabuse problem – I stopped eating animals. Yes, I stopped eating them, but, as you know, I didn't stop writing about them.

Oh, Lucille! I had written for so many years in praise of the consumption of animal flesh, as if eating a creature, raised in misery and slaughtered in filth, and then dignified by the name of Stroganoff or Wellington or Salisbury – as if this was evidence of the highest culture and the best possible breeding. Just try to imagine how I felt: Oliver Black, the alleged great man of morals, responsible for actively encouraging his fellow citizens to go forth and slaughter the innocent creatures of the earth. But they were only eating them, you might argue, not actually killing them. How would Emerson respond? "You have just dined, and however scrupulously the slaughterhouse is concealed in the graceful distance of miles, there is complicity." Dear God! How could I even begin to claim to be interested in Beauty, Liberty, and Truth, when my own ethic disregarded the vast majority of the living beings on the earth and included only our one little species? On what basis did I include only myself and my fellow humans? On the same basis that the slave trader justifies slavery, of course; what is right and good for the dominant individual or social group is transformed by rationalization, and then by institutionalization, into what is right and good for all.

The question thus became, what could I do by way of reparation for my sins? What could I do to make it right? There were four main things.

1) I could subtly direct my readers away from the meat dishes. I would praise the vegetarian items and downplay the importance of the meat dishes. Sadly, I wasn't nearly cunning enough in the beginning, and it wasn't long before Wendell Mullet, the australopithecine who's the head of the National Beef and Poultry Commission, discovered my game. He began blackmailing me, saying that he'd inform the world of my deception, and insisting that I write about the meat dishes *or else*. This I did, to the smallest degree possible; however, given that I haven't actually eaten meat in three years, I either relied on others for their opinion, which I then passed off as my own, or invented a convincing opinion based on my long experience and excellent gustatory imagination. It was wrong of me to do this, Lucille, I see that now – but I was a desperate man, caught between the proverbial rock and hard place.

2) I could assist Olivia with her noble animal rescue activities. There is an excellent reason why the number of cats she discovered between home and school was remarkably high; each cat was

a stray on death row, and each cat was planted between home and
school by me.

3) I could prepare food for my family so that my own home
could be free, as much as possible, from the agonies of the animal
kingdom. Olivia helped a great deal in this regard because of the
atmosphere she inevitably creates around her at the merest whiff
of roasting flesh. (You've seen it often enough, my darling – how
the kitchen grows frigid and dark – windows implode, wind
howls – and suddenly Olivia's head is spinning 360 degrees as she
floats around the room, speaking in tongues like a demon from
hell and looking for all the world like an eight hundred-year-old
troll.) And oh, to what pains I have gone to conceal my true aim:
replacing meat with meat substitutes when necessary, preparing
dishes such as Tomato Woodchuck and Welsh Rabbit (which contain no meat at all, of course, but were designed to throw others
off the scent), and trying to create enthusiasm for my own culinary creations – Tofu Howtowdie, Soy Gumbo, Bean Kebabs,
Tofu Fondue. The truth is that it's never been easier to be a closet
vegetarian, Lucille; what you didn't know is that you were all in
the closet with me.

4) I could send Branksome on a rescue mission to undo some
of the wrong I had done by encouraging animal consumption in
the first place. Was this really such a harebrained scheme? There
seems to be no political will to end factory farming, and people
seem to be largely uninterested as long as the bacon's on the table.
Sending Branky around the globe as a freelance, roving animal
rights activist dedicated to liberating factory-farm animals from
their human despots, and finding safe and humane alternatives
(mostly rescue ranches and various barnyard shelters), helped to
assuage my conscience whilst admirably suiting Branky's feral
temperament and giving it a little push in a more ethical, if less
strictly legal, direction. (Branky always did prefer the mute fel-
lowship of animals to the endlessly chatty company of human
beings; it was no surprise that his second wife – the one from the
Chinese industrial outback – spoke no English, and Branky not a

word of Mandarin. Ah, sweet peace.) It's a little-known fact, Lucille, that there is a mighty network of animal rights activists dedicated to the nonviolent liberation of the animals we keep for food – that I, through Branksome, could become a part of this mighty crusade was an enormous privilege. How I loved to hear news of the success of our schemes – all proudly tested on animals – and of Branky's amazing triumphs. Seventy-six freed in Turkey! Thirty-four in Chile! Eighty-nine in Uzbekistan! Experience taught us that the authorities tend to be suspicious when they find a man with a duckling in every pocket, a chicken under his hat, and a piglet down each pant leg, so naturally we kept him moving in order to decrease the likelihood of getting caught with various faunae concealed on his person. And it's true that the work was rife with moral ambiguity; there was, for example, the shady business of Branksome giving feed containing animal by-products to thousands of sheep in Australia, thereby spoiling them for their intended market – the kosher slaughterhouse – where no initial stunning of the animal is permitted, and throats are simply slit, after which the animal is hung upside down and bled to death. He was almost caught that time, as he was so many others, but he usually managed to escape (and his evasion of the Australian authorities as he tells it, in what he calls the native Australian manner – as unorthodox as it is unbelievable – running across sheep backs like a basilisk on water, releasing a jar of deadly funnel web spiders in his tracks, and then escaping to safety on the back of a giant croc – was, if true, ingenious). No matter what his methods, ultimately the important questions are these: How many creatures has Branksome delivered from situations in which they were denied the ability to exercise their basic behavioural needs? How many creatures has he rescued from the butcher's knife? I estimate that, solely due to Branksome's heroic exploits – funded, I'm afraid, solely by me – tens of thousands of animals are now happily living out their lives on various rescue ranches around the world, animals who now serve no human purpose whatsoever, but who are instead living out the plots of their own biographies.

This is victory indeed! Or so it feels to me, though I hasten to admit that others may not share my joy. New ideas and the resultant changes in lifestyle are never immediately embraced by the masses. Why not? Because, in this universe, it isn't just inanimate objects that keep going in the same direction unless a force is applied to them. And the old ideas and the old ways of doing things are artificially elevated to a status they do not necessarily deserve by that one little word – *tradition* – and tradition is taken for granted as a good thing, even when, as in this case, it is no more than a toleration of unnecessary cruelty. Do you realize, Lucille, that some people have constructed their entire culture around killing? Undoubtedly to such people, the whole notion of animal freedom seems like a colossal waste, and even a perversion of nature. Imagine a cow, for example, without a human purpose! A humble cow, roaming the forests like the majestic elk. Ridiculous! What right has it to even exist? Every right, I should reply, as much right as anyone else. The great philosophers of the moral status of animals figured this out long ago. The animals are free of me, Lucille. And may I also point out, from personal experience, how liberating it is to be free of them. To love, without contradiction, is relief indeed.

Just as I love you, Lucille – without contradiction. If only my love was fully requited, as I believe it once was, but is no longer. And so we turn away from my secret life to yours, my darling wife, and to the fact that there have been other animals in your life too – animals of the human male variety – perhaps a whole string of them, but certainly one particular man at present – a younger man, a better looking man, and a man who possesses all the requisite features of cool in ways that I never could. He once threatened to take you away from me – that he's managed to do it is a surprise on par with my astonishment that pickles and ketchup also make excellent bedfellows. It all adds up, though – the odd hours, your avoidance of me, your perpetually distracted air, the missing love-notes, the obscene sketches of *that man*.

Oh, Lucille. My beautiful treasure, my precious love. Tell me this – what in heaven's name are we supposed to do now? I myself have no answers, but for the moment, I beg you, I plead on bended knee with you – please don't leave me on my own with our three pubescent sons. I thought that in marrying you I would get to live forever with a delicate flower of a woman, not with three sweaty, hulking boys – three uncouth, ill-mannered hobbledehoys – whose main function in life is the conversion of bananas into testosterone. If anyone ought to leave, it should be me – after all, why should you and the children be witness to the public flaying I am sure to receive once the truth is out? So if you want me to leave, then leave I will. If you want to divorce me, that is also your right. Just name the date and the courtroom, and I shall be there with the primitive video of our wedding, to be ceremonially rewound at top speed, after which we'll have the cutting of the divorce cake, the trampling of the bouquet, and the pronouncement, "You may now kick the bride."

As for me, I intend never to leave you, Lucille, though the Riesling runs dry, and the soufflés fall, and the cookies crumble into the sea. I intend to honour the vows I made to you twenty-five years ago, if not to the letter, at least in spirit. I believe we both uttered a lot of religious gobbledygook in church that day – I tacitly agreed to be the head of the house, for example, just as Christ is head of the church – and having absolutely no intention of leading, I could promise in good conscience to be as effective a guide as a man dead two thousand years. But what I really promised you, my poppet, are the following two things: 1) to make your life better than it would have been without me in it, and 2) to be forever by your side, no matter what folly should intervene. I meant it with all my heart when I uttered the words "so long as we both shall live." The question is, did you?

So, no more secrets, my darling Lucille. Finally you know the awful truth I have kept from you; perhaps now is the moment to confess the equally awful truth (i.e., your affair with Rafe Wilde) that you have kept from me?

Uxoriously yours,

Oliver

The Dream Post
Dead Man Disappointed in Heaven –
Request for Transfer Denied

Heaven – Forty-seven-year-old Mr. Morrie Bund and his wife of only three days, Moira, who died yesterday in a freak accident involving a turkey baster and a nail gun, is not at all happy with the afterlife which has been prepared for him.

"Me and the wife arrives at the pearly gates, all excited like, only to be told by Saint Peter that there ain't no marriage or giving in marriage in heaven. Apparently, we ain't one flesh no more, and that old 'so long as we both shall *live*' wheeze is enforced in these here heavenly parts." This, however, is not the worst of it, according to Mr. Bund. "I looks down, discovers I got a new body, all spiritual and incorruptible like, just like some kinda angel in fact, including that I ain't got no pecker – I won't need it, they tells me, on account of I ain't capa-ble of sin no more. And then, to top things off, they tells me to get to the Marriage Supper of the Lamb, pronto, 'cause it's the Lamb that's gonna be my husband, and me and Moira, and every other Tom, Dick, and Harriet is gonna be His Holy Bride. Well, what the fucking hell is this? First of all I find out that I ain't got no pecker, and second of all I find out that, instead of being married to Moira here, I'm the goddamn wife of Jesus Christ, who, if I ain't mistaken, is a man. So whaddas that make me? It makes me a castrated queer, is what – and so my question is, how in hell is this heaven?"

When asked to be transferred to Mormon heaven, where men become gods with their own kingdoms and wives, or to Islamic heaven with its busloads of beautiful virgins

("So long as my Moira's drivin' the bus, I don't mind fulfillin' my duties"), the man's request was flatly denied. "Every man is naturally a little nervous when he finds out he's a bride," Saint Peter explained, "because he doesn't know what it's going to be like. Will I get pregnant? Will He bring home a disease? Will it hurt? Just the sort of questions that all brides have."

"Hey, wait just a cotton pickin' minute!" Mr. Bund was overheard arguing with Saint Peter. "There ain't no sex in heaven!"

"Show me in the Bible where it says there isn't sex in heaven," Saint Peter replied.

"But ain't this some kinda spiritual union?" Mr. Bund whined.

"That's right," Saint Peter replied, "hence your new, spiritual bodies. Now, if you'll just enter the pearly gates you'll find a table just inside with bouquets and garter belts for each of you . . ."

"All right, hell, then! Please, let me go to hell!" were Mr. Bund's departing words.

According to Saint Peter, disappointment with the after-life is not uncommon. "Upon popping out at the other end of the tunnel of light, the dead are often surprised to find themselves in a sort of celestial railway station, with separate gates for Muslims, Christians, Hindus, and all the other world religions." When asked about a gate for atheists, Saint Peter explained, testily, "There is no gate for those who made the mistake of not believing in anything – those, in fact, with no imagination – so the atheists and agnostics spend eternity as clerks and ticket-takers, and serve them right. If you don't want an afterlife, I say fine, you can just have more of what you had before. All right?" Other common complaints include overcrowding ("Nobody wants to be contained in a sterile cube of only a few thousand furlongs"); a tree of life that bears twelve succulent kinds of fruit, but from which nobody needs to eat anymore; and the fact that heaven is illuminated not by electric lights, but by the glory of God, which has no off switch, making it difficult to get a little shut-eye.

From: oliver.black@thedawnpost.com
To: nathaniel.midge@thedawnpost.com
Subject: Swallowing the Anchor

Dear Mr. Midge:

I shall be brief – as swift as the guillotine, the pistol, the bow. Please accept my resignation from the position of restaurant critic for *The Dawn Post*, effective immediately.

Sincerely,

Oliver Black

From: rafe.wilde@thedawnpost.com
To: oliver.black@thedawnpost.com
Subject: Earth to Oliver

Oliver:

Now who's been nipping at the brandy bottle after having gone recklessly off his meds. You think I'm playing around with your wife? Wow. You'd think I would've noticed something like that. Of course it *is* true that I have *you* to thank for getting me together with the woman of my dreams. She's an artist in the true sense of the word, and a knockout in the true sense of that word too. Ka-pow! You always said I should try dating an older woman – well, this one's a whopping forty-eight. Is that old enough for you? She's blond, she's beautiful, and the best part is that ever since falling in love, I'm seeing the whole world in a new light. I'm on this perpetual, nonpharmaceutical high, and I just want to gaze at the stars, and sing in the bath, and forget about this whole stupid revenge business. I admit that for a while my primary aim in life was to get the goods on you – which I did of course, after our dinner at the Pythagorean Pub and Grill, when, thinking I'd be too wasted to notice, you published *my* observations as your own. And then, when I realized that you almost never wrote about the meat dishes if you could help it, and I figured out that you were some kind of vegetarian who was keeping the whole thing hush-hush, I admit that I could hardly wait to pull the rug out from under you, and not only the rug – I wanted to disassemble the whole damned floor and leave you without a foundation to stand on. But you know what? I just don't care that you're a fraud anymore. Blowing the whistle on you is the farthest thing from my mind. I mean, it's directly because of *you* that this wonderful thing has happened to me. Without *you*, I never would have met *her*. Actually, and I don't want to get gushy here, but the truth is – you're like a father to me, Oliver. I owe you – big time.

Rafe

From: oliver.black@thedawnpost.com
To: rafe.wilde@thedawnpost.com
Subject: A Snake in the Grass

No! *No!* I don't believe it! *My* wife is blond, *my* wife is beautiful, *my* wife is forty-eight and an artist! Besides, I saw the drawings! Don't try to deny it!

From: oliver.black@thedawnpost.com
To: branksome.black@rebel.net
Subject: Indignation

Dearest Branky:

Ha! He denies it! Rafe Wilde *denies* the charge of illicit

canoodling with my darling Lucille! You're a man of the world,
Branksome – you tell me what cat-and-mouse, or rather, rat-and-
spouse game *is* this? What's he playing at? As I said in a previous
e-mail, we were getting along like a house on fire when he abruptly decided to abandon the house and lock the doors from the outside – why, then, is he now throwing the doors open, sweeping
me into his arms like the superhero he isn't, and carrying me out
of the burning wreckage to safety? It's all just an elaborate mind
game, isn't it? A hoax, a ruse, a canard with my darling duck as
the decoy. That's it, isn't it Branky? The truth is that Mr. Wilde
delights in playing with other peoples' minds – unsurprising, of
course, since he doesn't have one of his own with which to amuse
himself.

And that's not all, Branksome! For not only does he deny participation in any extramarital rannygazoo, but he denies also any
interest in ending my career – why this sudden indifference, I ask
you? It's a moot point now anyway, ever since I placed my career
lovingly in the centre of a munitions factory and proceeded to lay
siege with an inflammatory review. Yes, Branksome, I wrote my
final column for *The Dawn Post*, and predictably, the sparks flew,
generating no less than a raging inferno of controversy. And how
did I fare in all this? Well, I suppose I feel a bit like those three
biblical chappies who strolled out of the fiery furnace without a
hair on their heads being so much as singed. The difference between me and them is that when *they* emerged from the oven,
each was given a promotion by the king, whereas when *I* crawled
from the ashes, *my* career exploded in flames and is now sitting in
an urn on the mantelpiece waiting to be scattered to the four
winds. It's black armband time to be sure – so why is it I feel like
clicking my heels together and bursting into a rousing chorus of
"Zip-a-Dee-Doo-Dah?" It's because I feel, above all else, the
overwhelming emotion that contains all other emotions of positive aspect – and that emotion, Branky, is *relief*. True, a boat ride
across the river Styx is all that awaits the filing cabinet crammed
with *twenty-five years* of restaurant reviews and culinary verse

(i.e., my life's work) – yet I thank my lucky stars without ceasing that the whole ignoble business has at last been brought to a resolution. Finally, my days of calling for a priest to perform a requiem mass over my dinner are at an end. No longer must I pretend to be untroubled by the idea of being no more than a buzzard flapping about the dining-room and ever on the lookout for fresh carrion. You know, Branky, the adjective necrophagous is used to refer to animals who feast on flesh killed by another; I don't see why this word should not also apply to human beings who do exactly the same thing, do you? So no more parading about as a necrophagist, writing restaurant reviews that are, in essence, obituaries. I am free to live as my conscience dictates – and a dictator is exactly what one's conscience ought to be.

You should know too, Branksome, that after I wrote my final review, I set my hand to what might be my final letter to Lucille, revealing all, including the nature of our farm-animal rescue mission. I can't imagine what she must think of her beloved Oliver now. Certainly she's bound to think *you* are a raving lunatic – but is it crazy to care so deeply about the welfare of the individual? Impractical, yes – but insane? Certainly caring for the individual is the norm when it comes to our pets – creatures with warmer beds, more nutritious food, and better health care plans than the vast majority of human children can ever expect. Let no expense be spared for Fluffy, for Spartapuss, for Patch! Nothing is too good for the noble Coco! Everything under the sun is available to the pet with a disposable income – from massage therapy, to guided meditation, to metaphysical counselling, to space travel (and Laika is perhaps not the happiest example here), to good old fashioned Freudian analysis – for how else can one cure, let's say, a rabbit with an Oedipal complex? (As for Bossy, for Bessy, and the nameless billions on death row whose only crime is to be particularly tasty with a side order of fries, they are abandoned to their hellish fate.) I mean, what else is there *but* the individual, I ask you, Branksome? There is the species, yes – but the species doesn't feel fear or pain. The species feels *nothing*. I am all for biodiversity, because it is this more than anything that will ensure the continuation of life on the planet – but what really interests me is the quality of life of the individual creatures that make up our world. What does it matter if a species survives if it survives only to suffer? A life, *any* life, devoid of pleasure – a life of dissatisfaction, of wretchedness, of the thwarting of natural desires – such a life as this can only be a millstone.

Is *your* life a millstone, Branksome? I very much wonder, as I've heard nothing from you since your dramatic escape from old choky in a laundry hamper. Did you manage also to escape wedlock with the prison-guard's daughter – and with the washer woman for that matter? A marriage certificate is *not* a thank-you note – I shouldn't have to keep telling you this, Branksome. Anyway, I do hope this e-mail finds you devoid of the old ball and chain (both the literal and figurative variety) and free to pursue the liberation of every last creature on the planet – for it is nothing less than freedom for all that is our ultimate aim. Branksome? Branksome? Yes, my heart bleeds for you, as will your feet after they scour the earth seeking shackles to loose, and fences to trample, and barn doors to assail – but let us not have any little pity parties now, hmm? If you must feel sorry for someone, let it be me – a man who appears to have lost his beloved Amelia forever, and who is about to fall upon his upturned blade by writing a letter of resignation to the president of the International Restaurant Critics' Association. Wish me luck, Branky, in this final act of what might rightfully be called hari-careeri.

Write immediately,

Oliver

From: oliver.black@thedawnpost.com
To: hyacinth.butterworth-scone@thefaultline.org
Subject: Abdication

Dear Ms. Butterworth-Scone:

I am writing this letter consumed by the special dread that
accompanies the perilous task of bearding the lion in his den –
though naturally the food critic speaks of breading the lion in his
den, a no less dangerous labour. Ah, but what a curious recipe for
breaded lion is this! Stew in his own juices: a dash of abashment,
a sprinkling of dignity, a soupçon of ignominy, and several
pounds of raw relief. It is with this curious concoction of simmering emotions, then, that I must inform you of my intention to
forego the award for International Restaurant Critic of the Year.
It is inconsiderate and dishonourable of me to decline on such
short notice – of that I am well aware – but I find I can continue
with this grotesque pantomime no longer. You see, I am a tireless
lifter of veils, Madam, and it occurred to me one day to lift the
veil that conceals the true nature of the meat industry, because it
was the meat industry I was unwittingly supporting by my plethora of positive reviews. And what do you suppose I saw when I
lifted the veil? Did I see Beauty? Liberty? Truth? No, I did not. I
saw filth, putrescence, blood, and death. I'm afraid I let my better
feelings get the best of me, and I renounced the consumption of
meat altogether, vowing never to allow another creature, no matter how plump and juicy, past my rueful lips. Thus began my de-
ceit. I began lying to my faithful readers, writing about meat I had
never tasted, making a great to-do about the salad bar, the roast
vegetables, the pre-dinner buns, the packets of sugar – sometimes
there was little else to talk about other than the tiny buckets of
nondairy creamer. I can assure you that the life of the vegetarian
restaurant critic is a lonely one, not to mention beggarly; his is a
bare bread-and-butter existence, devoid of gravy entirely – for if a
restaurant critic can no longer write about food, there isn't a lot

left for him to do.

But what course ought I to have followed, Madam? I needed to earn a living, and yet my conscience kept straying back to the reality of the slaughterhouse, and not only to the animals who are sent there to meet their doom, but also to the people who are paid to engage in the revolting occupations the abattoir has to offer. I ask you this, Madam: Did you bring your daughter into this world so that she could stand in front of a whizzing conveyor belt, ripping the innards out of chickens at a rate of five thousand per hour, and rewarded only with a paltry wage and a handsome case of carpel tunnel syndrome for her troubles? Did you bring your son into this world so that he could spend eight hours a day sloshing about in ankle-deep blood and biological sludge, stripping skins off carcasses, hacking out tongues with a cleaver, stripping the flesh off decapitated heads? You didn't? Well, somebody did. Wasn't that thoughtful? But – oh dear. You don't suppose the women who supply the shambles with compliant worker bees are uneducated, minority, immigrant types, do you? Well, even if they are, at least their children have jobs, you might argue. But butchery is only a job, Madam, in the same way that paid assassination is a job. There is nothing noble about it; the work itself is obscene, the conditions foul, the outcome an abomination. Do you believe in jobs at any cost? I'm afraid I don't. The loathsome drudgery of the slaughterhouse is not good enough for anyone. We were all meant for better things. It is a waste of life – both animal and human.

Goodness, I hope you weren't about to eat; speaking candidly about the origins of our food is enough to put anyone off her dinner. You will forgive me if I've upset you, I trust; I write with vividness and candour not for the purposes of proselytizing but, rather, to explain myself fully and to justify my decision to leave restaurant life behind and, with it, the long-coveted award for International Restaurant Critic of the Year. (There are tear stains on my pillow, I can assure you.) After reading the reasons for my refusal, you are probably glad to be rid of me; you undoubtedly think I'm quite off my nut, that I'm a dangerous apostate with outrageous views who has taken his principles to some bizarre extreme. It's funny, though, how radically sane I feel. *Is it me who has gone bonkers?* Or is it crazy to suggest that it is *society* that has gone bonkers, when killing is the conservative position and pacifism is the rebellious extreme?

Please forgive me for so abruptly declining this illustrious award, but I'm quite sure that the slavering silver medalist will be only too happy to step into the breach. You may also consider this my official resignation from the International Restaurant Critics' Association, and if my fellow members ask why their beloved Oliver is missing from the roster, tell them, simply, that he no longer has the stomach for it.

Thank you, Dear Lady, for your understanding regarding this awkward matter.

Sombrely, but not regretfully yours,

Oliver Black

The Dream Post
Slaughterhouse Employees Face Challenges

Brooks, Alberta – The Octuple A Abattoir was abuzz with activity this week in preparation for the tenth international Bring-Your-Kid-to-Work-Day. "Obviously, meat workers face special challenges on this day," said spokesperson Bud Clot, "and the important thing is to lay the groundwork so that the kids understand what Mommy and Daddy do, and why."

"You see, Pumpkin," a father might say to his daughter, "what Daddy does is he hacks the tongues out of cow heads for eight hours a day. This may sound strange, but cows really don't need tongues, do they Pumpkin – not when they don't even have heads. This makes sense, right? It's true that I didn't grow up dreaming of the tongue-removal business, and I don't have to do this, no one is forcing me – but Daddy deliberately has a shitty life so you won't have to have one. Does this make sense? Your mom bags intestines all day long so that you won't have to bag intestines ever. Do you see the logic, Pumpkin? We justify our daily horror-movie existence by telling ourselves that this will somehow make your future brighter. For some reason, we feel it's A-okay if we waste *our* lives in this hell-hole, and we assume that when you grow up and have kids of your own, you won't adopt this very same philosophy, we don't know why. Do you see, Pumpkin?"

There was a carnival atmosphere outside the plant on the day, and loveable old Shambles the Clown was there to greet the children and juggle kidneys. The under-fives enjoyed the piñata – a life-sized cow that each child in turn beat the shit out of until it yielded its treasure. The "Scare-us Wheel" delighted the older children since, like the line itself, it never stops, and the children are simply hung by their belt loops on giant meat hooks and spun around until, like their parents, they can't think straight.

Unfortunately the day soured somewhat when the children were actually taken inside the plant. "Admittedly we made a big mistake," said Mr. Clot, "because the children just weren't prepared for what they saw." The big mistake was the ill-advised decision to take the children to the management offices, after which many of them emerged pale and visibly shaken.

"I never knew jobs were so boring," commented one wide-eyed tyke who, like the others, was horrified by the tedium of administration.

"It's like school," said another horrified tot, "except there's only one subject, and you have to do it all day long or they fire you."

"All those forms!" cried another. "And those were just the waivers! My God! The waivers! The waivers!"

The kids cheered up considerably when they were escorted into the belly of the plant and allowed to sled down ramps to the killing floor on inner tubes made of inflated calf intestines. "It's veal-ly fun!" quipped one clever youngster. And happily, the day ended with extra merriment when loveable old Shambles ran over some animal rights activists in his clown car.

From: rafe.wilde@thedawnpost.com
To: oliver.black@thedawnpost.com
Subject: A *Snake* in the *Grass*? *Moi*?

Oliver:

Whoa, chill out, Pops. I think I see what the problem is. You mean you saw those sketches of the Great Rafe in the buff? A woman down at the Temple did those, for the ceiling. She's using me as one of the models for the entrance to this, um, temple thingy. Is that your wife? Mmm, nice. But she's not the woman I'm talking about. *I'm* in love with Gabriella Savage, you know, my old piano teacher – and she's leaving her long-time partner, that colossal boob who's the chef at La Jonquille, Octavio Babineau (but we just call him O.B.) to be with Yours Truly. God! Who knew piano teachers were so sexy? I'm telling you, Oliver, if the local branch of the Piano Teachers Association ever hosts an orgy, they can count me in! No, I don't mean literally. I think I know what to do without some naked piano teacher saying, "And a one, and a two, and a three, and a fore . . . *play!*"

Oh, and about your wife – you know she's become a religious nut, don't you? She spends most of her time at the temple – mostly painting, but also sitting, listening, staring, becoming one with everything – no wonder she wasn't at dinner the night I came over. I guess she is a bit like Gabriella, come to think of it – blond, shapely, about the same age I'd guess. I know her name starts with L – Lisa? Linda? Lucy? Something like that.
    Rafe

From: rafe.wilde@thedawnpost.com
To: suzanne@heartmail.com
Subject: Goin' to the Chapel

Hey There, Suzanne:

Can you believe it? Only a few more hours of single life left before you join yourself forever to a guy who's going to keep *you* waiting at the altar for an hour and then have the nerve to double-bill *his* insurance company. Ha! I'm just kidding, really, although I *do* hope he remembers to warm up the ring before he slips it on your finger. But in all seriousness, I want to offer my sincerest congratulations on getting hitched, and don't you worry that nobody except a qualified pharmacist will be able to read his signature on the marriage certificate – I'm sure it's probably still legal. Anyway, I hope you like the wedding gifts. Those Starsky and Hutch mugs meant a lot to me, you know. And my metro-nome did too, but I thought the doctor would find all that tick, tick, ticking kind of soothing – you know, the Old Ticker, get it? The his-and-hers towels are brand-new, by the way, and note that I went to the trouble of getting them monogrammed – one says Suzanne, naturally, but since I didn't know the doctor's name, I just told the monogram lady to sew an illegible scrawl. Or is that the same joke twice in one e-mail? Anyway, don't forget what I showed you – you want to set your iron to steam and use deliber-ate but small circular motions, not those big angry sweeps you used to use when you ironed my towels. Oh, and because I know you always wanted one of your own, also find enclosed a photo and gut-wrenching letter from five-year-old Babatunde, your brand-new orphaned west African foster child, who, by a strange coincidence, has a dicky heart valve.

Love ya,

Rafe

From: oliver.black@thedawnpost.com
To: lucy.black@artnet.org
Subject: *Ah!*

Lucy!

Oh Dear God, Lucille. Oh my dearest love. Where are you, my precious? I desperately need to speak to you in the flesh, but since you are out (again), this e-mail will have to suffice. Oh, Lucille! How could I ever have doubted your fidelity? How can I ever apologize enough for accusing you of having an affair? And with Rafe Wilde of all people! Ah! Forgive me for insulting your good taste. You would no sooner fancy mating with a knave such as he than a gazelle would fancy mating with a hedgehog. How I could possibly have harboured any suspicions, especially knowing you as I do, is unimaginable to me now. I blame the evidence, which led me right down the garden path and directly into the potting shed, where I evidently went rather potty indeed. I expect you'll waste no time in wheeling me offstage and into a long-term care facility for paranoid husbands – although now, after having accused you of having an affair and being proved quite wrong, my fear of persecution has skyrocketed, and I believe I am more para-noid than ever. The truth is that I am absolutely terrified of losing you, my treasure, but losing you in a manner quite unlike the one I had initially imagined.

For although I now know that you were not having an affair with another man (if you can call him a man), I finally know what the secret is that you've been hiding from me. Don't try to deny it any longer, Lucille. Although I cannot begin to understand *why*, at the very least I finally know *where* you've been whiling away the hours. I finally know the truth, and the truth is, Lucille, that religion has got you in its grasp! Rafe Wilde of all people (if you can call him people) has informed me that you are usually to be found at a *temple*, perhaps sitting on a pouffe and caught up in a mystical trance, like some sort of dazed zombie. My poor poppet! You're trapped in some variety of religious cult! Am I wrong to imagine that you're under the spell of some charismatic little bald Indian man in a loincloth and turban? Some chanting, enchanting, cross-legged, snake-charming, tax-evading yogi? Oh, my darling! I only hope I'm not too late! Let us hope that, even as I write this, you are not caressing the hem of the swami's Versace robes and speeding off with him and his harem of truth seekers in one of his forty-two limousines, thence to levitate by Lear jet to his fifteen hundred-acre mountain ashram in the wilds of Atlantis. I wonder, have you already emptied our bank account of its contents? I rather hope not. I remember reading of one fraudulent Bhagwannabe who would only accept the largest of bills because the lower denominations and, especially coins, gave off frightfully bad vibes. Ah yes – the lam of god, who taketh away the sums of the worldly. Just don't do anything tantric, will you, Lucille? These swami types have as many arms as an octopus (you see it in their paintings) and are as famous for their lechery as they are for their lawsuits, so if he makes any obscene suggestions such as "vibrating together at a higher energy level," I hope you'll give him the old one-two just as you would any lascivious rake, loin-cloth or no loincloth, limo or no limo.

It is an agony to realize that you felt you couldn't confide in me, Lucille, that you believed you couldn't tell me your deepest secrets. No doubt you thought I would judge you, ridicule you, chastise you, and that you would have to bear the weight of my pronouncements. And it's all because of the negative press I've given religion in the past, isn't it? I admit I've had some jolly fun at the expense of religion, but only because it's all so nutty. Still, I'm afraid that standing in judgment became rather a habit with me; it is a hazard of my (former) profession, this impulse to

continually rate, to weigh, to compare and contrast. Must everything be put upon the scales?

Well, actually, yes, dash it all, and especially when it comes to
questions of belief. I had imagined that you thought so too,
Lucille, which is why I'm utterly blind-sided by this sudden
change. Upon the stormy seas of life, logic has always been your
anchor; it hardly seems possible, then, that all of a sudden my
queen of reason, my Diana of deduction, my Freya of philosophy,
my dame of doubt, my squaw of skepticism, my tomato of truth
should throw her principles overboard like so much flotsam. Do
you remember the eleventh talk in my afterdinner (but before
dessert – ha, ha) Family Lecture Series entitled "Right Belief – Or
a Good Swift Kick," and the amusing comparison I employed to
drive my point home – that is, the Norse belief that if one dies a
violent death, one will live for eternity in Valhalla, getting cut to
ribbons daily on the battlefield and then miraculously healed and
reassembled just in time for the evening porkfest – as opposed to
the belief that when one dies a violent death, one is in for an
eternal romp with virgins on tap? "This is why there are no Norse
suicide bombers," I sagely concluded. How well I remember your
vigorous nods of agreement and your merry laugh! I always
thought we saw eye to eye on questions of religion and belief – I
mean, just look at the poem we wrote about it – "The Religious
Are So Amusing," we called it, and it was *you* who rhymed chickens with Dickens, pew with boo, nun with fun. Obviously, I was
roundly mistaken.

But never fear, my darling Lucille. I will break you out! Somehow. I don't know much about deprogramming the brainwashed,
mind you, but I'm hoping my experience with the boys will come
in handy. I expect a little Bertrand Russell, an especially strong
cup of tea, and an ice pack should just about do it.

Doggedly yours,

Oliver

The Dream Post
New Age Believers Cause
Old Time Headaches for Police

Los Angeles – In a press release earlier today, police admitted to being flummoxed by an increase in New Age bamboozlers and spiritual scallywags of various descriptions.

"As an example," explained spiritual offense officer Jud Gement, "a ring of New Age swindlers is breaking into establishments catering to those beings who are vibrating at a higher frequency than your average Joe; then they're stealing souped-up, spiritually energized crystals, making various spiritual contacts in this temporal world and realities beyond, and before you know it they've got some poor spiritually undernourished being on its knees (if it has knees) paying the big bucks for it."

Especially valued are Elestial quartz crystals, which contain the absolute and ultimate wisdom, and are the keepers of ancient metaphysical information (though Officer Gement points out that "their true value cannot be fully realized as yet, as there is no read-out device and nowhere to plug in a keyboard. But just give those bastards time . . .").

Officer Gement not only handles major misdemeanours but also deals with the smaller domestic complaints that arise, say, between competing prayer groups. "I've seen some pretty rough stuff," he explains. "When peace breaks out in a previously war-torn area, and you've got a couple of rival prayer groups claiming responsibility for it, things can get pretty ugly. You don't want to get between a couple of enemy supplicants when they lock horns, believe me. It's not like you can just douse them with cold holy water – I've usually got to call for divine intervention, often a SWAT team (Strike With Angelic Tenderizers), and that's not cheap."

Especially vicious are those prayer groups that can change past events through their entreaties to the Divine. "Remember the Treaty of Utrecht?" asks Professional Prayer Commando Soren Knees. "That was us." The incarnation of Christ? "Us again, I'm afraid. There's this other prayer group that was praying for peace in Vietnam in the sixties, and look what happened – they bungled it totally. All I can say is it's a good thing we handled the Cold War."

Other New Age headaches for authorities include badly balanced chakras ("The danger can't be underestimated – there's just no way those people should be allowed on the road . . ."), the improper anchoring of the higher self to the physical body ("Do we need to introduce legislation? Isn't our 'Buckle Up' campaign enough?"), and, of course, the illegal trade in fairy parts ("Sometimes the entire fairy is ground up, other times just the gall bladder is surgically removed . . .") – despite their obviously endangered status.

From: rafe.wilde@thedawnpost.com
To: alma.wilde@command.net
Subject: Don't Say I Didn't Warn You

Dear Mom:

Okay, okay, since you insist on knowing, I'm going to tell you the name of my new girlfriend, as long as your affairs are in order that is, because I know your *vital* signs are all going to be *stop* signs after you read this. You know how I told you that, because of your incessant nagging, it's your fault that I went to my music lesson and got lured into a bizarre cult? Well, I also got lured to the roof of my apartment building, where the woman of my dreams stripped me bare and made love to me on the top of the old piano you sent me, and which you may remember I stuck up on the roof so it wouldn't contaminate my apartment. Isn't that the greatest, most twisted thing you've ever heard? It was your little guy's kinkiest sexual encounter yet, although it would have

been better without the pigeons, and especially without that traffic reporter buzzing us in his helicopter – I think he even mentioned us on the radio as a collision in progress. So hang onto
your bun, Mom, because the woman on the roof was somebody
you know, a trusted authority figure, who took advantage of my
relative youth and vulnerability for her own sticky ends. Okay, so
– are you sitting down? – the new love of my life is – do you have
your pills? – my old piano teacher – better put one under your
tongue now – Ms. Savage.

That's right, Mom – it's Gabriella Savage, and don't even
think of spamming me with your outrage and disapproval, because I'm telling you this is the Real Thing. Oh, I know what
you're going to say, what you always say when I start going out
with somebody new. It's not, what do I see in a *woman* like *that*
but, what does a *woman* like *that* see in *me*? I'll tell you what. It's
not just the fact that my skin is like porcelain and I look more like
the statue of David than ever (although way better endowed, obviously – I've always assumed that whoever sculpted David's thing
must have done the Sphinx's nose on the same day – I mean,
where is it?). It's not just my charm, wit, sophistication, or my
ability to iron a towel into two dimensions. It's not just my ever-
growing collection of seventies memorabilia, or even my sexual
dynamism, which might favourably be compared to gravity as a
force to be reckoned with. It's not even just our mutual love of
music, although it's music that initially brought us together and
that continues to be a source of inspiration, of expression, and of
some of the worst slanging matches you've ever seen. (Hey, it's
not like you can become a new music lover overnight – I'm still
getting used to the possibility of more than four beats in a bar,
more than three chords in a piece, and bicycle bells as vital members of the orchestral family. But don't worry – it's never long
before we're back up on the roof again. Ha!) I guess it's a complicated mix of qualities, but according to Gabriella herself, the
thing that she loves *most* about me is that I'm willing – just that
I'm willing – and it just goes to show that all those romance

novels women are forever reading are bang on the money. You always start out hating the bitch with atom bomb–like intensity, and all your fantasies revolve around putting hair remover in her shampoo, and she hates you back because you're a disgusting pig of a man who responds to her like he would to a flu pandemic, and every date with her has all the attraction of a magnet to the flame – and then the scales fall from your eyes (musical scales, in this case), and you realize she's not a dragon-lady, she's actually a goddess, and she realizes that you're not a hell hound but a hero, and the emotional blast furnace you've been standing in all this time isn't aflame with loathing but with loving, and that for some inexplicable reason you've somehow misidentified the most basic of human emotions. You know, maybe that's why it didn't work out between me and Suzanne. Maybe she just never hated me enough – although I'd better watch my step because judging by the recent phone call I got from her, I think she may hate me enough now. I'm thinking of sending her a book on anger management, actually, and one on etiquette too, with the chapter on the gracious receiving of wedding presents highlighted in bold.

So everything is fantastic on the romantic frontline for once, and I don't want to feel *you* psychically pulling me by the ear off the battlefield and threatening a courtship-martial, got it? I don't want to catch so much as a whiff of nagative psychic energy coming from your direction (and I mean *nag*ative), all right? You would've had a right to stop me dating my piano teacher at twelve, but not anymore. And you can stop hassling me about this cult business, too – you can call off the deprogrammers and stop worrying about any funny stuff going on. It's not about voodoo or human sacrifice or mass marriages or anything like that. We don't go in for saviours, miracles, magick, bibles, priests, gurus, sacraments, divination, astrology, scrying, channelling, chanting, auras, prayer, chakras, chi, souls, silver cords, rainbow bridges, UFOs, fairies, karma, reincarnation, afterlife, Atlantis – none of that. Nobody believes that everything is happening for a reason around here because there's some sort of divine, foreordained plan. Nobody's waiting for the second coming or evolving to a higher level of vibration. Nobody's walking on blistering coal beds or wearing inner vision masks or shoving crystals up the wazoo. Actually, a lot of religion, including that new age stuff, is just superstitious crap. Can you believe it? Who knew? I'll try to explain it all another time, but right now a verse of love poetry has suddenly sprung into my brain, and I have to write it down before I forget.

Here's a bed where we can be
As cozy as two squirrels
In a nest high in a tree.

See what happens when you clear your mind? If you just . . .
Oh geez, Mom – I gotta run. There's some kind of classical piano music wafting in my open window – and it's coming from the roof! Oh, *yes!* Can you believe there was a time when I thought classical music was just boring and ugly? Now I know different – classical music is to me exactly what a can opener is to a cat – the most beautiful sound in the world. Woo-hoo, Gabriella, here I come! Time for a little one piano, four hands, if you catch my meaning.

Your little guy,

Raphael

Chapter Ten

From: oliver.black@freenet.org
To: branksome.black@rebel.net
Subject: "It is difficult to get the news from poems
    Yet men die miserably every day
    For lack of what is found there."
    —William Carlos Williams
        Feast of All Saints and Every Good Thing

My Dear Branksome:

I hope this letter finds you well and happily engaged in the work, not of belling the cat, but taking the bell off the cat entirely and setting it free to experience its own glorious existence. And speaking of cats, how overjoyed I am to report that my dearest Amelia has reappeared as mysteriously as she disappeared days ago. Having lost her blimplike shape (no doubt from going days without food, poor dear), she can perch once more on my right shoulder, like a guardian angel who protects one from stray moths, mice, and pesky balls of yarn. The relief I feel at having her home again is immense. "Certainty, certainty, heartfelt, joy, peace, joy, joy, joy, tears of joy," said Pascal, admittedly in a different context – nevertheless these words capture my sentiments exactly.

How fascinating this new project of yours sounds, though it's hard to make out your chicken scratch on the back of a package of Doctor Doolittle's E-Z Breed Bovine Inserts. If I understand correctly, you've wandered into a bit of a grey area once again. Do you really think it's ethical to pose as a vet, Branky, spending your numbered days with your arm waving about inside the back end of a cow? I *am* sympathetic to the situation in which these sorry beasts find themselves on Pregnancy Test Day; if the cow is found to be pregnant, all is merriment and rejoicing, and Mother is kept on for another year, since it is calves that are the key to the rejuvenation of the farm the next spring. If, however, the cow is without child, she is led away for one last meal before being slaughtered in cold blood the next day. Now, do I understand that your tactic is to convince the unsuspecting rancher that, due to the tragedy of a sterile bull, every single one of his cows, without exception, is without calf? At which point your comrades pretend to lead the beasts to slaughter but, in reality, swiftly cart them away to rescue ranches where they can live with their children in peace and safety? Hmm. The ancient Greeks would have approved of a hero like you, Branksome – a fellow who is larger than life, who is on a quest that takes him out of the boundaries of his own society, who has a monster (of sorts) to slay, and who is under no obligation whatsoever to behave in a moral fashion. Modern peoples, however, would not look upon you with such an approving eye; thus I hope you'll take my advice, Branky, and put as much distance between you and those bovine backsides as possible, otherwise I'm very much afraid you will find yourself wading, metaphorically, through their contents.

As for me, oh so much has happened since my last letter to you! As you know, my career is finished – and as for my marriage? Oh, Branksome! I shamefully accused Lucy of having an affair, and with Rafe Wilde no less (everything still goes black for a moment when I think of it), only to discover that my darling has been entirely faithful to me. Why all the mysterious behaviour then? You'll choke on your gum when you hear this, Branky, but it turns out that she was involved in what can only be described as a *cult* – you know, little robed men with topknots and the like. I confronted her with this information in an e-mail, at which point she came to me claiming that she always knew I wouldn't understand, that I had to come with her to her *temple*, and that only then could she make me see the truth. Ugh! *Temple!* I felt embarrassment at the very word! What next? Cauldrons? Runes? Prayer flags? Drums and cornhusk dolls? I confess I have never felt such bewildering intellectual estrangement from a loved one, which is saying rather a lot given the alienation I have often felt from my tattooed, pierced, dread-locked, drug-growing, porn-gazing, banana-toting, head-banging sons. Still, I've never been able to refuse my darling anything, and so I agreed to accompany her to her "temple," though in truth it would have been far easier if she'd been taking me to a shady bar to meet some mysterious suitor. An actual paramour is jealousy incarnate and gives a name and a face to one's marital problems. Unlike nutty spiritual beliefs, an illicit lover has a jaw that can be broken, a set of ribs that can be cracked, and a head that can be paraded about atop a spike. Very gratifying indeed. However, instead of wielding, say, an actual sword against my opponent, it looked as if I would be restricted to wielding the sword of reason once again – less satisfying overall, but on the bright side, no prison term.

Imagine my surprise when Lucy drove us not to some plush, onion-domed, golden-bricked, and marble-columned headquarters but, instead, to a monstrously large and grotty sugar cube of a building – a warehouse advertising a place called Beds Beds Beds, and located in the slums only a block away from Billy-Bob's Burger and Bun. Horrors! I was paralysed with dread and refused to enter, so afraid was I of what I would find within. White robes, shaved heads, bells, chalices, crystals, pyramids, incense, gongs – beds? – and all the other banal trimmings and trappings. I was terrified of finding vacant stares, Branksome, of finding minds emptied of rational thought and brains replaced by so much rice pudding. Eventually Lucy took charge of the situation and with one hand placed gently in mine – and the other one twisting my arm savagely behind my back until I could do nothing but cry uncle – we walked through the doors and into the very heart of Lucille's secret life.

To say that the effect of this place upon me was explosive would be comparable to saying that the Big Bang was a pretty damned decent display of fireworks. I fairly swooned as I looked about me at the exquisite architectural lines and the exotic shapes and colours. I'm afraid the magnificence of the place far outstrips my ability to describe it. Perhaps the best way of summing up the feeling would be to say that I was overcome by instant synaesthesia. The walls sang, Branksome, and I could feel the music on my skin. I could taste the colours, I could smell the shapes. And just as if the old optic nerve bundles were wrapped around pulleys, my eyes were drawn inevitably upwards to gaze rapturously at the ceiling of the domed vestibule, upon which was painted an ornate fresco, executed, of course, by my own Lucille. I noted in particular the two angelic sort of figures hovering over the door to the nave, and I saw immediately in the one to the left the face of the divine Gabriella Savage, and unbelievably, in the angel to the right, the face of Rafe Wilde himself. Rafe Wilde, Branky! I was so surprised to see that bit of human dross dressed as an *angel* that you could have put me in a glass with tomato juice, a dash of lemon, equal parts Worcestershire and Tabasco sauce, a pinch of salt and pepper, a cube of ice, and a wedge of lime, and called me a Virgin Mary. Gabriella and Raphael. Two angels, united. One wants to laugh at the irony of it but, at the same time, weep at the beauty of it. I tell you it is my wife's best work, Branksome. And spanning the distance between the two angelic forms, lettered in gold, was a quotation – and let me warn you now that, like the Veggie Buddha Restaurant – and, you will find, like this letter – there seem to be quotations everywhere (which, particularly in the case of a restaurant, is an excellent idea – just in case your dining partner is a colossal bore, you can find out what Aristotle or Tennyson have to say, and the evening is not entirely wasted). And the quotation bridging the angels was this:

The faith that others give to what is unseen,
I give to what one can touch, and look at.
My gods dwell in temples made with hands;
and within the circle of actual experience
is my creed made perfect and complete.

I recognized the quote (Wilde – no, the other one) but I still didn't have the slightest inkling of what all this might be about.

Imagine my surprise when we passed through a gothic archway, entered the nave of the place, and found within a short row of people sitting on colourful tatami mats, all with heads bowed, all *sitting*.

"What are they doing?" I asked Lucille.

"They're sitting," she replied. Good Lord, not again, I thought. Naturally my mind hearkened back to our Mexican sitters, and I realized that whole situation was deeply ironic, but somehow it didn't seem funny this time (and even less so when I recognized Rafe Wilde as one of the sitters). Understand that I have nothing against people sitting about on colourful little mats and keeping tabs on the internal machinery, if that's what's required to keep the thing running. To be extra generous about it, I believe that some people can't meditate too much – criminals, for example, who cannot possibly sit on little mats chanting Om and at the same time be cracking safes and snatching purses. No, I have nothing against sitting meditation, Branksome, and fully recognize the benefits to be had by both mind and body, but still I felt a little disappointed. It's just the same old thing. Or so I thought, until I noticed one slight difference – each of the sitters was wearing headphones. This *was* something new. "To what are they listening?" I asked, and imagining that each believer was hooked into some sort of dreary mass indoctrination by a new age guru/sales consultant, I suddenly felt the urge to flee more powerfully than ever. The only thing that kept me from bolting were Lucy's dulcet tones, though the fact that she had me in a half nelson didn't hurt either.

Allow me to pause here, Branky, and make space for a little reflection. As you know, the old time religions, though good enough for Paul and Silas, are not good enough for Oliver Black. I apply the strictest standards in order to judge whether or not a belief is worthy, and I do it because wrong belief is such a danger to all of us, and not just to the individuals who hold such beliefs. However, I foolishly tarred all religions with one brush. It is the same sin of which Rafe Wilde was guilty when he so cavalierly dismissed modern art music. But what is it that the Sufi mystic Rumi once said? "There is fool's gold because there is real gold." Something like that. Consciousness must forever expand to include other conceptions – of music, of animals, and, indeed, of religion. Not that there is anything new about the religious ideas floating about inside the Beds Beds Beds warehouse; the historical roots of these ideas run deep, but they've been waiting centuries to be formalized and enacted. Actually, the whole thing has been right under my nose all the time, and it amuses me to think how many times Lucy has delivered lectures on the very subject. Of course, I wrongly thought she was indulging in pure theoretical speculation, but her speculations on the subject were only theoretical to the same degree that my speculations about animals were theoretical. What is the good of being an armchair philosopher? Ideas require action, if not by oneself, than at least by one's footloose younger brother who had nothing better to do anyway.

So what are these recently revived religious ideas? Ah, before I answer, Branksome, let me respond to your objections before you even have a chance to voice them. You are going to contend that such ideas are not really *religious* ideas at all, because they have nothing to say about God and the afterlife, and they are not contained within the pages of any holy books. Oh how wrong you are, Branksome – how profoundly ignorant. There are, in fact, great steaming piles of religions entirely devoid of books of any sort, and even godless religions that believe the afterlife is – quite literally – rot. However, what all religions have in common, Branksome, is this: they all have suggestions for right living. They all say you're going about it all wrong, and you really ought to give this other thing a try. You'll be better for it, both in this life and the next (if there is a next). In other words, all religions provide a diagnosis of the human problem, and all religions prescribe some sort of a solution. The problem side of the equation has traditionally been stated as either sin (in the West) or ignorance (in the East). This new religion, however, understands the human problem to be neither sin nor ignorance but, rather, starvation –

though clearly not starvation of the body, since most individuals in the West, and not only my sons, regularly eat more than they can hoist at every meal. (I saw it all the time in my former profession, Branksome, and I blame those overambitious food scientists and their sinister New Jersey flavour factories, coupled with the advent of the drive-thru fat food restaurant – where the portion sizes are so large that one's vehicle is simply weighed at the order window and again at the pick-up window, and one pays the difference between the two in dollars per pound. I tell you that America is rapidly flattening under the weight and will surely sink into the Pacific about fifty years ahead of schedule.) No, Branksome, it is hunger of a different sort, and as Lucy led me about the magnificent interior explaining the philosophy of the place in detail, I became convinced both of the reality of the problem, and the brilliance of the solution.

Allow me to delay revelation for a moment more and, instead, ask you to put your books under your desk and retrieve your thinking cap from the lost and found, so that I might spring upon you a little multiple-choice quiz. Happily there is only one question, and that question is this: What is the thing that might be said to be the Bridge that spans the gap between the temporal and the mundane on the one hand, and the eternal and the spiritual on the other? Think, Branksome, think. Is it amassing great piles of gold? Is it sex and procreation? Is it professional organized sports? You snort derisively, but judging by the amount of time they spend at it, millions would appear to believe these are sufficient unto the day and the next day besides. No, it is none of these, but do you know what is? Lucy does, and it is this very thing that is revered at the temple, because it is the answer to the starvation problem experienced by all who feel assaulted daily in this world of concrete and noise, of billboards and smog and slush and lies and corruption and slaughter and misery. Et cetera. A world in which shares of Beauty, Liberty, and Truth are cheap and the stock ever falling.

Well, how did you do, Branky? Hmm. See me after class and

we'll adjust the antenna and chin strap on that beanie of yours.
Meanwhile, here is the answer sheet, against which you may
check your own response. Humanity's great affliction, according
to Lucy and her peers, is *the starvation of the senses,* and this
leads, inevitably, to the starvation of the soul. You see, Branky,
contrary to what the popular song would have us believe, Life is
in no way like a symphony for the modern human. (Naturally I
refer to men and women alike, but since it's you to whom I'm
writing, Brother, allow me the liberty of referring solely to "him"
rather than the customary, but I always think hermaphroditic,
"him/her.") His senses are jammed with traffic fumes, jack ham-
mers, chatter, bananas – the coo of the mourning dove is foreign
to him, as is the smell of the rose and the sight of the stars sweeping across the heavens. Thus is his soul bollixed, Branksome, and
make no mistake. Occasionally, he might chance upon a bit of
Mozart played by a group of buskers as he clutches his briefcase
and rushes the crowd like an offensive line backer in order to
catch the 5:15 train – and, when it pulls away without him and
he's stuck waiting for the 5:25, he might accidentally peruse a few
lines of Shakespeare stapled thoughtfully to a notice board by a
crusading English major – he might even have cause to cast his
eyes across one or two Klimts during the office party that evening, held on the premises of a cash-strapped art gallery. But, as I
said, the senses are tragically plugged, and it isn't long before the
cooing mourning dove could smash headfirst against the window
of his soul and he wouldn't so much as flinch. And what the poor
blighter doesn't realize is that the music, the poetry, the paintings
– that it is *these* things that are the answer to his famished spirit.

And this is the big idea, Branksome, as old as the hills and as
sure as I'm sitting here, with Richard Wagner himself perched on
my lap and giving his whiskers a proper washing. The solution is
art, Branksome – but not art as inessential recreation. This is
where we've got it all wrong. We've treated literature and art and,
especially music, not as the gateway to the sublime, but merely as
a business whose purpose is to foist so many baubles and trinkets

on the public; thus we are guilty of the sin of simony, that is, the buying and selling of sacred things, those things set aside for our spiritual well-being. No, Branksome, the answer is this: art as religion – and the idea, as Wilde once put it (no, not *that* Wilde – the other one) is "to cure the soul by means of the senses, and the senses by means of the soul." It is art that is the bridge that spans the morass between the mundane and the spiritual, between the temporal and the eternal. You will protest again – I know it. "You're not talking about religion," you're thinking. "You're talking about art appreciation class." No, Branksome, you're wrong, and if it's not the antenna, then perhaps we ought to polish up the chrome fender and give the mud flaps a hosing. For there is worship here, and what *they* worship is what *I* worship – Beauty, Liberty, and Truth. There is faith here too, for it surely takes an act of faith to believe Beethoven when he says, "Those who have properly understood my music will never be troubled by the world again." There is the search for immortality, in the sense of *something* of oneself living on after one's death – as Wilde says (again, the other Wilde), "great works of art are living things – are, in fact, the only things that live." (Yes, I realize he is taking liberties with the verb "to live," and I'm afraid there are strands of DNA that make a far greater claim for immortality, but let's not be too literal.) The point is that, through art, the dead can communicate with the living, and the invisible with the visible. And those who worship at the Temple of Art come for the same reasons that any believer goes to church – for the purposes of transformation (because both religion and art are about transformation after all), to attain union with the transcendent, for enlightenment, and to find the peace that the world cannot give. "The purpose of art," says Glenn Gould, "is the gradual, lifelong construction of a state of wonder and serenity." This sounds suspiciously like a religious claim; I would assert that it is exactly that.

    I tell you that some of the most enlightening hours of my life were those I spent with Lucille guiding me through a building

whose internal architecture seemed to map my own soul –
through libraries, art studios, practice rooms, a concert hall – and
listening to her extemporize on the underlying spiritual nature of
artistic expression; but *nota bene*, Branky, that what she means by
"spirit" is not humans as incorporeal beings, or minds without
bodies – a sort of total amputation if you see what I mean – but,
rather, spirit as the essential energizing principle of a whole, obviously embodied person, with the word spiritual standing in proper relation to this nonsupernatural principle. You see, Branky?
It's all so much better than conventional religion – there are no
Freudian illusions here, no mass neuroses, no superstition. There
are states of rapture, yes, but far from being delusional, these
altered mental states are the closest thing human beings can get to
telepathy. When we read a book, we read the writer's mind – in
like fashion we hear the composer's consciousness, we see the
artist's soul. The brain-states of the great artists can become *my*
brain-state, and through this thought-transference comes understanding, nourishment, and the inspiration by which to live.

Oh, Branksome! Revelations struck like thunderbolts, and my
consciousness expanded until I thought it would burst like an
overinflated balloon. It wasn't Lucy, but Oliver Black who was in
need of a strong cup of tea and an ice pack. Passing by our sitters
on the way out then (each of whom was listening to music of his
or her own choosing, by the way, for there are no distinctions
between high and low art here, only between that which engages
and that which diverts), I noted that Rafe Wilde was still sitting,
still plugged in, still alert, and overcome with curiosity I asked,
"To what is Mr. Wilde listening?"

"To John Cage," Lucille answered.

"John Cage!"

"That's right," she said. "'4 Minutes 33 Seconds.'"

"But he's been sitting there for *hours!*"

"I know," Lucille replied, adding, "He's got it on repeat."

Ah well, Branksome. Even if you do think this "art as religion"
business is a load of hogwash, at least you'll agree it's a better

answer to the question of Lucille's whereabouts than the scenario I had feared, with its plot as deep as a Carry On movie. So where does my relationship with my one and only currently stand? I'll tell you, Branksome, that initially things didn't look too good, what with my wife becoming what is known as a person of faith, and me having made merry at the expense of people of faith so often in the past. Naturally, my poor Lucille assumed that I would be contemptuous of her, and for this reason she was terrified of confiding in me. Ah! This was her great mistake caused by my greater folly. It *is* true that my immortal beloved is, in truth, a religious nut; but like filberts or cashews, she is the kind of nut that is entirely good for one. And this new religion of hers is the goods, Branky, speaking to me in a way that no other faith ever could. It requires only one thing to improve it, and that thing is – well – *me,* actually. I'm afraid I still side with the Jains and their line about noninjury to living creatures being the highest religion – though instead of "religion" I prefer the word "axiom," since vegetarianism does not involve religion or faith or belief. "I believe in one God" is a statement of belief; "Animals suffer" is a statement of fact, and vegetarianism is simply the moral response. (It's only the staunch omnivore who has an interest in muddying the waters between ethics and belief, so that he might dismiss vegetarianism on the grounds that it's just another wacky religion, and therefore of no concern to him.) The point is that avoiding unnecessary suffering must be paramount; Albert Schweitzer, who is batting a toy mouse about my feet at this very moment, put it well when he said that even artists cannot exist only for art since "the ethic of Reverence for Life constrains all, in whatever walk of life they may find themselves." Does my agenda contradict Lucy's then? No, Branksome. Lucy and I have always wanted to live in the best of all possible worlds – a world of Beauty, Liberty, and Truth. Lucy has sought to usher in this Edenlike vision through art; I have attempted to make small inroads through ethics. Beauty, Liberty, and Truth is the common ground between us; it is where art and ethics shake hands and agree to have lunch next Thursday. And so there is room for a moralist like myself at Lucy's temple. *Quid est vita sine philosophia*, eh Branky? I'll tell you – life without philosophy is like a fully stocked pantry without a can opener, that's what.

And so, as for my relationship with Lucy – well, let's just say – *the socks are off*, Branksome. It's Amok Time for Mr. and Mrs. Black, and yesterday we actually managed to free ourselves from our responsibilities and our descendants for an entire six hours, so naturally we made plans to "renew our love" all day long! Oh bliss unbounded! Before we began our marathon, Lucy grabbed a fortifying cup of hot espresso and placed it on the bedside table – but, sadly, we were so excited by the whole situation that by the time we had both – well, you know – Lucy's espresso wasn't just still *hot* – it was *still steaming*. "So what should we do now?" I asked. "You mean for the other five hours and fifty eight minutes?" she replied. Ah well. It was most unfortunate, because I had recently browsed through one of those tarty men's magazines at the checkout counter and, in anticipation of just such an event as this, had committed to memory an article on the thirty-seven best ways to drive your partner mad with desire, and I didn't get to do any of them – although Lucy reassured me that I ran through all thirty-seven in two minutes flat. What a wonderful woman, Branksome! Allow me once again to recommend the obtaining of a wife. In my experience all you need is a red convertible, Samuel Barber, a dash of luck, and nature will take care of the rest.

So sorry about the length and depth of this e-mail, Branky Old Boy. I hope you had nothing else planned for the day; although, speaking of plans, you couldn't find time in your busy cow-frisking schedule to come home for a bit, could you? You might visit this temple for yourself, bask in Lucille's radiant presence, give a listen to Black Chalice's new CD (called *Beatus Black* – and, yes, I've taken out extra medical insurance for the boys in case of incorrect pronunciation), dandle Olivia on your knee and placate her with sweets, all the while avoiding the old striped shirt and manacles. As for my immediate plans, I have directly to proceed with the composition of an e-mail, one that is not a sword through *my* heart but, rather, a sword through somebody else's, and I'm telling you, Branky, he's getting off lightly with just the one.

Anyway, take care, Dear Brother, and if nothing else works, try screwing the light bulb on top of that thinking cap of yours a little more tightly – it's probably just a loose connection.

Sanguinely,

Oliver

The Dream Post
Rumours of Temple Dedicated to the Arts Angering Religious Leaders

Vatican City – A rumour that's been circulating for some time now, suggesting that there are dangerous heretics out there who are trying to replace religion with the arts, is alarming and angering many religious leaders.

"It was never about art!" cried the Pope, stomping around on the mosaic tiles of his palatial surroundings. "The important thing is Christ's sacrifice on the cross, as you can see in these magnificent stained glass windows," he said, "and in these drawings, paintings, mo-saics, ceramics, tapestries, and prints. Ow!" he added, after stubbing his toe while wading through a sea of Bernini sculptures. "Our religion is *not* about art. Our religion is about important concepts, like is God one guy split into three guys or three guys in one guy? Lots of people have died over this question, and you can see why. And, no, I am *not wearing* art," the Pope replied after questions were raised over his resplendent apparel. "Look – in a regular suit I look like the Godfather, okay? This is not the image I want to convey. Besides, do you know how comfy these papal raiments are? Mmm!"

When asked what an alien landing smack dab in the middle of the Vatican might think about the significance of art to the church, the Pope replied, "Well, of course it would get the wrong idea, but that's because our religion is about invisible things – God, salvation, atonement, transubstantiation, that sort of thing – and, frankly, we like to keep it that way. Invisible things are in our comfort zone. But an alien wouldn't understand that. An alien would only see these deceptively opulent, art-filled surroundings and would consequently come to totally the wrong conclusion."

"That's why we got rid of the art and made our churches as drab as possible!" chimed in a visiting Pentecostal pastor from a southern American state. "Oh yes! We could see the Devil's hand in these graven images, these golden idols, these false gods, and so we said no to Satan! No to idolatry! No to *sin!* Hallelujah Jesus!"

When asked about the music in his church back home – the piano, organ, seven-piece contemporary gospel band, and the fact that music occupies at least half of every service – the pastor replied, "Look at the time!"

"Exactly!" said the Pope, removing a couple of da Vinci originals from the path to his glittering papal throne. "Hearing all of our beautiful music wouldn't help that alien make up its mind about what our religion is really all about. And there's so much of it! At Matins, Lauds, Terce, Sext, None, Vespers, and Compline *every single day* – our priests and monks and nuns rarely *stop* singing, it seems."

"That's because the Holy Ghost reaches people *through* the music!" the Pentecostal pastor added. "God created music for his glory! Hallelujah Jesus!"

When it was suggested that religious ecstasy is really just musical ecstasy in disguise – because, among other things, music activates the mesolimbic system, which produces dopamine, and culminates in stimulating the nucleus accumbens, which is the brain's pleasure centre – and that it's therefore likely that God is getting the credit for the effect the music is creating, the pastor pointed and replied, *"Is that SATAN behind you?"*

"And then there's all our holy literature," continued the Pope, "which we make our children memorize along with the alphabet, and which we recite as if the words themselves had magical powers. We're even called people of the Book – you might as well call us people of literature. Sheesh!"

"But the Bible is the word of the Lord," cried the pastor, *"not* the word of man! Hallelujah Jesus!"

When it was pointed out that the Bible fits the definition of what literature is, regardless of whether or not it was thought up by man or merely dictated to him, the pastor replied, *"Is that a GIANT SQUID?"*

"Thank heavens we don't dance," said the Pope, as he watched a pack of visiting dervishes whirl across the Sistine Chapel, "otherwise that alien would think we really didn't have a leg to stand on."

When it was suggested that if religion isn't about art, maybe the Pope would like to sell the Vatican art collection to the public and give the proceeds to the poor, the Pope quickly retreated to his papal apartments, where he was later seen stroking his collection of nativity figurines and whispering *"My Precious."*

From: oliver.black@freenet.org
To: wendell.mullet@agricorps.org
Subject: Termination

Mr. Mullet:

I reject meat on both moral and aesthetic grounds. It is on these same grounds that I reject you, Sir. As you are undoubtedly aware by now, all of the sins of Oliver Black have been revealed to the world in the form of a written confession; thus has evil been vanquished, not by the sword of truth, but, rather, by the pen. You might say that I've put the pen back in repentance, Mr. Mullet, and what it means is that I am forever free of you and your fellow blackmailers and thugs. You have no power over me anymore; thus I shall no longer be giving so much as a shekel to the Beef and Poultry Commission. Hurrah! The truth has been made known, and as advertised, the truth has set me free.

Tell me, Mr. Mullet, how is it that an anthropoid such as yourself has no empathy at all for your fellow creatures, both human and animal? I expect you know that forty thousand children starve to death every single day in their bleak homelands; would you feel any outrage at all if you knew that most of the corn and grain in this world is grown to feed *not* children, but livestock? Your cattle and pigs and chickens eat it all, Mr. Mullet, while forty thousand children starve. Every single day. I've no doubt you are well aware that it takes about a pound of grain to make a pound of bread, but that to make a pound of beef takes sixteen times that much grain; does this not cause the brow to furrow, even a little bit? I could go on all day lobbing facts like bombs, but I believe that you are the sort of fellow who, as Churchill once said, can stumble over the truth and immediately pick himself up off the pavement, carrying on as if nothing had happened. I wonder about this quality you possess – the quality of not giving a good God damn, so to speak. Perhaps he was unloved as a child, I think to myself – and knowing you as I do, this is spectacularly easy to imagine. Maybe he was desensitized to others during a stint as a child soldier, or maybe as a child vivisectionist with frog and scalpel. Maybe he had a bad experience with a piano teacher. Who knows? I think the most probable answer, however, was written decades ago by the immortal doctor, a poet far greater than myself, a man who was, indeed, the champion of his profession. And the poet writes:

"But I think that the most likely reason of all
May have been that his heart was two sizes too small."

Good riddance, Mr. Mullet.

Triumphantly yours,

Oliver Black

From: rafe.wilde@thedawnpost.com
To: alma.wilde@command.net
Subject: Soulapalooza

Dear Mom:

Whoa! I can't believe you've finally finished clearing out the holy shrine of Little Rafe. Thanks for sending me the final box of stuff, and especially for my *Star Trek* action figures, including the whole extra wardrobe you once sewed for them for when they go on shore leave. I didn't recognize Spock at first – honest to God, I thought it was John Travolta in *Saturday Night Fever.* Nurse Chapel's got a classy Jackie Kennedy thing going, but Jesus, Mom, you knit Captain Kirk a leisure suit that's so bulky he can barely put his arms down or his legs together – imagine a jacket and pants crocheted out of rope – that's what we've got here. So I've taken it off and replaced it with that snazzy tennis outfit – just right for fun and games on the planet Triskelion.

So let's say that this is your official thank-you note for all the stuff you've sent me, okay? And, because I hate writing these hellish things, let's say it's also a pre-thank-you note that covers all gifts from this date to 2065 inclusive, at which point the status of your thank-you account will be reviewed. All right?

Anyway, sorry I haven't been writing so much lately, but I've been spending a lot of time at this temple thingy, so now I've got this kick-ass inner peace thing happening. I can't possibly answer all of your panicky questions about it, Mom, but trust me, no one's scamming anyone, okay? In fact, it's not like organized religion at all, if you think of it that way. Ha! Or you can think of it like a church service if you like, one in which they've taken out the ridiculous (i.e., the sermon) and just left the sublime (the music). Music's not just another stimulant, you know, Mom, although nothing else can change the entire chemistry of the brain like music can. It's the direct link, the passageway from one mind to another, the channel for the direct communication of emotions and ideas and states of mind. What you want to do is fuse with it, and then bingo, you've got ecstasy and tranquillity. It's all about enlightenment and transformation, you know what I'm saying? I mean, listen to this: I'm finally learning to cherish each moment, because you never know if the next moment's going to come. See? See the difference? The old Rafe would have substituted the word "woman" for the word "moment" in that last sentence, but I've gotten beyond all that. Not that the Great Rafe is ready for Pope-hood just yet (although if I *were* Pope I'd make the church return everything they've stolen and set all the nuns free, obviously). The point is that after all these years of being a music critic, I'm finally getting the hang of sitting around and listening to music. I'm letting the sounds be themselves, like Cage says to do, although just letting the sounds be themselves brings up the relevance of the role of the music critic. I don't know if I can hang onto my job, Mom, and I don't know if I want to. What's the point? At the risk of sounding like Oliver Black, I have to say that reviewing popular music is beginning to feel about as significant as rating my favourite pasta, you know? There's spaghetti, macaroni, fettuccini, manicotti, rigatoni – but it's all just pasta. It's all made with exactly the same ingredients. There's other stuff out there, and lots of it. (At least, that's what Gabriella says; and although most of what's out there is still unpalatable to me – i.e., it sounds like complete shit – Gabriella assures me it's an acquired taste, and she says it's only a matter of time before I'll be instantly transported to paradise by even just one single note of classical music.) And besides, if I'm spending all my time as a critic, I won't have enough time to engage in my true art form, and you know what that is, Mom. You've *always* known.

I mentioned that name again, didn't I? Oliver Black. It's like a tic or something; I seem to have contracted an Oliver Black-specific form of Tourette's. Well, you'll be overjoyed to know that I finally made my peace with him – *after*, and *only* after, I made him agree never to send me another e-mail. Mind you, he's twice as irritating in person; the guy's a hard-boiled old crank who wants *his* thing to be *everybody's* thing, his thing being (as usual) ruining everybody's fun, not to mention their appetites. Why can't he just let the rest of us bumble innocently through our days without making us feel guilty about every damn thing? Personally I couldn't care less about Oliver Black's beef, or his mantra, which these days is eliminate suffering, eliminate suffering; I say if he's so into eliminating suffering, why doesn't he shut the fuck up and stop making my life a misery for a change? Why doesn't he try not wrecking every good experience? Christ Almighty. The guy doesn't even have to be in the same room as me anymore, when, suddenly – BANG! – I've got his face three inches from mine giving me *that look*. Oliver Black has become the *face* of my *conscience*. He's haunting my refrigerator; he's the invisible guest at every meal. I can't even enjoy a bucket of chicken anymore without Oliver Black's head popping out of it. I mean, come on – it's chicken! You can't tell me they're not for eating – chickens are *made* of chicken! Jesus! What does Oliver Black *not* understand about this? Anyway, the guy's a tyrant (which really isn't so surprising when you consider how many tyrants have also been animal lovers). And it isn't just about food; it's one clash after another about any subject you care to name, and others you won't even have imagined. Like the time I brought a CD of Number One Classical Hits to the temple thingy, which I'd gotten *free* in a box of corn flakes. Isn't a free CD in a container of breakfast cereal a good thing? Don't we want more people listening to *Ode to Joy*, and *Maiden's Prayer*, and *Rustle of Spring*? Apparently not. Oliver just grabbed it from me, shook his fist at it, and yelled something like "Simony!" and then wouldn't speak to me for the rest of the day. Go figure.

Anyway, just because I'm such an ace son, I want to say thanks one last time for all the memorabilia, although Gabriella says I don't need it as badly as I need to be free of it, but *she's* the one with about thirty-five miniature busts of composers, just sitting around the house like gruesome little shrunken heads – I keep telling her she should paint herself black, string them around her neck, maybe start her own cult. And speaking of Gabriella – thanks for not having a spaz and for even going so far as to suggest that my old bedroom be turned into a guest room for when Gabriella and I come to stay. Great idea, but does it have to be bunk beds until *after* we're married? Woman-on-top and woman-above are not the same thing, you know. Having your girlfriend suspended three feet above you out of reach – no, sorry, I don't believe in long-distance relationships.

No, the bed you've got to get – and read this carefully, Mom, because this is the single most important thing I've ever said to you, or anyone – is *exactly the same model of bed that Gabriella owns*, which is the greatest, most comfortable bed on the entire planet, but that's not the only reason I love her (I hope). It's called the Hypnos 2000 and the whole sleep strategy is based on actual science – on the science of snuggles, the technology of tranquillity, and the mechanics of cuddly coziness. We absolutely love this bed, me and Blankie. And it's all environmentally friendly, all digital, all with total 24-hour-a-day online support. Sure it cost ten thousand bucks, but who cares? It's worth it for the Kevlar frame, titanium dual shock absorber nodules, Bucky ball coils – you could launch this bed to the moon with one of its own springs, they're coiled that tightly. But it's the mattress that's the true story, stuffed with abandoned feathers from plump and pampered free-range eider ducks, ducks who only shed feathers devoted to moulding themselves to your body and remembering its exact shape for all eternity. This is my death bed, Mom, the bed I'm going to die in, because I'm never going to sleep anywhere else. Lucky, lucky Gabriella.

Speaking of which – no, I haven't asked Gabriella to marry me yet. But that's only because she beat me to it.

Ha!

Want to come to a wedding, Mom? Yeah, I thought so.

Peace out,

Raphael

From: oliver.black@freenet.org
To: selwyn.black@freenet.org
      merlin.black@freenet.org
      damien.black@freenet.org
Subject: Father Still Knows Best

Hello Boys:

Good Lord, we've been through a rough time lately, and I want to take this opportunity to thank all three of you for your understanding, your patience, and your generous forgiveness. It can't be easy to realize that the Old Man is not the paragon of perfection you always believed him to be. And you might well think that because I've been advising you to live lives of excellence and virtue, at the same time that I myself have been living the life of a fraud and a hypocrite, that I have no right to offer my counsel and will thus lay off the letters of fatherly advice. If you think this, Boys, let me tell you that you couldn't be more wrong. After all, I am still your father, and a father must be as watchful as the giant Argus, who had a hundred eyes in his head and never slept with more than two eyes shut at a time. And besides this, if even Oliver Black can go astray, how much more likely is it that three wide-eyed, impressionable neophytes such as yourselves might go careening off the rails?

Still, although I intend to continue to guide you like a sheep dog nipping at the heels of his charges, this e-mail will be my last letter of reprobation for a while, owing to the fact that your mother says I ought to cool it for a bit and show you that I have at least a little faith in your ability to turn yourselves into decent human beings. As I've mentioned before, even when you were babies, your mother was forever whisking away educational materials I had made for your benefit – most notably my series for infants with titles such as *Walking for Dummies*, *Talking for Dummies*, and the like. She thought it might send the wrong message, and so you continue to wind yourselves up in Mother's apron like the three little pigs seeking protection from the Big Bad Wolf. Don't think I'm not aware that you complain regularly to your mother about my treatment of you boys, suggesting that I'm far too hard on you, too controlling, too rigorous and overbearing. This is nonsense, of course. Ought I to leave the raising of three boys to blind chance? Good Lord, no. I merely want to ensure that, upon sending each of you soaring from the nest, I don't unwittingly release into the world a sociopath wielding an axe, a copy of the white pages, and a rubber duck. It's the least I can do.

However, before I sign off for this indefinite trial period, allow me to get just one last minor point off my chest in the form of a question. And that question, Boys, is: *Why?* Why is it that whenever you leave the kitchen, I find not just the refrigerator door but, indeed, every single cupboard door, almost without exception, gaping open? It's a small point perhaps, but it's been irritating me for years, and I simply cannot take my leave of you without an explanation. Could there be some ancient instinct at work? Perhaps your subconscious demands that you open every single door in order to check for predators that might be lurking, say, in the pantry, behind the tins of baked beans. Boo! Or perhaps, when your ancestors were grazing upon the fruits of the savanna, it was evolutionarily advantageous to see everything available to them so as to make better dietary choices; who wants to feast upon a pile of grubs when there's a dumbwaiter with a five-course meal upon a ten-piece table setting, and a bottle of Dom Perignon chilling in the ice bucket – or its primaeval equivalent – just behind the next grove of trees?

I said every cupboard *almost* without exception, didn't I? The exception is the door behind which we keep the cleaning supplies, about which you appear to be positively phobic. "Ah! What's that? *Not a sponge!* Everything going black . . . must – get – headphones – and – remote – control – to – block – out – parental – requests – and – be – constantly – entertained . . ." Dear Boys, what can possibly be going on in your heads, if anything, when you see your mother on her hands and knees with bucket and sponge, as if at prayer – her knuckles alternately red from chemicals and white from clenching a sopping invertebrate (fake of course) – and you hear her calling upon the patron saint of domestic servants, St. Martha (no, not Stewart, and don't be such smart apples) to bless her with the brute force necessary to remove the spaghetti welded to the kitchen floor? What can you be thinking as you watch her, like pampered Russian princes vacationing at the fleshpots of Egypt, idly observing their maidservant from atop their thronelike beanbag chairs? What you're thinking is this: "She's doing what she likes to do – we're doing what we like to do. Everybody's happy."

Ah, Boys. Your mother and I are cognizant of the fact that we are not just raising three individual young men, but three future husbands – or, possibly, wives depending on your sexual orientation – though in your case the matter seems settled, given that the walls of your bedrooms are papered with a harem of posters of spectacularly endowed and (I've got bad news for you) surgically enhanced and airbrushed humanoid females, who have nothing better to do than to pose in that ridiculous way that is guaranteed to turn a man's brain to pudding and cause him to part with all the cash in his piggy bank. Ask yourselves this: how much money have I spent on posters of pouting females? My point. I agree that it *is* true that women who look like the women in those posters *want* you, but sadly, they don't want you for what's in your pants, unless what's in your pants happens to be your wallet. This is one of nature's most entertaining little jokes, and the fact that so many men don't understand the punch line is essentially what makes the world spin on its axis.

Sorry, Boys. I seem to have gone off on a bit of a tangent, so moved was I by the spirit of divine edification. What I really meant to say, what I'm saying every time I offer advice and correction is – I'm proud of you. I'm proud of all three of you. Really I am. The piercings, the tattoos, the irresponsible sex, the incessant eating, the blatant disregard for your mother and me – none of it really matters. You are the sons of Oliver Black, and I really couldn't have asked for three finer young men. You're not bad people. Not at all. You're just bad at *being* people. Thankfully, there's still time and with my help . . . well, we'll just see how we get on, shall we?

Your loving dad,

Dad

The Dream Post
God the Father Leaves Children to Their Own Devices

St. Cloud, Minnesota – In a shocking worldwide address entitled "He's Just Not That Into You," God the Father explained that it's time for Him to move on, to leave the universe once and for all, and to explore intimate relationships with other beings.

"You people haven't exactly been a good time, you know?" said God. "You're whiney, you're neurotic, and you're never going to learn to rely on yourselves if you think I'm going to step in every time you get a hangnail," God explained. "You've got to learn to figure things out for yourselves and stop calling my name every time you're about to get your heads shot off, or whatever. I'm all for atheists in foxholes, all right?"

"You need a different God," the Almighty continued, "because I don't feel like I can commit to just one planet, okay? I mean, you were an attractive species, but – well, you've put on a lot of weight, haven't you, and although I thought we had something special, I see now that I was mistaken. Besides, I've met another species. Cute, shapely, sixteen-dimensional – we just connect, you know? It's a two-way street with them. They know what a god needs, and it isn't unceasing prayer, that's for damned sure. You smother me, you people, and if you're not nagging me you're sucking up to me, telling me how great I am, until I just want to smite you – which, admittedly, sometimes I do. Hey, a deity can only take so much brown-nosing. It's embarrassing, you know? Have you no self-respect?"

When God's people complained that they need comfort and solace and assurances about the afterlife, God could barely stifle a yawn. "I never realized how repetitive you are," said God, "besides which you don't need any of that from me. All I ever gave you was a little hope anyway – there were never any guarantees. This business of 'faith being the evidence of things unseen' was always just a tragic misuse of the word 'evidence,' wasn't it. Surely you people can see that."

When various theologians protested further, saying that if the Almighty leaves the universe, we'll be doomed because people are radically contingent beings sustained in being by His love, God blew a gasket and kicked each of them in the shins. "Do *you* understand this twaddle, because *I* sure as hell don't. It's meaningless! What sustains you is the universe, the environment, your human culture – that's it. Add God-love and you've added nothing – the list of sustaining ingredients is the same, got that? Jesus! Would you people quit trying to pass off your crazy hypotheses on the back of legitimate ones? And that's another reason

I'm leaving," God continued. "Our religious beliefs are just too different."

God's children pleaded one last time to make Him stay, but the Almighty turned a deaf ear. "Besides, you can do better than me. I'm not good enough for you. That's because I'm a figment of your imagination," God explained, "and in my wisdom I decree that the time for belief in imaginary beings is over."

"But if you're a figment of our imagination," cried God's people, "how come we hear you talking to us in scripture, out of burning bushes, even in the privacy of our own heads?"

"Christ Almighty!" replied God, "do I have to spell everything out for you people? Does the word 'imagination' mean nothing to you?"

God intends to pack His things and leave next Tuesday, but says He'll stay in touch and is hoping that we can still be friends.

From: oliver.black@freenet.org
To: branksome.black@rebel.net
Subject: Omnium-gatherum

Feast of Saint Dwynwen

Dearest Branksome:

Like the first issue of *Zeno's Paradox Periodical*, I thought you'd never arrive at my door. Ah! How wonderful it was to have you home again, if only for a few days! I admit that I was initially puzzled by your sudden nocturnal departure – puzzled, that is, until I read the front page of *The Dawn Post* the next morning. You've developed a bad habit of sneaking into pet stores at night and quietly freeing all the animals, haven't you? Must I remind you, Branky, that this is *not* our mandate? Must I point out that although the act itself is good-hearted, it is wrong-headed? Finding safe houses for the animals we raise as food is our goal – releasing flocks of budgies into the wild in order to mate with, say, the native sparrow population is not. The world doesn't need spudgies, Branksome; it needs freedom for all those birds who are currently held in bondage and are even now dependent on us for their very survival. For example, did you know that there are no domestic turkeys on the entire earth who can breed naturally? They cannot. They are all bred in the factory and they are all related. Some day there will not be a single one left, I hope; rather, we will be witness to wild turkeys soaring as majestically as eagles, or, if not exactly soaring, at least gliding respectable distances to locations of their own choosing.

I am happy to report that the award for International Restaurant Critic of the Year was given out last night, and not to me. My name was not even mentioned; I am persona non grata in the world of haute cuisine, and there will be no gold watch, no good-natured roasting, no feastschrift in my honour. Luckily, the general public has been somewhat more sympathetic, if argumentative. Several letters concerning what has become known as the Little Black Lie are printed daily in *The Dawn Post*, and it's a job just to keep up with the refutations. The main argument, as old and tiresome as it may be, is that the animals are going to be eaten by something anyway – why should they not die a little sooner and thence be eaten by us? I was accused of gross insensitivity when I suggested to one reader that we might well use the same argument on her: "Why don't we just bump *you* off in the prime of life," I wrote, "since ultimately you're just going to be food for worms anyway?" Oh dear. It only got worse when the same dear lady suggested that unnecessary suffering wasn't such a terrible thing, really, if it meant a tender chicken on the table for Sunday lunch. In retrospect, I see I ought not to have written, "Let us stuff you in a plastic bag, throw you down a flight of stairs just for the hell of it, and ask how you feel about unnecessary suffering then, shall we?" It was quite exciting, really – I was accused of thuggery, misanthropy, misogyny, and cannibalism all in one issue. I shot back a rebuttal immediately, accusing my readers of the sin of misology – and have since heard only from those read-

ers who have a good dictionary. (Go ahead, Branky – I'll wait.) I
suppose that ever since I witnessed my darling Lucy giving birth
to the children, I've taken the whole notion of pain far more seriously, and I not only understand in my mind but feel in the very
marrow of my bones that the only answer to the problem of suffering is the cessation of suffering. Animals are like us in that they
experience pain; therefore the unnecessary pain that humans in-
flict on animals (and each other) must, as far as possible, be elim-
inated. This, I admit, is dogma.

But never mind that now, Branksome. Let me relate instead
the details of a most joyous occasion that took the place of a ban-
quet in my honour. Given that it seems so much like the end of a
chapter in my life, and the beginning of another, I decided to
push the boat out in a big way – I rented La Jonquille and the services of Chef Octavio for the entire evening, invited all of our
family and friends, and threw a giant party in honour of the saint
who has been such a comfort and inspiration to me lo these last
three years. Whenever I began to fret about my disintegrating
relationship with Lucille, or about the desperate nature of our
mission, I would turn in my mind to Saint Dwynwen, the patron
saint of lovers and sick animals. I realize it was positively mediaeval of me ("Do I contradict myself? Very well then, I contradict
myself, blah, blah, blah"), but I would think of Saint Dwynwen,
Branksome, and somehow it gave me strength to know that others
concerned with love and beasts were thinking of her, too, and
calling on her for help in their time of need. I hosted Dwynwen's
feast, Branksome, and what a feast it was! La Jonquille was so
crowded with loved ones there was barely enough room to swing
a cat. (I was reminded never to use this particular expression in
front of Olivia, by the way, especially when she's wearing the
classic little black shoes with the pointy, reinforced steel toes.)
Everyone was there – Lucy, Olivia, Selwyn, Merlin, and Damien;
Pythagorus, Samuel Barber, Amelia Earhart, Bertrand Russell,
John Stuart Mill and all the other cats; Angel, Angel's mother,
Rafe Wilde, Gabriella Savage, Billy-Bob, Rafe's friend Suzanne,

her surgeon husband, and their newly adopted son, Babatunde (who's just had heart surgery, bless him); even Fabio alias Tex alias Isosceles was there in the capacity of headwaiter. There was a place reserved, symbolically, for Dwynwen herself (though occupied throughout – I'll explain presently), one reserved for St Anthony, Abbot (patron saint of domestic animals), and a symbolic spot reserved for St Nicholas of Tolentino – a man whose compassion for animals was so powerful that he once resurrected a roast chicken; arising from its bed of glazed vegetables on buttery feet, it tested its wings once or twice and then flew off the table – traumatized no doubt, but none the worse for wear. Imagine a small child pointing to the sky above the local Chicken-on-the-Way drive-thru and exclaiming "Look, Mama! A flock of roast chickens!" Clearly a man of greatness, though not the ideal guest at a barbeque.

So who was sitting in Dwynwen's chair the entire evening? It was none other than our own Angel, a young woman who has been taken from crayons to perfume and back to crayons again in only a few short months. Being a knockout has its disadvantages, you know, the obvious one being that it's so easy for one's beauty to eclipse one's brains, and certainly this is what happened in Angel's case. She's been treated as little more than a doll her entire life, as something to dress up, put on display, and play with as one sees fit. Certainly the boys never saw her as a complete human being, and even Rafe Wilde was guilty of this, though when I brought the subject up with him in front of Gabriella, he denied it vociferously. (Later, when I overheard the clever Angel suggesting that she print out his e-mails as proof, I was reminded of how pathetic it is to hear a grown man cry like a baby.) It turns out that Angel just needed a little support and direction in her life, and living under the Black roof, with two relatively sane parental substitutes, has had a beneficial effect. Angel seems to have worked the boys out of her system, thank goodness, although sadly the same thing cannot be said of the boys. Each was temporarily winded after the initial sexual marathon, but is no longer, and now a peculiar tension is in the air – one imagines the head-on collision between three falcons about to dive for the identical mouse. Stringbean is particularly chagrined – I think he believed Angel might be his only shot at fornication, and from the straggly look of him, I'm afraid he just might be right. Be that as it may, it is not the seed of Stringbean, but rather, Lucy's message of equality and sisterhood that has fallen on fertile ground. Angel is now a young feminist, but not only a feminist. I sat her down one evening and explained to her all about my saints, and I spoke with particular passion about Dwynwen – about her legendary beauty, her rejection of the suitor Maelon, and especially the fact that she became the patron saint of sick animals, and that her name is invoked in any attempt to heal an injured beast. Thus Angel is thinking of becoming a veterinarian – a sort of celibate, feminist, vegetarian veterinarian. In order to make a radical break with her old self, she has even asked that we stop referring to her as "Angel" (too generic, like being called Girl) and call her Dwynwen instead. Of course I am delighted to do so. She has even quit modelling and is throwing herself into her schoolwork, except on gig nights, when she plays tambourine in the band. It's therefore no longer clear whether Black Chalice's sold-out concerts are due to the music itself, or to Angel's skimpy outfits and incessant gyrating – but as Selwyn so philosophically replied when I put the question to him, "Who gives a fuck?" Who indeed. Mind you, I can believe Black Chalice fans are more excited than ever given the increasingly superior quality of the lyrics. Not that they're using unexpected words in their pieces (frumptious, whuffling, fribjous, sluffish – they reject them as fast as I concoct them) – but who would've believed that their most requested song would be the rock anthem "O Cookie, My Cookie?" And just look at the lyrics of the most recent Black Chalice song, penned by Selwyn himself.

If I Could Bottle Aristotle

If I could bottle Aristotle,
I'd pour a drink into your cup,
And you'd become so logical,
And we would never break up.
'Cause loving me makes sense, Girl,
Your heart and head are in a whirl,
Because you need philosophy,
Plato, Leibniz, Nietzsche – Me.
Oh yeah, Babe, oh can't you see,
Oh yeah, Babe, your will is free.
Absolutely, QED,
You need them and you need me.

I'm hoping such lyrics mean that Selwyn's revolt against reason is finally coming to an end. At the very least, he seems to be delving deeper, although he still refuses to take my advice about penning lyrics related to the true nature of romantic love. "I Wanna Punctuate Your Equilibrium," "Silly DNA Songs," and "I Dream of Jeanie with the Allele for Light Brown Hair" are not songs you should expect to hear any time soon. Lyrics such as these do not achieve the goal, apparently – the goal being to attract the fairer sex in droves. Ah well. As Wilde says (no, not *that* Wilde, the other one), "If music be the food of love – rock on!"

As for Merlin, he too is getting himself straightened out (except for his jutelike hair, which remains anything but straight, with all manner of beads and baubles glue-gunned into the coils), and despite his lengthy absence due to "polio," he is even completing the year at school. Just yesterday he informed me that he'd gotten 50 out of 50 on his mathematics final exam. One hundred percent, Branksome! Can you credit it? I was enormously impressed, of course – I only wish he hadn't gone on to add, "No, wait, I got a better mark than that – 60 out of 60!" Ah well.

And Damien? I'm happy to report that for the first time in his life, Damien failed to leave the milk out on the counter to spoil! Oh happy day! Have we finally progressed to the dawn of conscientiousness? No, Branksome, we have not. Damien didn't leave the milk on the counter to spoil because there *is* no milk to be left out on the counter to spoil. Milk, as well as butter, yoghurt, cheese, and eggs no longer fit into Olivia's vegan vision for our family, thus they have been forever banished from our home. I expect this information might cause you to wonder who's in charge around here. Ah, Branksome. Here is wisdom: The question is not, "Who wears the pants in the family?" The question is, "Who wears the little pointy black shoes?" Remember these sagacious words next time you visit.

And speaking of steel-toed footwear, it was a particular delight to have Angel's mother join us at table. The woman never changes (I refer not only to her attire), although when Angel ceased her modelling career, Mrs. Day was forced to find work in order to support herself and her copious adopted descendants. And who would have guessed that finding employment would be so easy for a mildewy sort of bog woman such as she? It turns out that Mrs. Day just happens to be the only person on the whole of the earth who has the entire Bible memorized, from the first "In the beginning" to the final "Amen," and as such, she's a highly marketable commodity. Did I not tell her to consider work as a memory specialist? I did indeed, and now she'll be going on all the big American talk shows, both to show off her skill at spewing verses picked at random, and also to stun the public with her ability to hold entire conversations by responding only with verses from holy writ. This is a rare skill indeed born of a formidable, if radically misguided, intelligence. It certainly amuses the young people; at one point during dinner when Mrs. Day turned to the boys and said something like, "Ye shall be troubled, ye careless ones, and ye shall be stripped and made bare, and shall lament for the teats," I'm sorry to report that rather a lot of liquid went shooting out of rather a lot of noses. And who can blame them? You'd think she'd know better – asking boys not to laugh after a word like "teats" has been sprung on them is like asking the sun not to rise.

Sitting beside Mrs. Day the entire evening was Rafe's uncle, Billy-Bob, owner of the Billy-Bob Burger and Bun international franchise. There are posters of his scarred, rough-shaven visage everywhere around the city, posters that look like they ought to say "Wanted" but say instead "Elect Billy-Bob in Ward Eleven." There's rather a lot of money to be had in this "man of the people" line of work, you know, but though Billy-Bob now has stained-glass pie plates, brass-handled spatulas, gold-plated potato mashers, and diamond-studded collars for his Chihuahuas, still he has not forgotten his humble roots. He'll make a fine city councillor – now if I can only convince him to eliminate flesh foods from his menu, all will be well. But don't hold your breath, Branksome – no one can say that Billy-Bob is not an animal lover (observe how he coddles his pets), but he loves animals in the same way that most people who say they love animals do – that is, he loves to have them for dinner, and not as invited guests either. Do I contradict myself? You bloody well do, yes.

You'll be pleased to note that not only Mrs. Day and Mr. Billy-Bob are finding new employment, but our own Lucille has secured that long-sought-after professorship at the university. It is she who will now be the chief breadwinner, and just in the nick of time (though I ought also to mention that the boys are now bringing in great gobs of cash, and I shouldn't think it will be long before Captain Black is splicing the mainbrace and goose-winging the jib, if you take my meaning). Obviously my long sojourn at *The Dawn Post* has come to a bitter end, but that doesn't mean my working life is finished, mind – it only means that, instead of painting with words, I shall be painting in oils. And in flour, baking soda, sugar and spice. It's true, Branksome. Oliver Black is the inaugural chef at the top-secret Temple of the Arts, the very place I suspected of luring my Lucille into a crazy religious cult. I am freely imposing Olivia's vegan vision of the world (a vision that has become my own) on the other artists at the temple, and although some were skeptical at first, one taste of my own special BLT sandwich (Beauty, Liberty, Truth) convinced them otherwise. I feel a true artist! And Lucy says that because I supported her artistic life for the first twenty-five years of our marriage, it is only fitting that, for the next twenty-five years, she support mine. Oh, Branksome! Our marriage is renewed! The Scrabble board has been unchained, the love notes are once again flying between letter boxes, and I'm hoping it won't be long before we finally act out the climax of our written passions! We're only waiting for an opportune moment, the time when it will be safe to enact the denouement without fear of interruption – which, if I've done the calculations right (let's see: four children still living at home, the youngest is eight) should be only a matter of a decade or so. Ah well. After all we've been through, I can wait a little longer. Besides, I'm still getting used to this new security. I'm like a vulnerable teenager, all giddy and uncertain. I keep asking, do you still love me? Do you *really* love me? I even had the audacity to ask my darling the other day, "Will you still want to make love to me when I'm a hundred?" "When you're a hundred, Oliver," she replied, staring lovingly into my eyes, "I'll be ninety-two." Then, expecting her to ask me something like, "The question is, will you still want to make love to *me*?" she said instead, "At ninety-two I'll take what I can get, thanks very much." Dear God, I love this woman, Branksome. How does the old song go? "You're forty-eight, you're beautiful, and you're mine." All mine, mine, mine.

Yes, renewal is in the air, and nowhere more so than in the person of Mr. Rafe Wilde. Like me, Rafe has been relieved of his position at *The Dawn Post* and is thus able to engage in other occupations. He's been liberated from journalistic drudgery and is now able to explore his true art form, which he at first believed was popular song composition. You know, Branky, in Bach's time the bar was set so stratospherically high that composers had to be intellectual rocket ships to reach the level of their predecessors.

However, because the pop music bar of excellence has been set so that even the most accomplished limbo dancer cannot worm beneath it (it being impossible to limbo below the earth's crust), many popular musicians bumble along oblivious to the fact that they're utterly devoid of original ideas and talent. There's a terrible confusion in the pop music world between the idea of the simple as opposed to the simplistic – and it was this confusion that was the insurmountable obstacle for poor old Rafe. He was trying to shovel his way to greatness, and he hadn't a clue that people were fascinated by his music in the same way that people are fascinated by any sort of horrible disaster. It was obvious that Gabriella was having serious second thoughts every time he began plucking the strings of his Stratocaster and bursting into song – actually, everyone was surprised when he would begin to sing one of his three-chord monstrosities with the lyrics so obviously shoehorned in, as we would all assume he was still just tuning up. You know well my views on unnecessary suffering, and so as a public service, I'm afraid Rafe rather had to take it on the chin concerning his music. This, as it turns out, was all for the best, because in ridding him of his dream of becoming the next John Lennon (including certain assassination by age forty), he was free to discover his true art form.

At first I was alarmed to find Rafe at the temple on his hands and knees, his hair in a sort of blankie-bandana, with a little toothbrush scrubbing away at the grout between the tiles of the mosaics in the nave. Grabbing him by the arm, I lifted him to his feet and cried, "Who is inflicting such a vile punishment upon you, Sir?" "Punishment?" he replied, bewildered by the question. And so Rafe Wilde has progressed from music critic to Sparkle technician, spending his days on his knees at the temple, polishing it to a shine that would cause a blind man to shade his eyes. It is his true gift, to be sure, and nothing seems to give him greater satisfaction than watching the feet of one person after another fly out from under them as they discover a well-waxed floor, as smooth and free of dust as Hubble's mirror, and as slippery as a skating rink. (Something like Rafe's skin, actually – how strange that I'd never noticed his flawless complexion.) His whole appearance is altered, especially his attire – gone are the tight jeans and the white pirate shirts, replaced by what couldn't be, but surely looks like, a sort of frilly, pink, flannel nightie. You may laugh, Branksome, but never in my life have I seen anyone look so calmingly cozy. So transcendently tranquil. So celestially snug. And how marvellous that, after spending so much energy on conforming, on the cultivation of cool, it seems he finally feels free to be his true self. His former girlfriend Suzanne seemed particularly mystified by Rafe's radical transformation, but once she recovered from her initial astonishment, a good deal of happy banter and good-natured teasing ensued – Suzanne, at one point, chiding Rafe for being a closet cross-dresser, and Rafe retorting, "Actually, it was Suzanne who was the transvestite. She just loved wearing my dresses." That sort of thing. Very sweet. I thought rather a lot of this doctor chap, too, and I wasn't afraid to say so – in fact, he's just the sort of fellow I'd want my Olivia to marry – highly educated, makes great wads of cash, has a taste for the finer things, and yet is a man toiling in the service of humanity, a true hero, a champion of the sick and downtrodden. I went on at some length to Mr. Wilde about this fellow's virtues until he cut me off, and rather sharply too. He's a bit touchy about this doctor and I think I know why – all evening, the good doctor kept brushing crumbs off the table, and where did they fall? Onto a freshly polished floor. One wept for poor Rafe – it was almost too much for the hardiest of Sparkle technicians to bear. Still, his former waspish self was nowhere in sight, and he kept his cool – another result, I believe, of having the angelic Gabriella in his life. Truly, Branksome, the positive changes that woman has brought about are wondrous and unprecedented – and can you believe it? Rafe and Gabriella are trying to have a baby, to slip one under the wire in order to "prove their love," as Rafe put it.

And so it begins again.

And, finally, to Olivia, with whom this adventure began. At

the time of this writing, she has officially taken over the entire
garage with Olivia's Beasty Outreach, her animal rescue service –
unofficially, she has taken over the cellar and the tool shed, and
we have to keep flushing animals out of other areas of the house
before they can take root. Lucy had kittens when she found
Amelia Earhart's in the laundry hamper (yes, it's true, Branksome!
My little Amelia wasn't lost, she was off having kittens – all of
whom look suspiciously like Christopher Hitchens, by the way),
and just this morning I unwittingly had a bath with a hamster who
had a rather exciting adventure on a soap dish – a tale with which
he will undoubtedly regale his grandchildren someday. As will I.
Olivia is still playing the piano, usually in the style of John Cage –
that is, prepared piano – prepared in this case not with wire and
rubber and ping-pong balls but, rather, with cats. How appropriate that it should be that calico ragamuffin Pythagorus, the first
person to discover the numerical ratios of the intervals of the
scale, who is usually stretched out almost the entire width of the
piano, washing himself in a sunbeam and purring like an eight-
cylinder engine upon the strings.

And on that note I shall bring this missive to a close. I want to
thank you again, my brother, for being my confidant and advisor,
and more than this, for your spectacular efforts on behalf of all
animals everywhere. Truly it is you who are the Good Shepherd,
gently guiding the sheep out of the paddock and leading them to
pastures new, where they are safe not only from the wolves, but
also from the shepherds themselves. Keep up the stellar work,
Branksome, and remember the next time you find yourself shiver-
ing under a thin, scratchy blanket on a straw mattress after a supper of animal byproduct and organic slop – living, in fact, much
like the animals you are so diligently trying to free – remember
then, as I say, to gaily snap your fingers, toss your head, and laugh
it off – not only because there seems to be no prison that can hold
you, Dear Brother, but because Saint Dwynwen herself tells us
that "Nothing wins hearts like cheerfulness." It is her most famous motto, which updated might easily be put: "Nothing wins

hearts like a little Black humour."

Fight the good fight, Branksome.

Your loving brother,

Oliver